ONCE ON A BLUE MOON

A NOVEL

LINDA MCGEARY

THE TRILLIUM TRILOGY

BOOK TWO

ONCE ON A BLUE MOON

ACKNOWLEDGEMENTS
To my husband,
Duncan McGeary,
for faithful support and encouragement;
Lara Milton, my editor,
Aaron Leis, a computer wizard;
Map design and Cover photo illustrations by Andy Zeigert
Images courtesy Wikimedia Commons
Thank you all.

DEDICATED TO
Vivian Cummins, my mother,
who lives in Tomorrow Land.
but inspires me still,
to love of story, poetry,
words and meanings.

Map of Blue Moon

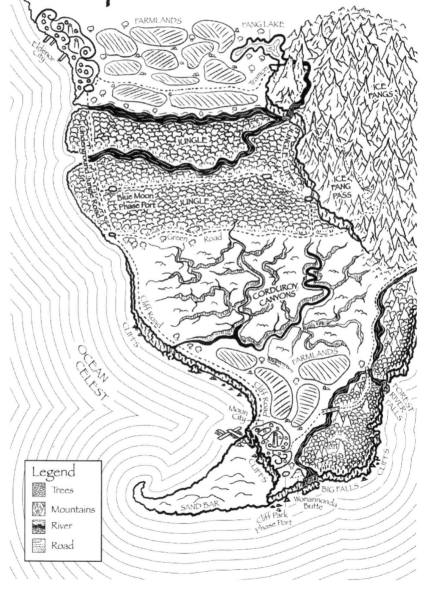

FARMLANDS

FANG LAKE

Eldenor City

ICE FANGS

Tramor

JUNGLE

Underground Jungle Road

ICE FANG PASS

Blue Moon Phase Port

JUNGLE

Green Road

Cliff Road

CORDUROY CANYONS

OCEAN CELEST

CLIFFS

FARMLANDS

FOREST RIVER FALLS

Cliff Pass

Moon City

CLIFFS

CLIFFS

BIG FALLS

Wonannonda Butte

SAND BAR

Cliff Park Phase Port

Legend

- Trees
- Mountains
- River
- Road

CHAPTER ONE

I am on the Blue Moon. With a strange man! And red-eyed snakes!

I felt a frisson of panic race down my spine.

Would I even live long enough to see the Blue Moon?

Life never informs you when it's about to take a sudden turn for better or worse, I thought.

For many years, I dreamt of the Blue Moon; now that I was certain I was on the moon, what I remembered were the horrified faces of my friends … and me vanishing from their sight, like they had vanished from mine. It was not something I thought about for long, though. *How has this happened* was next? Then came, *what must I do right now?*

I followed the young man beckoning me, made sure I did not brush up against any of the vines. More and more crimson-collared snakes kept pace with our progress. The heat and silence were stifling. Threat vibrated on my flesh yet I didn't know or understand what that threat really was. It unnerved me, to say the least. I kept my mouth shut, breathed sallow but steady, and moved fast—but not quite at a run—to keep pace with his long strides.

His purple braid hung all the way down to his … Well, how could I not notice? His bodysuit was skintight, the color of the foliage. He would blend right in if he stepped off the path, except for his pearly white skin and purple hair.

He was humanlike, but not human like me.

His head was the same size as mine, maybe a little larger, and the same shape, but his profile was slightly flatter and his ears smaller, closer to the head, with tiny pointed tips. They looked like seashells I'd seen on the beach at Califeia, like when a shell is cut in half lengthwise. His nose was long, with a sharp, slight ridge. Every time he turned to see if I still followed (I was being very quiet), he would smile with lips that seemed too large for his face, like his amazing large eyes that had vertical pupils, like a cats.

Everything about him seemed human: his shape and size, his hands, the way he moved. Yet he was totally ... the word Sabostienie leapt into my mind. I almost said it out loud in my surprise at the realization, but caught myself. I eyed a snake to my right that was keeping pace with me. I slipped my hand in my pocket and felt the sleeper weapon there. I kept it warm in my palm, just in case I needed it, as I kept following the graceful young man. I tried to be alert and ready for anything, but when you haven't got a clue about a place, that is pretty hard to do. Everything felt like a threat.

Sweat was rolling off my face, and I felt a trickle down my back by the time we came to a wall of black rock. The vines had been burned away in a five-foot swath around a steel door. There was a crunchy white stuff on the ground in front of the door, and a strong smell of fresh salt and something else I couldn't identify. All the snakes that had been following stopped and swayed, yearning towards us, their red eyes unblinking and hot. My heart pounded as the man pressed his palm to a blue gel pad and the door slid silently open. He pulled me inside, and it slid closed. We both released a big sigh of relief.

"You did well!" His voice was deeper than I'd thought it would be, with a bit of a rumble to it. "The only explanation is, you don't know about the Crimson Death. Or you have a death wish."

"Crimson Death? You mean those snakes ... " I saw his eyes go wide, and I looked down to where he was staring. On my coat sleeve was one of those red-eyed devils, rearing back to bite my arm. Before either of us could react, it struck, but the coat was too thick and the snake's fangs caught in the heavy fabric. In an instant, before it could free itself, I had the coat off and was stomping the red-eyed thing to death with my heavy boots. A putrid smell like rotten eggs rose from the dead thing and made me cover my nose.

"Oh, Great Wonannonda, you are *fast!*" the young man exclaimed.

I kicked the coat into the corner, backed up against the opposite wall and stared at the smashed mess on the floor.

"OK, then! It's not a death wish," he said.

"What the hell? Our snakes don't have fangs! *Crimson Death?* Are they poisonous?" I felt weak, and slumped to the floor.

"Well, not exactly. Their bite paralyzes, and then they crawl inside your mouth and nest in your lungs or your stomach. They get into your body by whatever means they can find and give birth to their young. The mother and then the babies, in turn, start eating their way out … and you're awake to feel it, but you can't move. That's what kills you."

"Oh," I said weakly, and felt sick to my stomach as I took in the horror of it. I stared at the bloody little creature. Carefully, I unlaced my boots, pulled them off without touching the goo on the soles and tossed them over by my coat. I didn't think I would ever look at my snakes quite the same way again, not if these were their cousins. No wonder the early settlers had an aversion to snakes, if any of them were like these. It made me realize that everything has a backstory. Nothing happens without a motive behind it. Find the motive and you may be able to understand the issue, or at least the thought behind the action.

I looked up at the man's white hands, reaching down to help me stand. Hesitantly, I took his hands and shot to my feet with his tug.

"Thanks," I said. "You saved me back there. Were they attracted to our noise?"

"Yes, they home in on voices particularly. We, your type and mine, have soft skin, easy to bite. The Crimson Death learned long ago that voices come with an easy first meal for their young. If you thought they were moving fast as they followed us back there, it's a good thing they are nearly blind, if you had spoken, they would have been on us before you even knew they had moved."

"You mean like that one?" I asked, pointing toward the goo.

He nodded, then stepped over to the side of the door and pushed some buttons on a small control panel of blue lights. I felt the floor jolt, and my stomach was in my mouth, and I felt like I was falling. Again I put my back to the wall. Nausea threatened to get rid of the stomach in my mouth, but when we came to a sudden stop with another little jolt, everything settled back into place.

"What where you doing in Death Alley, anyway?" he said. "My name is Zarek, by the way. And you're … ?"

I stared at the back of his head as he spoke. I wasn't sure I wanted to give him my name or tell him anything about myself, so I didn't answer his question. Instead, I asked, "What were *you* doing in Death Alley?" because I couldn't think of anything else to say.

He turned and stared at me. "My job," he replied, a bit of sarcasm in his tone. He turned back to the controls. "I keep the vines clear and kill the snakes when they overpopulate, and release the Truggils to run the Alley and eat the snakes when there are too many for me to handle."

"Where does the Alley go?"

"For someone I don't know, you expect a lot of answers without giving any," he said, then shrugged and answered my question. "It is swallowed up in the jungle. It goes nowhere. We keep it clear out of tradition. It used to go to something important, but the eons and the jungle have swallowed it up, too, whatever it was. The Father and Mother want the path kept clear to a certain point, so we do it. If it is important to them, it is important to us … and it is good for jungle training."

"What are Truggils?"

"Don't you know anything?" His luminous eyes ran up and down my heavy clothes, and then he frowned. "You're not one of ours, are you?" Suspicion clouded his face. "You're a port beamer, aren't you? A jumper. I didn't even think this port worked anymore. No one has used it in over a thousand years. Maybe longer." He gave me a hard over-the-shoulder stare, but continued. "Truggils are beasts your people exterminated nearly two thousand years ago, back on Homeworld, along with our habitat and a lot of our people."

"You're Sabostienie!"

He stopped what he was doing, turned to stared at me. "I'm usually better at reading people than this. You have surprised me now three times; that is a record."

"So why would my people kill off the Truggils if the Truggils kill off the snakes? I know for a fact my people hated snakes of all types. Still do."

"Because they were stupid?" He rolled his eyes and turned back to the panel. "The Truggils are a troublesome breed, unruly and ugly. They dug up planted fields and ate what they found. They scared your children as hordes of them ran through the streets of your towns. Their scaly snouts, clawed hooves and skin as thick as armor plating are impossible for the snakes to bite, unless they get lucky and strike around the eyes, where Truggils are soft skinned; then the snake wins. But mostly the Truggils eat the snakes. They find them a delicacy. It is still a mystery to our scientists why they can eat them and not become paralyzed as the snakes are digested, but they can."

I wrinkled my nose. "Yuck!" I said, and shivered.

"Better the Truggils eat the snakes than the snakes eat you."

"So, what you're saying is my people created an imbalance, and then the Crimson Death went after a new food source and found they liked it, and then overpopulated, bringing a plague of Crimson Death to my people, which caused them to hate snakes."

"Yes! You're quick, I'll give you that."

"And you just released a horde of Truggils to run the Alley, and hopefully eat a bucketful of those red-eyed devils."

He applauded. I blushed, and he grinned.

He opened the door and we stepped out into a white hallway. Much like the Wells' roadway walls, but these had a touch of glimmer, a soft glow that seemed to emanate from them.

"I'm not sure I like you," Zarek said. "You're quick to assess situations, you seem to know things, yet you aren't one of our humans, and you lack good manners."

"You're right." I blushed again. "I'm sorry, I was being rude. My name is Pendyse." I held out my hand. Zarek looked puzzled, but hesitantly took my hand, and we shook. His hand was dry. Mine was damp.

"My people say this tradition of shaking hands began when two groups met and wanted to prove they held no weapons hidden behind their backs," I said.

He glanced at my slingshot and the sword at my hip, both in plain sight. I remembered my sleeper weapon, still in my coat pocket. I went back into the box that moved, like the one in the Wells, only this one was faster, picked up my coat gingerly and dug carefully in the pocket.

"You won't need that," Zarek said, eyeing my coat. "We have climate control down here, and if you scratch your skin on a broken fang, it will still paralyze you, and there is no known antidote."

I very carefully pulled out my token and the sleeper weapon, then discarded the coat in the corner, along with my boots with the snake goo on them.

He stared at what I held in my hands, frowning, and then his eyes narrowed. "You have a Rectifier ... and a Key! You came from downworld, all right!" His tone was accusatory, and he took a step back from me. "You're one of those beamers the Mother and Father are talking about. You didn't come here the usual way, through the We ... " he stopped mid word.

"I didn't know there was a usual way. It was an … unexpected trip," I said. "Accidental. I don't really even know how or why it happened." I held up the token and stared at it. "Is this the Key?"

"Yes."

Zarek kicked the coat over the snake mess and pushed the whole thing, boots and all, with the toe of his soft boot into a hole that opened in the floor. When it was all safely inside, he closed the little door and pushed a button, and I heard the whoosh and crackle of fire. "Garbage disposal," he said.

"How do you know about 'Sleepers'?" I asked as we began to walk down the wide, cool hallway, which was immaculately clean.

"We invented them. We don't kill people, but we won't be killed anymore either, if we can help it." He gave me a sidewise glance. "And just in case that handshake was only for show, I must tell you I carry a Rectifier too—they can put most large animals to sleep, and what I do is dangerous work—and if you are thinking of using yours on me, you need to know … "

"… that the Sabostienie can't be put to sleep by the Rectifier," I said.

His dark purple brows rose slightly. "Surprise me again, and I may have to put you to sleep just because you're annoying me."

"What did you mean when you called me a beamer? Have others come through that gate?"

"Not *that* gate!" he exclaimed, and clamped his lips tight as if he was annoyed with himself and had said too much already. We walked in silence for a long time. There were occasional bay doors with pad-type controls similar to ones I'd seen in the Wells.

Finally Zarek spoke again. "You're different. You're not what the Roamers tell us your kind are like."

"And what kind is that?"

I stopped in the middle of the wide hall/roadway. Judging it could comfortably accommodate four work cyna-cycles side by side, I wondered if they had them here. It was similar to the underground roadways of the Wells, but so square and straight that it didn't seem Sabostienie-built, as they like the sweet curves of nature. That made me smile. *Here I have a Sabostienie in my company, and I'm thinking as if I am an expert on all things Sabostienie just because I've been to the Wells.*

"You're not one of ours from the … and yet … " He shook his head, perplexed. "If you are from above the desert, the Roamers tell us those people are all kill-crazy and would slaughter Sabostienie on sight just because we look different. I think you could kill me, but you don't seem to want to. You are a mystery to me."

"OK. You were a surprise to me too," I said matter-of-factly. "So, where are we going?"

"I should take you to Moon City. But strange things have been happening there lately. Beamers, people like you, have been found coming through an old, unused gate close to the city and have been causing trouble."

"Other people? People like me from above the Steel Desert, not from the Domed Wells?"

Again he stopped and stared at me with wide eyes and his mouth slightly open. "Do you know *everything*?"

"Do you have flies here?" I asked with a smile.

"Flies?" He shook his head. "What are flies?"

I laughed. "Never mind; I'm sorry."

"You make a joke on me!" His lips gave a twitch. "Rude, no manners, just like I said."

"I'm sorry!"

Then he laughed too, a deep rumble of sound that I liked.

"So, what are flies?" he asked.

"It is a way we have of saying someone is so surprised that their mouth is hanging open and they should be careful of the flies; like, close your mouth or the flies will get in."

Zarek nodded and touched his generous lips with protective fingers. "So are they like the Crimson Death, then?"

"Heavens, no!" I said in horror. "They are only tiny bugs with wings. They may bite, but it can only make you itch, and if you swallow one, they taste nasty." My face contorted, remembering the time I had swallowed one.

He smiled. "I think I will change my mind."

"About what?"

"Liking you. My people appreciate humor. You have a nice laugh."

"So do you," I said, and we resumed walking.

"Do you never tire?" Zarek asked a while later. "We have been walking for some time."

"If it is a long way to go, we can run. I wouldn't mind a good run."

"Run? You like to run?" A sharp, competitive light flashed in his eyes.

"Do you?" It was my turn to be surprised. Mark had been the only one I knew who had really *liked* to run with me.

Zarek grinned and shot away down the hall. I was quick to go after him. We ran full out, neck and neck, till we were both winded and had to stop. Leaning our hands on our knees, breathing hard, we began to laugh. We laughed so hard we fell down and rolled on the floor.

He finally sat up. "This is the craziest thing I have ever done. So undignified! I should turn you over to the Family. But I'm not going to do that." He tapped his chest and became serious. "There is something happening. Something bad. I know it, I can feel it." He tapped his chest again. "We think, we yearn, but what the heart feels is often the truth we must go by. I feel somehow you are a part of this present trouble. I just can't tell if you are a good part; but I believe you are."

He got up and went over to a bay door, pressed his hand to the pad and spoke. "Patefacio!" Inside, there were cycles and equipment, and several other smaller doors that led off from the large main area. We went through one of those doors and into a living space.

"Hungry?" Going to the kitchen, Zarek pulled out some packages of food from the cold box and put them in some kind of oven. They were soon ready, and I was surprised at how good they were. I ate it all and wanted more. We both had a second one. I also drank many glasses of the best water I had ever tasted.

"You will need new clothes," Zarek informed me. "You can't run around Moon City in those; those would be a dead giveaway that you're not from around here." Going over to a wall of drawers, he pulled one open and dug around, and came up with an indigo bodysuit made of the same kind of stretchy material as his. "We can stick here for a while and rest, then head up to the city. I want to talk to my best friend, Mergel, and see what is going on up there. And you need to … know things. So we will talk. For as long as it takes to prepare you for my world."

"What about your job? You can't just go missing, can you? Who would release the Truggils? Or keep the Red Death at bay?"

Zarek shrugged. "Crimson Death," he corrected, and gave me an upside-down smile, and a one-shoulder shrug. "I've wanted to do something else for a while now. But I'm good at this job, and I like the solitude. I have stayed past my time, though. I'll send word for others to come and take over while you go change."

As I headed for the bathroom with the clothes he'd given me, he said over his shoulder, "You will be my new job! Finding out why you're here. You know about Sabostienies already; do you also know about Wonannonda?"

I stopped and turned. "Yes." I gave him a big, genuine smile. "I live on an island in the fork of the river—a very large river—and I have a Wonannonda Tree there, in the middle of a grove of trees that have snakes without crimson bands that would never bite anyone. The One Great Telling Tree we had in our capital city died recently, but it gave me the Twin Saplings to keep safe and to take to my island. When we planted them, they grew together very fast, making one great tree."

I remembered the wonder, the amazement, of watching those trees grow, and then the memory of Mark's death clouded my mind and saddened my heart. In a somber tone, I added, "That was actually what brought me here. It was the tree that found the old Blue Moon phase port."

"And you had a Key. I am right!" Zarek exclaimed. "The head and the heart lead to the truth. Not only did you have a Key, but I believe you are the key to our jump to something new!"

CHAPTER TWO

Over the next few hours, Zarek and I shared details of our lives we thought might help with the problem of the Beamers. I thought they might be the Voice and her crew. We were surprised to discover we both knew Jorame and Wydra Oath. My father was right: there was much we didn't know about the Oaths, or about their double life, and of a mode of travel in a manner I could not comprehend but had now used myself. *And the first person I meet on the other side knows the Oaths, who I met less than a month ago, but would trust with my life,* I thought. Have *trusted with my life.*

"I know them well. They are Roamers for the Father and Mother," Zarek said with a laugh.

"You have mentioned the Father and Mother several times. Can you tell me more about them? What kind of rulers they are? And what do Roamers do, exactly?"

"Uh, well ... the Father and Mother are honored among our people. Like a king and queen; only not like your king."

"I hope not! Our king is a liar and a fraud," I said. "I've read about queens in some of the Earth books. They're like a female king who can also rule."

"Well, not so much with our people. They are equals. That is true, in reasonability and service, yes. They are also our spiritual heart. They cover all of life, like the crown of Wonannonda covers smaller trees to protect them from storms. They lead, they love and they protect, much like a father and mother do in a family." Zarek lifted his hands in an openhanded giving gesture, as if that was just a normal thing for leaders to do, for fathers and mothers to do.

It made me envious of the Sabostienies' ways. "So how do you know Wydra and Jorame? And what do you mean, they are Roamers?" I asked.

"They spend time here in Moon City every year. It's partly a vacation and partly time to report to the Father and Mother what they see while they roam. Their time spent at home in the Wells is preparation time for roaming the North Country, above the desert, to learn as much as they can about the state of mind of your nation's leaders. And to make sure they still don't know about us in the desert."

"Are Wydra and Jorame the only Roamers?"

"Only two at a time are Roamers, usually a married couple or siblings; Jorame and Wydra are twins. They took the Oath when they were fifteen years old." Zarek scrunched his brows and nose up in thought. "That was about fifty years ago."

"No way!" I exclaimed. Then I remembered Susan Pearl and her thousand years. "Oh," I said, thinking about how I had felt when I'd first met the Oaths, that I couldn't determine their age.

"Oaths all live long lives. They drink the purple tea. Not everyone is chosen for that life, or can accept such responsibility and grief. Wydra and Jorame were born here on the moon."

"What do you mean, grief?"

"The Father and Mother and the Roamers have to be committed to selflessness. You may think it would be good to live so long, but... they see everyone they love die, every fifty to a hundred years. Jorame and Wydra have already seen their parents go back to Wonannonda, along with an older sister and a few friends."

"Why doesn't everyone just drink the tea and live to grow old with them?"

"And how would that work? With everyone living longer, death rates would fall, but births would continue, and the planet's resources would be used up, and what would happen then? Starvation ... war ... violent death? We know what would happen because we did it to ourselves, several thousand years before your people came to our world. Things were very different for us back then. We were more like you, killing to take territory from each other, family against family, group against group, until we became sick with the killing and dying: sick in the soul, to the depth of our collective Spirit.

"We all said we believed in the same Father-Mother-Creator, but we each held our way of believing as the only way, the right way, and so we killed to win the upper hand for what we believed, all the while saying our Divine was a loving, accepting, merciful, forgiving Creator.

"But we were not loving, accepting, merciful or forgiving.

"We did not reflect what we said we believed in. And until we all saw that, we fought and killed. In that wayback time when understanding dawned on us, our ancestors buried their weapons and took an oath not to kill again. That has been our way of life since. It was a great struggle to come to that point, but we formed something good and continued on."

Zarek was quiet for so long I thought he was done talking. I opened my mouth to speak, but he looked up and continued softly, "It was hard for our people to relinquish the years we could have had, to limit the use of the purple tea to only a few, and to use it for only the best reasons: for healing purposes; not for oneself, but for the people. We have small families. Most have only two children; some have four or five, but that is very rare. We were told when Stephen Steel, a descendant of your Adam Steel, came to us with his group, all nearly dying from being chased into the Steel Desert, that your people make many babies in your country, and you may all come to the same end as we did, which could have an impact on our way of life eventually as well, even though we have been careful and have tried to live gently on the land. And out of your people's notice."

He stood, pushing his chair away from the table. "It is time to go. I have sent messages for others to come and take over. We should not be here when they arrive."

Out at the cycles, he asked, "Do you know how to drive one of these?"

Grinning, I picked an indigo cycle to match the bodysuit he had given me, straddled the cycle, put on the helmet and said, "On."

Zarek raised his eyebrows and nodded. "OK, then. Let's go!" He opened the bay door and we turned left, the way we had been headed before we'd stopped.

We rode side by side, talking through the helmet coms. "You said you sent messages for others to come. How did you do that?" I asked.

"Our technology, most of it, came from your people when they first landed here. They were very advanced. If we had had some of that advanced technology when we were warlike, you would have found no one here when you arrived two thousand years ago. It was a marvel to our people; like magic. But we adapt quickly, and we added our own sensibility to things. We learned to maintain the solar satellites your people had put into place."

"Then what happened? Why do my people have so little of this technology? Well, I do have two cyna-cycles now myself. I don't understand how they work, but I do know how to drive them."

Zarek laughed quietly. "I can see that!"

"I don't understand why our leaders decided to hide all this information and technology from us, to bury it. But then, I don't understand why they have made the laws they have or treat our people as they do. I want to change that. I want to learn more about your leaders, how your Father and Mother lead your people. I'd like to meet them."

"Yes," he said thoughtfully. "You are not what I expected or was told your people are like."

We drove in silence for quite a while till we came to a steel door. Zarek made it open, and we raced out onto a smooth, stonelike road. After riding fast for half an hour once we left the underground passage, we pulled off the road and set down to stretch our legs.

I pulled my helmet off and looked around. We were on a high hill at the edge of the world. I had no idea of direction here, but looking straight ahead, I saw white cliffs dropping away to the bluest blue ocean.

"Beautiful!" I breathed. "I do not think I have ever seen that shade of blue before."

"The color is due to the kind of algae that grows in our ocean. It's called celest. We harvest it; it's one of our main food sources."

I gasped. "I just remembered! It's my birthday today. I'm thirteen. What a glorious gift, the color blue celest, on the Blue Moon."

I looked to my right, back down the road we'd come up. Where we had come out of the tunnel there was a vast expanse of deep blue-green as far as I could see. It was like a green sea of trees that undulated in the wind. A large flock of strange-looking birds with ragged wings like butterflies rose from the green closest to us. For us to be able to see them at all at this distance meant they must be huge. They flew as one, floating like a scarf on the wind, turning together, a dark cloud of swaying, strange beauty that rose and fell, twisting and turning.

"The jungle," Zarek said. "Not an easy place to be unless you're underground—for us, anyway. Humans like the day better than we do, and a few find it a challenge to explore the jungle. Unfortunately, not many adventurers grow old. If the snakes don't get them, the Fire Flyers will." He nodded to the butterfly-like birds. "They breathe fire and eat what they cook."

"Sounds like a charming place, beautiful but deadly. Why do you have to go there at all?"

"We only have three cities on the moon. Our two main cities are at sea level, there," he pointed toward the far side of the jungle, which stretched away farther than we could see, "and there." He pointed, down to the coastline behind me. I looked in that direction and saw a city nestled in the low curl of a bay. Its lights glowed and twinkled in the dim rays of the setting sun.

"Let's go!" said Zarek. "We are still an hour away at moderate speed." We climbed back on the cycles and headed down the hill toward the city that appeared to hang at the edge of the world above the Celest Ocean.

"This is Moon City," Zarek explained. "It is like two cities in one, with two architectural styles married in a way that includes human and Sabostienie. The human styles have been here longer and are older, some of them, but we are a unified people, the two races.

"I will take you to my best friend Mergel's home," he continued. "Mergel lives on the rim; I think we should find out what has been happening in the city before we go to the Heart. When I talked to my sister Skitar, she said Mother had disappeared from the ... " He paused, as if wondering how much to tell me. I sensed that he was still not sure of me and was leaving things out of our conversations, but under the circumstances, I would have done the same, or most likely be much less revealing, if our positions were reversed. "That Mother had disappeared from the Heart, that there was some kind of trouble there in the city," he finished.

As we went down into the streets, we saw crowds of people running out of town.

"This can't be good," I said. "Is this normal?"

"No," Zarek said, sounding troubled. "Follow me, and stay close."

He turned onto a narrow, curving street, and I followed, watching the people fleeing. My hackles went up, and I itched to know what was happening.

After a few dozen twists and turns, we came to a beautiful building made with rounded, organic shapes, much like in the Wells. Here, there were no protective outer walls. Why would a peaceful people need walls? A bay door opened, and we glided to a stop.

An inner door opened and an older, rounder Sabostienie man came out. He had hair as white as his skin, with the characteristic strip running down the middle of his head and the sides bare, though his hair wasn't spiked up, but lying loose to one side. I followed Zarek's lead, slid off my cycle and removed my helmet.

"Mergel, what is happening out there?" Zarek asked.

"I am loath to tell you, but the Jumpers have taken the city. The Heart has been over run by men with hacking weapons. Some of our people have been killed. How many we don't know yet."

"Father and Mother?"

I was watching the two with dawning realization. Zarek had called Mergel "my best friend" a few times. I looked again at Zarek, the anxiety he was exhibiting and the age difference between them, and I flashed back to his statement, "Not everyone is chosen for that life, or can accept such responsibility and grief," and I knew in a heartbeat that he had, maybe at the same time as Wydra and Jorame.

"You are an Oath?" Even though I spoke softly, they both turned to stare at me; I suspected I had surprised Zarek again.

"Who is she?" Mergel snapped. "Why doesn't she know who you are?" His bright golden eyes narrowed, the pupils turning to no more than vertical slits. "Where did she come from?" He pulled a Sleeper from his pocket, and Zarek stepped in front of me.

"Put that away," he said. "She's my friend. Pendyse, this is Mergel; Mergel, this is Pendyse. You won't need that, I promise. Put it away."

"If you want to make me sleep through the troubles I might be able to help you out of," I said as I stepped from behind Zarek, "I would be obliged if you would do it somewhere there's a bed beneath me, rather than a concrete floor. I've seen how Rectifiers drop a person."

Slowly, Mergel put it back in his pocket. "We have much to discuss," he said, giving Zarek a sharp look. "Come in, then. Are you hungry?"

We talked as we ate something slightly bluish, but with a chewy, sweet, tangy flavor, and had a drink that made me feel like a thousand tokens.

"When we first discovered the Beamers on the old downworld phase port pad, we thought they were from the Wells, that they were testing the old port to see if it still worked," Mergel explained. "We thought they were friends. We saw soon enough that they were not. We put some of them to sleep, but they killed half a dozen of us before we could put down even half of them. They had about forty men with killing weapons. We were not prepared. Nothing like this has ever happened here before."

"Yes, we have become complacent because of that, I fear," Zarek said. "We have watched from the desert, but didn't think they could get to us here. I was on the Green Trail when I heard about the attack. I was on my way back when I found her in the middle of the old moon port."

"Did you finally subdue them?" I asked Mergel.

"No, most of them got away, into the forest on the other side of the city, leaving their fallen men. We have them in a secure place for now. But the ones who fled to the forest came back into the city an hour before dusk. I had just gotten home myself when I saw the people fleeing in panic, and stopped a woman and asked what was the happening. I was getting ready to go back when you showed up."

"Mergel, do you know anything about my sister?" Zarek asked anxiously. "I talked to Skitar, and she said Mother had disappeared."

"Skitar is safe. We don't know where the Mother is, though. I think she was at the Heart, but we don't know that for sure. We caught a man coming through that same port only an hour after the first group came through, and rectified him and took him to the holding place. We may have overdone the sleep level; he may not be awake for a while."

"Why don't you just hunt them down and put them all to sleep?" I asked, shaking my head. I couldn't understand why they would fall apart like this when they clearly had superior power. "Show me where they are and give me five people with Rectifiers, and I'll put a stop to this."

Getting up from the table, I went out to the cycles and opened the storage compartment that held the things I'd been wearing when I first arrived. I picked up my weapons belt and strapped it on. Zarek and Mergel both looked at me with the unease of children in the presence of a dangerous animal. I held up my hand. "Don't worry. I am not going to use them on you. These people came from my world, a violent place sometimes, to be sure, but with combined effort, we can subdue them. You have the superior technology to stop this."

"No, we don't." Mergel took a deep breath. "Few of us have Rectifiers; they are rare, especially here on the moon. Why would we need them here? We have no murder, no violence, no enemies; our need for them is limited. They work on the larger animals we encounter sometimes. They are mostly in the Wells, where the people live closer to … "

"To murderers?" I finished. "OK, I get that you are uncomfortable with my weapons. I would be uncomfortable without them. But I think I know these people better than you do, and they will not hesitate to kill again, and again, if we don't stop them one way or another."

"How many Rectifiers do we have?" Zarek asked. "I have one, Pendyse has one. And there must be one or two that put your eight Jumpers to sleep."

"The men with hacking weapons took one that I know of. I have mine," Mergel said.

"They won't know how to use it," I said. "Anyway, I hope they can't figure it out. At least they won't know it doesn't work on Sabostienie."

Mergel gave Zarek a look that asked, *Why are you telling her these things?*

"Trust me, I didn't; not exactly," Zarek said, answering Mergel's unspoken question. "She knows things … she told me. Like she picks them out of the air." An odd look passed between them. I felt like I was being left out of half a conversation somehow.

"May I see the men you captured?" I got on my cycle. "Did any of the men you saw wear fancy jeweled boots? Were any of them very old? Where are they now? Thirty-two awake creating havoc and mayhem; eight plus one asleep. Do you know if any are awake yet that I could talk to?"

Mergel stared at me for a long time, and asked, "You intend to go into the Heart and confront them? Are you sure that is wise?"

"They have to be stopped," I said grimly. "I will go alone if I have to. Just tell me where."

Zarek shook his head. "No! We'll go with you."

CHAPTER THREE

Mounted on the cycles, we rode into the Heart of Moon City. Mergel rode with Zarek and we went slowly and quietly. I could see how the people here had been taken unawares; they had no safety measures whatsoever on the moon. They believed themselves without enemies here. Unreachable. Safe.

I followed behind them, noticing how bright everything was. I had thought the Blue Moon was large and beautiful when seen at night from Earth … I no longer knew what to call the planet I was born on; it was not the true Earth... but from here the light reflected off what Zarek called Homeworld was even more spectacular than the Blue Moon was at home. The reflected light made night here a perpetual twilight. "Does Homeworld always shine this bright?" I asked Zarek, using the helmet communicator.

"Yes. We have none of what you call true dark. During the day, we face the sun; during the night, Homeworld."

We needed no light from the cycles, but the Homeworld light would also make us easier to spot if the attackers had set guards about. "When we get close enough, we should walk the rest of the way, if we can find a place to park the cycles," I said. "We can move in the deep shadows better without them."

"I agree," Zarek said, "but I know another way. It's not far now. We can go underground and come to the holding place in a short time. Be ready; we have a back way in."

We soon came to a tall, blank wall, with a niche large enough for the cycles and a small door in the corner. We had to duck down going through it. I didn't wonder at the purpose of having a door that looked like part of the wall, thinking of my family's escape routes.

Immediately inside were stone steps leading down. I counted as I went: fifteen down, then a left turn, and twenty-three down and then a turn to the right. We were in total darkness. I wanted to use my cell flash, but Mergel and Zarek said they could see fine in the dark, even though I couldn't see a thing. They put me between them and we went single file. I kept my right hand on the wall as we kept going down, fifty-three steps in all.

"From here it is straight and flat for half a mile, then back up," Mergel whispered to me as we continued. "We will go through the Heart. It will have light, but we will need to skirt around it, staying as quiet and hidden as possible, for that was the last place I heard the Beamers reported as being."

This tunnel was quite familiar feeling to me; it was much like those at home. We moved fast, like a seamless team of three, or more like one. It was an odd feeling, as if our minds were linked somehow. It made me wonder, could that even be possible? The things I didn't know about the Sabostienie could fill an ocean. But the one thing I *did* know was that I trusted Zarek, as unreasonable as that might seem. There was something about him. I felt a connection with him, as I had with the Oaths when I'd first met them.

We slowed, and stopped at the bottom of some steps going up. "At the top will be a place to listen and look out onto the gathering room of the Heart," Zarek said. "After we listen and watch, I will go out first and decide if it is safe to continue from there."

"I should go first." Mergel puffed himself up with a big breath. "If the Father and Mother are gone, or … well … you are more important than ever, if that is so. Let me go first."

I could not see this exchange because of the dark, but the current I felt flowing between them was deep, and I didn't have to see them to know they were both scared, for each other and for their leaders, their people. I recognized the tone and feel of it.

"Why not let me go first?" I said. "I grew up with violence, or at least the expectation of being around violent people. I have very good instincts and reaction times, and I have weapons. And if someone should be there and capture me, at least you will be safe. There is an element of surprise on my side, as they won't be expecting someone like me."

There was a pregnant silence. "We choose not to do violence," Zarek finally said.

"That is not our way," Mergel added, with a hint of judgment in his tone.

"But it *is* their way!" I argued. "And I might be able to spot them more easily than you."

There was another long pause, then they said, at the same time, "OK, but be careful."

"I'll show you where the watch hole is," Zarek said. "This was the hall of the first of your people when they came to this moon, around two thousand years ago."

"They were much more suspicious of their leaders and each other than we ever were. It's in their nature– " Mergel broke off. "Well, it was certainly in their nature then," he finished, I think in an attempt at deference to me. "Anyway, you can listen and look, and see if anyone is there in the gathering room."

When we arrived at the small opening and I pressed my forehead to the wall and peered through the token-size hole, the large room below was empty of people. Furniture was toppled, the more delicate pieces broken. Storytelling panels in silk and embroidery had been ripped from stone pillars. Some hung in tatters, but I could still tell what they were meant to be even if they were too ruined to tell what the stories were. The lights in the main hall were on. There was no possibility of people hiding in that well-lit area, but at the head of the room, there was a seating area with pillars directly behind it, and I could not see the wall below where I stood at all. This was not an optimal view. There were no lights on in the pillared areas at the head of the room. Nothing but shadow back there. No way to tell if there were lurkers in the dark recesses. Along the sidewalls were many huge, arched doorways leading off into more shadow. Next to the series of arches on both sides of the room stood long tables lined with chairs. Even with things tipped over, smashed and ripped up, I could see the beauty and grace this room had once held ... and there was a feeling of the Tree to it. That radiant presence filled me, but still I saw no one.

"There isn't anyone in sight," I whispered. "What is below us? I cannot see what that wall holds."

"It looks exactly the same as the pillars behind where Father and Mother greet our people, where we meet for celebrations and ... " Mergel paused. In the slice of light from the spy hole, his white skin glowed in the sharp illumination where it landed on him, and again I was struck by how different the Sabostienie people looked ... How this must have shaken up the invaders when they came through the phase port they used, expecting … well, expecting something not that different, perhaps. Maybe the Voice knew, maybe not. But what effect did this discovery have on the men with the Voice? And I was sure it was the Voice. "Behind the pillars where the seating area is—or rather, was: the Beamers have ruined it—that is where you will find the Father and Mother's living quarters," Mergel finished, as if he had intended to say something else but had switched course. "When we get to the bottom and I open the hidden panel, you go through, look around and come right back to us as soon as you can if you find no Beamers," said Zarek. "Knock on the wall. We will hear you and let you back in."

We went down the steps and came to a seamless wall, with a small, square vestibule barely large enough for the three of us to stand in together. I smiled in the dark, thinking of the ones who had built this escape hatch. I wanted to see if the outside was as smooth to the touch as the inside. I wanted to see if I could find the latch.

One side of the wall slid silently inside a recessed area and settled with a soft snick. Cautiously, I peeked to both sides, and stepped out into a small room that looked like a storage area for linen and tableware. The hidden door slid shut. I quickly felt around in the area where I knew the opening was, but found no latch or hidden hook. The doorway to the main hall was covered with a heavy velvet drape. Looking around the edge of the drape, I scanned as much of the large room as possible. Nothing. No one stirred. The silence made my skin crawl; it was unnaturally quiet.

Slipping out, I followed the wall to the first large, arched doorway and silently stepped into the shadows. There was a wide-open passageway lined with many doors, some open, some closed. Going from shadow to shadow, not making a sound, I came up even with the seating area, then moved out into the light and around to the back of the seating area. That is where I found the first body, behind a settee that was tipped over on its side. I glanced up to where I knew the spy hole must be, and hoped Zarek and Mergel weren't there. If they were, they would know I had found someone. Maybe they knew already. That odd feeling came back to me, as if they were seeing through my eyes, or were aware of what I felt.

Shivering, I moved on into the pillared area behind the head of the gathering room. There I found another body in a pool of blood, all pearly white skin and staring eyes; I noticed the blood was the same color as ours. This one was a woman, with the familiar hairstyle of the Sabostienie, but her hair was loose and had fanned out, white, in the drying blood. The sorrow I felt at not having had the chance to know her welled up in me. How senseless a killing! Peaceful people had been slaughtered, and for what reason—because they looked different? Why was the Voice here? Was it just to escape retribution at home? *What do they want?*

If the Sabostienie would not or could not defend them selves, then I would do it. I vowed it on the blood of this dead woman I would never know, vowed to stop these people at any cost, even my own life. *They have to be stopped for the safety of both worlds,* I decided. *If I can do that without killing them, I will, but if they give me no choice, so be it, they die.*

Turning to the corner, I stared into the darkness, wishing for vision that could pierce it like Zarek's and Mergel's, then moved on, cat paw quiet. The living quarters were empty but well lit, which revealed tall ceilings and silk wall hangings in brilliant blues, roses and purples. Against one wall stood a vanity and a chair carved out of what looked like a giant seashell that changed hues with every shift of light as I moved through the room. Going through a doorway in the back wall, I came to a balcony that overlooked the cityscape, all lit up as if for Winter Festival. It was the most magically enchanted scene I had ever laid eyes on. It took my breath away, and I paused at the splendor of it.

There were two types of buildings in the city: one was spired and peaked, with colorful roof tiles, and the other was composed of the rounded, undulating, earthy shapes I associated with the Sabostienie, also colorful, but more subtle, somehow, more pleasing to the eye for me. Mixed together as they were, though, they made a statement about life here, and I liked it. I went back inside and walked through a few more doors and rooms, checking for anyone. It was as silent as a mausoleum, and I began to believe there was no one alive here at all. Then a soft moan froze me in place. I tilted my head, trying to catch the direction of the sound. I retraced my steps and went back into the most masculine looking of the two sitting rooms; the sound had come from behind a massive desk. Quietly, I peeked over the desk.

Blood! More blood than I had ever seen from a person who was still alive. I hurried around the desk and knelt beside a man of great age and presence. Even while dying, he held me riveted with his cat eyes of piercing ice blue. He was a large man, dressed in robes, and where they were not covered in dark red blood, I could see they were made of fine cloth. He must be someone important.

"Is there anything I can do for you?" I took his white hand as it trembled. I shook my head and swallowed hard. The sorrow I felt overwhelmed me.

He swallowed too, and without a word from his lips, he spoke into my mind. *"They took Trisaine. They have killed me. I was Camison, Father of my people."* He clutched my hand with incredible force for one dying. He struggled for breath. *"The Mother yet lives. Save her if you can."* Blood oozed from his thin, pale lips. He blinked and tried to swallow. *"They have taken her to the Old Ship."* His eyes closed and his breathing slowed. *"They came for the Life Stealer."*

My heart ached for the pain he was in. I wanted to pull him from the brink of death and make him live again. Tears silently slipped from my eyes, and suddenly his were open, a red, wavering smile on his lips. "Pendyse."

"You know me?"

He lifted his other hand with effort and brushed a tear from my cheek, as if to comfort me while he lay dying. *"I know your heart. Save your tears for the living."* His hand fell back to his chest, and the fingers holding mine went slack.

And his life flew home to Wonannonda.

The Voice had done this, or had caused it. *What did the Father mean, they came for the Life Stealer?* I wondered. *What is the Life Stealer?* I stood up. He was too large for me to move, but I couldn't just leave him there like that. I went into the bedchamber and pulled a purple hanging from the wall. Taking it back, I covered his body with it.

"You can't hide what you've done!" Prickles ran down my spine. I turned slowly, holding my hands up, empty. "Father's dead, and you did it!"

A child, no more than five or six, if Sabostienies ranged about the same as us in size and age, stood at the edge of the desk.

"No. I would never do this," I told her.

"You have Beamer weapons. You have a wicked slicer on your belt, I can see it." said this beautiful child with wide purple eyes and lilac hair that grew in a strip from her forehead to the nape of her neck, long and flowing, her head bare on the sides. Her chin trembled. "I won't let you kill me too."

She raised her hand. In it, she held a Rectifier.

"Wait!" I held out my hand. "Please wait."

A flash of something hot and zappy traced over my face, arms and legs, and all along my skin, and shimmied down my spine. My switch was flipped; then I was out like a light.

CHAPTER FOUR

I awoke curled on a cold stone floor. Raised voices coming from another room. Not moving, I strained to hear what was being said. I thought I could pick out Zarek's voice. I unfolded my stiff legs and tried to sit up.

"They have been at it for an hour," said someone close by. I jerked around to find John Bouyahie sitting on a storage box, leaning against the wall, one knee drawn up, an arm casually draped over the raised knee. At a glance, I saw that there were bars on the other three walls. It looked like there were five or six cells on each side of us. Looking back at Bouyahie, I grimaced and rubbed my aching shoulder where I must have hit something when I fell.

"I wondered when you would wake up," he said.

"Who is arguing?" I stood up and stretched. "And what are they arguing about?"

"You, apparently. I think I should not take you and your sword so lightly. I hear you killed their leader."

"I did not!" I snapped. My hand shot to my weapons belt.

"They took them before they put you in here," he informed me. "They threatened me with that zapper device, and I sat down on the floor with my hands laced behind my head. Once with that thing was quite enough for me." He stretched and climbed off the storage box. "I do not think they use their brig for anything but storage, which seems very odd to me." He indicated the cells we could see. All had boxes, barrels and various unused or broken pieces of furniture in them.

"We need to get out of here," he whispered vehemently "I think they intend to kill us."

Shaking my head, I said, "No, they don't." I moved over and took the seat he had just vacated on the edge of the crate. "They are a peaceful people. They don't use their brig because they have no crime. They are shook up and scared; their leader was just murdered, maybe both of them." I rubbed my temples, then my eyes, wrapped my arms around my knees and gave Bouyahie a cold stare.

He stared right back. "What happened to you? The last time I saw you, you were a boy. In that tight blue getup, I can see you have lost your package and gained buttons." I drew my knees up tighter against my chest. "That makes me doubly curious about finding you here, and realizing that Allois did not tell me everything about you after all. She was protective like that about her offspring. She made me make promises … " A look of pride for his lost wife crossed his face. "So, how did you come to be here?"

"It's a long story. Perhaps now is not the time."

"I have my own long story. I followed my brother, the Voice, and the king and a group of their men. We have to get out of here. I have to find … " He broke off, and I turned at the sound of a door opening and footsteps heading in our direction.

Zarek, Mergel, the little girl, an older man and woman who looked like a couple, and two official-looking men, all Sabostienie, came up to the bars and stared at us.

"Zarek, what is going on?" I asked, jumping off the box. Everyone but Zarek and Mergel moved back from the bars, fear writ large on their faces. "Why am I in here? You must know I did not hurt Father Camison!"

"Yes! You killed him!" the little girl said. "I saw you there."

I knelt down in front of the child a few feet back from the bars, so as not to scare her more. "What did you see?" I spoke softly, with as much calm as I could, thinking of how Jillio, Quill's littlest sister, would react in a situation like this. "Can you tell us exactly what you saw?"

"We heard a great lot of noise. Mother thought it might be more Jumpers. Then we ran into Father's library and they hid me under his desk. Told me not to make a sound."

"You didn't tell us that," the woman said.

"It was really scary, Greatma. I hadn't gotten to it yet."

"What else happened?" I barely breathed as I spoke.

"Men … lots and lots of men came in and broke things, and called Father and Mother under natural."

"Do you mean unnatural?"

She looked up and to the left, as if in search of a spider's web in the corner of the room, then nodded. "They screamed a lot. One old, old, really mean man stabbed Father and took Mother away." The little girl seemed younger than I had first guessed. *Her height had maybe fooled me*, I thought with chagrin, as I had always been tall for my age, too. Then she began to cry. In spite of the child's size, the woman picked her up to comfort her, her legs wrapping around the woman's waist.

"Then you must have seen me come much later and talk to the Father," I said.

"I told you!" Zarek snapped at the two men. "She didn't do it. Her weapon was clean. And she had just left us. We had linked with her, and I didn't feel any bad in her. Why would someone put a shroud over someone they had just murdered? A shroud is a sign of respect. She wasn't trying to hide what she had done, Willobee. Did you hear them talking?"

Willobee shook her head, her lilac hair shimmering in waves down her back. She spoke in a muffled voice against the woman's neck. "When the bad men all went away, I snuck after them so I could tell where they took Mother … but they went out and I couldn't keep up, so I came back here to be with Father. That was when I saw that one." She pointed at me. "That one tried to hide what they had done. She had weapons. She wasn't one of our own, so I put her to sleep with Father's Rectifier."

Mergel took a key out of his pocket.

"No, Mergel! What are you doing?" one of the men cried as Mergel put the key in the lock.

"She didn't do it," Mergel said. "Zarek is right." The door swung open and I walked out. John moved to follow, but three Sleepers instantly focused on him and he backed up, hands in the air.

"Pendyse? Uh, can you put in a good word for me?" he said. "I want the same thing you do. I want to find these men and stop them. Whatever it is they are up to, they mean no good for any of us. They will keep killing until we stop them." John said. "You stand a better chance of stopping them with me, than without me."

I turned and gave him a hard look.

"For your mother, then," he said. "For Allois."

"I'd like to talk to the other men you are holding. Is that here or somewhere else?" I asked the group of Sabostienie. "And this man can be of more use to us out here than in there. He comes with me."

"I hate to tell you … " Mergel paused, then said, "but the men we put in the holding place got out somehow. The bars were broken open, they were old and weak."

"The king and Voice came with their men and broke them out," John Bouyahie said. "I heard them down at the end of this corridor but I sure as hell did not want them to find out I was here with no way to protect myself. They would have killed me. I am persona non grata with them. So I hid among the boxes when they all came past looking for a way out of here." He pointed at the door the Sabostienie had come through. "They went that way."

"Come with me," Zarek said, and headed in the direction Bouyahie had indicated the Voice had taken. We all followed. Behind the door was what looked like a map room, with a great quantity of maps on the walls and tables, with charts and maps. At that moment, the door on the opposite wall burst open, and Jorame and Wydra rushed in.

"Thank Wonannonda you are safe!" Jorame came to me and almost hugged me, but then just took my shoulders in his hands and shook me. "What were you thinking? Why would you mess with technology you don't understand without us around?"

"How did you get here so fast?" I asked. "Is everyone OK back home?"

"We will talk about that later. Tell me what happened." Jorame gave me another gentle shake.

I pull out the old token from my pouch. "I had this in my pocket. I think it was what brought me through the phase port. And yes, you're right, I had no idea what it would do. It was purely accidental."

"No. It was fate," Zarek said. Both Oaths glanced at him, and gave their greetings to him and the others, and a hard eye to John Bouyahie.

"If Zarek had not come along when he did, I would have been eaten by the Crimson Death," I explained.

"Oh, dear Wonannonda," Wydra breathed. "Thank the Creator you weren't." A shudder of pure revulsion passed over her from head to toe.

"The Father is dead," Zarek said flatly. "Beamers from Homeworld came through the old park phase port, and killed … " He turned to one of the official-looking men. "How many?"

"Twenty-three; twenty-four, now that we have found Father. We don't know what has become of Mother." The man slumped in defeat. "How will we continue without them?"

My mind flashed to the reaction of some of my people to the death of Telling Tree. There was the same kind of deep bond here. Only this was for people. "Father Camison told me to follow them and save Mother Trisaine if I could. That they were looking for the Old Ship, and something called the Life Stealer."

A collective gasp sucked the air from the room as John and I looked around from face to horrified face. "What?" John and I said in unison.

"What is the Old Ship and the Life Stealer?" I asked as an inkling of terror prickled at the back of my mind. "We need to go. Now!"

"Oh, God." Jorame dropped into a chair at one of the map tables. "Could this possibly get any worse?"

"No time to sit. Pen is right: we have to prepare to go," John said. "We have to stop them as quickly as we can, before they find this Life Stealer thing, whatever it is."

"Willobee, can you show us which way they went?" A need to move raced through my blood as Willobee wriggled down from the woman's fearful, clutching grasp.

"They came back here, to this room, and took a map the Mother told them they would need." She headed out of the room and back through the living quarters, down some steps and outside to a courtyard, then into the street.

We all followed her.

We traveled down the street for a ways until she stopped. Willobee pointed. "That way. I couldn't keep up without them seeing me, and I was afraid."

The sun was beginning to rise. The glory of a purple and pink-golden sky made me breathe easier. The words, *"Be at peace, I am with you,"* rode a current of soft wind that caressed my face. I took a deep breath and settled my mind.

"OK," I said. "We need to prepare for all contingencies. Food, gear, weapons." The others shifted and murmured uneasily at the mention of weapons, but I just turned and headed back to the Heart. They followed, like a flock of agitated geese, John beside me, his long strides matching my own.

"So what are you thinking?" His dark, brooding face was close to mine as we marched shoulder to shoulder.

"You don't know about cyna-cycles. You're in for a treat. We can catch up to them, easy. But we should not be lulled into thinking this is going to *be* easy. We will be going against what has become the nature of these people, the Sabostienie. They don't kill. We may have to. There is going to be pressure on us not to."

"That will not bother me. And it will not stop me either," John reassured me. "No matter what comes, my brother is a dead man, along with anyone who gets between us. Other than that, I will do what I can to keep you alive, along with your friends. Allois would want that." He gave me a raised eyebrow and a sidelong look. "You have some very strange friends, Pendyse Ra'Vell."

"My world is expanding, that's true!" A small smile tugged at the corners of my lips. "And making strange friends seems to be a talent of mine. Strange, but interesting."

Zarek trotted up on the other side of me. "We can gear up some work cycles and stock the storage compartments with food and weapons of our kind … and your kind, and catch up to them in very short order, I think, if we can figure out were they went. They can't get far on foot."

"That's exactly what I think, too," I said. "John and I will head out as soon as that is done. Do you know where this Old Ship is?"

"Don't think you're going alone!" Zarek's pupils were fine slits, showing large amethyst irises with a deeper purple fanning out from the vertical center; his lips were a stubborn, compressed line. "Mergel is coming too. And Jorame and Wydra."

"What we are going to have to do … may not be … " I began haltingly.

"What we will have to do remains to be seen," Zarek said.

"Would you look at that?" John Bouyahie stopped in the middle of the street and was staring at the building we'd just come from. "It is the barracks!" He shook his head. "Look at it. It is exactly like the building in Telling Wood that housed the Kings guard. Your Father and Mother lived in a military building," he said.

I saw it, too, and realized the great hall, the side passageways and all the doors and rooms off to both sides were barracks for fighting men. The Sabostienie had transformed a training place for fighting into a gathering place for celebrations of family and friends to live together peaceably. The symbolism was not lost on me.

"Someday, Zarek, you are going to tell me the history of your people," I said. "I want to know everything."

"If we all live through this, I will gladly tell you whatever you want to know, and turn you loose in the Heart's Library." He fell silent as we entered the building. No one spoke as we headed for the kitchens.

Once there, we talked about cycles and what to pack. They gave me my weapons, and I put them back on my belt. They showed John a stash of weapons they had taken from the eight men they had put to sleep. When the king freed his men they hadn't been able to find those weapons to take away with them.

As we finished up, Mergel said, "We will make time to honor our dead before we go." Mergel touched Zarek's back in a comforting way. "Your sister, Skitar, her husband and Willobee, along with a few others, have already gone up, and they are preparing for your father's Sending."

I stopped what I was doing and stared at Zarek. "*Your* father?" I said, "Your flesh-and-blood father?"

He looked away and swallowed. "Yes," was all he said, and he continued packing the trail food we would eat on our trip in case it took that long to catch up to the Mother. *His* mother.

"Zarek ... I am ... " I didn't know what to say. I had been where he was so many times before, and yet I had nothing to say. I knew nothing would take away the sting of pain, the realization that he would never see his loved one again. I went to him and gave his shoulder with a gentle squeeze and a pat. I didn't know him well enough to do anything more. I hardly knew him at all.

"You said he spoke to you." He turned to me then. "Did he say any thing else? Anything more than about the ship and the Life Stealer?"

"He told me, 'The Mother yet lives. Save her if you can.' He spoke my name out loud; all else he spoke in my mind. He said that he knew my heart, and to save my tears for the living."

At that, Zarek gave a tremble of a smile. "That is something we say at every Sending: life is for the living; save your tears for the living." He blinked and a large tear slid, sparkling like a diamond, down his face and hung for a moment on his sharp white chin before plopping onto the stone floor. I followed it down, my gaze locked on the seeming slow motion of that drop of salt water. A world of pain in a single tear, down, down, splash, one tear scattered into many, the pain of many; I saw it all in one tear.

"You are the designated next Father, aren't you?" I asked, barely above a whisper. I felt my heart would break for him. I knew what responsibility passed down too soon felt like, too. He nodded and brushed at his eyes. He may have been fifty or sixty years old, but in the scheme of things in his world, it still may have been too soon.

Mergel hefted a full pack onto his back and eyed us as he slammed another loaded pack into John Bouyahie's chest. John grunted at the unexpected burden. "Here, you carry this." Mergel snapped.

We picked up our packs and the two extras for the Oaths and headed out to the courtyard, where there were six work cycles resting on the ground, ready to go, already packed with the other necessities we might need for the journey. I didn't know exactly where we were going, which made planning seem impossible. The dangers would be obscure to John and me.

"I guess we are as ready as we can be," I said. "For now, John, you should ride with me, or one of them, until you get a feel for the way a cycle moves."

"We will tow the three cycles not driven," Mergel said. "Jorame and Wydra have gone up to the Sending place. Our people have moved our dead there already. Everything is prepared."

"Can all of you speak mind to mind, like the Father spoke to me?" I asked as we climbed onto the cycles, John awkwardly clambered up behind me. For a large man, he was the soul of grace in motion, except for now, when his lack of ease became palpable.

Mergel gave me a tight-faced look. "Who told you we could mind speak?" He shot Zarek a scolding glance.

Zarek only shook his head a bit and shrugged. "I told you she was good at figuring things out." He shrugged. "Some of us are better at it than others. Jorame and Wydra are very good at it between themselves. Some people can only mind speak, or mind link, share the touch with people they know very well. Father and Mother can … could … Mother will hold out for as long as she can, but she will already know Father is dead, and that will be very hard on her. They have been together for over seven hundred years. They were close; no distance could ever break their mind link. Not even when one was on Homeworld and the other was up here." Zarek mounted his cycle, hiding his face inside his helmet.

"So, are you saying you can hear all our thoughts?" John asked.

"No. Of course not!" Mergel said. "On," he told his cycle, and it lifted a couple of feet off the ground.

I felt Bouyahie tense.

"Put your helmet on," I said. "We can continue this conversation as we go. On." I said, and lifted off the ground as John clutched at my waist, his jeweled boots jerking against the sides of the cycle until he found the footholds, and then he put on his helmet.

"No one would read a thought unless it is given," Zarek said.

"Zarek and I mind link easily because we have been together since birth. Best friends before we could even speak words." Mergel was attaching the gravlock to one of the extra cycles as he spoke, broadcasting to all the helmets.

"Wait a goddamn minute here," John snapped. "You are not even the same age. What are you talking about, since you were born?"

I sighed. "John, they are the same age." I backed up and gravlocked to another cycle, even as Zarek did the same. "You read some of the disk books, didn't you? The Voice and the king drank tea made from the Purple Pearl. They are very, very old. You knew that, surely."

"Well, yes, but … seeing it like this is different than knowing the Voice is ancient; I can see that for myself. With Zarek, here, he looks hardly older than you. How old are you, anyway, Zarek?"

"We have slightly longer lives than humans in the natural course of things. As Pendyse's ancestor, Susan Pearl, discovered, the purple tea adds about a hundred years chronologically to about every five years of aging. I was fifteen when I took my Oath."

"So how old are you?" John asked again. "In years lived."

Mergel answered. "We were born on the same day sixty-eight years ago." Mergel shot out ahead of us all. "I may have thirty-five or forty-five years of life left, if I don't get killed on this crazy mission. I hate the jungle, but I love Mother."

We were all quiet then, lost in our own thoughts as we followed Mergel.

The road led us to the edge of the city, to a place high up on the bluffs on the opposite side of the city from where Zarek and I had come in. The road wound around the base of a cone-shaped rise, and a spiral trail went up and around it. At the top was a large amphitheater of the purest white stone. The open side of the amphitheater faced the ocean. At that outer edge was a white marble stage where the bodies would be lifted up. Hundreds of people, maybe a thousand, were gathered, and filled the semicircle of seats that had been carved out of the white marble butte. Many colorful robes and headscarves blocked the sun from their sensitive skin and fluttered in the early morning breeze.

After parking the cycles, we went and sat in the front row. I looked down toward the ocean to see the glass oblong boxes rise out of the floor of the stone, to stand on their feet end. Each a white wrapped body held upright by the narrow glass walls. Twenty-four bodies in all with Father Camison wrapped in purple in the center, so many, even one small box in the middle next to the Father.

One of the men who had been with us at the brig stood up and walked to the front of the stone stage area, raised his hands and called the murmuring to silence.

"We are here to Send our loved ones home to Wonannonda, our maker and true Father and Mother, who loves us and all living, who is larger than this sky, deeper than this ocean, willing and ready to receive us when we leave this life," he said.

"This life is for the living." The swell of hundreds of voices rose around me. A shiver went down my spine.

The man lowered his hands and said, "Save your tears for the living. We Send our loved ones to a place we can only imagine, and we honor them with lives well lived."

It struck me how similar our death ceremonies were, both peoples sharing simple, quick partings. How could that be? Two such different peoples: was the same Creator our common link?

The man who had spoken came and sat with us, and slowly, blue and red vapor filled the glass boxes, curled, hugged, clung to and changed the bodies into a sparkling rich cloud of opalescent shimmering air, like frozen fog, only denser. It took a long, silent time, but when this change was complete, the walls of the boxes dropped down into the stone floor, and the breeze caught the shimmering clouds and drifted them out over the ocean.

They merged and hung in the air, danced, shifted and swirled in the most glorious light show backed by that beautiful blue water below us; then the glitter began to drift and spread out and down until it was gone from sight.

Without a word, we all began to leave. A profound feeling of peace enveloped me. I wanted all the people to feel it, and with all my heart and will, I sent it out to everyone. Zarek turned and stared at me in surprise and awe, his mouth open, eyes wide.

"You are doing that! You are Sending."

Smiling, I focused on wanting everyone to feel this peace, even these strange new people I had only just met.

I said, "Peace to you, my friend."

CHAPTER FIVE

The six of us gathered around the cycles as the people drifted down the spiral road. Even though there were hundreds of them, they dispersed quickly. The brevity of the service, even for one as important as the Father, somehow felt right to me. I also felt optimistic that we would find the Voice and her crew. I wondered if the Voice's real, true name was Zee, the name I had read in Susan Pearl's journals. I wanted to call her something else, not the Voice; she would no longer hold that title. Not for me. Not because she was a woman, but because her heart was false, because she was all for herself and her son, and cared nothing for her people. For a leader to care nothing for the people was appalling, unthinkable and unconscionable.

"Well, are we going after the Spider or not?" John Bouyahie whispered to me. He was putting on his helmet, making ready to leave. "Or are we going to stand around here all day and look glum?"

"Spider? Why Spider?" I asked. It was almost as if he had read my mind. I looked at him suspiciously, wondering, *Is there something in the moon's atmosphere that aids in mind touching?*, but his face was covered by then and the faceplate only showed my own suspicious reflection. This mind touching thing could be freaky as well as beautiful, and for the most part I didn't know that I liked the idea that people might just snatch some random thought out of my head.

"Relax, kiddo," he laughed. "I do not have to read your mind to know what you are thinking. It is written all over your face. I cannot read minds, but I read faces very well."

"But I was just thinking of the Voice's real name—what I think it might be, anyway. I want to call her something else; she does not deserve to be called the Voice any longer. You called her Spider. I think her name might be Zee."

"Oh. Well, I see how that might seem odd to you, but I assure you I did not get that thought out of your head, and Spider has been my private name for the Voice long before I knew he was a she."

"You two make my head ache," said Mergel, climbing onto his cycle.

"Come on. The crowd is thinning out. We can leave now." Zarek got on his cycle too, and then so did the rest of us. All except John: he stood there with his helmet on, looking at the huge metal beast as if he would rather kill it than get on it.

"Do you want to ride with me for a while? We can tow your cycle. Would that be all right?" I asked the others.

"Sure, if the old man ... "

John interrupted Wydra with a snarl. "Old man! I will show you what an old man can do. You will take back those words, woman."

She laughed and said, "On."

To my surprise, John got on the cycle and said, "On." When it rose two feet off the ground, it began to wobble, or he did.

Wydra backed up to his side. "Put both hands on the directional bar. You won't even need it as you get used to the ride. Then you will be able to relax more and all you will have to do is say 'left, right, forward, back.' Or just lean into a turn and the cycle will sense where you want to go. No, no, no, don't touch that ... "

John's cycle and John shot straight up in the air twenty feet and hovered there. He yelled all the way up. Wydra shot up after him and got him calmed down.

"OK, I will ride with you and we will tow my cycle for awhile," Wydra said. "That way you can get to know the cycle and gain a little experience."

"I think that would be wise," John said in a shaky voice. "How do I get it down?" The cycle dropped down to the two-feet-above-ground level, and John yelled all the way down. There were a few muffled chuckles as Wydra gravlocked her cycle to his and climbed on behind him.

"OK, Big Boy, ease out nice and slow. We don't want to run over any life celebrators," Wydra said.

Zarek led the way. I was behind him, with Mergel, Jorame and John behind us in single file. We worked our way through the crowd until we were down off the bluffs, and then picked up speed through the city until we were close to what I thought was Mergel's home, I asked. "Are we close to Mergel's place?"

"Yes. But how … ?" I heard surprise in Mergel's voice.

Then Zarek was laughing. "She does that all the time; surprises you."

"I have a gift for directions—although I don't know where your east, west, north or south are. Which is which?"

"We are going northwest right now," Zarek said. "More north than west. If you look at your instrument panel, you will see, on the far left, a small readout that shows you exactly in what direction we are going."

"And if you look next to it, at the little green readout," Wydra picked up, "push that little button under that readout, and it will tell you if people are within a set radius of us. We can scan for John's Spider and her clutch. That readout can even tell you how many are present, and whether they are male or female, human or Sabostienie."

"Can it tell us where the Old Ship is?" I asked. "Maybe we can go straight there and meet them instead of following them."

"The Father and Mother lost the ship on purpose," said Zarek. "Our history told us it had some dangerous weapons on it that could not be … undone … so we left it where it landed and encouraged the jungle to swallow it whole. The jungle guards it now. We think your people meant to keep it as a possible escape if the planet or the moon was not as habitable as they hoped. That long ago, there was no jungle that far west; it was inland and didn't come all the way to the sea at that time, not like it does today."

We arrived at High Point Lookout, the place where Zarek and I had stopped the day before and gazed down on the jungle that stretched inland to the east for hundreds of miles. The wind was high and the blue-green vegetation moved like an undulating, turbulent ocean.

"Oh, my God," I heard John whisper. "What *is* that?"

"That's the jungle." Mergel shook his head. "Not a place sane people go."

"We should be able to find them before they reach the jungle," said Jorame. "Do you think your mother knows where the Old Ship is?" he asked Zarek.

"If my parents did know that, it was not information they shared with me. All I know is they wanted to keep it out of sight, or out of reach. Maybe you would call it a secret too dangerous to know. They must have wanted it lost in the jungle for good reason."

"Could Death Alley have anything to do with that secret too dangerous to know?" My question hung in the air for a moment before it was answered.

Then Zarek said, "We know the Old Ship is in the jungle. That is about all. But that is an interesting question."

At the High Point Lookout on the coast road that led from the underground jungle roadway and out to Moon City, looking to the east I saw a path that I hadn't noticed the day before that split into two paths and led off, one toward the middle of the jungle, and one that lead toward the mountain edge of the jungle. The mountains looked like tall, sharp teeth. A vast tract of land stretched out between the sea and the mountains, the jungle along its northeast side. The land between the ocean and the mountains wore ridges and gullies, a web of fissures that was sparsely vegetated. To the south and back toward Moon City were verdant green farm fields.

"Now let's go find John's Spider," Zarek said. "We split up into pairs, and each pair will take a different path to the jungle. Keep your people finder on at all times, and as soon as you catch sight or scent of them, radio the others. It shouldn't take too long. Wydra, you stay with John; take Clift Road. Jorame, Mergel, together on the east path. Pendyse and I will take the middle path. That is the most likely one they would take, I think. The most likely place for the Old Ship to be is somewhere in the center of the jungle. With this kind of topography, it won't be easy to pick up a signal from the communicators when we are down in the Cords. The rock walls can block the sensors if we are down too deep, so we should check in every half hour. Stay keen. We know the dangers out there; the Beamers don't."

Zarek set off, and I followed him down the center path, and saw the others move away as well. We were out of sight in no time at all, the land a maze of small canyons we couldn't see out of once we went down into one. A little strip of sky, and rock walls was the whole view.

"There are many offshoots that branch out from the main zigzag path. Stay close behind me; I know the way. You don't want to get lost in the Cords," Zarek said, then clarified, "The Corduroy Canyons."

We slowed to a reasonable speed when we reached the beginning of the zigzagging fissures that went deeper and deeper. It was dark and dank, and clammy-cold down there. *It is a good thing we have on climate-control suits*, I thought, *more protection from things that bite, too. Maybe not protection against things that start fires, though.*

"How far do Fire Flyers range?" I asked. At that point we were riding side by side, as the trail was wide enough to allow it. Zarek looked over at me, but I couldn't see his face through the visor of the helmet. "I wish I could see your face," I said.

He touched the side of his helmet and his visor went clear. "On the side of your helmet is a button. Push it and the visor will turn clear. It is darker down here, and putting the visor on clear will help you see clearer without the sun shield turned on. Our eyes take in more light than yours. We have to protect them from broad daylight as much as we can; our skin, too."

"Can we rise up out of the canyons, like John rose up? To use the sensors and send messages to the others?"

"Yes! You are very observant. I have wondered if you and I could mind touch with words. It would be unusual, but we have trained humans, like Jorame and Wydra and others, to mind speak to each other, and sometimes to us. The Oaths, all Oaths, can mind speak to each other. Even the ones who retire keep that ability once they've learned it."

"Your father spoke to me, and he knew what I was thinking."

"That was Father. Father and Mother, if invited, or in cases of emergency could mind speak with any of our people, whether human or Sabostienie, but they had had hundreds of years of practice. There are ways of opening up the mind ... "

"What ways? Teach me."

"We could take a break and stop at that flat ridge up ahead, see if our sensors pick up anything and check in with the others. We can try to mind speak. I certainly felt you open and send feelings of peace this morning." He gave a sad smile. "We can try," he repeated, but he didn't seem very hopeful. "It is usually something that takes time and many attempts to learn."

We carefully rose up twenty-three feet and moved onto a flat ridge. Looking over the land from that perspective, you couldn't tell it was riddled with fissures at all. It looked flat from there, except for the drop beside us.

I stood at the edge of the ridge, helmet off, shading my eyes. "We have nothing like this landscape on ... on Homeworld," I said. "It is starkly beautiful." Then I remembered the Steel Desert. "Well, there is the desert and the Wells."

Helmet off, Zarek came and stood next to me, gazing at me and not the landscape. "I have a feeling your eyes take beauty with them, where many others would see only desolation."

Slowly, I turned and stared at him. The dazzle of his white skin gleamed in the bright sun. His eyes were the color of the Trillium Sea back home, with the barest of cat-slit black pupils, the iris turning deeper purple at the outer rim as well as around the pupil.

"Well ... it *is* beautiful," I said.

"You are one of the lucky ones, I think. Not everyone is gifted with the natural eye to see beyond what appears on the surface to what is beneath, within; eyes and a mind that recognizes there is beauty even in the homeliest of things, like this land here."

"Your eyes are quite amazing, too!" My pulse had an odd beat to it, and I could feel my face flush as I stared at him.

He turned to stare out at the flat-looking reddish brown rocks and the wind-bitten weeds of the same color that stubbornly clung to those rocks while I stared at his flattish profile. Not much of a nose, small, with a sharp bridge, and fine tipped; small seashell-like ears with pointed tips; lips with a slight purple-pink tint to them. His deep purple hair was a thick, wiry two-inch hedge along the top of his head, with a braid that hung down the middle of his back. His appearance was beginning to grow on me, I thought, not as shocking, actually pleasing.

"Do all the Sabostienies' hair grow only on the top like that? And not on the sides?" I ask. "I have noticed ... "

He smiled and turned back to me. "Yes."

Going back over to the cycles, I watched as he cast out the sensors to pick up any humans nearby. "Nothing for a fifty-mile radius," he grunted, then tapped a thing that looked like a cell watch and spoke into the face of it. "Wydra, Mergel, take a break and do a reading, if you can pick up my call. We are maybe not quite a third of the way through the Cords at this point."

"Hey." Wydra's voice came out of the tiny wrist thing, which amazed me. "We are on the Green Road between the jungle and the Cords. John is doing all right with the driving. He is a little bit like Pendyse's friend Rifkin was at first, not sure he likes the speed." Then she laughed. "But he's no coward! We'll take a reading and get right back to you."

"Mergel. Are you there?" No answer.

"Maybe they haven't reached a place they can lift up onto yet," I said.

"I'll try again before we drop down into the Cord."

Zarek made a sun shield bubble over our heads and sat on the rock ridge. He patted the ground in front of him and I sat down, cross-legged. "Take a deep breath, relax, just breathe in and out," he instructed. "Slow and easy, center on the heart. We did that for a while. "Notice how many scents there are around us. Slowly scan the ground and notice how many different shades of color you can see."

I did as he said, breathing deeply. Dust, a dry plant that had a kind of sickly sweet scent, then a bitter taste at the back of my mouth, another deep breath, my eyes tracking slowly over the rocks and bushes near by. Something large and coiled, just out of visual range, made a scrape of sound. I went rigid, staring in the direction of this slightest of noises.

"Don't worry, it's just a bush baby, nothing to be concerned about," Zarek reassured me. "I'm impressed you noticed him. Now do that again, with your eyes closed. Feel with your other senses, relax … and open your mind to nature. No questions now, form no thoughts, just open to impressions of the nature around you."

That was hard, having no thoughts, but I tried. I let my thoughts drift away, breathing deep and trusting Zarek that whatever a bush baby was, it really was harmless. I told my mind to *Release your thoughts, let them go.* I began to lift, to let go. I felt like I was floating.

Eyes closed, mind open, deep breathe. The sickly sweet smell came from a crevice three feet to my left. It wasn't a plant smell: it was coming from a bug at the base of the plant. I could hear it chewing the stem of the plant, could smell the tangy weed scent of it and the combination of the bug and plant. Shifting my senses to the bush baby, smelling a slight rotten egg scent, then I noticed another smell very close to it, like the urine of a furred animal. Tiny feet scratched in the sand, ever so quietly. Something shot out of another crevice and bit the furred thing. I jumped, my eyes flying open, and I saw the roiling coil of a very, very large snake. I was on my feet in an instant and on the back of my cycle with my feet up in the next. I watched the thing, as thick as my arm and twice as long, wrap around a rodent of some kind.

Zarek watched from where he sat. "Truly, they are harmless. They only eat these small sand roos. Now, if you were a sand roo, I would tell you to run. But the bush baby would rather flee from you than take a bite. They're timid creatures. Really."

Still, I crossed my legs on the seat of the cycle as I watched the grey-silver snake swallow a rat the size of my two fists. I was acutely aware of each sound, smell and sight. I noticed colors in the minutest of flowers, brilliant yellows and whites, greens, fringed in red and purple. I was blown away at what I had missed at first glance. Even the grains of sand had distinct colors to them.

"Ah, yes, your eyes are open," Zarek said approvingly. "Come back and join me. We have a little more time. You catch on very quickly."

I got off the cycle and sat in front of him again. "Now we open to each other. We hold hands, and look only into each other's eyes, but you listen for my heartbeat, I listen for yours. Once you think you have caught the thread of mine, close your eyes and concentrate on the sound of it. Count the beats, feel the rhythm of it. Open your eyes when you think you have it."

We touched hands lightly, and I was soon lost in the changing shades of purple in those fathomless eyes, and listened for the drumbeat of blood that would tell me who he was at the deepest level. Soon I caught a soft *thump, tada, thump, tada,* that sang through me. It grew louder. I closed my eyes and the sound and feel of *thump, tada, thump, tada,* coursed up my arms and into my chest to mingle with my own beating heart.

Dada, dada. Dada, dada. Dada, dada. There was a fine, sharp staccato of double beats, just like my heart always felt to me, but at a quicker tempo than normal. Then suddenly the two came together and sounded like *thump, dada, dada, tada, thump, dada, dada, tada, thump.* The rhythm sped up, and we pulled apart in shock and stared at each other.

"What was that?" I gasped.

Zarek only stared at me, his fine nostrils extended, his pupils expanded to make his eyes appear almost all black. I felt a tug on my soul, as if some part of him were lodged in my heart and couldn't get out. I could hardly breathe. I jumped to my feet, backed away and turned to stare out over the rocky landscape.

After a while, he came up behind me. "I'm sorry if that scared you. I have worked with many people, helping them learn mind touch, but that has never happened to me before. I ... "

"What *was* that?" I repeated. I felt so strange. I wasn't sure what I was feeling, or whose feelings I was feeling. Were they mine, or his?

"I don't know, but please don't let it stop you from opening to the touch. I believe you have a great capacity for this, more so than many of my own people who have grown up around it their entire lives. I suspected it might be so, but … Well, you truly amaze me."

We stood in silence at the edge of the world for a few minutes longer. Finally, Zarek said softly, "Don't worry. I will never force you to open, and I will never take a thought from you that you are not ready to give. I promise you."

He turned, went to his cycle and got on, lifted off the ground and tapped his radio device. "Mergel, Jorame, report. You are overdue."

No answer came back. He looked worried. "Wydra, John, are you there?"

"Here, waiting," Wydra replied. "I have not been able to reach my brother. Have you heard from them?"

"No, we haven't. We have been sending, but there's been no response." He turned and looked at me. "What do you feel it means?"

"Well, I don't know your technology, and in this kind of landscape, you said it could be difficult to make contact. It might mean nothing, or it could mean trouble." I shrugged. What did I know of here? Then I felt the bush baby sliding back into its crevice to digest the roo and thought, *maybe I could know more than I realize.*

"If your Father and Mother could mind speak, or touch, from any distance, what is your range with them … with your Mother?" I corrected myself. "Have you ever tried to contact her from this far away?"

"Well, we don't really know how far away they are. We have communicated with coms, yes, but not by mind touching, never at some unknown distance. Still, it never hurts to try. Nothing is ever learned without trying." He set the cycle back down to earth and slid off it, went to our sitting area and sat down again. "Come. Sit with me."

CHAPTER SIX

"Hold your mind open, just be … Breath … Be."

"Be?"

"Air." Zarek closed his eyes. "Breath and air. That will help support me and extend me out while I search for Mother's mind."

I reached out and took his hands. His eyes popped open and we held each other's gaze for the briefest of moments, and then both of us closed our eyes. There was a quickening as our hearts began that syncopated rhythm, a link to another being like I had never felt before. Setting that feeling aside for later examination, I let go of thoughts and words, slipped into the breathing pulse of the life all around me, being the pulse, and then I began to stretch out, to grow thin. I thought I might lose myself before I could reach … being air … and then I breathed in slow and deep … and was air.

I floated over the land, invisible. I was the air itself, nothing but a pair of eyes, seeing, looking. What I saw was like the visions in Telling Tree's Heart.

Then I understood the greater connection of mind touching. Below, there was a group of humans and one tall, regal Sabostienie woman standing next to a work cycle and towing platform with men loaded onto it. Zarek's Mother climbed onto the cycle. John's Spider, the woman Zee, who had been the Voice, climbed on behind the Mother, and they lifted off and moved forward at a moderate speed. Then with a sense of great speed my sight was pulled down the zigzag track and I saw Jorame and Mergel, sitting on a ledge ten feet up a ridge wall, the pathway clogged with hundreds of some kind of armored beast, rampaging through the canyon toward Zee's people, and the Mother.

Then my sight faltered and snapped me back into my own body, and I was staring into Zarek's eyes again.

"Almost," he said. "So close; we touched. Mother knew I was there, but we didn't quite … "

"I saw them!" I said excitedly. "Did you see them?"

"No, mind touching is not seeing. It is …"

I interrupted him. "*I saw them!* They have a cycle, and the towing platform is out, and that is why we did not come upon them out in the open before we came to the High Point Lookout. Before we split up. They are not on foot! They are on the east path with a cycle. I saw Jorame and Mergel, too, trapped on a small ledge about ten feet up a deep Cord. Their canyon's full of black armor-plated beasts running toward your Mother and Zee's men."

"That … " Zarek stopped and shook his head. "That is impossible! We don't *see* things. We feel, we hear; we don't *see*."

"Well, you didn't tell me that! So, I saw." I stood up, went to my cycle and got on. "Maybe it's a whole new thing you didn't know you could do."

He came over to me, looking thoughtful, and tapped his wrist communicator. "Wydra. Jorame and Mergel are all right, but trapped in the canyon by a horde of Truggils on the rampage behind the Voice. They are on the east path; they have a cycle with a platform. That is why we have not caught up with them. We should have guessed there was no other way for them to move so far so fast."

"I still haven't been able to contact them myself," Wydra answered. "I am relieved they were able to get through to you, though."

"They didn't. They are still out of com range. I was teaching Pendyse to mind touch *and she saw them.*"

There was a long pause. "Did I hear you right? Did you say she *saw* them?"

"Yes!"

"But … no one … "

"I know. I guess I didn't give her any kind of preconceived parameters. She didn't know that that is impossible."

"Oh."

"Come on, people," I heard John snap, "If she saw them, then it is not impossible. Get over it, and get on with it. If Jorame and Mergel are behind the Spider and her men, how do we get in front of them and trap them on the path? And what are Truggils?"

"OK, Wydra, you might want to take over the driving and speed up," Zarek said. "Meet us at the intersection of the east path and the Green Road. We will wait for you there; we'll squeeze them between the Truggils and Mergel and Jorame behind them, and us in front. Go!"

We dropped down onto our path and also sped up, but I was not as fast around the corners as Zarek. When I tried to keep up, I scraped the sides of the cycle against the canyon walls several times, once taking some skin off my left leg along with a length of protective suit. It hurt like hell, but I kept going.

"Are you all right?" At first I thought Zarek was speaking to me through the helmet communication device, but then it dawned on me: that was a mind touch. *"Are you hurt? I heard you cry out."*

"I didn't! Not out loud." I spoke into the helmet's mouthpiece, too shaken up to even try to answer him back in mind speech. "Do you realize you just spoke to my mind?"

"No! I ... " He was silent as he pulled over beside the rock wall and set his cycle down. I pulled up behind him. He came over and examined my leg from the knee down to the ankle. The scrape was bleeding down inside my suit into my boot. He took the time to cut the leg of the suit away to clean and bandage the wound. "You don't want to be bleeding openly near the jungle; it's not safe," he warned. "There are animals that love the smell of blood, are drawn to it. What bleeds warm red is good for dinner."

"I am all right now," I said. But I wasn't pleased to be called dinner for some wild beast. "We need to go."

Zarek wore a worried expression. He hesitated, then said, "Come on. You're with me, I'll drive you ride. We'll leave your cycle and come back for it later."

Seeing me hesitate, he added, "Don't worry, it will be here when we get back."

I shrugged and climbed on behind him. "What about my weapons?"

"All we need are the two Rectifiers you have and the two I have. We are well armed against mammals ... except for maybe your kind."

Once underway again, we went faster than I had ever gone. I squeezed my eyes shut so I couldn't see the rock walls so close and held on tight. The weaving of the cycle roiled my stomach, so I held onto Zarek, pressed against his back, and followed his movements, which seemed to help settle my swishing stomach and mind.

We burst out of the Cord and onto a straight stretch of the Green Road and sped up even more. I couldn't bear to think what would happen to us if we hit something, or someone, at this speed. Anything I had done with Jorame and Wydra was positively sedate in comparison. It made me wonder how John Bouyahie was faring. If he thought going twenty feet up in the air was wild, how was he dealing with this?

I wonder if they are still towing John's cycle or if they've left it along the road somewhere like we did mine. And what of Jorame and Mergel? Zarek said that Truggils are not dangerous to us, but they are much bigger than I imagined them to be. If you were in their way … but Jorame and Mergel should now be behind the Truggils. Zee, the king and their crew are on the pathway ahead of the Truggils. That should prove interesting.

We reached the junction of the Green Road and Ice Fang Pass and East Corduroy Path just before sundown. We sat down to wait, hiding the cycle out of sight at the edge of the jungle. I heard an eerie scream come from the giant green foliage up high and behind us, which made me jump and spin around, searching the trees and vines.

"What was that?" I asked.

"It will be dark soon. That's when the night things come out. We will have to make a dome and wait," Zarek replied.

"Are you avoiding my question? What made that horrible sound?"

"One of those things that like the smell of blood." He gave me a teasing look, and then said, "It sounded like a Fire Flyer, or a maybe a Nar Cat. You have the cats on Homeworld, I know, but I believe I've heard you train them as war animals. Here they are wild, and as big as your Nar Hounds, I hear tell. But I've never seen a wild one. Not even in the jungle. They are like ghosts."

"Are you *trying* to scare me?" In the gathering gloom, I could see an expanse of white teeth as he grinned.

"Don't worry, I won't let anything eat you."

"And you're sure we got here before Zee? We haven't missed her crowd?"

"No. There is no sign the Truggils have been through here yet, so I'm sure we got here before them. Mother will be doing all she can to slow them down."

"Maybe under cover of darkness, we could sneak up on their camp and take them in their sleep. We would have the advantage of surprise."

"We don't want to be in that zigzag rock alleyway when the horde comes through."

"Well, there is that," I admitted.

After some time nursing my scraped leg, I began to feel a slight tremor in the ground beneath my feet. Zarek lay on the ground and pressed his small, shell-shaped ear to the dirt. I did the same. There was thunder in the rocks, and when I looked up, Zarek had caused a shield to cover us where we lay. Before too long, the ground was shaking like an earth trembler. The horde burst out of the canyon like black Steel Desert sands pushed by a wild wind. They swept around us like a river around a rock and flowed off into the jungle. They just kept coming, so many of them; not as big as my hounds, not as small as a wild dog, *but scary enough to believe they might have done some damage to the ones we are after*, I thought with a certain amount of satisfaction. Then I remembered that Zarek's mother was in there with them.

"Can the instruments of the cycle Trisaine's on tell if something like that horde of Truggils is coming?" I asked. "Would your mother know how to protect herself?"

Zarek sighed. "She would. And she would protect the others, too."

"But why?" That appalled me. "They killed your father, and some of your people, for no good reason! Your people, even in defending themselves, didn't hurt any of them. Those people … " I swallowed the taste of bile. "The people from my world, they will kill her; they will kill again, just as John said, and I was hoping the Truggils would take some of them out, to even our numbers. It would make things easier. We are at a disadvantage here; you know that, don't you?"

"Oh, Pendyse. She will do what is right because it is right, not because it is easy. If you only do what is right when it is easy, where is the moral center in that? If you only do right when there is no threat to life and limb, then do wrong to save your own life at the expense of others, then where is the value in any life at all? If you kill one person, you kill the world. If you save one person you save the whole world."

A flash of guilt and shame swept over me, then a rush of anger flared up. "I get that, Zarek. But … " Frustration rattled me. "But mercy must be balanced with justice. It is not right that murder goes unanswered, that it is allowed; doesn't that make us a part of the bad things that happen, if we don't try to stop them from happening? Even if that means taking a life in self-defense or in defense of the helpless, or making the ones doing such horrible things face the consequences of their actions? Don't there have to be laws to hold a society together, to protect and serve all the people?"

"And who is to say when justice demands a life? Are you wise enough or good enough to know when that is? When does justice become revenge?"

I thought of the men I was responsible for sending to Tomorrow Land, or to the bottom of Lake Fell, and shuddered. Did I feel good about that? No, it made me ill, but at the same time, even though I would rather not have to do it again, it did not entirely feel wrong, either. I felt like I was doing the right thing, even though it was not easy. "Isn't that what we are here for, to stop some horrible wrong thing from happening?"

"Yes! But do we have to kill to do that."

"I think sometimes you do," I said sadly. "Who is Willobee? How is she connected to you?"

"She's my grandniece, my sister's great granddaughter. Why?"

"What if she was being held at knifepoint and you had no Sleeper in your hand, only a weapon that could kill at a distance? Would you allow her to be cut to ribbons before your eyes, or would you try to save her with the death of a murderer who would not stop at her death if he was not stopped by his?"

The last of the stragglers from the horde thundered past us. Slowly, silence returned, and then, little by little, I became aware of small sounds starting up again in the jungle behind us, night things stirring. Heart weariness overtook me. Zarek had not spoken, and the intimate closeness we had experienced earlier was gone. I felt our alien difference like a gulf between us. Such a promising friendship; but I found it impossible to think of laying oneself bare to death like that without …

"Come on, I think the Truggils are all gone now," Zarek said, interrupting my thoughts.

We climbed onto the cycle and slowly maneuvered toward the place where we would find the Mother, Trisaine. How would she have protected her captors? I couldn't imagine.

"Have you tried to talk to your mother again?" I asked.

"We are getting very close. I can feel her thoughts just out of reach. I will be able … there she is."

We rode through the dark, making not a sound. I felt but could not hear their conversation. I felt it like a whispered thing just out of hearing range.

"You will be glad to hear six men were killed due to the Truggils," Zarek said, "four outright. No matter how Mother tried to calm the men and get them behind the cycle into a ripple cave in the cliffs, when they felt, then heard the horde coming, they panicked, and it was chaos. The two men who were only wounded a man in jeweled boots finished off at the command of your king and his mother, your Voice."

"No. Not mine." I shook my head in adamant denial. "I claim no part of them."

"But you do take part with them! Violence breeds violence. Ignorance begets fear, fear begets hatred, and hatred leads to destruction."

Quiet then, I clung to his back as we slid through the dark, feeling heartbroken and not able to say why. I felt so alone, like I had when Quill had left. I longed for James, Hannratti and Rifkin. I longed for home and all of this to just be gone, to never have happened. I wanted to run wild and fast and never stop.

We began to slow, then stopped. We slid off the cycle, and as we walked, I began to hear voices and see the glow of light from their cycle, which seemed to be stationary.

Zarek bent and whispered in my ear. "Mother is expecting us, and Jorame and Mergel are just on the other side of them. We will coordinate through Mother and hopefully put them all to sleep."

"Shouldn't we wait for John and Wydra?" I asked.

"No!"

Ever so quietly, we crept deeper into the Cord. The Mother's light from the cycle made tall, grotesque shapes of the men as they moved around among the rocks. We were so close now; we could easily subdue those on this side. I was waiting for Zarek to give the word that Jorame and Mergel were in place and ready to drop them all when we heard shouting and the sounds of a struggle. Someone shouted, "Breach, behind us!" There were the sounds of bodies falling, grunts of effort and the slither of blades from sheaths. I didn't wait; I ran in with a steady stream of sleep blasting through flesh. I was terrified—not of dying, but of losing my friends, of them being hurt.

Someone was screaming like a berserker as I plowed into men twice my bulk, and I realized it was me, I was screaming.

"Breach, other side! Other side!" cried a booming voice right next to my ear. I turned the Rectifier on the man and the shouting stopped.

"Light, more light, witch!" That was Zee, the Spider, the Voice. "Now! More light, or I'll gut you myself!" The night canyon flared to life, blinding my Sabostienie friends' sensitive eyes for a moment. In truth, all of us held as still as a stone tableau in a battle museum for a few seconds, then it was back to the free-for-all. I couldn't keep track of anyone, we were so outnumbered, although I did notice there were a good many bodies on the ground. I put a few more down before we were overwhelmed, and things got quiet again.

I looked around for my friends, frantic to see them alive. Mergel lay on a rock not far from me, Jorame standing guard over his inert body. A sword was pointed at Jorame's throat. And couldn't help because I was being held in a headlock by a huge man, a giant by anyone's standards. He loosely held me in the crook of his elbow as if I were a ragdoll, my toes barely touching the ground. Then I saw Ojilon Bouyahie down for the count, and was very grateful, but I couldn't see Zarek.

"Well, well, well." Zee sauntered up to me, the curved blade that had dispatched Michkin held in her hand. "Look what we have here. A fish out of River Rush." Her cackle of laughter froze my struggles and I let myself go limp, a dead weight on the man's arm.

"Ugh," he grunted, and dropped me. I was up in a flash and lunging at the old hag. She spun and sliced toward my face. The breath of the blade whispered beside my cheek as I bent backward out of the way, or it would have taken my eye. Then the giant had me in a headlock again. "Want me to snap his neck?"

They don't realize yet that I am a girl. I didn't think that would last long. My worst fear shimmered in the back of my mind, but I wouldn't let it surface, and I would die fighting before I would let them do that to me. I would not even let the word into my conscious mind. Again, I felt so grateful that the crazy Bouyahie was not awake; then I remembered that Wydra and John were somewhere along the road beside the jungle and wondered if they would have enough sense to stay out of the stewpot we were in, If they would know. It made me remember when we were in Remode and I had had the strange feeling that the Oaths knew each other's thoughts. And they did. Now I wondered how far they could go with that. What was their range?

"Put them all over there against the rocks by the dead monster. Is it dead?" Zee pointed her chin in Mergel's direction. "Someone check." One of the men went over and slapped Mergel hard in the face. There was a slight movement. Another slap had Mergel gasping as he sat up.

I looked at Trisaine, her serene beauty marred by distress. We held each other's gaze, and then I heard her in my mind. *"My son tells me you are a good person and have been sent by my Camison to save me if you can, but if you have to make a choice, save my son instead. He is the future of our people; I am the past."*

"Are you listening to me, you little shit?" Spittle was misting my face; Zee stood inches from me, screaming. "You cannot stop me. Your family has been a thorn in my side for hundreds of years. You are the last one, and only a little thorn. No one will dare to oppose me once I get my hands on the Life Stealer, a weapon that will kill anyone who gets in my way; but the genius of the Life Stealer is that it only kills people and leaves the buildings standing. Not like cannons or explosives. Just people … Poof. Just like that. All that's left for us to do is clean up the mess."

"You are truly despicable!" I spat out.

Her face twisted with rage, she raised that curved blade to my face.

"The king!" someone shouted. "The king has been stabbed!" The king stumbled into the circle of light and fell to his knees, blood bubbling from his mouth, blood running between his fingers, which were clutched to his stomach. He slumped over and rolled onto his back.

"No! No, no, no!" screamed Zee, throwing herself on her son, then shrieking, over and over, "Who did this, who did this? Find him. Edward, oh, my son, Edward." As he slipped away, she howled and raved.

All the men who remained awake rushed about, looking in crevasses for some hidden stranger among them.

Zee sprang up and pointed her knife at my eye. "You did this. You … " She hissed.

"I have no blade. I came with only a Sleeper, no other weapon," I pointed out. "And your man had a hold on me when it happened." They were words flung against a wall of jagged, unreasoning rage; there was nothing there but insane raving. I turned my head away from her, and a rush of relief shot through me as I saw Zarek, held with his hands tied behind his back. The man next to him was pocketing Zarek's two Rectifiers.

"Look what you have done, you evil, vile, dirty child. My beautiful son!" Zee was wailing again, and no one seemed to know what to do.

My eyes tracked over the remaining men, five, eight, thirteen, then they lit on the king's favorite grandson, Lawrence, standing just at the dim edge of the circle of light, and in his hands ... blood dripped from a knife. A look of shocked fear exchanged places with wily greed; back and forth those emotions played across his face, until the giant man noticed him.

"Lawrence! What have you done?" the man bellowed.

Zee turned from me and faced this favored child, this young man. Had they initiated him to the purple tea yet? Was he in the inner circle?

"Not you!" She shook her head in denial. Her shoulders slumped. "Not you." The velvet rattle of her voice became hard as stone. "No, it cannot be you." Still holding the knife she had had at my throat, she rubbed her forehead absently with her other hand. Then, without a word of warning, she streaked across the short distance between them, and plunged the blade up to the hilt into Lawrence's stomach and shoved down.

He slid off the curved knife and fell, jerking and twitching, "You promised me," he cried, thrashing. "You promised ... I could be king." He cried, his pain spilling from him in a tangle along with his guts and his anguished plea, "Don't you ... love me ... any more?"

This whole family line is as crazy as a four-wind twister, I thought, but somehow my heart went out to him. What must it have been like, living with them for family? But even now, he pleaded for her love ... and she turned her back on him as he lay dying, begging for her to love him. My eyes stung with unshed tears.

"Look at the pretty mess you have made of my adventure," Zee said to me. "I am going to find that Old Ship our ancestors came here on and get that weapon, and if you live through this night by some miracle, just try to stop me. I'd love to be the one to shove a knife into your belly... but I'm too tired right now." She took a deep breath and wavered on her feet. "Men, choose four of your most vicious friends who they put to sleep. Set them up against the rock wall with swords in their hands. Put our monsters and monster lovers next to them, and we will see how they fare with no weapons to defend themselves with when they all wake up."

"But if we leave them here, when they finish with these abominations, how will they find us?" one of her men asked.

"Does it matter?" She glared at the man who had asked the question. "They will have served their purpose. If they can follow our trail and catch up, all the better, if not, so be it. They will have served our quest valiantly and been lost honorably."

The rapidity of her shifts in demeanor, her mercurial mood swings, was way outside normal. It would be a miracle if she didn't change her mind and kill us all herself.

I looked at Zarek. If ever there was a time for mind touch talk, it would be now, and I tried with all my will and might. *"When they shoot us with the Sleepers, you and Mergel fall, too, and stay down until they are gone. Do not move! They don't know you can't be put to sleep."*

I started to repeat this when I heard, *"I have it. I will pass it on. Be well, till we can breathe together again."*

CHAPTER SEVEN

Light and heat pried my eyes open. Men were shouting; the clash of swords rang in my ears. Wydra screamed. I rolled over, still groggy and half-paralyzed, seeing, with a sideways glance, John Bouyahie with a sword in his hand slashing wildly at one of Zee's men, who was swinging a sword at him. A quick survey of the area revealed that the other three men John's Spider had left to finish us off were dead, blood pooled on the ground around them.

I sat up. Wydra staggered over to me and struggled to help me stand. "I can't make Jorame wake up," she said in jerky sobs. "John is wounded, and I don't know how long he can hold out. Those four men attacked us." Running unsteadily to her brother, she tried again to rouse him; then, when she couldn't, she tried to drag him out of the way.

"Wydra, where is your Rectifier?" I asked. "*Wydra.*"

She looked around, wearing a dazed expression, and then I noticed the bloody smear along the side of her face and down her neck. Seeing a sword only a few feet away, at the fingers' edge of a dead man's hand, I bent and picked it up and joined John in the fight. He was a bloody mess from dozens of small cuts on his arms, legs and hands. I tapped his adversary on the shoulder with the sword. He jerked and spun around. John dispatched him to Tomorrow Land while he was still able. The man fell to the ground, and John dropped, too.

I checked to make sure the man was dead—how many times had our fencing master told us, "You never turn your back on a dead man, not until you know for sure he *is* dead"? —then I went over to Bouyahie, who was lying on the ground gulping air as if he had been deprived of breath for a long time, sweat beaded on his crimson-streaked face, making watery pink tracks into his hairline.

He was a mess.

When he was able to sit up, he looked at me and grinned. "You just saved my life, Ra'Vell." He wiped a bloody hand across his face, as a tired man would at the end of a long, hard day's work. "Although I could have used your help with the other three a little earlier." He sat up and checked out all his bleeding cuts and the sliced-up mess of his white climate suit. "I liked this thing, too; it's damned cold out here at night," he said ruefully. Then, tilting his head, he added, "And hot as hell in the day."

Laboriously, John got to his feet, and, wavering, shuffled over to Wydra. "You OK? The way that one hit you with the pommel of his sword, when you fell, I thought he had killed you." He wrapped Wydra's petite frame in his arms. I couldn't tell if it was to comfort her or hold himself up. "Are you … " Then they both tumbled to the ground.

"Oh, great. I'm out here alone with four dead men and who knows how many others lurking about, and you three decide to take a nap." I looked around the cliffs and rocks. "And where are Zarek and Mergel?" I scanned in all directions and walked backward to where my three friends were on the ground. *I so wish I had my slingshot or my bow right now*, I thought. I felt naked without them, totally without means of protection. I managed to drag Jorame behind a large rock so he'd be out of sight if there was anyone around besides us. Going back to Wydra and John, I shook them, and John stirred. Wydra did not. She looked very pale.

"Wydra!" Taking her arm, I tried to pull her up. Her head lolled to the side. *She's a dead weight, and I already spent my strength on Jorame, and I'm not yet fully recovered from the Sleeper blast.* "John, help me get her behind the rock over there."

John opened his eyes and sat up.

"What happened?"

"You passed out. I think Wydra may have a concussion. I need to get her over by Jorame, behind that rock, out of sight." John could barely stand up himself, but together we managed to pull her by the arms and drag her over the sandy, stone-ridged ground. Wydra's hip jolted on a ridge, and she groaned and her eyes flew open.

"What … " She said groggily.

I stopped, bent down and brushed her blood-sticky white hair off of her forehead to see what the damage was. "Wydra? Look at me." I held up one finger and moved it back and forth in front of her face. Her eyes tracked it, and she sat up with some effort.

"Jorame … " She looked around for her brother. "Where is Jorame?"

"Over here," we heard him say with a grunt. "I am all right."

John helped Wydra up and they wobbled each other over to the rock. I headed for Wydra's cycle, moved it closer to the big rock and made a shield that covered us all. It would protect us from above in case any of Zee's men had been left behind or came back this way to make sure we were dead, or to pick up their friends. *But wouldn't Zee have done that already if she were going to do it at all?* My brain felt fuzzy, and I sank down onto a bench-like rock against the cliff to take a breather.

"So, what has been happening since I've been asleep? Where are Zarek and Mergel? They didn't go after Zee by themselves, did they?" I said as a frisson of sick panic rose in my gorge.

The effects of the second sleep were far worse than the first, and I wondered what long-term effect might come with shots from a Sleeper. After I examined our wounded, I went to the cycle to find the medical supplies, then came back over to clean Wydra's head wound and apply a square antiseptic bandage. Then I turned my meager talents for healing to John Bouyahie's wounds.

"You're going to have to get out of that suit," I ordered.

Wydra snorted a laugh, and I gave her a furrowed-brow look as she said, "Yeah, Johnny, skinny out of that suit," eyeing John with an appreciative peek from under her bandage. He gave her a lifted brow and a crooked grin, and began to strip. Heat blistered my cheeks at this little exchange. Jorame's eyes narrowed as he watched them, and when he glanced at me, I pretended not to notice.

Once John was down to his smallclothes, I was able to clean his many wounds. A few were deeper than the others, but for the most part they were superficial, though he'd suffered a lot of blood loss, by the look of it. When they were cleaned and sterilized, purple spray bandages put on the less serious wounds and bigger, white, antiseptic gauze bandages on the deeper ones, he looked like a large white-and-purple polka-dotted, hairy boy.

"I don't think I will ever see you as an intimidating, scary man again," I said, and Wydra laughed out loud while Bouyahie scowled at both of us.

"Do we have another white suit that will fit me?" he asked. "I really liked that thing. And I can hardly run around in my smallclothes."

After he was redressed and comfortable, Wydra looked at me and blanched. "Oh, Great Wonannonda, Pen, you're bleeding! How did you get hurt?" She stood and came over to me. I looked down to where she was staring.

"But I wasn't hurt … Well, my leg was scraped on the canyon wall, but … "

"Oh," she said. A look of comprehension flashed over her face, and she took my arm and moved me away from the men, to the other side of the cycle. "I think … well … this happens to all girls. You do know about the monthlies don't you?"

I felt my face instantly flush. I glanced over at Jorame and John and back at Wydra. "Why now?" I wailed in a whisper. "There could not be a worse time for this. I knew it would have to happen some day, but … " I sighed. "I suppose no time would ever be a good time."

Wydra lifted her hands to my face, and she pushed my shaggy black curls behind my ears. "Stop that! That's boy thinking. You had to think like a boy far too long. Sweetheart, this isn't a bad thing. I know it's inconvenient, but someday you will be happy for this. It means you're growing up, you've become a woman … and you'll like that. Trust me! You'll be all right." She dug in her cycle's storage compartment and gave me a small package, another white suit and some cleaning supplies, released the shield, and said, "Come on, I'll show you how to use these."

Later, back under the shield, Wydra and John began telling us what had happened.

"I was foolish," John said. "I did not check the bonds of the four sleepers myself, and did not realize Zarek and Mergel would not tie them properly tight, or leave their swords so close to them. I was … distracted. They got loose … " He glanced at Wydra and looked embarrassed. "We were talking while we waited for you two to wake up." A man-woman look passed between them, and I wondered … then dismissed it. It couldn't be, not in the middle of all this. Not in this short a time.

"One of them hit Wydra and knocked her out," John continued. "That was their first mistake! They should have taken me out first. But they don't know about these people," he looked at me, "you know, the no fighting thing."

"It isn't the no fighting thing," said Jorame, "It's the no killing thing."

John gave him a look from the corner of his eye and continued. "The man was standing over Wydra with intent to kill, and I got up and knocked the sword from his hand and kicked him away from her. That is when the second and third ones attacked me. I saw the fourth one over by Pendyse and Jorame and threw my boot knife … and I never miss. Killed him dead on the spot." Wydra's gaze dropped to the ground, hiding her eyes, her expression blank, hiding … what? Relief? Disapproval?

"By then the first one had recovered, and then three were on me. I had to put my back to the cliff so they could not get behind me, and Wydra had dropped the Sleeper when she was hit and could not find that … that Rectifier thing, but she kept searching. They kept cutting me, a quick dash in and slashing at me. My reach was longer than theirs, so my arms were where they focused their attention, my arms and my legs. I finally killed one of them, and then there were two. They were wearing me down, I was losing too much blood, becoming lightheaded, and when Wydra could not find the Sleeper thing, she finally gave that up and jumped on the back of the one who you tapped on the shoulder, and while he was busy with that hair-pulling, slapping, scratching biter," John stopped and smiled at her, and held up his hands with a small shrug, "I got the one she left me. And when she was thrown off the last man's back, I attacked him, and that was about when you woke up, Ra'Vell."

I stared at Wydra with astonishment. She didn't look up. Maybe it was embarrassment she was hiding. *Hmmm. Maybe the Sabostienie* can *fight.*

"Where are Mergel and Zarek?" I looked from face to face. "Did they go after Zee?"

"No," John said, "they went to get your cycle. It was some time ago that they left; they should be back soon. The Spider took Jorame's, Mergel's and Zarek's cycles. We now only have three and will have to double up." Wydra gave him an under-the-brow look, head tipped down slightly and a little half smile. What was going on with those two?

It was beginning to annoy me.

I liked Wydra and didn't entirely trust Bouyahie, even if he did trust me to keep his son safe on Ra'Vell Island. I had taken Lodar in because he was my half brother, not because John Bouyahie told me to do so.

Still, I thought, *don't we have to start trusting people from the other side of the line at some point? Or has he well and truly crossed over to our side? Can he ever be fully trusted? Once he gets to his brother, Ojilon, what then? Will he still fight on our side? What exactly did he intend after he caught up with Ojilon?*

Time stretched on. I felt increasingly uneasy. "Shouldn't Zarek and Mergel be back by now?" I asked, finally. "How long did it take us to get here last night?" I stood up and gazed as far down the zigzag trail as possible, then went to the edge of the shield wall and came back. "Really, no one is around anywhere. Maybe I should go and see if I can find them."

"Just stay put, kid!" Bouyahie snapped. "You are not running off and leaving us stranded here with no means of protection or transportation and no supplies. We will wait a little longer. Wydra and I need some sleep. You forget we haven't had any, while you two have been napping all night. By the time we got here, you two were out and Zarek and Mergel were guarding the sleepers. So they haven't had any sleep either. Just sit tight; they will get here."

We waited for another two hours while John and Wydra napped on one sleeping bag rolled out behind the rock. Jorame and I sat in the sand, our backs against the cliff, eating some of the packaged food and talking in low tones. "Have you ever been put to sleep with a Rectifier before this?" I asked.

"Yes. It is part of our training. If you are going to use a weapon, you should know what it is like to have it used on you," he said.

I gave him a long, silent look, then sighed. "I know the consequences of using a sword or a slingshot. I don't have to have them used on me to understand that. I know someone's death often follows the use of blade or ball—my brother and Mark remind me of that every day. I don't have to suffer those consequences myself to understand or imagine what it would feel like."

I closed my eyes, not wanting to see the image of Mark's dying face but unable to stop it from coming to me anyway. "I admire your ways," I said. "I may even believe they are right on some level, but ... " I shook my head. "I cannot—*cannot*—let them do this to my world, or your world. They will not stop, even if we ask them to play nice, because they don't think like you or me. They don't want what you or I want." Looking at Jorame's handsome face, framed by sandy brown hair with white streaks, I saw his green eyes glistening with ... what? Compassion? Sympathy? Sorrow?

"We know what they are like," he said. "We have been roaming your Nueden for a long time. We see and report the atrocities and murders done to your people by your people."

"How can you see that suffering and do nothing?" Standing, I kicked at the sand and turned to him. "Isn't that as bad as killing those people by omission, by not lifting a hand to help them? What good is your superior technology if it can't help keep your neighbors as well as yourselves safe?"

"Which ones?" He came over to me and placed his hands on my shoulders. "Until we knew your father, and you, and your friends on your island, we didn't see much good above the Steel Desert. We thought you were all pretty much crazy, one group not much different from another, everybody vying for power and riches, willing to do most anything to get them or keep them. So which ones were we supposed to help … and at what cost to ourselves? And what of free will? This is the life and law your people chose for themselves, no matter what *we* think of it."

"No! Not always. For the majority, it is a way of life forced on them; they have no power to stop it. They are afraid of reprisals if they get out of line." I shuddered, then sighed again, looked down and closed my eyes. "Maybe if they knew something different was possible … that they could live free, out from under the wicked things tyrants do … "

He curled his finger under my chin and tilted my face up to his. "We have our fears, too. Why do you think we have Roamers at all? It's because of the kind of sick thinking that almost wiped out the Sabostienie when our kind first came to Homeworld. We never thought they would come to the Blue Moon. This is our worst nightmare. Losing Father … and … "

"Your nightmare is just beginning, but my people have been living their worst nightmare for hundreds of years now. Does that make you feel any less fearful?"

"Pen … please … " He ran his finger up the side of my cheek and brushed my curls away from my face. He pulled me close, making me shiver for no good reason. I also felt like crying for no good reason.

"Let's not argue," he said, and kissed my forehead. I looked up at him and saw the traces of stress at the corners of his mouth. "I … want us to … "

Over his shoulder, I caught sight of Mergel, then Zarek as they came up behind Jorame. My pent-up emotions sprang free. I was flooded with relief, and I slid out of Jorame's embrace and ran to Zarek and Mergel.

"Where have you been? We've been worried sick about you two." When I looked back for confirmation from Jorame, his face had closed up and his stance was stiff. "Haven't we?" I asked, not understanding what I was seeing. Then Wydra was standing beside her brother. She gave him a quick look of concern. John, came up behind her, looked irritated, grumpy at being woken up from his nap. There were too many emotions for me to sort through, and somehow I was feeling responsible for the looks on all their faces, but didn't understand exactly why.

"We had to take cover from a pair of Fire Flyers," said Mergel. "They had us pinned down for a few hours before they gave up and moved on." He threw his leg over the side of the cycle and slid off.

Zarek did the same. "At least we used the time wisely and got some sleep." His glance stopped on the four dead men, and I saw a flash of anger light his eyes as his pupils narrowed to vertical slits. "What happened here? I thought we had decided we wanted them alive," he said to John, "that they were to be questioned, so that we might find out exactly what they are looking for and how and where they plan to use it."

"Well, that might have been possible if they had been tied properly, but they got loose, and I had a hell of a time fighting off four experienced swordsmen, who were trying very hard to kill my two sleepers here and Wydra, to say nothing of myself. It was them or us! Would you rather have come back to them alive and us dead? If it had not been for Pendyse helping me out with the last one, you might have arrived to only one survivor, and that would have been him." John pointed to the last man to die, and Zarek's gaze came around to me, softening. His expressive eyes rested on me a little longer than was comfortable.

"Are you alright?" he asked me. Then he looked at each of us in turn, asking, "Are you all alright?

"I lost my Rectifier," Wydra said. "When I needed it the most, I dropped it in the sand and couldn't find it." She glanced around on the ground, as if it would materialize under her feet.

"We should make them with some way to attach to the climate suits or whatever we're wearing, so if we drop them in the heat of battle they can't get lost," I said absently, looking around on the ground with Wydra, hoping I could spot the precious device.

When I looked up, they were all staring at me as if I had a third eye. "What?"

"That's actually a brilliant idea." Mergel grinned at me. "We only have three left if we can't find Wydra's. Let's all look. Each one of us take a section and we will systematically go over every inch of the ground where she was when she lost it. We'll crawl if we have to, but we need that Rectifier."

Half an hour later, we found it poking out from under the big rock we had been sheltered behind. Then John suggested we use some twine and medical tape to make a necklace of sorts; that way, it would be around its owner's neck when it was needed. It was a flimsy fix, but we could see how the device could be improved when the next generation was manufactured.

The Sabostienie would need more of them. A lot more!

CHAPTER EIGHT

At the edge of the jungle, we stopped to eat and discuss whether we should go on in the dark or set up camp for the night while we still had some light in which to do it. To our right were the peaks of the Ice Fangs, Mergel told us. If we went that way, over Fang Pass, we would come to a small town, Tramon, in the foothills of the high country, the highest elevation on the moon where people lived.

While we were still eating, I was itching to be on the move. "Why not keep going? Go for as long as we can stay awake," I said. "They have too great a lead on us to stop now."

"We have to catch up," said John. "I am of the same mind as young Ra'Vell on this, and if we have to ride through the night, so be it."

"You say that only because you don't know the jungle." Mergel stuffed a piece of green bread and cheese with a blue tinge to it into his mouth, talking as he chewed. "As hungry as we are right now, there are things in there that are even hungrier all the time." He pointed over his shoulder with the knife he'd used to slice the cheese. "And they especially like the night. That would be things like the Fire Flyers we told you about, and the Crimson Death—you know of them firsthand, Pendyse—and then there are the Gorges, which can smell your blood a mile away, especially when you're wounded." Mergel eyed John and his visible bandages.

Wydra gave me a sharp look, then glanced away. She was probably thinking of my … condition.

"Even though they are virtually blind in the daylight, if they smell blood, they will come out in the daytime, too," Mergel continued. "They have the longest, sharpest teeth and claws, and if you should get away from one after an attack, you won't last long, because their claws secrete a neurotoxin that will slow you, and the pack will hunt you down. They may move slowly, but you will eventually move slower. In the end, they always get their meal. Then there are the wild Nar Cats …"

"Good, then, maybe those hungry things will eat our enemies and we can all go home." John lay back were he sat and stretched out in the warm white sand, his hands behind his head, his feet crossed at the ankles, and closed his eyes, as if the litany of teeth and claws didn't bother him at all.

We sat or lounged at the mouth of the Cord as we ate and rested.

"On second thought, I'm willing to wait for daylight," John said after awhile. "I do not want to be some wild thing's snack in the dark." He sat up suddenly. "But we only have three sleeping rolls, and they are not all that wide."

"Pendyse and I will share a roll," Wydra said. "You men will have to figure out what you're going to do." She shot John a sly little look, like a poke in the chest. There was something going on with them, I was sure of it. I glanced away and met the gazes of Jorame and Zarek, both staring at me. My glance slid sideways to Mergel, which seemed like the only safe person to settle on. He was saying something about the solar satellites, which riveted my attention.

"… we can turn the satellites off, and even if they get back down to Homeworld, they won't have an easy time getting the Life Stealer, whatever it is, around to steal those lives if they can't travel on the Zap."

"Yes, but won't that interrupt your own power here on the Blue Moon and in the Wells?" I asked, puzzled. "Won't that stop all electrical systems?"

They all laughed, everyone except John and me, the only ones not in the know.

"OK," John said as he rose to sit on a rock to put him self at eye level with the others. "Clue us."

"We live by the same power system that energizes our cynacycles. It is a solar- and planet-based synergy. They are perpetual engines. It is clean and always available." Zarek explained. "We have been using synergy power for, oh, six or seven hundred years now."

"But I don't understand." John frowned. "Why would you keep the satellites working if you are not using the solar power they generate?"

The light dawned in my mind. "It's because we use it!" Warmth bloomed through me in a suffusion of amazement. "They keep it going for us!"

"No ... that makes no sense." John recoiled, shaking his head. I could see him struggling with the concept of such goodwill toward people who, if they had known the Sabostienie existed, would have gone to extreme measures to wipe them out. "Why would you do that for us?" he blurted. "Why would you do that for one day, even one hour?" He was shaking his head, his expression one of hardened disbelief. "Knowing how Nuedeners would feel about you if they knew you existed?" He looked at Wydra. "Is this true?" he asked the only one he seemed to trust.

"Yes," Wydra said simply, with a little movement of her head toward one shoulder, a half shrug.

"If we had let the solar satellites run down, your people would have suffered more than they already do," Jorame said, looking at me. "Our people chose not to interfere with the governance of your people, no matter how repulsive we found parts of it. We believe in freedom of choice, even bad choices. We did not want to throw you into a dark age. We hoped your culture would evolve to greater understanding ... more compassion and social equality ... someday."

"And we think we are seeing that happening on your island, Pen." Wydra said.

"So we keep them going." Mergel stuffed another piece of cheese in his mouth and munched.

"But that would make you slaves to a people who would hate you, and the actions of the Spider prove they *do* hate you, now that they know you exist," John argued. "They killed your leader. I just do not understand why you would keep the satellites going."

"We may be servants, but we are not slaves," said Zarek. "We serve all people, yours and ours. We choose to do these things. If your people tried to force us or use us as slaves, then our service to you would end."

All of them looked around at each other and nodded. Zarek continued. "Service is something given freely. It is personal energy we choose to expend on behalf of your people. Slavery is energy your leaders have chosen to take from those who are weaker, those who have no power. If that were our choice, we would simply choose death over slavery."

"No, you would not," John said sharply. "I do not believe that! No matter how bad it is life wants life."

"Don't you see? Taking something that is given freely contaminates the gift, twists it," said Zarek, "has the power to turn it into resentment. We have the same emotions you humans have, but we have spent the last four thousand years learning to control and channel negative energy into more positive actions. Do we ever disagree with each other? Frequently. Do we argue? Yes. Do we stomp around sometimes and shout? Yes! Then we sit down, discuss things and work out a solution that all can live with. When people of differing opinions are talking, they are not fighting. We may not all be one hundred percent happy with it one hundred percent of the time, but no one loses everything, and we all gain from this social contract, this body of wellbeing and respect.

"Do we call each other names? Do we fight and damage each other? No! That would be like tearing our own arm off and eating it. How would that benefit the body?" Zarek finished.

"It might keep you alive if you were starving," John said, not yet willing to give up or give in to what Zarek was saying.

"We would rather die than hurt our own people ever again, or yours! Or ourselves by being poisoned by resentment."

"Getting along is much harder to do than killing each other." Mergel stood up. "You have to start trusting, acting trustworthy, and you have to trust the other side will too. That is unbelievably hard to do; anyway, according to our history, it is. That takes real heart. I've never had to do such a hard thing, to lay down a weapon in the face of an enemy who is also putting down a deadly weapon. What we are trying to do right now … well, it is totally new territory for us, too."

"For us all!" With Zarek's statement, we fell silent, lost in our own thoughts.

The dark was creeping up on us when Jorame and Wydra stood and began to set up camp. They positioned two cycles at the mouth of the Corduroy Canyon and one in back of us, down the Cord a ways. They dug a privy hole in a small niche of rock at the very back of our campsite, which would give us some privacy. We settled in close to the two front cycles, as they put up an invisashield that covered front to back creating a dome over us, extending down to the ground on both ends. We were snug and safe from all the night things with hungers I didn't want to think about, but couldn't stop thinking about.

The unknown was hell, in all its permutations.

I felt confused and uncertain. There was so much I didn't know or understand about this place and these people. I felt more affinity with John at that moment than with my new friends; my own nervous tension even seemed like a stranger to me. After I stewed in circular logic for a while, trying to get a handle on my battling emotions, my feelings ranged from these people are impossible to a great admiration for them, peace finally settled over me, and I knew one thing: the all-encompassing Spirit of Wonannonda was with us. If I put my trust in that Spirit, I would find what I needed to know, as I needed to know it—of that I was sure.

The tension inside me uncoiled, rose to the surface of my consciousness and sloughed off like my Nut Snakes shedding their skin. I began to relax, and thought of all that I had yet to discover, and realized that in the days ahead, there would be a gold mine of things for me to learn. I yearned to see this Library Zarek spoke of. *Heart's Library,* I thought. *Makes me think of the Heart of Telling.*

As we settled our bedrolls close to the front cycles, our source of heat as the temperature began to drop thanks to being so close to the Ice Fangs, John said, "Yes, but … " as if there were no gap between our last conversation and the one he was opening up. "The men we are following won't hesitate to kill us if they get the chance. They are acting on human nature. I'm not partial to the idea of dying just yet. I have a son I want to raise, and I have to make sure his uncle will never have the chance to do to my son, Lodar, what he did to Lodar's mother," he glanced my way at that, "and what he has made perfectly clear to me he will do if he can. I am not going to let that happen, even if I have to kill him myself to stop him. Even if they kill me in the process, I will ensure the safety of my son."

"We understand those feelings," Wydra said, compassion and concern in her eyes. "We also are not partial to dying. We also want to defend ourselves and our friends, and will, within our means, and in our way. Rectifiers have served us well for hundreds of years. But some of the components to make the Sleepers have become very rare. If we can, we will take back the ones the Voice—or the Spider, or Zee, or whoever she is—the ones she took from us. At least that way they can't use them against us."

"And how are we going to do that?" The look on John's face was doubt personified. "Without killing them?"

"With surprise, stealth, leverage: whatever presents itself to us at the time," said Wydra.

I ran my hand over my slingshot and sword, glad to have them back on my hip, even though I knew they made my friends uncomfortable. If everything went awry, at least I might be able to stop what the worst of my people plan to do and save Homeworld, for I did not believe they would give up without killing some of us, and that broke my heart to think about. I looked around our small circle, discovering that I loved each one of them, even John; loved them for what they were and what they weren't, just as they were, and to my great astonishment, I was flooded with an even greater love, a love that I knew as the Divine overarching presence of Wonannonda.

I was so full of the mystery of that greater love that I thought I would burst if it didn't stop pouring into me; love not just for these people here and all those at home, but even for those we followed. Slowly, it began to recede, leaving me feeling hollowed out, and I saw my little, personal, love as only the beginning of understanding of what love is.

Wondering what I would put in that huge open space in me, I felt bereft, empty. Even though I could barely endure what had been given, I already longed for it to return, even knowing I was not ready for it.

Morning came all too soon, and we were on the move as the sun glinted off the Ice Fangs, slicing through the huge, wet, diamond-glazed trees and the flowering bushes with vibrant-colored blossoms of rainbow hues that were twice as tall as my Nut Snake trees. Vines that wrapped around tree trunks and snaked along the ground. Ridged roots that curled themselves into fin shapes and circles at the ends, with tight little shoots coming out of the centers to grow baby trees.

The jungle was a beautiful but frightening and deadly place, yet I could see how people would want to explore it, to drink in its natural glory.

"It will be easy to follow them. They have used the flame shooter to burn a path through the jungle." Jorame showed us how to do that with the cycle he was driving, Zarek behind him. I was on Mergel's cycle. We were not going as fast as we would have on a smooth surface, riding abreast, the scanners on full alert status for people or beasts, so far, so good.

"So ... what are Gorges?" John asked through the helmet coms.

"They are five-foot-long reptiles on four feet. They are very colorful; if you see one, you'll know what it is. Or maybe you won't.

They like to drop on their food from the trees. Truggils and people are some of their favorite meals … " Mergel said with a shudder looking up.

That was when we saw our first skeleton, a man picked clean down to bloody, white, serrated bones, the tatters of the king's robes scattered about the tree roots he was decorating.

"Do they eat carrion?" I asked.

"No, that would be the Nazeel birds. They are harmless to us, but they do follow the Gorges." Mergel pointed. "Over there, now that was a family of Gorges that did that. Those two men were alive at the time they met up with the Gorges."

There were two broken skeletons, one at the base of a tree and one of some poor soul who had been trying to climb out of reach and gotten tangled in the vines.

"Carrion? The king was carrion?" John sounded shocked.

"Didn't anyone tell you?" I looked over at him as we rode along very slowly, almost at a standstill.

"No," he said.

"Well, his grandson, Lawrence, killed him. Then the Voice killed Lawrence, who I think was wearing that garish red outfit that is over there, snagged in those bones." I pointed out what was left of another body. "Should we be going so slow?"

"We are OK. Nothing on our scanners … wait, what was that?" Mergel pointed at a blip on one of the readouts.

"That looks like a large deposit of metal of some sort." Zarek reached around Jorame and tapped their scanner. "Maybe we have found the Old Ship your people came here on."

"It is still a good distance up there." Jorame tapped the distance calculator and came up with an amount of time for traveling there at the slow rate we had to go.

"Can't we go any faster?" Irritation edged John's voice. "We can't lose them now. Come on, so what if the ride gets bumpy? Let's move it!"

We picked up our pace a bit, but were still going only slightly faster than before we slowed to see the bodies. As we moved along, we saw a few more scattered along the way. We didn't stop to look.

A couple of hours later, we pulled up beside a flattish, dish-like object that was as large as the king's whole compound back on Homeworld. We couldn't see the top of the ship, it was so huge, and the jungle was burned away from it all along the front side. We cycled around it as far as we could go, to the other side of the huge thing, which was up against a cliff on the far side. There was a path there that was burned into the jungle, heading off to the northwest.

We rode back around the ship till we found a large ramp that had been open for eons.

"I'm not leaving the cycles out here," Zarek said. "We all go in. No one gets left behind. Be ready with the Rectifiers. Whatever the composite of this metal is, it's messing up our scanners. I can't tell if they are in there, or if we only have beasts living inside. These doors have been open for a long time. The jungle has moved in."

"Just to put your minds at rest," Mergel said. "Even though there are many small beasties that live in the jungle, the ones we mentioned are the worst... oh, then there are the rats, smaller than most of the ones we've told you about, but vicious biters. You won't die from their bite, you'll just wish you had—unless you don't treat the infection it will cause. They love to live in dark places just like this, and they are very territorial."

Mergel paused then said in a tight voice, "I hate rats."

Inside, with all our lights on, we could see the scurry of something on bony legs that were long for the size of its body, with a long whiplike tail, about the size of a small lap dog.

"Yep! Rats!" I could hear the shudder in Mergel's voice.

The space inside was tall and wide. There were smaller metal things that looked like some kind of vehicles with wings, and many boxes up against the far wall, and a good-size path right down the middle.

"This looks like a cargo bay at the Zap, or some kind of carriage garage." John pointed to the left, far down the open space to the edge of our light and said, "Over there is one of our cycles."

We headed in that direction, silent now and watching in as many directions as we could, for the light didn't pierce every dark corner.

When we were just about at the end of this huge space, the ceiling erupted in screeching and the flapping of many small flying things that slammed into us and headed out the opening.

"Tone it down, Pen. You're breaking our eardrums," Wydra shouted. "It's only Leather Wings, the little cousins of the Fire Flyers, but they don't breathe fire. Don't worry they only eat bugs, lots of bugs. For that, we like them."

I hadn't even realized I was screeching along with the Leather Wings. I shut up, clamping my lips tight, determined not to make another sound, embarrassed.

John laughed. "I am glad to see something scares you, Ra'Vell. I was beginning to think you were not quite hu ... normal," he said, bouncing his glance off Zarek and back to me. I was glad the helmets contained most of the sound of us talking, and of me screaming. I wouldn't have wanted to be the cause if Zee heard us coming and trigger a trap.

At the place where our stolen cycle was parked, we saw a people-sized door, too small to allow cycles through. We parked and all of us got off our cycles. I followed Zarek's lead and took off my helmet.

"They aren't here." Zarek said.

"How can you be sure of that?" John sat his helmet on the seat of Wydra's cycle and came around to join us in front of the door.

"Only one cycle here." Zarek was checking it out, looking to see what was left in the storage compartments. "Well, they didn't eat the food, at least. Bedroll is still here. Med kit." Rummaging around, he jumped back as a rat ran between him and the cycle, heading toward Mergel. Wydra shot it with the Sleeper and it dropped to the metal floor with a hollow thunk. I bent down to examine it, poking it with the tip of my sword.

"Oh, no, no, no, don't get so close." Mergel snatched at my arm. "Come away; don't mess with that nasty creature. They have vile germs not even your sword wants." He hawked and spit on the animal. "Where there's one, there's at least two. Its mate is around here somewhere, and maybe a family," he said as he peered into the shadowy corners. "If they are not here, let's go. We need to go." His eyes looked a little bugged out to me, so I humored him and stepped away from the rat, even though I really wanted to get a closer look. It had the face of a fox, and ears like one too, but the body did look like what we call rats, a rodent species. These were definitely bigger, though.

"Did I tell you that infection by their bite, left untreated, will make you kind of ... uh crazy?" Mergel pulled me back even farther. Suddenly, as if on cue, a man burst through the door, roaring like a Nar Cat, and plowed into us, knocking Wydra down and slamming into John, who swung him around so fast I couldn't even see the motion, only the results. The man was on his knees in a headlock. John was choking him out. When he dropped to the floor with that same hollow thunk as the rat, John helped Wydra up, hurried to her cycle and grabbed some rope. The man was tied, hands and feet, before he came to. His eyes were red-rimmed, and he began to spout gibberish. One word in ten was understandable.

"Hell … bomb … nothing … dead … " It went on like that, and then Mergel injected him with something from the med kit.

"You don't think I'd come to the jungle without bringing the thing that can keep us sane, do you?" he asked.

"Well, I am glad for that!" said John. "Maybe he can tell us if they found what they were looking for. And where they went."

"Not likely, not if he was bitten before they went in there." Mergel lifted the man to his feet as he came to. He struggled and almost fell. Mergel held him up. The gibberish started again, but it was quieter now, less frantic, as if having people around calmed him. Mergel finished cleaning up and dressing the bite that had oozed a pussy yellow, sticky mess.

"Your right, we can't leave him here." Zarek patted Mergel on the back.

John gave Zarek a puzzled look at that exchange. I knew Mergel had just mind touched with Zarek. I had nearly forgotten they could do that. I looked at Jorame and Wydra, and wondered if they were talking to each other silently, too.

"OK. I did not hear Mergel say anything. Are you guys mind chatting or whatever you call it?" John asked.

"We've been friends for a long, long time," Zarek explained. "I know him very well, that's … "

"You are not old enough to know anyone for a long, long … " John stopped and gave Zarek a squinty-eyed look. "Oh. Time. I keep forgetting," he finished with an introspective expression, and lapsed into a thoughtful silence.

"We need to see if we can discover if they found what they were looking for. Time to go adventuring," Jorame said. "Whether we like it or not."

CHAPTER NINE

After re-parking the cycles out of sight behind a stack of huge, empty crates, we found a handcart with a flat bottom and got the crazy man onto it. He kept saying, over and over, "Rat mat, rat mat, rat mat," then he would laugh like crazy and say it again.

"Do you think his name could be Matt?" I asked as we pushed our way into the dark passage on the other side of the door.

Jorame, Wydra and Zarek led the way with their Rectifiers and cell lights pointing up the curving hallway. Mergel pushed the flat cart with the crazy man on it right behind them. John and I brought up the rear. We walked backward to keep an eye and our lights positioned behind us. My Sleeper was on a string around my neck, at the ready.

"No, no go. Rat bit. Rat mat."

"At least more of his words are making sense," I said to John.

"You call that making sense?"

"Do you know who he is?"

"He looks familiar, but … " John shook his head. "I don't think so."

The man barked his words like a dog. "Big rat, rat, rat."

Looking over my shoulder, I saw the man rubbing at his pant leg where the bandage covered the rat bite with his tied hands.

"Mergel, how long does it take to come back from crazy once you get the treatment?" I asked.

"Hours … days … I can't say; it's different for every person. Depends on general health and fitness. I was a child when … " He broke off and stopped in the middle of the hall. "How did you do that?" He turned to me. "I never talk about that horrible experience." He shivered, turned back to the cart handle and began to push the man again.

"Matt, was anyone else bitten?" Running backward till I was close enough to look the man in the eyes, I repeated "Matt," and he looked at me and grinned. "Mat rat. Mat, rat, rat."

"Was anyone else bitten?"

"Rat mat, bit one bit two." Then his head lolled to one side and he was out.

"Is that normal? Just to fall asleep like that? Or is he dead?" I demanded.

"He's a small man. Maybe I gave him a bit too much hetnothal. I'm a teacher, not a healer."

"Cut the chatter!" John snapped. "How are we suppose to hear anything coming if you guys are going to carry on like a couple of women—oh, I forgot, you are one, Ra'Vell. Get back here and be quiet."

I noticed then that we were passing door after door. Anyway, I thought they were doors; there were no visible means of opening any of them, though. The deeper we went in that curved echo chamber of a metal dish, the more oppressive it felt, like things were too tight in there. But that was illogical: some of my tunnels back home were tighter than that, and I'd never felt that way in them. Not even the first time.

I wanted to ask Zarek what he thought about them. Thinking about our time on the Cord edge when we mind touched, I focused toward him. *"Are these doors?"*

He jerked to a stop, turned and looked at me. Then I heard him say in my mind, *"Yes. I am sure of it."* He turned and caught up with the twins.

"Should we try to open one?"

"No!"

"What are you looking for?"

"I'm not sure. But when I find it, I will know."

We slowed at a place in the wall where it was all crumpled and the metal skin torn and jagged.

"Looks like it fell from the heavens." Mergel examined the breach. "The ship slid into that ridge of rock, I think, and tore a hole in it's side."

"There is sunlight out there, just a bit, but I can see where it's coming through." I jerked back, eyes wide. "There are skeletons in there too. And I don't think they're any of the ones we're looking for. These skeletons are just bones on the floor. Old, really old, I think. Some of them look as if they have turned to powder."

"Then don't worry about them. They are already in the next world." Bouyahie pushed past us down the narrow hall, sword drawn. We followed, going single file through the smashed-in area. Jorame and Zarek had to push and pull the cart through, making a horrible metal-on-metal screech as they forced it through. We all winced at the too-loud sound, but the crazy man slept on. Not even a twitch. Mergel checked his pulse to make sure his heart was still beating. It was, to Mergel's relief.

On the other side, more rooms lined the walls. This time I noticed something that could be a palm pad beside one of the doors. Everything was covered with the scrim of dust and grime of the centuries, and there were small growing things, now and then, at the edges of piles of blown-in dust and dirt. As we moved farther away from the breach in the ship wall, things were cleaner, and we could see the palm pad more plainly now.

"One of the doors is open!" Zarek whispered. "John, shine your light over there."

He did, but it was only a small, bare room with metal bunks hanging on the wall, the top one detached at the near end, falling down, with a nest of some kind in the far corner.

"What are you looking for?" John asked. "If we knew, we could split up … "

"No. We stay together. There will be no splitting up."

There was a scurry of small feet behind us. We turned as one and saw one big, fat rat and four or five smaller ones in the shadows, following us.

"The family." Wydra took aim and got them all in one Sleeper sweep. They fell forward like mesmerized worshipers. "That should hold them till we get out of here," she said. "Let's move on."

We picked up our pace and hurried along. Eventually, we came to a staircase that led both up and down.

"Would a dangerous weapon be up or down?" Zarek looked first at John, then me. "What is your opinion?"

"Down." John and I spoke at the same time. We looked at each other and laughed. "I hear great minds think alike," he said, and slapped me on the back.

"But what are we going to do with him?" Jorame tipped his head toward the rat mat man. "We can't get that cart down those stairs. They're too steep and narrow."

A claw-scratching noise came from the next floor up, which made our decision easy. John grabbed the little man off the cart and slung him over his shoulder with a grunt, and headed down the stairs. "I hope this ship hasn't heard of metal fatigue."

He went down backward. I could see that his center of balance was better that way, but he would reach the bottom with his back to a dark, unknown space. I didn't like that. So I went down fast, facing out. At the bottom, I pulled my sword and got out in front of John and Rat Mat to guard the stairs while the others came down. Wydra was last. She came down facing up the steps. Her Sleeper, which had been hanging from her neck, was in her hand, and she was ready to put down anything that might be following us, as long as it wasn't a Gorge.

Without warning, a Nar Cat leaped from behind the stairs and roared weakly. It was moving stiff and slow, its eyes unfocused, wobbling on its legs. At the same time, three Gorges slithered down the stairs from above. One landed on the cat's back. It yowled, and swung its sharp spiral horn striking a glancing blow off the first Gorge. A second Gorge tore at the purple-and-black-striped Nar Cat's flank. The cat's cry and his eyes reminded me of the buck in the kill hole back on Homeworld. The eyes of the dying pulled at my heart, just like the buck that I watched as his life slipped away that horrible night in Forest Deep, the day I went to the Telling Tree alone.

"This is no time to stand staring," John said. "Run!"

We ran.

John fell behind, huffing under his burden. I slowed and turned to look behind us. The third Gorge was coming after us. I couldn't see it, but the sound was distinctive: click, clack, slither, click, clack, slither. The lizard creatures had a long tail that swished with the swaying gait of their slow running slither. They were not fast, but this one came on sure and steady; then it was in the arch of light cast by John's cell flash. The shimmer of every color rippled on its back. I sheathed my sword, pulled my sling out and put a ball in the pocket, pulled back and let fly, and hit the thing right between the eyes. It jerked but kept coming. Second ball: I aimed for the eye this time, and hit it square on.

It slowed again, but kept coming, black ichor dripping from its ruined eye. A third ball hit the other eye. The thing let out a loud *wubb, wubb, wubb*, and with a slap of it tail, then a hiss, it died as it was still moving toward us.

"Don't stop!" John yelled. "Let's get the hell out of here."

Funny what things you notice at a time like that. John had just used his first contractions. They were more economical when in a hurry, I noticed.

As we caught up with the others, we heard the horrible sounds of the fallen Gorge being ripped apart by claw and tooth and eaten by its own kind. Nature's economy.

Down the hall, we came to a dead end.

Zarek went to the last door at the end of the hall. He banged on the door, and then kicked it. He turned in a circle as we heard a slither behind us. Even though this part of the hall was clean, the pad was occluded, so he rubbed with his sleeve on what I thought looked like a palm pad. He spit on it and rubbed some more, and put his hand up against the pad.

I prayed it would open. I did not want to have to kill any more Gorges; they were very hard to kill. The eye was the only place that seemed to be vulnerable, and what if I missed? And Mergel had said the Sleepers didn't faze them. *Figures.*

I went over and put my hand on the palm pad, and said "Open." Nothing happened, then the word patefacio popped into my head, so I said "Patefacio." To my surprise, the door gave a growl and a rumble, and moved about twelve inches and stuck.

"How'd you do that?" Jorame shoved Wydra toward the opening. Mergel followed, lighting up the interior of the large room with the cell flash. Jorame went in after him. "John, hand me the rat man."

They passed him through the door just as we saw the snout of a Gorge coming around the bend, slow foot after toe-clacking foot. John was a big man, and he had to really work at it to get through that narrow opening, but he managed to push the door open a few more inches. I wouldn't doubt he had torn off half his bandages in the effort, though. By the time he was through the space, the Gorge was only ten feet away.

"Move it." Zarek pushed me toward the opening.

"No, you first." I placed a ball in the cup and positioned myself to take aim.

"No, you."

"Oh, for God's sake, get in here and argue later!" John roared. Reaching out, he grabbed my arm and pulled me through. Inside, I repositioned, getting ready to fire as soon as Zarek was inside and moving to the side of the door, where there was another pad. I hit the creature on the snout, snapping a couple of teeth off. It made that *wubb, wubb* noise, and I could hear more claws on the metal floor, and the swish of tails.

"Get the damn door closed!" John bellowed.

Zarek rubbed the pad clean, then placed his hand on it and said, "Claudo." Nothing happened. There were three more Gorges coming around the curve now, and the one in the lead was near. Load, aim, and let fly, and the ball hit it in the right eye at close range. Then the hiss and *wubb* was at the door. Losing an eye had hardly slowed it down. "They must have skull bones harder than rock," I said.

"Close the damn door," John shouted.

"Wubb, wubb," I growled, imitating what I hoped was their threat sound and not a call to dinner, then I hissed at them as I moved to the pad and slammed my hand against it hard. All the Gorges out there stopped for a moment, maybe at my sound. I used the word Zarek had said, "Claudo." The door gave a shudder but didn't close, and the Gorge in the lead came halfway through the opening, turning its head and snapping its broken teeth at my leg. Zarek and Jorame were both there, Jorame with a piece of broken metal door plating, pushing it against the lizard's face, Zarek with a stick of some kind, hitting it on the head over the sheet of metal as they tried to push it back out the opening.

"Please," I whispered, prayer like, "Claudo."

There was another rumble and shudder and the door snapped shut, cutting the Gorge in half. It pulled itself forward on its two front legs, trailing its innards in a bloody streak on the floor, hissing before dropping dead.

We all let out a collective sigh of relief, staying clear of the thing; finally, Mergel went close enough to poke it with Zarek's stick. It didn't move, and when we were sure it wasn't coming back, we turned our attention to the room we were in.

It was round, with a high, domed ceiling. The air was stale, but I could see that no dirt had filtered in here. Things were dull, but you could see places where a shine still persisted.

In the center was a column of glass that went all the way up to the dome and down into a spiral well to the floor below. Elegance, beauty; words were not enough to describe the feelings the white metal, curving stairs going down moved in me. They reminded me of the last place I had seen at home on my island.

An elegant enigma wrapped in mystery.

"Great Wonannonda!" Mergel breathed. "'Aquilo Divinus … Lux Divina.'"

The others gasped, looking at the white wall behind us. John and I turned to see lettering much like our own, but I didn't know what the words meant.

"'Aquilo Divinus,'" I read.

"'Lux Divina.'" John's eyebrows rose, and he turned to Wydra. "What is this? What does it mean?"

Tears were striking down her face, "I'm not sure."

"Then why are you crying?"

"Because I know what those words say."

"As do I, as do we all."

"I don't." I said, "John doesn't."

Zarek stepped forward and touched the wall where the words had resided for … how many thousands of years?

"'Divine Wind.'" He brushed his hand over the letters. "'Aquilo Divinus.'" He caressed the other letters as well. "'Lux Divina. Divine Light.'"

He turned to face us. "This isn't the ship your people came on. I think it's the ship *my* people came on."

CHAPTER TEN

We found another way out. We took with us from the ship *Divine Wind, Divine Light* three books we had found, real books, with translucent pages, and two maps that were made of the same substance. It was like glass, but not breakable, thin and clear, but as strong as steel.

We made our way back to our cycles by an exit down the spiral stairs to the lower level, and set up camp in two empty crates tipped on their sides and pushed together, with only a narrow gap between them to use as a door, circled by the cycles under an invisashield. It was cozy.

John sat with his back against the crate wall. Wydra sat between his legs and leaned back against his chest, her elbows resting on his upraised knees, his chin resting on her head. Some unspoken change had happened on this part of our journey. Unspoken or unheard: whichever it was, they had become a couple. Jorame seemed a little unsettled by it, but it passed without comment by any of us. It was simply accepted. Who would speak against what comfort any of us might take, when any of us might be dead in the next day, hour or minute?

"Tell us why you think this is a Sabostienie ship and not a human ship," John urged Zarek.

"To begin with, if it were one of yours, wouldn't the name of the ship be written in English? The language you speak? And why are our letter signs so similar? I have thought for some time how strange that is. Every now and then there are words that sound so alike, even with a very close meaning, between our two languages. Sometimes they're exactly the same, or so close to it there is little difference." Excitement bubbled in Zarek's voice.

"You mean like divine and the two words in your language, divinus and divina?" I asked.

"Yes!" Looking my way, he nodded. "There are actually quite a few: imago and image, a likeness. Sub and subtract, under, beneath, below, less. Ager and agriculture for farming; the word inventor is exactly the same and means to discover or make something. Lamentor and lament, to bewail, to weep and wail."

"Liber, libri," said Mergel. "Book, or library."

"Yes, yes, that's exactly what I mean. Haven't you ever wondered why this is so, Mergel?" Zarek asked.

"Well ... couldn't it be cross-contamination of the two languages of peoples in close proximity?" Mergel mused.

"How? The only contact we've had with any humans is with our own Sabostienie humans. And they came to us hundreds of years ago with their words. When we taught each other our speech and cataloged as many words as we could, making the language dictionary ... those same words or similar words were *already there*."

"OK. But what does that mean?" John asked. "So we have a few similar words that have similar meanings." He shrugged. "So what?"

"Don't you see?" Zarek smiled. "What do you think the odds are of two groups of people developing words in common, to say nothing of a similar alphabet, when they have never crossed paths before? And from two different worlds."

"Astronomical," Jorame whispered into the silence.

"Astronomical is right." Zarek's purple hair bobbed and his white skin glowed in the cycles' light, a play of light and shadow, as he faced each of us and nodded. "Yes. Astronomical." He took a drink from his canteen and continued. "We had to have come from the same place. The same world! Don't you see?" he said, grinning. "Auctor and author, originator ... immortalis and immortal. The same."

"I have been meaning to ask about that," said John. "I have been chewing on something I overheard Mergel say to you back in the Cord, about how this was like when you were kids camping there." He glanced over at Mergel, then back at Zarek, and back at Mergel. "You are an old man ... "

"It is impolite of you to say so, but yes, I guess a forty-year-old would think of me as old. I *am* sixty-eight."

"I know about the purple tea, but how does it work?" John interrupted, looking mystified.

"And if it hasn't sunk in yet," Mergel continued ignoring John's question, "to make it perfectly clear, so are all of us … except for you, and Pendyse, of course." He gave me an open-handed gesture and tipped his head towards me. "We all grew up together; we went to the same Teacher House and were best friends."

Wydra winced. "Well, you knew I was older than I look. We have talked about the tea." She craned around to look up into John's face. He looked momentarily shocked; then he broke into laughter and kissed her soundly on the mouth. "Cradle robber," he said when the kiss ended.

We all looked elsewhere, avoiding this sudden show of affection, and when I glanced up, Jorame and Zarek were both staring at me. Embarrassment heated my cheeks, and I looked away again.

"So it's really the Purple Pearl?" John Bouyahie asked. "I think I almost did not believe you." He shook his head. "Well, how can you blame me? Really, even when I read about Susan Pearl, I don't think I believed it. I thought it might … well, I don't know. It is just so unbelievable."

"Yes. We drink the tea every day." Wydra straightened and turned her back to him again, his chin going back on top of her head, her perfectly spiked hairdo now flat and lazy, falling to both sides, after our two days away from city amenities. I had a flash of my mother in his arms just like that. Father said he had had a letter from her that said she loved another man. That she loved them both, that she was happy, and for him to stop looking for her. She had loved this man. And he had never taken another woman after her … until now. My friend Wydra was falling or had fallen in love with him, too, too suddenly and unexpectedly for me to be totally comfortable with it.

What do you call your mother's husband? Is he related to you? I began to see him in a different light, one of connection … and even if he could be one of the scariest men I'd ever met, he laughed with a real laugh, like Grandfather. I saw the contentment on his face and hers, and felt suddenly happy for them.

My thoughts touched upon the face of Quill, and I realized the pain I felt in regard to him had changed, shifted somehow. He was a piece of home, and a sudden longing for my island pierced me as I came back to the conversation.

"Insula is island. In our history," Jorame was saying, "we have a story about an island called Insula Atlantis, and it says that is where we are from, or where the people who adopted our people came from. We always thought it meant your island, Pen, because the Sabostienie have a history there, too."

"I always wondered whose feet had worn the passages so smooth," I said. Thoughts of my home's past gave way to concerns about its present. "But now I just wonder if my friends are all right," I added.

"With everything that has happened, we forgot to tell you," Wydra said. "We knew the minute we saw the place you disappeared from that it was a phase port, and told them we knew where you were and that we would bring you back safe as soon as we could."

"They were worried and scared. But they are all right. We told them to do as you would do and carry on," Jorame said, and then added, "Sorry we forgot to tell you." He smiled a sweet smile. "Next time we'll do better."

"That reminds me of another word, investigo, to track down, investigate," Zarek said. "And that is what we need to do to find out all of our connections and beginnings. Mother told me once that our true name was Sabbatstella, which means Star Sabbath—we were the Star Sabbath People—and that in the wayback years, somehow it was changed to Sabostienie. She didn't know why, or what the 'stienie' meant; she did know it was what our enemies across the mountains called us, though, so it was possibly not nice, but eventually we all became one people, so we all carried the same name. Sabostienie. She didn't know why we were called the Star Sabbath People either. She said we slowly went through slight physical changes over the thousands of years we've kept historical records. Maybe once, we looked more like you."

A worried silence settled over us.

"I pray for the Mother," Wydra said after awhile, shades of sadness in her tone. "Would you try to mind touch with her, Zarek?"

"Yes. We might be close enough, and she could tell us what has happened with the ones we follow," Mergel said.

We all became deeply quiet. I closed my eyes to help Zarek stretch out to find her.

We sat silent for a long time. I felt Zarek's thoughts leave, and I followed him out of my body. I saw our circle within the two crates tipped on their sides. I went out of the ship and over the jungle, pulled by a power named love. *Mother.*

The Mother met Zarek outside the human camp. Zee's men didn't have a shield. She hadn't shown them that. They were gathered around another metal ship very different from the one we were in. What was left of the words written on the side read what I thought said *Ark of*. I could sense that it was not far away by cycle, and I could see that Zee was down to six men, Ojilon being one of them. They all looked a bit crazed, stressed to the breaking point, haggard, as if they had not slept at all. They were tattered and dirty.

The Mother was left to herself, leaning against the metal ship as far from the men as she could get and still be in the circle of glowing fires, each as tall as a man. I could see the moment when the Mother and Zarek's minds met. I could not tell what they thought together, so I began to examine the camp. They had two cycles left; one was loaded with a medium-sized box. The woman I thought of as Zee was playing with a palm-sized ball of some white, almost clear material. *That must be the Life Stealer*, I thought. *How does it work? How does it steal a life? How many lives can one tiny ball of a thing steal?*

My sight went back to the mind touch of mother and son, and I saw the moment when she let go, became a sparkle in the night sky and drifted up, up and up … meeting another sparkling presence among the stars. I knew it was the Father. Their essence met, and mixed, glowed … they were together again.

The pull I had felt to come here was reversed, and I flew back to my waiting body.

When we opened our eyes, Zarek wore a look of such utter pain on his face that I half rose, my hand stretched out to him.

"What's wrong?" John stood too, lifting Wydra, and then we were all on our feet.

"Mother is dead." Zarek turned his back to us. "They are both gone now. My connection to them is broken."

He had not had time to grieve for his father, and now there was no hope of rescuing his mother.

"The Spider is down to six men," I said grimly, "and they are worn down. Ojilon is with them. We could … "

"You were there. You saw," Zarek said, still turned away from us. "She told me those six are quite out of their minds and she was ready to leave them and join Father, who has been waiting for her. But she was expecting me. She had gathered as much information for me as she could. She knew I would come."

"Damn," John breathed. "Maybe now is a good time to attack, kill them all."

Zarek turned and stared at him. In fact, we all stared at him.

"We don't kill! Remember?" Jorame said.

Zarek closed his eyes sat down hard; the pain on his face, in his whole body, made me ache for him. We all sat down again.

"Mother laid out what to do," he said. "They have a box full of Life Stealers. It is a small weapon, actually, no bigger than the palm of your hand. According to what she was able to learn, they are round, palm-size bombs of some sort, which will kill people and animals but won't destroy places. The buildings will be left standing, unharmed. There is some sort of trigger device that sets them off."

I was stunned at the scope of the evil these people were willing to do to get what they wanted. It was unthinkable. *What is it they want?* I couldn't even imagine. "Why would our ancestors make such a weapon?" I wailed. "I don't understand."

Zarek held my agonized gaze for a long time.

"Mother said she heard them saying that it was meant to clear the land of any possible inhabitants or troublesome animals that roamed the countryside when they first got here," he said at last. "They didn't discover us for a little over a hundred years. By that time, the weapon was forgotten. History was already being rewritten. But it was recorded in some accounts the Voice found, and she began making plans and started to search for phase ports around the country and for where the ship might be found on the Blue Moon. From what Mother overheard, they plan on taking some of the Life Stealers back through the port they beamed here by and return to Homeworld tomorrow leaving a crate of Life Stealers here for safe keeping. I told her we were going to shut down the satellites so the Zap can't transport them to your island. She said their plan is to take the cycles, loaded with the bombs, so even if we do shut down the satellites, they will still have a means to place them all over Homeworld, to anywhere they think the people are troublesome. They plan to do it here, too, as they leave. Their scope is not just Homeworld anymore. They want the moon too."

He stopped and covered his face with his hands, his shoulders shaking with silent sobs. We sat suspended in his grief. Then he blurted out, "She said we may have to choose: the death of all our people and yours, or changing our way of life and beliefs in order to stop them from killing us all. That we may have to... kill them to save our worlds."

Pandemonium broke out, the Sabostienie all talking at once. "How can this be?" "No. The Mother would not say such a thing." "Why would she change ten lifetimes of beliefs?"

John and I stared at each other, silent and grim-faced.

"We may have thought we were getting away from hell when we left Earth," John finally said, "but it looks like we brought hell with us."

Sabostienie tears ran freely, and I found myself crying with them. John was the only dry-eyed one among us. I, at least, had an inkling of what this news was costing them.

"She said it is partly our fault," Zarek said. "That all we did was watch while this malignant evil grew worse, a cancer we could have cut out while it was new. We did nothing."

When things settled down a bit, Zarek continued. "She said now is a time of new beginnings, whether we are ready for it or not; a time of reforming ourselves again. If we can, we are to become one people: the moon, the Wells and Nueden. We should leave now and get back to Moon City well before them. Even with shields, traveling after dark in the jungle is very dangerous, but if some of us die trying, the ones who make it will have time to set a trap for them. We must not let them get to Homeworld, or destroy life here." Tears gathered, glistening in his eyes but remained unshed.

"What about her body, for the sending." Wydra asked softly, almost inaudibly.

"She said it would be to dangerous for us to try … She said to let it feed the jungle."

Silence. What could anyone say to that?

We began to load up.

"What are we going to do with Rat Mat?" John asked. We all looked over at the still tied-up sleeping man, who hadn't moved a muscle, which seemed odd to me.

"We have to take him with us, of course." said Mergel. "He wouldn't stand a chance left here alone. Not even untied."

"What's the point in that? Your Mother said to kill them; he's one of them." John gave Mergel a steely glare.

"No!" Mergel clamped his lips shut, staring right back. "She said we had a choice to make; she didn't say outright to kill them. Besides, he was not one of the six she was talking about."

In the end, they put the rat mat man on an extended platform, and we headed out in the dark. They lit the way down the burned jungle path, and we had almost gotten back to the Cords without incident when it happened.

Wydra and John were leading the way. Jorame was on the next cycle, and Mergel was on the cycle behind him carrying Rat Mat. Zarek and I were at the tail end. We had a narrow field of invisashield over the line of cycles in hopes of avoiding the worst the jungle could hit us with from above. We had locked speed with the lead cycle, making us one unit, like a train. Keeping my eyes on the path ahead, I noticed that something was happening to Mat on the platform. There was something writhing on his stomach. A tangled ball of wiggling … a small purple and white, crimson-banded snake landed on our wind guard. Then another. Then several. Some fell away, and we couldn't see where they fell. Somehow, a Crimson Death had gotten to the man and infested him. Now some of its offspring were on our cycle and some on Mergel's.

"Crimson Death!" Zarek yelled. "Mergel, release the pallet. Snakes are coming out of Rat Man's stomach. Drop him. He is already dead."

"Do it now," I screamed, "before any get on your cycle behind you!"

"Breaking off lock speed!" Zarek yelled. "We'll lift up so the body doesn't hit us. We have our own snakes to deal with. Keep going. No one stop. We will meet you at the Cords. Keep going. Don't stop!"

We lifted up and were buffeted by huge leaves and vines that nearly pulled us off the cycle. I kept my eyes on the remaining snake, which was now working its way over the top of the shield. It went flipping over onto the visor of Zarek's helmet. We brushed at it with bare hands, and it dropped away to the jungle floor. Relief flooded through me, even as every inch of my skin crawled.

Settling back to the normal two-feet-above-ground level, we saw a streak of flame behind us. The body we had just dropped was burning. There were two Fire Flyers settling down for a feast. Another was screaming overhead. "We are going to have to pick up the pace. Mergel, are you clear of snakes? Check your readout. We have a Fire Flyer on our tail. Speed up before more join him." Zarek said.

"Double your shield capacity and pour on the speed," Jorame ordered. "Breaking all lock speed. Move it!"

We watched as the line of cycles separated, their lights flashed and they picked up speed, hurtling down the path faster than was safe; but speed wasn't what I was worried about, or even the Flyers: I was still looking for snakes. Even with a scan, I still wanted a visual check. Once I was sure there were none on us, or our cycle, I breathed a lot easier.

It seemed like an eternity, but we finally reached the mouth of the Cord and stopped. We put up a good solid shield, checked Mergel's cycle for snakes and rechecked ours. Once we were sure there were no Crimson Death left anywhere under our shields, we all settled down a bit.

"Turn off all the lights. That may discourage the Flyers," Zarek said. "We'll take a rest. Maybe sleep a bit if you can. We'll go down Green Road back to Cliff Road. The Flyers will get hungry and lose interest in us in a bit and leave for better hunting. We need some rest."

"I'll take watch," I said, too jacked up to sleep, to even think about sleeping. But the others seemed to settle together in a lump against the rock wall, our cycles making a tight circle around us with full invisashield up. I sat on a rock and thought about Zarek, the Mother and the Father.

"Zarek ... I'm so sorry."

"Me too. But we'll figure it out. We'll save our people. Now get some rest. It may be your last chance for who knows how long. For right now, we are all alive. Hang onto that."

CHAPTER ELEVEN

We pulled into Moon City at noon. I wondered about the man Matt, hoping he had not been awake when the Crimson Death began to eat their way out. I hoped he had still been out from the medicine Mergel had given him. What a horrible death, and none of us could figure out how the snake had gotten to him. When? We hadn't seen a single snake. That it had gotten one of us.

We had no more close calls after that, and went straight to the Heart. Parking in the courtyard, we all ran up the steps to find Zarek's sister, Skitar, and her husband, Bex.

"Zarek," Skitar said with a sigh of relief. "We have all been so worried about you. And the rest of you," she acknowledged as an afterthought. "What has been happening?"

"One of you must go to the Tech Center and shut down the satellites," Zarek said. "We must put the Homeworld at a disadvantage … for now," he added after the horror-stricken looks that the two of them gave him.

"But why?" Bex asked. "Won't that cause havoc?"

"Better a little havoc now than a lot of death there and here if we don't," said Mergel as he went to his friends and put a gentle hand on each of their shoulders. "The Mother is gone now too. But she told us what we must do to save ourselves and to save Homeworld."

"There will be much work ahead," Wydra said as she joined the growing circle. John and I stood a little ways off as the Moon City people discussed what had to be done. They wanted the city evacuated.

"Move them into the forest, as far up as you can, to Forest River Falls area. We don't know if this is necessary, but we would rather be safe than sorry we didn't," Zarek ordered. He was the Father now; even though he only looked fifteen, he was their leader. "If ... or when ... we can, we have a great deal to talk about, but right now we just want the people all safe. And we have to set a trap for the Beamers, for they are coming back to the city, and will be here maybe within the day, though greatly diminished in numbers, as the jungle took most of them. They did not know what to look out for."

An expression crossed Bex's face of determination, and resolve, to save their people.

They went on their way, down a spiral staircase I had not noticed on my first trip through this vast hall of gathering. I so wanted to see the Tech Center, but we left the same way we had come in, got back on the cycles and sped out to the Park Phase Port, next to a river and the forest that followed the cliff edge along the ocean.

Shortly, every work cycles the city had was loaded with Sabostienie people headed up the river to the forest, higher up from where we were settling in for the wait.

We hoped the stream of people would make it out of sight soon. We didn't want them anywhere around when Zee and her men came back through the city and out to the phase port.

We positioned the cycles around the open metal circle close to the pillars on the forest side, away from the city, as that would be the most likely direction they would come from, and then we cloaked ourselves in a shield. We would be invisible to them as they came back, until we were ready to drop the shields and have a clear shot at them. We hoped to put all of them to sleep before they could beam down.

"How do they expect to use the port without knowing about the instrument panel I see in the alcove over there?" John asked.

"How did you get here?" Mergel asked.

"Well, I found a small box of tokens by the port back at Nueden, one like I had seen the Spider play with a few times before. I just took a chance ... and the next thing I knew, you guys put me to sleep. So that token will take them back too? That is all you need? Where is the safety system in that?"

"Well, for the last thousand and a half years," Jorame said dryly, "we haven't had to have one. These are shortcut tokens for people who travel between the two planets so frequently it is just easier to have a preset token to take them to the gate they use most often."

"That may be convenient, but we will have to come up with better security system now that they know you're here," John said, giving Wydra a tight little smile. "We can't have people like the Spider just dropping by to wreak havoc on your people whenever they please."

"Do you have a way to void out any previously programmed tokens?" I asked. "Some way to eliminate any possibility someone unexpected might pop in for a visit unannounced?"

"What do you think?" Mergel looked at Zarek. "Is that possible?"

"Why not?" Wydra said. "We program tokens for other sites all the time: we don't always use them for the same port, and they can be reprogrammed. So why not deprogram them at the instrument panel?"

"Yes," Zarek nodded. "Yes, I believe we can deprogram the tokens, even if we don't have them with us. Or more to the point, we can reprogram the station port. I think if we change the port setting, that might block any of the old tokens without having to have them present. There is no way to tell how many are out there, let alone try to get them all back to reprogram."

"Like yours, Pendyse—that was a one-way pass," Mergel said. "If they had used that one, the snakes would have had them for breakfast." He looked thoughtful for a moment and mumbled, "Mores the pity they didn't." Which made me feel sad for my new friend, having such feelings.

As the time stretched on, we discussed many of the changes that would have to come now that things had changed. New pathways would have to be opened up, communications between our people, so they could get to know each other.

We agreed we would need to take things slowly, to adopt a "test and protect" approach.

Then all talk stopped as we saw new movement from the south side of the city, just as the sun was giving a spectacular display as it dipped into the ocean and Homeworld rose and shone a ghostly trillium and green, huge and beautiful.

Then came Zee and her men.

When they got closer, we could see that they had only two cycles, the lead one loaded with the box I had seen on the palette. They came right up to the metal circle of the port floor, but not onto it. They were arguing. Only the three of them remained: Zee, the giant of a man who had wanted to snap my neck like a twig back in the canyons, and Ojilon. We had decided we would put them all to sleep, but we would have to drop the shields to do it. We couldn't do anything from behind the protection of the shields.

"Of course it will work," Zee said. "Look, they have no fight in them. They are cowardly, weak creatures."

"But where are they?" Ojilon wanted to know. "I want one of the women, maybe more. I want to see if I can get a son on one of them."

"That is disgusting! They are abominations." Zee turned away from the other Bouyahie and to the giant. "Move the machines onto the port when I get back. I want to make sure they know it is us coming through and not to kill you idiots."

"What's to stop them from killing you?" Ojilon sneered at Zee, which made her pause on the rim of the port, thinking.

We de-cloaked just as Zee was about to step onto the metal floor of the port. She fell back behind the giant. John gave a scream of rage, sprinted across the port and threw himself onto his brother. The rest of us paused in confusion for a second too long. The giant pulled out some kind of hand weapon I had never seen before and pointed a long black barrel at Zarek. Mergel jumped in front of him just as there was a huge bang and a flash of explosion. Mergel fell backwards against Zarek, and they both dropped. The giant face and chest was on fire, screaming and John and Ojilon were rolling on the ground.

Wydra ran to John and Jorame to Mergel, who was also screaming in pain, but alive. Zee pocketed some small white orbs from the open box and stepped onto the platform. I did the only thing I could. I tackled the old bones, hoping to knock her off the port before it could activate.

When I came to lying face down in the dirt, the king's guardsmen were standing in a ring around the port, and Zee was shrieking, "Do not kill the vile thing! I want him alive. I want him to see his precious island folk all die because of him." She still didn't know I wasn't a him, and that was fortunate I thought. Even in these circumstances, I could appreciate that amazing piece of good luck.

Zee turned to me. "You will not be out of my sight until your people are all dead, you meddling piece of ... "

"Did you get the Life Stealer?" one of the men asked, distracting the shrieker.

I was still lying in the middle of a cavern when another man jerked me to my feet, and shoved a long coat into my hands. "Put this on! Cover up," he ordered. To my astonishment, I recognized him as one of James's brothers, who had been at Rifkin's father's kennels when the Oaths and I had come through on our way to the Wells. He knew I was female and was telling me to hide it. I did, and he moved away. The torchlight cast uneven flickering shadows on the rough walls.

"Where are the other men?" I heard another man ask.

"They are dead. They are all dead," Zee said without emotion.

"*All?* My brothers went with you, old man ... and now you tell me they are all dead?"

"There were people there. Monsters. Not like us. White. Shiny abominations. Weird hair. And we had to go to a wet, slimy, forest, a place of horror past all believing. That was were we had to go, and the snakes, and flying monsters that breathed fire, and other things you do not ever want to see. They all surround the Old Ship. So shut up about what you do not understand." The wizened old woman who used to be the Voice still had some power, for the man backed down, for now at least.

Someone asked, "What about the king, and his grandson? Did you at least get the Life Stealers?"

"Not as many as I would have liked!" She spun around, looking for me. "Where is that meddlesome Ra'Vell boy?"

I stood in the shadows, and she didn't even notice I now had a heavy long coat on. My Rectifier must have been pulled off in the fray, as I no longer had it around my neck, the flimsy twine broken.

"You have caused me more trouble than all your ancestors combined, you brat." Zee shuffled over and slapped me hard across the face, then across the other cheek when she saw that the first slap had done little to cow me. I wobbled, nearly knocked off my feet by the second blow. The old woman could still deliver a wallop. But I steadied myself, drew up to my full height and stared down at her. "They did not teach you a thing about respecting your betters, I see," she observed.

"Oh, no, they taught me well," I replied. "When there is someone better to respect, I gladly do. Like the two leaders you killed up on the moon. Now, they were people to respect."

She screamed and punched me in the gut. This knocked me backward against the rough rock wall that felt like home and gave me strength. Again, I regained my footing.

"I only killed the man when he would not tell me what I wanted to know," Zee said. "The woman was more ... helpful, you might say. And I did not kill her. She died on her own, *the bitch*; she did it on purpose, too, so she would not have to help us any more. That return trip cost us dearly because of her, so I left her body to be eaten by her nasty little pets." An insane look crossed Zee's face, and she tilted her head as if she were listening to someone. "Yes, that would be a perfect end for him. A visit to the jungle ... all ... by ... him ... self." She nearly spat the words in my face, then a mad cackle erupted from this weathered woman who looked like a man, and the laugh ended just as suddenly. "Come on, boys, let us begin."

After we traveled through tunnels and man-made connecting passageways for about twenty minutes, we emerged in a building on the northeastern edge of Telling Wood.

We stopped to eat and rest. There was some concern about the slowed steps of the Voice, and the men felt it was time for some of them to go on alone. I saw James's brother leave with a group of the men, leaving us with only four guards. John's Spider and I sat in comfortable chairs after she had eaten and we slept for a while; of course, I was tied to my chair, literally a captive audience at this point.

"It took me centuries, *centuries*, to find this place, and even longer to find some tokens for the port here," Zee said. "I had read about these things in the books your Susan Pearl was hiding."

I saw she wanted to be stroked for her persistence and her cleverness, and I wanted to know as much as I could about her past. It surprised me that her men didn't seem to care that she was a she—that is, if they knew. *Do any of her people read?* I wondered. *Or haven't they heard the rumors yet? Or maybe they don't believe them. But why wouldn't they at least question what they heard? Or maybe they have.*

Stop it, I told myself, and turned to face her. "When did you learn there was a port on my island?"

She laughed. "I have known about that port for, oh," she lowered her voice so the guards couldn't hear her, "about a hundred years or more. Time gets away from me these days. I know, clever boy that you are, that you know how old I truly am, and that you tried to ruin me with the people."

"I did not try!" I looked her right in the eye, reverting to male speech patterns. "I did ruin you! You just do not know it yet."

"You may think that," she snapped, "but people love to collect around a person of power. And I am that person. I have had power longer than you can imagine. When a nation feels weak and afraid, it gravitates to a decisive leader. And if the people are a *little* afraid of that leader, all the better."

"The Father and Mother of the Sabostienie believed it is love that people gravitate to."

This brought a coughing cackle of laughter from the old woman. "Love? No wonder those fish-belly people are such cowards. Love makes no one strong. That is your problem, boy: you believe in fairy tales."

"What happened to you?"

"Happened?"

"Yes ..." I whispered, "What happened? You were young once, like me, in a less harsh time, I would guess," I glanced at the guards on the other end of the large room gathered around a crackling fire in a huge fireplace, talking amongst themselves. I noticed they didn't seem to want to be close to power. "Why did you turn so completely against your own kind?"

"My kind? You mean women?" She huffed, her face screwed up like she had a bad taste in her mouth. "Women happened to me. That's what taught me about *love*." She vomited up the word like a sickness. "*Love,*" she said again, her face twisted, "brings nothing but pain and suffering. You should know that by now."

My thoughts skittered back to the face of Quill, my ... what? What could Quill have been, what had he been? Would he ever be my friend again?

"I see you have tasted the bitter fruit of love," Zee said slyly.

"I have also tasted the sweet." I smiled. "You cannot always make people feel for you the way you may feel for them. And, really, you are only lying to yourself when you say you do not love."

"No, you are wrong about that. Since that first time, I have never loved again!" she insisted.

"What about your son?" Silence. "What would you call that?"

"None of your business," she snapped, her cold-eyed stare drilling into me.

"How did he become king? How did you do that?"

"I find your curiosity typical for a Ra'Vell. You people never knew how to keep your noses on your own faces and out of other people's business."

"Well, what difference does it make now?" I asked reasonably. "You are going to kill all my people and me in the end anyway. Why not tell me? Let me see what Zee's life was like, how she assumed the mantle of power over a whole nation. I do not think you will give me the chance to tell anyone your story. But ... " I shrugged.

Zee snorted. "You think me so weak-minded that I would fall for that clumsy childish attempt to reveal my secrets—secrets I have kept for hundreds of years?"

"But you did not keep them," I pointed out. "Your son knew them and wrote down many of them in his journals. They are no longer secrets. So what would it hurt for me to know Zee's beginnings? Even with the Purple Pearl, you are reaching the end of your life. No one lives forever, not even you. Have you ever told anyone, besides your son? Let me be the bowl you pour your poison into. You can break me when you are done and no one else will ever know your whole story. I just want to understand why I have to die."

Her eyes turned a darker shade of brown as she stared at me for a long time.

"A bowl to be broken." She whispered. "To be filled with poison and broken. I like that."

Then she began.

"My true name was Ozeenita."

CHAPTER TWELVE

"My family and friends called me Zee. I liked that better than Ozeenita, so I kept it. My friends, my family … keep them? Not so much. I had just turned fourteen. You could not tell it by what I look like now, but back then I was beautiful. Long, thick honey blonde hair, striking brown eyes, and lips that bowed in a kissable fashion—and yes, I had been kissing. We were in *love*." She spat those last words out at me like a curse, and laughed.

Her hands moved together down the length of her lap as if she were smoothing some fine fabric. "My father was an important man, even richer than the king, and I was in love with the prince. He was in love with me. We looked exquisite together. He was so handsome. I thought my father was negotiating a marriage bargain with the royal family. The Steels. Well, he was. But not for me and my prince."

She fell into a silence I was almost ready to nudge her from, if I could, when she started up again. "My sister and my best friend convinced the prince that I had been kissing others besides him. It was not true, but they persuaded a couple of boys to say it was. They told my prince I did more than kiss, that I loved a good romp under the covers.

"Those *spiteful* girls were jealous of my beauty and good fortune. *They ruined me.* They even told Father that the old king had been pawing at the trough, a man twenty years older than my own father. It was *disgusting*."

Zee's lips turned down in a bitter, sour expression. "I did not see that coming. If I had, I would have run away. Yes, the king made unseemly advances toward me, but I always rebuffed him, kindly, but I *hated* him. Everyone knew he was without moral scruples. I only put up with his presence because he was my prince's father.

"When my father came and told me he had struck a match, and that I would be a queen, I was so happy. I still thought he meant me, and my prince. I danced with joy, I *actually* danced; I twirled around in my happiness, and my skirts belled out like a sweet velvet flower." Then a hard, vicious look crossed her face. "I always thought I was his favorite ... but I thought wrong. Men cannot be trusted—but then, neither can women. Especially women. They are not forthright; they gain power from beneath, unseen and unexpected. *They are more devious than men by far.* They will do anything to get power. They are evil and perverse. So, in order not to be usurped from the position I had gained, women had to be put in their place."

Then came another long pause as memories clouded her eyes.

"'You will marry the king in a month's time,' my father said. 'He does not mind that you are sullied.' And I thought he was joking. But no: he had arranged for my younger sister to marry my prince, in a year's time, and for me to be shackled to that sagging bag of bones that had bad breath and rotting teeth ... in only a month. My young life would be wasted beneath his withered flesh. How had this happened to me? Begging did no good, and I vowed I would never beg again: people would come to me begging. The world would come to *me*. And mine would be the voice they heard telling them what their lives would hold." Her grin stretched wide across her wrinkled face, the wrinkles of too many years, collected in brackets around that cruel mouth.   "That was when the idea to become the Voice first came to me.

"When I rushed to my prince to tell him what our fathers had done to us, I found him with my sister. Laughing. *Laughing with her.* He told me I was not good enough for him, and that they were going be married, and they would be moving to the Oregon Province to live on an island close to Ravenwood City. It was a property my father owned." She shot such a venomous look my way that I felt my blood chill. Could she be related to my people, this vile creature, or was she just playing with me? The sneaky, shifty cast to her face made me wonder if any of this was true. Did she even know the truth, or remember the truth about her own life after all those years?

"So you see, the island should have been, *was* rightfully mine, but they stole it from me. They took *everything* from me. But I got even with them." She spoke in little more than a hissing whisper.

"Yes, I became queen, a woman with no visible power. None! And even as old as he was, the king would come to me every night until I was so large with child that he could no longer mount me. Then one of our maids took his fancy, my *righteous* husband, and he bothered me no more for a time. The priests of the Book and the keepers of the Tree were blind to all his wicked ways. From that, I learned that power blinds people. Yes, they were all defiling the truth and groveling at the feet of a vile man. But I showed them. I learned well how to use secrets and fear.

"My son Edward was born, and the king came back to my chamber door. I poisoned him slowly over a six-month period till he died, but not before he got me with twins. Everyone thought he had died of old age and overexertion with his young wife. The priests tried to force me to marry a man worthy to be king until Edward was old enough to rule, but I would have none of their offers. I was the queen, and the people began to fear me, as some of my enemies dropped dead without visible cause." A malicious hatred spread across her face. "I made sure people feared me, too. *I* was the one who made the Devil into a woman." She lit up with pride at this accomplishment. "I wanted them to hate women, to blame them for all their woes, to strip them of the power of their deceit. It only took a small push. I wanted them to fear me, yes, all of them. And they did."

I bet they did, I thought. They would have hated one woman, anyway, for Zee had made herself the Devil.

"Poison became my art, and now you are my bowl to fill as I please, and I will feed it to your people. I told you I got even with every last one of them who made my dreams a pile of dung, and I will get even with you as well. My father died in agony with a little help from my cup, after my sister's wedding. Before my sister and her prince moved to Ra'Vell Island, during the year before they married, I poisoned her womb. Thanks to finding Susan Pearl's journals and her herbilogical studies, I killed any possibility of future children they might have had together—but that did not stop him, oh no; he turned out to be just like his father, still made babies with all the loose women who lived there on *your island* already." She gave me a hooded stare.

"In that year before they married, something astonishing happened to me. I met your ancestor, Susan Pearl. Of course, at the time, I thought she was a man, an old holy man, a traveling monk who crisscrossed the land. We had known of him for a very long time. That monk made me curious. 'How could he be as old as people say he is?' I asked myself, and began to follow him, and when I found a stash of books and journals in a small monk's cave not far from here, *I discovered my life.* And the means by which I would achieve the idea I had had to be the Voice of the Tree. It was genius.

"I started drinking the purple tea and cultivating the plant. I was only eighteen years old then. After forty years, people began to make comments that I was not aging. They began to think me unnatural, maybe even evil. As if I could suck the very life juices from the people around me. I *was* a woman, after all. I encouraged them in their fears and suspicions. Some people, who got in my way, simply disappeared. I was still working on my grand plan back then. I would be the most powerful person alive, and they would all come to me. *And they have.*

"I am the Voice they hear, the one they listen to, the one they obey. There has never been anyone like me, and will never be another as powerful as me." She lowered her voice back down to a purring whisper. "And *I* was a woman! And *I* had split man from woman! They will never recover. No matter what people like you might try to do to heal the rift I created, it will never happen." Again she wore that proud look on her face, as if she had accomplished something wonderful instead of something devastatingly evil.

"When my babies were in their late twenties, I cut off my own breasts, and transformed myself into a monk. I lived in Susan's cave for a few decades while people died or forgot me while my children ran things in the kingdom, at my command. Edward was king. The twins joined the priesthood and began to set up rules about how to approach the Tree and who could approach the Tree—certainly no longer women."

Zee squared her shoulders and puffed out her frail, flat chest that had once been adorned with breasts while I thought of that horrific scene. I could almost hear the screams that must have filled the air during that act. As if she could hear my thoughts, she said, "The Purple Pearl tea also heals wounds beautifully. It may taste as bitter as death, but the feeling once that taste is gone is marvelous. Too bad you will never know it."

Repulsion roiled in my gut at her story. I was appalled by what she was telling me. Does anyone ever see himself or herself as evil? Or is it such a gradual slide into rationalization that you lose yourself to your own cause, whatever that might be? That scared me more than she did.

"When I came back to the city," she continued, "I was seventy-five years old, and looked younger than my twins. I had only shared the purple tea with Edward. The twins were true believers," she laughed. "They would have drunk poison from my own hand knowingly, willingly. They believed me to be the Voice of God the Creator. They believed me when I told them God had spoken to me and told me what to do. They set up the Code, the Creed and the Law for me. We made the House of Nine, and Edward and I ruled it, even the Book and the Tree, for over a thousand years. *We* made this." She spread out her spider-thin arms to indicate everything. "*WE DID.*"

She was breathing hard now, wheezing. "And you came along and tried to ruin it. Better than you have tried to kill me, to shut me up, to move me off my mark. They could not, and neither can *you.*"

"Are you so far gone that you can not feel the heartbeat of your own people?" I asked, weary to the bone of the story I had asked for.

Sneering at me, she said, "Far gone? *You have no idea!*"

The Voice stood up. "What this world gets, it deserves. Down to every last one of you. Your family has plotted against me for decades, and they have paid for that, and *you* will pay for it to your last breath. I will see my bowl full of pain and poison, enough to choke you, before I break you."

"Untie this piece of dung!" she screeched to her men. "We are leaving. Now. Rest time is over. I want to test my Life Stealers!"

We walked for an hour and a half before we came to the city center. There were burned-out homes and whole ones, and the Voice had the guards knock on doors, and any people they found at home they brought out; they cleared out the Women's Free Houses and the Palaces; they gathered as many people as would come to join the army of the Voice, to take down the enemy to the west. That was what I heard all up and down the crowd of people that coalesced around the Voice and her guards.

"We will go to the Zap and fill to standing every last car and coach ... " Zee commanded.

One of the men whispered something in the Voice's ear. Then she did a dance of rage that was almost comical until she drew out her blade and stabbed the messenger through the throat. A collective gasp rose from the people and they backed away from the madman/or woman before them as the messenger slid from the knife and fell with a gaping wound, blood pulsing out to darken the ground.

I figured she had just discovered that the Zap was out of zap, and no one would be moving that way. She ran over to me screaming, "Your fault! Your fault! Your fault!" She flourished the knife in front of my face, gritting her teeth in rage. "You plague me with your magic!" She swung her knife at me just as I pulled back, but her blade snicked along my cheekbone close to my right eye, making a shallow cut that burned like fire. A frisson of fear of poison raced along that fire, as blood covered my cheek.

She came to her senses, or what passed for sane, and called for wagons to be brought out and loaded with all the provisions needed for an overland trip to Fell Lake. She was going into one of the homes to sleep for the night, but first, she had me tied to a tree and told the men if anyone freed me, they would pay for it with a horrible death.

My cheek bled and stung abominably, but no one came to tend it. Who would dare, after what they had just witnessed? I was tied standing up and slept as I could. At some point right before dawn, John Bouyahie and James's brother Ferris, the one who had given me the coat, came and woke me. I ached in every strained and screaming muscle.

"Ah, kid," John whispered. "Look what they've done to your beautiful face." He tipped some water onto a cloth and dabbed at my cheek. "What were you thinking, to go after the Spider like you did? You fell right into her web."

"Pen, I wish we could let you go, but … " Ferris looked around at the men asleep on the ground and the ones on watch, who were half asleep. "There are just too many of them. We are moving people to the east of the city now; we are not sure what that devil is planning, but we are taking any who are willing to go with us in the opposite direction she's taking. I heard the Voice say those weapons have a ten- or twelve-mile radius. We have hundreds of people gathered at the kennels and are moving them out as soon as we get back there. Heading east. We hope that will keep them safe from what ever she is planning."

"Wydra, Jorame and Zarek are most likely already on the island," John said, "to warn your people and get ready to save your hide. So be prepared for anything. We don't know what they will do, but your friends will come for you. So don't go all heroic on us; just keep yourself alive."

"Give me a drink." My dry throat was raspy. John gave me a generous swallow of water. "What of Mergel?"

"Alive. They had to take his right arm off, though. Whatever that thing was ripped right through his side."

"Ojilon?" John tipped the canteen up to my lips again and I swallowed gratefully.

"Dead," he said flatly. "He will not bother anyone again."

"Hey! What are you two doing there?" One of the guards finally noticed my two angels. "Get away from him."

"We were only giving him water. Even a condemned man can have a drink." Said John.

As they moved away, I felt hope surge in me. Some of the people in the city would live. I knew Zee only had four orbs. I didn't think she was so crazy that she would kill herself in order to get all her enemies in one swipe.

"Wonannonda bless," I breathed to their departing backs.

As the sun rose, the camp began to stir. Before it was full daylight, things were in motion. Zee was up, shouting orders. We moved out shortly after that. I rode with the Spider and five of her guards in a plush wagon with her personal supplies pulled by four large, grey mares.

After we had gone maybe five miles from the city, I stood up in the foot-well of the wagon and looked back. I wanted to see how many people were coming with the Voice. What I saw was a long, single-file line of people, standing or sitting, all the way back to the city, while the majority of the crowd kept following us. What had she meant, by test?

Puzzled, I said, "Looks like you are losing them."

Zee cackled, but said nothing. Every few miles or so, I would look back, and more people would be standing or sitting in line. I would shake my head and she would cackle again, and the hair on the back of my neck would rise and I'd get gooseflesh up and down my arms. My gut was telling me this did not bode well for those people.

Close to fifteen miles out, we stopped and set up camp. The sun was beginning to set, and I could see the line of people stretching back up the rise to the city, which was on the highest point of land in the area. The population of Telling Wood had been over 400,000 before the burning started after Telling Tree died. It looked like a lot of those who had remained after those events were now spread out on the plains, setting up tents.

Zee climbed up on the wagon seat and stared off toward the city shining in the late-afternoon sunlight. "It is time for my test!" She pulled out a small handheld device that was the size of a reader, only flatter.

"What are you doing?"

She sneered at my question, and then grinned. "You need to see what my little beauties can do. I need to know their range."

I shook my head, my hand out. "You can't do this!" I said, my voice steady. "These are your own people; some of them love you. Please don't do this."

"Pendyse of Ra'Vell, you forget yourself. You have spent too much time with monsters and abominations. *We men do not use contractions!*" she screeched, and pushed the button.

A wave of soundless distortion shimmered the air, and then a thick vibration rolled out from the center of the city and settled into my bones, rattling me all the way down to my feet. Then the screams began, and above it all, I heard, though my hands covered my ears, the laughter of that black-garbed *thing* that stood on the wagon seat with her arms out as if she were embracing a marvelous wonder to behold. Right up to the edge of the wagon behind the one she stood on, people—men, women, children—and the line of them all the way back to the city were lying on the ground, crumpled and dead. Half the people who had come with us had not moved far enough from the city to be safe. Zee had almost been taken to Tomorrow Land herself.

The ache in my chest throbbed like a second heartbeat, but I did not scream or cry, or lose my head. With great clarity, I realized that this was what I was here for, to be a witness to this, and to prevent this madwoman from totally destroying every living thing on this world.

Even the horses tied to the many wagons behind us had fallen dead in their traces. Dogs' bodies lay among the people. The ground was carpeted with the dead, all felled by some kind of silent shimmering sound wave. I walked to the end of the wagon and saw hundreds, maybe thousands, of dead, blood trickling from ears and eyes, noses and mouths. And I thought of the Crimson Death, how it burrowed inside to hatch its young to eat their way out; this sound—or non-sound—did much the same. I saw grey-pinkish goo oozing from mouths stretched wide with screams of pain, frozen in death.

Leaning over, I vomited, retching and retching even though all I had been given all day was a little water. And up on the wagon seat, this set Zee off again. She laughed and laughed. Everyone else who had not fallen dead kept completely silent. All eyes were on that one stark figure, and then she spoke.

"How do you like the taste of my poison? Am I not the most powerful leader of all?"

My voice rose above the silence. "No true leader would cut down her own people and laugh about it."

"*I ... am ... not ... a ... woman!*" she shouted, jumping up and down on the seat of the wagon till I thought she would topple off. When she regained her balance, she glared at me with a burning hatred.

I stood straighter and glared back. "I am so glad of that, *Mister Spider*, for what woman could kill her own children and not die of it herself? It would give women a bad name if you were one."

She threw back her head and howled with laughter. "Mister Spider! I like that; yes, indeed. Mister Spider." Then the laughing mouth became a straight and bitter line and a sudden silence ensued as she climbed down from the wagon, walked over and stared up into my face. "I will wrap you in gauze, my pretty little man, and put you in my pantry to eat later, but thank you for the interesting name." She turned away, and yelled, "Guards! Put up my tent. I am tired and hungry. Bring me some wine, too." Then she turned her back to the guards, and said over her shoulder, "Oh, and nothing, I mean *nothing*, for our guest. Not *even* water."

When she walked away into the crowd of people, they parted like waves from the bow of a ship. I could see their fear, but I also saw hate on many a face, and I knew she had gone to far this time. She had revealed too much of her true nature: she was a caricature of a human, and inside her there was nothing ... nothing but empty darkness.

CHAPTER THIRTEEN

Fires burned all night. It was the start of the week of true dark, where no moonlight kissed the land for nine nights. Every time I looked toward Telling Wood, grief welled up in me; it seeped into me from the very ground. At this time many of the people who were still alive and had come with us out from the city had turned back, heading home, burning bodies as they went. Sleepless, I watched them go. The fires they set for the burning of the dead would flare up, burn bright for a time, and then slowly become dark holes in a darker night.

I couldn't tell how many people had gone, but, using the fires to judge time and distance, I figured they were about halfway back to the city and it was maybe three o'clock in the morning. That's when I heard a rustling in the prairie grass beneath the wagon, coming up behind the wheel I was tied to. A child whispered, "Do not move; do not give me away. I have some food and water for you." A small hand snaked through the spokes with a canteen, and I drank gratefully. From my other side came his other hand with a piece of winter fruit, then bread, and then another drink of water.

"Thank you," I whispered, after swallowing the water. "Bless you for your kindness."

"This is not kindness; this is, *I hope you kill the monster,* and you cannot do that if you starve to death first. You are the only one who stood up to it. It killed my father, my two brothers and my friends … and … " The child choked up. "And I do not even know how it did it."

"She is not an it," I said. "She may have become a monster, but she didn't start out that way, she is simply a woman who lost her way and has become what she hated." I didn't know why I was defending her, but I didn't want this kid to become like her. "Hate eats the hater, so don't hate, or you could fall into her fate and become what she is … and you wouldn't want that. All it takes at first are small choices to go down that same road. Don't feed the evil that can grow in any human heart."

The hand came slowly through the spokes of the wheel and fed me more bread, then a piece of meat. With the smell of burning human flesh hanging in the air, I almost gagged at the thought of meat of any kind, but forced myself to eat it. Whatever was to come, I had to keep my strength up. And who knew how long it would be before I could eat again? So I ate more than I really wanted.

The child was quiet as he fed me, until I said, "Stop. I'm so full now I might burst if I ate another bite. You have saved my life, and I can't thank you enough."

"Why do you talk like a girl?"

"Because I am one."

"No way! You are so brave!"

"Who says girls can't be brave?"

"Well … "

"What is your name?"

Silence.

"I won't tell anyone. My name is Pendyse Ra'Vell. My friends call me Pen."

More silence, then a squeak of a whisper: "Andraykin. My friends call me Dray." There was a wet, sucking-up-of-snot sound, and a nose being wiped on a sleeve. "I have heard of you, but I heard you were a boy. And good with the sword."

"It's true, I am good with the sword, and the slingshot, and bow—well, just about any kind of weapon—and I did live my life until recently as a boy, because it was the only way my family could keep me, the only way I could get an education and move around freely. But I'm done with that, and if I live, I am going to help change our world. Make it a better place. Would you like to help me do that?"

There was a thoughtful pause, then he said, "You can call me Dray."

"I will, and you can call me Pen."

"I will keep your secret." There was a light scurry of sound, and he was gone.

With my stomach full, I must have slept for a bit, even though I was very uncomfortable sitting up with my back against the hub of the wheel. When I woke just before daybreak, the people who had stayed were moving about and talking in low tones; the mood was dampened and quiet. The camp was only a hundred strong, if that, as hundreds of people had left in the night to find their way home, more than I had originally thought.

I was curious to see how Zee would react to this news.

And if these were all the people left with the hollow woman who called herself their leader, did that mean they were "true believers" who would drink poison, willingly, knowingly, like her twins? Or were they just too scared to leave, or too mean? Or did they sense the end of their leader was near and wanted to step in and take her place?

Watching the morning begin, with cook fires stoked and food smells overlaying the horror of burnt human flesh, I noticed a gathering of men who looked like hungry wolves who were surrounding a tired stag, but were still wary of the massive antlers. But this was no stag; they were lurking at the tent flap of the Voice, and they were not wolves, but eleven men. I began to feel the prick of a new terror. I knew the enemy called the Voice … the Spider … Zee, more or less, but who were these rough-looking, hollow-eyed men in fine travel gear? They looked like a cross between gents and soldiers. Why hadn't the Spider brought these men to the moon with her, these men looked like they could have gotten the job done? They looked like eleven John Bouyahies … no, they looked like eleven *Ojilon* Bouyahies. That thought made my skin crawl over my bones like restless ants.

Here were eleven hollow-eyed men with scorched souls.

Eleven men who are like the Spider, only much younger, I thought, *without conscience or empathy,* and I knew I was looking at the end result of our culture's breakdown, which the Spider had set in motion all those hundreds of years ago. How many men and women in this world were like them? And how could we ever achieve peace with those whose only hunger was to have their own way, to gain power over others, to do what ever they wanted?

They kept glancing around like they were taking stock of who was left and what supply wagons were still there. I followed their glances, taking stock of them taking stock. These were not men I wanted to know I was of the opposite gender. My mind went to the child, Dray. I should have told him to go back to the city, and to convince whoever was left with him to go, too. This camp was no place for a child Mark's age.

The Spider emerged from her tent, stretched, yawned, and then went still as she caught sight of who was waiting for her. Then she moved among the men with the studied grace of a manipulator. I watched the tension slide from their shoulders as they traded loaded glances behind her back. Being just out of hearing range, I could only catch a word here and there that was spoken a little louder than the others. The men all laughed as the Spider said something I couldn't hear. She had somehow put them off their guard. She was making herself one of them, at least on the surface. It was fascinating to watch her work her twisted magic of sizing these men up and putting them at ease. But I could see the fault lines, like on a cracked pot. They were not one, even with each other. They were twelve for themselves. And they would be allied for only as long as it was good for each one of them. They were lone wolves, and would turn on each other in a heartbeat if any one of them thought it would serve his plans better.

What *were* their plans?

These men were perhaps the most dangerous type of element on the face of this planet, and I didn't like it. I saw the Spider pull the square, book-shaped trigger pad from a deep pocket in her robe and fiddle with it with a twisted grin as she looked into each man's face. She indicated the other pocket, where I had seen her stow the last three orbs. The men shifted, and the tension was back in them, big time. One by one, quietly, they got up and left, going in different directions.

Hmmm, I didn't like that either. And I wanted to know what she had said there at the end.

From that point on, she was never alone. Her guards were the handpicked men she always had around her. "True believers," I suspected, men who would take a knife or arrow for her. How did she foster such devotion, being such a hate filled person?

We traveled in the direction of Ra'Vell Island, this pared-down army, for three days before we came to a small community in a circular grove of trees, with a spring in the center of the tiny village and fenced gardens outside the grove. It was a pretty, pastoral, homely sight, and I remembered wanting to stop here when I was with the Oaths on our way to Telling Wood. Was that only twenty-six or twenty-seven days ago? I had lost count. *I think there are only three or four more days of true dark, before the Mother brings her light to us for nine days,* I decided.

Camp was set up just outside the village.

The people of the town came to greet us. They brought food and drink to share, and salt to shake on the ground between the Voice's people and them, as a sign of meeting in peace and hospitality. That was an old custom, one I had read about but never seen. The head man said, "Welcome to Isuladune."

I liked these people. They reminded me of the Sabostienie. And I saw the looks the men from Nueden gave the women and girls.

It worried me. If they had been my women, I would have hidden them away at first sight of a large encampment of mostly men. Nice people don't think other people can hide such black hearts as some of these men carried in their chests. But I knew better.

Dray came to me every night with food and water, at different times of night so a pattern wouldn't form. No matter how I tried to get him to leave, to go back to Telling Wood, to take who ever his remaining friends were and go home, he would not.

"Even if I wanted too, they won't," he said.

"Dray, please, do not talk like that. If someone were to hear you, it could be dangerous for you."

"I know. Just like you, I don't talk this way except to you, and you to me. We have honesty between us." Dray fed me a piece of cheese. "I have eyes and a brain. This is no time or place to announce you're a changeling. You're too smart for that."

"I slipped up back when the Spider set off her weapon; I do not want you to slip up and get hurt by it," I explained. "I am grateful for the food, you know that, but she has been giving me water now, and is getting suspicious that I am not falling apart without food. She makes me walk all day to test me. I do what I can to fool her, but she is not stupid. So, watch yourself. I mean it when I say I couldn't bear it if anything happened to you because of me."

When Dray left, I listened to the night sounds, the fires' crackle and snap, the people snoring, a man and woman laughing after coming together. It was at times like this that I felt most lost, and yet most myself, thinking, on my own, even though I was tied to a wagon wheel every night, with a couple of guards sitting at a fire within sight but not hearing. At least during the day I only had a rope around my neck and my hands tied in front of me as I walked beside Zee's wagon. She didn't know or understand that I liked that better than sitting with her in the wagon. I could feel that I had lost weight lately. I didn't have much fat to spare to begin with. But at least I could be thankful, for what the ropes put to sleep at night, the walking revived in the mornings. For the most part, people paid no attention to me. I felt invisible, except I knew the Spider was very aware of me, so I kept my secret identity alive.

Drifting off with my head leaned back in the crotch of two spokes I was almost asleep when the screaming began.

Tent flaps were rustling, voices being raised; the whole camp came awake and, using the cell lights the camp kept for emergencies, people were trying to discover what the trouble was. The Spider got up and came to check on me. She stood next to the wagon with her sleepy guards as the camp was searched.

One of her priests ran up, shouting, "Someone killed two of our men. They cut off their … " He made a cutting motion down by his privates. "Gone! A bloody mess!"

A second man came up. "Four men are dead. We have the three men who did it. Here they come."

This made Zee's guards wake up and stand at attention.

"What is the meaning of this?" Zee hissed, her voice cracking with rage. "Who are you, and why are you sneaking around in my camp killing my men?"

Not only had the people brought the killers, but they had also dragged the bodies of the four dead men along with them. I was shocked to see they were four of the eleven men who had gathered outside the Spider's tent that morning three days ago. And the men being held were some of the men who had welcomed them to camp next to their village, Isuladune.

"Tell me! Now! Why did you kill my men?" Zee said in a much calmer voice now that she saw who had been killed. I felt a secret gloat emanating in waves of satisfaction off the Spider as she felt her web lines wiggle, and I knew she was ready to pounce in perfect spider fashion.

One of the men shook off the hands of the guards and stepped forward to the point of a sword. "These four men killed my son and raped my wife and daughter. In my village, that is a crime punishable by death."

"They got what they paid for!" shouted another man from the village, who was still being held. "We welcomed you in, we poured salt, and you defiled our women and our hospitality!"

"Well," said the Spider, "I guess you should have offered your women to my men in the first place if you really wanted to be hospitable. That is how it is done in the city. And you are all lawbreakers according to Nueden law. You have never been registered or named a town under the charter."

"We are not harming anyone. We live simply and take care of our own. We are a peaceable people."

"Well, now, these four men," she waved a hand loosely toward the dead and savaged bodies, "would beg to differ with you." Zee cast a reflective gaze over the village men, and then, giving a huff of disgust said, "Kill them! Kill everyone in this village. And leave their bones to bleach in the sun."

"No!" I shouted, appalled. The five men were shocked into silence. I shook my head, disbelief rattling me down to the essence of my soul. "How can you do this? These people are innocent. They only protected their own."

"You would say that, Ra'Vell. One lawbreaker to another, huh, is that why you would save them?" She licked her lips and ginned. "More poison, my dear boy. Poison for my cup." She turned back to the crowd. "Kill them now."

I curled up into a tight ball, my knees against my chest, and buried my face against my knees, squeezing my eyes shut. But there was nothing I could do about the sounds. The sounds of shattering bone, of blood spilling; and the screams.

Brontis, our man at Ravenwood Castle, had sometimes talked of war, but it could never have been as bad as this. *Even Remode, where Brontis grew up, a sick place of death and defilement, could not match this slaughter*, I thought, but maybe that was only because I was here, living in this moment. I was in it, and could do nothing to stop it. I felt the pain of every trapped person who had no ability to defend themselves. It chafed my heart, and I felt the poison Zee intended to fill me with pour into my soul. I did not want to keep it. But hatred roiled in that cup I had become.

Zee kicked me, once, twice. "Open your eyes and see what lawbreakers deserve." She kicked me again. I opened my eyes. Yes, I would record this new horror created by the one called the Voice, the Spider, who made a meal of death and laughed about it, trying to make it appear delicious. *Dray was right. She is a monster, an it,* I thought. How many times do I have to see it, to believe it? But she had once been a baby girl. What had happened to her? Even if I were to take her story as the whole truth and nothing but the truth, what had caused her to twist in this mad fashion? Doesn't everyone born have worth to begin with? Why would they throw it away?

In order to create peace, don't we have to know what unmakes a human heart? And peace doesn't come from hate. Hate is death. Love is life. And with that thought, the Wonannonda Tree bloomed and grew large in my mind. In the midst of the screams from both sides and the images by torchlight I never wanted to see, though even in this, I felt a calm settle in me, and heard the whisper, *"Be at peace. I am with you. And I am with them all. They are with me."* And love poured into me. Love for all these broken people, broken in body and soul, along with those who were innocent of any wrongdoing. I saw their worth and the loss of them to our world, and the receiving of the departed spirits by the Great Father-Mother Creator into a loving embrace. I could not tell what their fate would be after that reception, only that they would be dealt with according to the lives they had lived and the choices they had made.

The townspeople were not as much like the Sabostienie as I had first thought. When they saw their leaders cut down for dispensing justice, they fought, and people on both sides died. The Spider and her guards never left my side as the carnage raged. I prayed for Dray and his friends. I hoped they were alive and well out of it somewhere.

"Wonannonda, guard their souls," I whispered.

"Was that a prayer, my little priest?" The Spider bent down to look into my dry eyes. "Oh, you think you are such a cool one? I have told you my story. Sometime before this is all over," she grabbed my chin and forced me to look into her dark brown, sunken eyes, "you must tell me yours." She tilted my face this way and that. I saw something flash in the depths of her eyes, and then she tossed my chin with a bit of a slap. She stood up. "I must insist!"

She hobbled back to her tent, and her guards went in with her.

As soon as they were out of sight, I heard Dray behind me. "I have never been so scared in all my life. The silent deaths were bad, real bad; my family … but this … it makes no sense."

"I'm glad you feel that way. Because this should never make sense, Dray." I was so tired; I put my head back between the spokes and closed my eyes. "Are the people you're with all right?"

"Yes. They stayed out of it, back at the edge of camp. We did not know what was really going on. We had to hide in a ditch at one point, because men with swords came by, and in the dark we could not tell who they were. So we just stayed quiet."

"That's good," I whispered.

"What happened, do you know?" Dray asked.

"Yes."

"What?"

"Some men hurt some of the townspeople," I said, "and the village men came and killed the men who hurt their people. Then the woman some people call the Voice said, 'What these men have done was unlawful,' and commanded the whole village to be put to death."

A silence followed.

"Oh," Dray said, and quietly shuffled away.

Sad, drained, and as uncomfortable as I was, I slept.

CHAPTER FOURTEEN

I was slapped awake. Jerking, I sat up from my uncomfortable slumped position. What greeted my sight was morning sunlight and the ground littered with bloody bodies. The few women still with the camp were given the job of gathering the bodies and burning them. Zee was down to fifty-three men; of course, the Voice did not count the women. As a captive, I was not counted either. Counting all of us, there were only sixty-nine.

This small village was full of fighters, untrained, maybe, but they had a righteous anger and a right to protect them selves or at least attempt to, even though they had failed. There was no bargaining with the enemy at their door; it was fight and maybe some would live, or let Zee's men kill them all without trying to save themselves. My chest hurt just looking at the dead. The wind drifted the acrid smoke of burning flesh toward me and it stung my eyes.

"Get up," the Spider said. "You are coming with me to look at what you have done."

I said nothing in response to such illogical talk, but rose tiredly to my feet. What use was there in denying her crazy claims? I stomped my feet to get the circulation going. They were tied with about nine inches of slack between them.

"Untie Ra'Vells feet only," she snapped at the guard who had slapped me awake. "Give me the rope." The guard handed my tether over to the wrinkled hand of the maker of death, and she led me away from my wheel of torture. I could hardly stand straight I was so stiff.

We walked around the grassy commons of the neat, well-kept little town. There was a circle of brightly painted cottages just inside the ring of trees. A spring rose up from the rocky rise at the highest edge of the large circle with a pleasant burbling, peaceful sound and came splashing down to a small pool in the center of the village circle. It must have been a good place to live, with its fruit and nut trees, gardens and water.

I averted my eyes from the bodies until my gaze snagged on a small girl, maybe ten, nightdress thrown over her face, body bared.

I turned slowly to the Spider, shaking my head. "You can blame me, but this will always be on your head. And I believe, somewhere in that black heart of yours, you must know this was wrong. At every juncture of choice in your life, you have made the wrong one."

Turning from her, I scanned the place, taking note of the dead, to see them, honor them. That was when I saw it: the shrine at the high point, above the spring, among the trees, a shrine that was an exact duplicate of the one on my island. Keeping my face perfectly still, I noted a boy, maybe my age, dead, slumped against what might have been a secret passageway down to … what, caves? Hiding places? It did look like he might have been guarding a passageway. Taking another look around, I saw only a few women and children dead on the ground. More than this would have lived in this place, surely. I wondered if the Spider noticed.

My heart raced, my thoughts leaping with possibilities. I felt sure some had survived and the bones of their dead would not bleach in the sun as the Spider had said. Life has its ways. I wondered how many had survived. Looking over at the Spider, my face stony, I noticed her men looting the houses of food and anything that looked interesting to them. Giving her a cold-eyed stare, I vowed to myself I would never utter another word to her.

The Mother had been right, there was no redeeming this one, and even though her body walked among us, she was already dead. Had been for hundreds of years.

I just stood there and stared at her, and said nothing.

"Well? What do you think? Do you like the poison you carry for me?" she asked.

Not blinking, I took a step towards her and stared right through her, as if she weren't there at all. She blinked and stepped back a pace. I walked around her, brushed past her ever so lightly, without one word.

Rage took her, and she jerked the rope around my neck, making me stumble. Righting myself, I ignored her. "I … asked … you … a … question." She bit out each word. I remembered her saying those exact words to Michkin before she killed him at Telling Tree.

She would have nothing from me but my blood. She would not have the honor of being addressed as a living person. She was putrescent flesh as far as I was concerned, more so than the dead lying on the ground at my feet. I scanned the cottages and the camp just outside the ring of trees. The smell of the dead roasting in piles made me breathe in small, shallow breaths as I tried to avoid the stench and the acrid taste that settled in my nostrils and on my tongue and coated my throat. *If she kills me, this will be my last memory,* I thought. I stood at the end of Zee's rope, troubled at that thought, and changed the direction of my thoughts. I placed my mother, my brother Pelldar and his son, my nephew Mark, in my mind instead: not dead, but alive and smiling. I saw in my mind's eye all those who meant something to me and held them firm.

She jerked me off my feet and kicked and stomped me; I was pummeled by pain. That was a good sign, I thought, as she had killed Michkin before she had started kicking him.

The Spider threw the rope at one of her guards and snapped, "Tie this piece of dung up on my wagon seat. We are leaving. Whoever is left behind can catch up with us or not, I do not care. All I need to take Ra'Vell Island is one of my little beauties. As long as we have this one alive, they will open the gate for him, and he will take in a Life Stealer and I will clear out the vermin once and for all."

I didn't look at Zee. I didn't let my face register an emotion, not one.

Hours later, she was still trying to make me talk to her. She would jab or slap me, punch me in the gut with the butt end of her curved blade. I was reliving all the good times I'd shared with my friends: how we met, the things we had done, where we spent time together. I was turned off to this time and place. In spite of what John had said that first night, when I was tied to the tree, that Jorame, Wydra and Zarek would come, I figured I would be dead before they got to me. I knew if the Spider took us on the straightest course, we would also come across the other little village that was on this track, and I couldn't bear to think of what might happen there. If only there were some way to warn them.

Two more days passed. I didn't see Dray in all that time, and hoped he and his people had turned back. The Spider had lost all of the women and twenty or so of the men, as close as I could figure.

We came to the second prairie village and found it empty. Such relief washed over me that my head felt light and buzzy. Even though they gave me water every day now, they gave me nothing to eat. The Spider had said, "If you want food, you can ask for it."

That night, as my aching back was tied to my bed, the wheel, as the sun slid into the purple plains grass, setting it to a fiery shimmer, I sighed tiredly. The Spider had me walking again, which I quite preferred to sitting next to her, even though I was exhausted by the end of the day. I fell into the depths of sleep almost immediately.

It seemed like I had only closed my eyes for a moment when I felt a small hand on my shoulder, and my heart sank. Stirring from the aches of dreams and constant pain, I sighed, "I thought you were well out of all this."

"My friends left, but someone needs to feed you."

Bits of bread, meat, cheese … I ate a little, having had nothing in the past two days.

"That was so good, the best food I have ever had. Mark used to … " I stopped. Unexpected memories of him could still punch me in the gut and bring the sting of tears to my eyes.

"Who is Mark?"

"My nephew. He was killed. Murdered a month ago. Only a month ago … that seems so long now; so much has happened."

"I have news," Dray whispered close to my ear. "Zarek says, 'Open up. You have closed your mind down and you need to open up.'"

I twisted in my confining bonds to look at Dray. I had never really seen what he looked like. To me, he was only a whispered voice and hands, small, fine-boned hands thrust through the spokes. Even now, I could only see half of his face: one eye, hazel; long, thick brown lashes; half a smile with a deep dimple.

"Zarek?" My heart pounded. "Zarek is here?"

"Yeah. And he … is so … *wild*." Dray shook his head and grinned. "And there's a couple in white suits like the one under your coat. And they have these machines." Dray's eye sparkled as if he had seen magic, was a part of magic. He grinned again. "They have a plan. But you need to open up. So Zarek can tell you." His small hand patted my shoulder as he said, "I've got to get back to them. I rode all the way here on that cycle thing from the first round town where so many died. We saw to it the villagers were burned and sent to Tomorrow Land. It was beautiful, Pen, sad, so sad … but somehow sweet, too." His face was hidden in the fall of his dark auburn hair burnished in the firelight that hid his eyes. "A lot of kids are orphans now, like me."

I wanted to comfort him, but my hands were tied. All I had were words. "Me too," was all I could say; then I remembered my father was not dead. And there was also John Bouyahie.

"I've got to go," Dray said.

And he did, but I was wide-awake. I took a deep breath of the clean, sweet purple plains grass, closed my eyes, opened my mind as wide as I could and visualized Zarek's face, and Jorame and Wydra.

"Pendyse, can you hear me?" Zarek said in my mind.

"Oh, yes! Sweet life, are you all OK? Are my people all right? Did you see what the weapon does? There wasn't a whisper of sound, just this swoosh of a shimmering wave of some kind, and this horrible pressure in my head. I was right there at the edge of it, just feet out of range. We can never let this happen again, ever, even if stopping it kills us—but not you; you must live to help the people heal. Please take Dray back to the spring village, that should be far enough," I thought in a rush.

"Are you finished?" Zarek's mental voice was reassuring. *"Dray did another little job for us before he came and fed you. He served a very fine wine to the Spider and her crew, and as soon as they are asleep, he is going to slip in and relieve the Spider of her weapons."*

"Don't forget the trigger. Tell him to get the square book-like thing she keeps in her robe pocket. The orbs are in the left pocket, the trigger in the right. If he doesn't get the trigger, she can still set those orbs off a good thirteen or fourteen miles away. Get them out of range, fast! There are three!"

"She wouldn't risk it with her own life at stake," Zarek thought at me.

"You don't know her! I have just spent the last six days with her, and yeah, I think she would. She is so full of hate that it has gutted her soul, emptied her of any human empathy. And she is old, and she knows she can't live forever. I foolishly brought that point to her attention a few days back. So, yes, don't doubt for a moment that she would do that if she thought she was at the end of her road. If she could get me and my friends, even a few, I believe she would do it in a heartbeat."

"I don't think she has any idea how fast the cycles can go." Zarek's words touched my mind. *"I will take Dray and the orbs and be halfway to Isuladune before she even knows they're gone. Trust me."*

"Oh, I trust you! It's her I don't trust."

"Once we have them and Dray safely out of here, we will come back for you. Your people have a surprise for the Spider."

With that, Zarek was gone.

Trying to penetrate the dark of the waxing moon shadows, looking around to see if I could spot any of my friends, I noticed a guard asleep, slumped by the Spider's tent flap.

My first full view of Dray as he snuck into the tent was of a scrawny, shabbily dressed boy, his hair a hacked-up mess.

A street kid! That surprised me. He had Library diction; there were no barbed street tones in his voice. I would have sworn he was Gentry born. I hoped we would all live through this night. I was sure he would have an interesting story to tell. I wanted so much for him to live, and I wanted to hear his story from his own lips.

Out he came with a bag in his hands and, like a shadow himself, he slipped into the dark and was gone. I hoped the Spider would sleep until dawn, giving my friends a good long time to get as far away as a cyna-cycle could take them.

I didn't know if those orbs could be destroyed or if there was a second trigger device; thinking about it nearly laid me out in a panic. *What If ... No!*

I took a deep breath, closed my eyes and remembered the new Telling Tree on my island, remembered the peace. Even in the midst of terror, even tied to a wheel hub, I knew the seeds of peace grew in me and in others, just as the tree grew on my island. Brother Swayne had seen himself serving me, and House Ra'Vell, into his old age. I had to hold onto that vision. The visions were real. The Spirit of Wonannonda was real. Life would get better for all of us ... but who knew where it would go before it got better?

At least the Spider didn't have the orbs anymore.

I closed my eyes and opened up to my surroundings. *"Fly,"* I sent out to Zarek. *"Fly like the wind."* I settled into as comfortable a position as possible and let my mind feel the camp. There were only a few who were awake. One of them was heading toward the Spider's tent right now. I couldn't see him, only sense him.

Then I heard it, and felt it beneath me: the thunder of horses' hooves coming from the west. Three men on horseback arrived just as the man who was coming up to the tent, reached the door.

"Halt!" the man by the tent shouted. Then I recognized him as one of the men I had seen days ago, who had scared me as much as the Spider. There was no one stirring inside the tent. The man had drawn his sword. I was not at a good angle to see the new arrivals till one of them jumped to the ground. Even on the other side of the horse, when he spoke, I knew instantly who he was.

Zidell!

With him was the other man I had last seen in my prison, Ezra Jerril. I could see their shadowed faces from the low burning campfire next to the tent. When the third man came into view, I could not believe my eyes. It wasn't a man at all, but the redheaded girl James had taken a liking to. Podrick. Podrick dressed as a boy, with her hair cut very short.

"I am here to see my uncle, the Voice. I have valuable information about Ra'Vell Island and the caverns," she said in a deeper voice than I remembered her using before. It made my mind reel.

Zidell stepped up. "I am Zidell, high priest of the Book and the Tree."

"Haven't you heard? The Tree is dead, the king is dead … and the Voice is a lying traitor … and a woman."

A few of the guards and some of the chosen were beginning to stir now and gather around the campfire, stoking it up.

"Do not blaspheme the Voice of Creator!" Zidell raised his fist to the man's face. "Who are you to speak such lies? That godforsaken island was full of such lies, but you ride with the Voice himself. How can you say such things?"

One of the scary man's seven other companions came up behind him and they had a quick whispered conversation. One of them went into the tent. "They are all sleeping!" he shouted.

"Then wake them up!" the scary man shouted back.

The second man brought out the Voice-Spider-Zee, dragging her by an ankle; she emitted a loud snoring snort and stirred, trying to wake up.

"What have you done?" Zidell shrieked in a rage, flying at the big man, reaching for his eyes, only to meet the thrust of a blade held in the scary man's fist.

Zidell slid from the short sword to the ground, a look of disbelief on his face. "How … could you?" he gasped clutching his stomach. "What have … you … done?"

More men arrived with lamps and torches.

One of the Voice's loyalists ran to the struggling bag of bones and helped her to sit up. It was surprising, how many still believed she was a he, and deserved adoration and worship.

"My … " Zee gasped and grabbed clumsily at the pockets of her robe for the orbs and trigger. "Where … Who?" Her eyes couldn't focus, and her head lolled back. The loyal priest who held her up began to feel in the pockets too, and looked up at the scary man. "Did you take them?"

While all this was going on, Podrick and my former prisoner, Ezra, were pulling back, trying to slip out of the circle of light.

"Stop right there," a quiet, rough voice said. "Come on back into the light."

Another of the seven men accounted for. So far three of them were visible. *Where are the other four?* I wondered.

Podrick and Ezra were brought up to the scary man. "You said you have information about the island?" he asked.

"It is for my uncle, the Voice; for his ears only," Podrick gestured toward the incapacitated Voice.

"*His* ears are a little addled right now, and you must be going deaf." He laughed, giving his men a meaningful look I could not interpret. "Maybe it is a family trait." Then he glared down at Podrick a full head shorter than him. "Or were you just not listening?"

The second man sniggered. "These two do not believe, swordbrother. Why not show them?"

"Yeah." One of the other ones said, "Let us show them all."

The Spider was trying to stand but couldn't. The scary man stepped up to her and slid his short sword into the front of the Voice's robes. She froze, still as a statue, and then there was the rip of fabric as the sword, sharp as a blade can be, cut the robe away from the scarred, shrunken chest of a woman. The scary man cut the robe all the way down to her feet, along with her undergarments, revealing the final proof.

"But … " Ezra began, then he shut up, glanced at Podrick, whose face was like stone, her eyes the only active part of her, trying to find a place to dart, I suspected.

Neither of them knew yet that I was there. Even though it was a cool night, I felt a line of sweat trickle down my spine. What would they say to the seven men when they found out?

CHAPTER FIFTEEN

"It is the middle of the night, Gene," one of the seven said. They had all come out of the shadows by then.

"The orbs are gone. Someone got to them before us. They can't have gone far. Search every tent." The scary man said. "No one sleeps until I find them."

"Yeah, we can question these two in the morning, when we have some light to see what we are looking at. You know I hate doing things in the dark," said one of the seven.

"Shut up!" the scary man said. *Is he Gene,* I wondered? He seemed like the leader of the once eleven, now only seven, scary men.

The Spider had drawn her knees up to her scarred chest and wrapped her arms around her bony legs. She was slumped over, whimpering. "Why ... can ... stand up?" she slurred. "Someone ... stop them."

"Tie those two up! Check every square inch of the tent to make sure the witch did not hide the orbs in there, somewhere. Drag the others out and search them too," Gene ordered.

As two of the seven men jerked the resisting Ezra over to the wagon where I was tied, he saw me and began to scream, and fought to kick me and pummel me about the head and shoulders. "Pendyse Ra'Vell, this is all your fault!" He was wild, kicking, as two of the men tried to contain him. Ezra grabbed a knife from one man's belt and sliced the man's face, then turned toward me. The next thing I knew, Ezra's head was in my lap, detached from his body. I squirmed to get out from under it, and Gene, the head lopper, kicked it away. It bounced like a ball into the dark out of sight, but the headless body lay at my feet.

"We need the kid now more than ever," Gene said. "Getting the island will be harder without the orbs. We do not need information from a secondary source when we have the main fount." He turned toward Podrick, glaring. "Are you going to cause problems too? Should I just dispatch you to Tomorrow Land now and be done with it? If I tie you to your uncle, the Voice's fancy wagon, will you try to kill the kid too?"

She held up her hands and shook her head. "No trouble. No trouble at all." Then she held out her hands to be tied, and they slung her down on the ground next to me, tying her feet and body to the outer edge of the large wheel a few feet from me. Laughing, the two men pulled the ropes so tight that she screamed in pain.

"You two can keep each other company till morning," Gene said. "You have till then for us to make our decision about what to do with an extra mouth to feed, one we probably do not need." He squatted in front of Podrick and grinned, leering at her. "I like pretty boys." He glanced at me, then back at Podrick, rose and walked back to the tent. He helped the men search inside it, and they stripped the Voice's guards and checked their clothes. Once that was done, they left them lying naked on the cold ground to sleep off their drugged stupor.

I didn't look at Podrick, but I asked her, "Is the Spider really your uncle—I mean, aunt?"

"The Voice is my God, and my protector," she spat out. "And you have … you have … caused this humiliation to come on her. I don't know how you did it, but I know it is your fault. It is not right!"

"How did you free my two prisoners?"

She laughed, a rather hysterical, high-pitched burble not unlike what I heard from the Voice on occasion.

"You rabble-rousers were easy to fool." She lowered her voice to the merest of whispers. "Sandill was so eager to *save* all us poor, defiled girls that she believed every story I told her. And your people … Oh, Great Creator, that was pure fun! James … "

I turned my head to look at her, studied her beautiful but twisted features now covered with dirt, grime, and a trickle of blood from where the rough treatment had marked her. She sneered at me.

"I killed him, you know, after we made love … *Love*." The word was a snarl, her lips turned down. "If you can call the fumbling, bumbling, grunting mess we did *love*. But he fell for it like the stone that crushed your grandfather." The look on her face was pure venom. "When we were done, I gutted him like a fish."

"You're a liar," I said very quietly, fear spilling into my soul. Not another one. It couldn't be. "You lie."

"About what, that I killed James, or that I know all about how your grandfather died? I was there with my father, Alan Bouyahie. The Bouyahie you killed." She laughed again. "The Voice and I fooled him too. He did not even know I was a girl," she hissed in so quiet a tone I could barely hear her myself, though I was sitting right next to her. "One of the inner circle of girls the Voice raised to infiltrate the Web, the Wave and the Weave." Sarcasm flicked from her lips on specks of saliva. "The Voice has been raising priests for hundreds of years, from some of the best families, families who have been turning sons *and daughters* over to 'him' for training ... And, well you know what the world thinks girls are for, but the Voice would occasionally chose an exceptional girl to turn boy. I was that exceptional girl in this generation. I knew everything, and you have ruined all that."

"Too bad for you then ... isn't it?"

She looked at me, puzzled and taken aback. "How is that bad? I have had years with the Voice. She has taught me everything I need to know. I knew she was a woman. She thought it was the funniest joke on men, that a woman was their leader. She was grooming me to take her place when the time came. I think it is about here. I do not think '*He*' will last much longer without the bombs. So it is my time now. I will just take over."

The sneer was back, and the cocksure tilt to her head as she glanced about at the shadows. "Maybe I'll tell them you're a girl. You know what they would do to you, don't you?"

"Reveal that, *Podrick,* and I won't be the only one on the ground with my legs spread."

"Too late!" she said in a singsong voice as the night exploded with the clang of metal on metal and the screams of bloody battle rose in the dark. "I think I shall enjoy watching you get ripped apart," she said, smiling sweetly, "even should I get the same fate."

I couldn't tell what was happening or who was fighting. Could this be my people and the plan to rescue me?

"Over here!" Podrick yelled. "Free me and I'll help you kill these bastards." Her words were rough, her face twisted with fury. "Free me and I'll fight with you!"

A young priest, no more than twenty, came running toward us, flipping the knife in his hand to a position for sawing at rope. He pulled the ship knots loose from the back of wheel spokes and gave Podrick the knife after freeing her hands. She sawed at the bindings on her ankles and leaped to her feet with a triumphant shout. Glancing back at me as she ran into the melee. She called, "I'll deal with you later, Ra'Vell."

By the waxing moon's light, which was thin, I watched men die, not knowing who was on what side. The frustration and fear turned my stomach to acid, and all that lovely food that Dray had fed me wanted to escape as badly as I did.

The fighting came to an end just before dawn. The eastern edge of the horizon was barely a shimmer of gold when Gene came and stood before me on wobbly legs. "Glad to see you are still with us."

"So, what next?" I asked.

He gave a real belly laugh. Then his expression turned to stone. "You are going to give us your island. That is what is next." He turned to walk away, then stopped and turned back to me. "And if you have any ideas about not doing that for us, I just want you to know, we—my associates and I—have sent word to loyal friends in Dunsmier, the military city—"

"I know what Dunsmier is," I interrupted.

"Well, know this: they are coming to reinforce my small band, and your untried people will not stand a chance against us. We want your island, and we are going have it. We are going to the Blue Moon. We will have their technology, all of it, or I swear to burn down this world and everyone on it, and the moon, too. So do not think you can resist what is coming. Advise your people to give up now and we might let you live."

He turned and left.

A whole new kind of crazy had just come to town. And I was sick to death of people telling me they were going to smash the world. They were all power-hungry megalomaniacs.

By the time the new crew had stripped anything useful from the dead or dying, it was getting on toward noon. They had untied me. Overconfident that I was too cowed to even think of escape now that I saw what they were capable of, they let me walk beside the wagon with no fetters on my hands or feet. They were right; what could I do? I couldn't outrun horses or arrows. I knew that. So I would wait. And watch for my people.

As we left, I saw they had not even bothered to burn the dead. Podrick's naked lush body lay on the ground, lacerations on almost every inch of her very white flesh. The loyal priests of the Voice were all in a heap, the Voice unceremoniously tossed like a bony rag doll on the top of the pile, her ripped robes flapping in the wind, revealing her longest-kept secret. *You get out of life what you put into it,* I thought. *Somehow, somewhere, it all has a way of coming back to you.* I closed my eyes, sending a prayer to Wonannonda for my friend James.

I had the feeling these men did not believe in anything unseen, only in the power they could grab with that of the fist, the boot, and the sword. It was unbearable. It tangled in my mind like cage worms in a jar of meal.

The same kind of danger still pervaded our world; maybe even a worse danger. There were just different people in charge of handing it out now. And I knew I would never help them take Ra'Vell Island. And the island had been unbreachable in any war ever fought in these parts. These men didn't know our history if they thought they could take my island.

Zee's people I knew the lay of, but this new crew, were complete strangers to me. I hadn't even known such a group existed. They seemed like men from Remode before I burned it down, only way more organized. I fervently hoped there was another such happy accident in my future where these men were concerned.

We traveled without incident for the rest of that day and the next two. By the time we could see the bridge spires in the distance, Gene and his men numbered only fifteen; they were missing four of the original eleven. I had picked up all kinds of information just by being quiet and listening to the men talk at night.

The eleven had trained together in the military city of Dunsmier in the province of Dakota, just south of Oregon and the city of Ravenwood. I wondered again if my Keeper Brontis knew any of them, as he had been trained at Dunsmier as well. It made me feel a little more oriented to this new set of circumstances. They were military, an elite band.

For the thousandth time, I wondered when or even if my rescuers were ever going to show up. Here we were, nearly at the gates, just at the sandy ridge of the East Fork of River Rush.

While Gene's men set up camp, he came for me.

"Now is your time to be useful," he said. "Tomorrow morning, you will tell your gate guards to open up for us and give us the keys to your kingdom, little master. Or we will wait till reinforcements come with enough explosives to bomb your people out of existence, now that we have lost the orbs that would have made it easy on everyone, a painless death with everything left intact." He looked at me, with a squint of speculation. "You were right there in front of the Voice's tent. You must have seen who took them. Who was it?"

I glared at him, ignoring his question. "You blow my people up, you blow up the phase port to the moon. Then what would you have?" I wasn't going to let him know I knew how to get to another phase port. If they ever got to my Blue Moon phase port and through it somehow, the Crimson Death would take care of them. Which was another thing I wouldn't tell them about. I almost smirked at that, thinking it would be a death to good for them.

"Does that mean you choose not to help us open the gate?"

"That depends. You tell me how many reinforcements you are expecting."

He grinned. "So force of numbers is what impresses you, is it?"

I looked him straight in the eye. "I have to know what my odds are, either to fight or surrender." I stared hard at him, scared spiteless as I was, I let my gaze go hooded and tried to pick up anything that might be in his mind. "Tell me the truth! I will know if you lie."

He laughed; I seemed to amuse him. "You are a gutsy little bastard." He grinned.

"Well, I can only die once. And I figure you had better pick your shot, because you can only use me against my people once. And dead, I am no good to you at all. That is, if you want to do this the easy way."

A glimmer of meanness crossed over his face, the charm gone, the humor gone, and I feared I had gone too far. Then a look of utter disgust followed, and he said, "Five hundred strong."

The minutes his words hit the air I knew them for a lie. "You mean fifty?"

Abruptly, he turned and walked away.

Score one for the truth. Somehow I had seen that number as if it had been emblazoned on his forehead, like a vision in the Heart of Telling. I whispered a prayer of thanks.

At the tent flap, he looked over his shoulder, a quick glance my way, a crease between his brows. It was my turn to grin at him.

Once he was inside and out of sight, I sat down suddenly and began to tremble from head to toe. I shook so hard my teeth rattled together.

The sun was low in the sky, its glare glancing off the sand and the saw grasses whipping in the wind. I calmed myself and felt the urge to open my mind.

"Get ready! Get down. Lay down, under one of the wagons. I don't want to hit you with a Sleeper sweep by accident. We have them surrounded." Sweet relief started me shuddering all over again as Zarek's mind touched mine.

"I am already there," I shot back as I rolled under the wagon next to me.

"Hey, what do you think you are doing?" the man guarding me growled as the sand next to us erupted into the forms of three armored men. My guard fell asleep before he hit the ground, unable to shout an alarm. Two more guards were already down. I grabbed my sleeping guard's sword and felt jubilation race through every part of me. I no longer felt defenseless. It was a false feeling, to be sure—many die with sword in hand, and I would have preferred my slingshot—but a sword would do.

I couldn't keep count of those who had fallen, but it was at least half of the sixteen men present; then I saw Will rise up from the sand with a Sleeper in his hand and face a man who screamed, "We are under attack!" Then the man went down. Will grinned a toothy grin. "Stay there!" he commanded me. "We don't want—"

Gene stepped out of the tent. Confused screams were being cut short as dozens of my people shot Rectifiers at the men I had been forced to live with for the past few days, until they were all down except Gene. He had his hands up, disbelief in every line and muscle.

"Don't kill me!" he said, shaking his head. "I don't want to die, not like that, not without a sword in my hands. Not with whatever means of death that thing deals."

I rushed to Will's side, flung myself into his arms and gave him a big bear hug.

Will kissed my cheek and set me on the ground. "Girl, we have been waiting for you! What took you so long?"

"I have never been more glad to see you, Will," I said.

"*Girl?* What the … ? No way!" Gene shook his head in disbelief.

"Yes!" Will and I said together. I saw Rifkin ride in on my small cycle with Wydra, John and Jorame. They all came over and gave me hugs. Jorame kissed me on the forehead as he released me. Zarek stepped into the circle, and the setting sun shone gold on his white skin. "So glad to see you again, Pen." And he wrapped his arms around me. I returned the embrace.

The big man, Gene, stumbled, gaping at Zarek. "What the hell *are you*?" The color had drained from his face, and his arms hung limp at his sides.

"We are the people who are going to take back the world," Zarek said. "The killing stops here." He raised a Rectifier and put Gene to sleep.

CHAPTER SIXTEEN

As the sleeping men were loaded on to the cycle pallets, Rifkin eyed me, "You're a mess Pen," he waved a hand in front of his face. "And you need a bath in the worst way." Then he laughed, "But it's great to have you back."

"A bath would be nice." I said and asked him, "Where is James?"

Rifkin shrugged. "He was down with the dogs last I saw him. We looked for him when we were getting ready to come out here to hide ourselves. We have been keeping an eye on your progress. He most likely decided not to come late to the party because it might give us all away."

"Ummm," I grunted as I helped him lift one of Gene's men onto the platform. I dusted off my hands. "When was the last time you saw him?"

Rifkin eyed me. "What's up? You seem … I don't know. You should be elated about your rescue, but you seem … well … troubled."

"Did you know that Podrick was not what she seemed?"

A frown passed over his face and settled in his cobalt blue eyes.

"Now you look troubled!" I half-laughed, not wanting to believe what Podrick had said, keeping James alive in my mind for as long as I could. Standing on the balance point, not letting it tip in either direction, alive or dead, a stasis of feeling.

"Well, I know she has him twisted around her little finger. He is completely besotted with that woman. They are hardly ever apart. And something about her has me feeling … well … I don't know … suspicious. And there is some bad news. Our two prisoners have escaped somehow. They must be on the island, but we haven't found them yet. Or who let them out."

"They're dead," I said flatly. "The Voice too. And all the priests who were with her."

Rifkin stared at me. "You mean ... Podrick is dead? But ... I don't understand, how ... ?"

"Two nights ago, she rode into the camp, along with Zidell and Ezra."

"Wait, I think everyone should hear this." Rifkin gave a whistle with his thumb and finger, a loud, piercing crack of sound that caught everyone's attention. "Hey, Pen knows what happened to our escapees!" he shouted. Wydra, John, Jorame, Zarek and the others gathered around me.

"Two nights ago, while Pen was with those men ... " Rifkin pointed at the sleeping men piled on the platforms. "Go ahead, Pen."

"Podrick, Zidell and Ezra rode into their camp." I jerked a thumb toward the heap of sleeping men. "That was the night Dray gave the Voice drugged wine, along with her bodyguards. Dray had just gotten the orbs out of there when the leader, that one," I pointed at Gene, "came to take them by force. Podrick and the others rode in about then, and Zidell went berserk and attacked a man who had a short sword, and that was the end of Zidell. When Ezra saw me, he attacked me; I was tied to a wheel hub at the time, with no way to defend myself. So the leader there, Gene," I indicated him again, "lopped off his head. That is why I have dried blood all over the front of me," I said with disgust. I paused to catch my breath, and then continued.

"Anyway, about that time, they tied Podrick to the wheel next to me, and she told me she had helped them escape ... and that she had ... killed James." I almost gasped out that last bit. A deep silence fell.

"We thought they had run off together," Will said at last. "Why would she kill him?"

I slumped down on the edge of the platform, my legs giving out. My head felt light. I was so tired and heartsick. "She was slated to be the next Voice. Carrying on the tradition of a woman in charge of men who believed she was a man. They thought that was funny." I brushed at my eyes unable to keep believing, Podrick had tried to hurt me by lying.

After that, we crossed over the bridge and put our prisoners on stretchers to carry them down to the prison cells. It was a silent business.

Everyone seemed to be immersed in a well of deep thought. They tried to get me to eat and go to bed while this work of heavy lifting went on, but I was too heartsick, and even as tired as I was, bruised and battered, I couldn't rest. Even after a long hot shower which made me feel human again, but I couldn't settle down until I had James's body so we could send his spirit to Tomorrow Land. I had come to believe that was just symbolic of the meaning of life after life, but his physical absence weighed on me like a hundred-pound stone on my back. I couldn't shake it. I felt like it would crush me if I didn't do something.

I couldn't stand the thought of him lying on cold stone somewhere in the caverns, food for the rats. At that thought, I threw off my covers, pulled on some clean clothes and headed for Rifkin's room. When I got there, Hannratti was already there, red-eyed and weeping.

"I can't sleep. I have to find his body," I said. She gave a loud sob at that. "I'm sorry ... I'm so sorry, Hannratti."

"Hanni; James called me Hanni. A girl's name," she sobbed. "I'm not a boy anymore."

I pressed my lips tight and tried not to join her, tried to be the brave one, to hold us all together, as I noticed Rifkin had red-rimmed eyes too. "Do you think one of the hounds could find James if we took her to the last place you knew he had been?" I asked him.

He sat up, instantly energized. "Of course. Why didn't I think of that?" He sniffed, and ran an arm under his nose. "We'll take Ripper, she has the most experience. Hanni, you stay here."

"No. I may be a girl, but so is Pen, and James was my cousin and friend as much as yours. I'm going."

The three of us, sniffing and blinking, went to the kennel. I hadn't seen my puppy in a month and was amazed at how big she was, how beautiful. Her fur had lengthened and was like snow in the moonlight; a fine glossy sheen overlay the deep purple cap surrounding her horn. She was too big to pick up easily, so I knelt and buried my face in the ruff at her neck and breathed in that sweet, clean smell. She licked my face and we nuzzled. Her yips and whines of greeting gave me heart. Finally I was ready to go.

We took Ripper and made the long hike to the barracks by Rock Harbor, where James had been staying with Podrick. Rifkin found some of James's unwashed smallclothes to give to Ripper to smell, and we turned her loose. Nose down, tail up, she headed back the way we had come. She would catch a scent, then lose it, and then catch it again. Finally she stopped at a narrow tunnel, seldom used, as it only led to a few small, unused storage cells. She shot off down the passageway to the very last cell. Entering that cell, we found James, naked, but unmarked.

"She said she gutted him like a fish," I whispered.

Ripper licked James's face and he stirred. We all yelped in surprised, then ran to him. He was chained hand and foot to the wall, with shackles only four feet long. He was half-dead from cold, thirst and hunger, with food and water set just outside his reach next to his neatly folded clothes, to taunt him with what he couldn't have, I suspected. Creator forgive me, but at that moment, I was glad Podrick was dead; she was as evil as the Voice, daughter-spawn of the eater of evil itself.

Rifkin grabbed the canteen of water and pressed it to James's lips, pouring it into his slack mouth. James gulped and spluttered, choking, but it revived him a bit, and he took some more and swallowed it. I picked up his coat and covered him, checking his chains and looking around for the key. "No key that I can see." Turning to Hannratti, I said, "Hanni. Take Ripper with you and go get help from the barracks; get chain cutters and a stretcher. Bring help."

She ran.

"Ripper, go with Hanni," I commanded. Ripper shot out after her.

"James. James." Rifkin kept repeating his name and shaking him gently.

"That's … " James swallowed another gulp of water. "My … name." Another sip. "Don't wear … it out." His voice was dry and raspy.

Rifkin and I whooped with joy, tears streaming down our faces.

"I'm glad … to see you too," he said, voice cracked, but audible.

"We've got help coming, brother." Rifkin's voice was as rough as James's.

"What took you so long?" James muttered in a small coarse voice.

And then we were laughing. Even James gave a croak of mirth. I breathed deep, overcome by the sweet sense of life revived at finding James alive. The tilt the world had taken on now squared itself again, and I felt the new energy of hope fill me. Podrick may have meant to deal us all a blow by having us find him too late and learning we could have saved him if we had only looked for him sooner. Well, we had found him. Podrick had failed.

After help came and we got the shackles off James and his clothes on him, and some more water into him, we carried him back to the barracks. There, he had some clear soup and a bit of bread, after which he felt more like himself.

"She tried to kill me," he said as he told us what had happened. "And she would have accomplished it, if you hadn't come." He paused. "I thought she loved me." He shook his head, "I thought I loved her." He nodded then. "Yep, that sex stuff is a powerful magic that can make you overlook a lot of things that are right in front of your eyes. But you ignore them because you want to believe in the magic. That isn't love. I had three days to think about it. Did she really free our prisoners? She said she was going too."

"James," I whispered, "Podrick is dead."

He blinked once, twice, took a deep breath, and said, "Well, I can't say I'm sorry about that. Before she left, she showed me her true self. She was full of poison that would have spilled out over our country; she was very good at making people believe things. She had me completely fooled. All I can say is I'm sorry she wasn't what she pretended to be. What I thought I loved was that story of herself that she told me—the one she had made up." He looked away. "I wonder what was the truth. How did she become what she was?"

We all spent an uncomfortable few moments in silence, and then he continued. "She drugged me when we got down there to be alone. When I woke up, I was naked and in chains. She told me her plans, spent quite a long time on that. She kissed me goodbye and said, 'I hope you die slow. No one will find you till you are nothing but bones.' Then she left me with food, water and warmth just out of reach. That was what saved me. I became so angry at her, at myself … and then I thought of all of you, looking for me … I yelled myself hoarse. And no one came. Everyday I yelled hoping someone would hear me. That was when I thought I might really die after all, but somehow, every time I woke up, there were these words in my head: *'Don't give up! They're coming.'*"

I felt a lump the size of a plum in my throat. "I am sorry she did that to you," I said, thinking of Quill. Of how the pain of lost dreams can hurt. "But, I think," I said, "what hollows us out can make us deeper, more spacious people if we choose to let it."

"Yeah, but why do we have to gain wisdom in the worst ways?" Rifkin quipped.

I slept that night in the barracks with Hanni and James. Rifkin took Ripper back to her pups and the message of finding James alive back to Will and the others.

In the morning, four of the guards carried James on a stretcher from the barracks at Rock Harbor up to his room in the castle. Wydra and Jorame checked him over and stayed with him while the rest of us met around Chet's kitchen table. There was a crowd of people there to welcome me home and hear our stories, and find out what plans were being made to deal with the soldiers who were coming from Dunsmier Dakota.

"Now, I have answered all of your questions; can someone please tell me how we got so many Rectifiers?" I asked, my eyes on Zarek. "Where did they all come from?" I could see one hanging by a thick chain from every neck in the room, even Chet's.

"Oh, let me!" Hanni said. "Quill was cutting that black stone to help rebuild the women's town, ReMaid, and the Oaths were there. They had taken some of the women and children who came to the island from other places to ReMaid, and they discovered … what did you call that stuff?"

"Linnaeus stone," said Zarek.

"Yea, Linnaeus stone, the rare substance that the Rectifiers need in order to work. They shipped a load to the Wells, through the phase port under the tree. That is where they are making them. In the Wells," she clarified, "not under the tree."

"We have the first run done already, and most of us have one," said Will.

"And you can see we put them on chains," grinned Zarek. "Just like you suggested."

"Some of us wear them around our waists," Rifkin said, "as a chain around my neck sort of freaks me out." He glanced around the room. "If you're in close quarters in a fight, I don't want someone using the chain to choke me, but I haven't been able to convince—"

"You're absolutely right, Rifkin," I interrupted. "That's not something I thought about when I put one on a makeshift line around my neck. I lost that one in the scuffle with Zee when we beamed down from the moon. The twine broke … if it had been a chain … " I looked around at the people who had one hanging from their necks, then I looked at Rifkin's. "I like that! The chain is strong-looking," I said, "sturdy, with a snap claw hook, long enough so you can wear it around your waist; that makes good sense. Then we can keep the Rectifier out of the way, in a pocket, with no danger of being strangled by the chain. We have some dangerous men in our brig down below, and we don't want any of them having a chance to kill any of us and get their hands on a Sleeper. We also have the problem of pretenders. We have no idea if there more people like Podrick who might want to free them for some reason."

"I have already set two guards on duty at the brig's main door, and that guard duty will be a permanent post to be filled at all times," said Will, "so that won't happen again. And as soon as the hounds are old enough there will be hounds on guard duty as well."

"There could be many more who want to make a grab for power and dominance than just those men," I said. "What we want to promote is freedom for all, and a way for everyone to have a choice in how they live their lives. This is not going to be a quick fix. But Zarek's people have lived for thousands of years now without wars, or mass killings or murder. I want us to learn from them, find out how they did that, how they started doing that. I know we are a people who love our weapons, and our skills with them, and it will be very hard to lay them down. I know it will be hard for me. But I will do it, as soon as we make this island secure."

"What do you mean?" Will looked puzzled. "Our island is secure."

"Not until we make sure there are none among us who would betray us, as Podrick did."

"And how do you propose to find that out?" Will asked, hands on hips.

"The Heart of Telling." Glancing around the kitchen, I saw smiles, frowns, surprise and doubt on the faces of my closest friends and allies. "Trust the Spirit of Wonannonda, and we will grow in truth and wisdom." Brother Swayne smiled.

"Only those who have access to the prisoners or military positions will need to go before the Heart of Telling, I think," I said. "It will keep us all safe from any plans to stop us before we get started."

"OK, then, I will go and make ready when we're done here," said Brother Swayne.

Hanni looked around the room. "The Heart of Telling will know." Her round, rosy face and blue eyes held hope, and then doubt. "We can trust that Great Spirit, can't we, Pen? It didn't tell us Mark was about to die. If it had, we could have saved him. But what if … "

"We can ask," Brother Swayne said. "We may not always get the answers we want, but we can always ask. The answer may be yes; sometimes it might be no. That Great Spirit is love, and love has its own reasons. Whatever they are, you can most assuredly trust that love."

Over the next few hours, Brother Swayne spoke with the soldiers who came up from the caverns and from every post around the island that was vital to our defenses. He asked them, "Are you willing to lay your heart bare before the Heart of Telling? To express your allegiance to truth, peace and freedom?"

There were only three women who refused, and one man who the Heart of Telling showed was a thief and a pickpocket. The three women were put off the island out the east gate, and the man was thoroughly searched and put in the brig to decide about once we dealt with the Dunsmier soldiers who were on their way here.

My friends had not been idle while I made my slow, captive way home.

Brontis, Castle Ravenwood's Keeper, now had radio communication with Will; they both had a wrist communication link device like the ones the Oaths and Zarek wore. I hadn't had any time alone with any of them yet; everyone was too busy planning and carrying out preparations so we would be ready for the new arrivals. Brontis had sent word that they had just camped outside of Ravenwood City, not far from the castle. "They even had the gall to send him a runner to request shelter for their Command of fifty. It is raining there," Will said, "and you were right: they only have one Command with them."

I smiled to myself. I had been pretty sure I was right when I had said to Gene that there were only fifty men coming to join him.

"OK, then, we have until tomorrow to get into place below Rose Rock Village," I said. "It will take them that long to reach there from Ravenwood. We don't want them wrecking the place if they get there before us. I know the perfect place to face them, halfway between Rose Rock and Ravenwood."

Will gave me a Nar Cat that ate the fancy bird smile. "I know exactly what place you mean. Perfect!"

"The Rumpled Hills," I nodded. "Plenty of cover for us, and a long, narrow stretch of road coming up through them. Yet it looks deceptively open, and somewhat flat."

"That is the way they would come in order to meet up with their friends at the East Fork Bridge," said Will, tapping the map we had laid out on Chet's kitchen table. All of us gathered around it while Chet's staff cleared the breakfast dishes.

I closed my eyes and rubbed my neck. Last night had been the first night in … how many … that I had slept in a real bed, lying flat, but I felt like I could sleep for a week and not catch up, I was so tired and sore. Small lacerations and bruises covered most of my body. I was more black and blue that skin toned.

Jorame and Wydra came in from tending James. "He's sleeping. He will need some time to recover from his ordeal," said Jorame, "but we gave him some medicine that will speed that along."

"I was just saying, we will stay in Rose Rock tonight and get in place before dawn, to stop the troops that are coming our way," I pressed my fingers to my temples.

"That's cutting it kind of close, isn't it?" Wydra asked. "Shouldn't we be in place in case they fast-march? We have seen how your soldiers can move quickly from one place to another."

"She's right." John walked around the end of the table and looked at the map. "We should camp here, actually in place, with a watch on the southeast end of the Rumples who can alert us when the soldiers approach."

"That would put us at the high end of that gentle slope that goes up to Rose Rock." I nodded. "Yes, that's good."

Shortly after that, we broke up to go about the tasks of preparing to leave the island. John went to see his son, Lodar, and Dray, who was staying with Klea, Mark's mother. I hadn't seen them yet, but they were safe. I smiled to myself, happy to know this.

Wydra, Jorame, Zarek and I were the only ones left in the room. Chet and his crew were off banging pots and pans around, such a homey sound. I sat at the table, just wanting to sleep, but to tired to move. I ached everywhere.

"*We have decided!*" Zarek's thoughts spoke to me. "*You are a mess; you have bruises and cuts that have not been tended to. We want you to drink some of the purple tea. It will heal what wounds you have quickly and give you new energy for the task ahead. But drink only a small amount. You don't want to become dependent on it.*"

Wydra brought out a small flask and handed it to me. "Drink."

I stared up at her, at her pretty pixie face and her white strip of hair standing up all spiky. She wouldn't ask me to do something harmful. I took the flask, gave it a sniff. There was a slight tart smell. I tipped it up and drank it down, fast, what little amount there was of it. My mouth revolted instantly, puckering at the horrid taste. Tart was not the word for it; I wanted to retch, it was so bitter, sour, with a slight moldy aftertaste. My ancestor Susan Pearl must have been nuts to try this a second time, I agreed with all those people she had tried to convince to drink it … then I began to feel light infuse my whole being, a zing and a kick that raced along blood pathways to reach every part of me. I watched a bruise on the back of my hand disappear. A cut right next to the bruise became less red and swollen. I stood up, pushing back the chair I was in with so much energy that I knocked it over accidentally.

"Whoa!" was all I could say as it sped through my system. The sensation was like nothing I had ever felt. One small gulp could do this? I began to see the appeal … and the danger. This feeling ... it was like being superhuman. Beyond the desire to live for what might seem like forever, there was just this feeling of wellbeing. To see healing happen right before your eyes! I extended my hands, looking at them as if they were some amazing miracles belonging to someone else.

"Are you all right?"

"Yes." Looking at Zarek, I was surprised to see the worry in those large, liquid cat eyes of his. *"I have never felt better. Let's go do this."* The aches, the pain and the tiredness were all gone. Gone. Just as a medical property, this was so far beyond anything I could have imagined. "I see why this is a controlled substance," I said aloud.

"That's the thing," Wydra smiled. "Most people are suspicious, non trusting; they only put their tongue to it, and the taste is so vile and overwhelmingly bitter, they refuse to drink it. So it sort of controls itself."

"Does it always taste this bitter, even for you when you drink it every day?

"Yes, but you get used to it, because of what it gives you at a cellular level."

"Oh." With nothing left to say, I glanced down at the hand where the cut had been. Fresh, unmarred skin was all that was left to see. Not even a scar remained.

CHAPTER SEVENTEEN

I was standing alone at the crest of the hill, the road rising up to meet me, with fifty hardened-looking soldiers marching my way. Dressed in men's clothes, not to hide myself this time, but because they were what I was most comfortable in, my hands causally in my pockets, I stood in the middle of the road, hand on my Rectifier, its nose sticking out of a hole in my pocket.

"HALT!" I shouted when they came within thirty yards of me. The whole troop began laughing. I didn't hold that against them. I would have laughed, too, if I didn't know what was tucked away within the folds of my coat. They were at a distinct disadvantage, I knew. Grandfather was right. Knowledge was power.

They kept coming.

"HALT!" I held up my free hand and shouted again. "You have no one to meet. Gene and his men are not here!"

That did stop them.

"Who are you, boy?" the lead man barked. "Do you carry a message from Captain Gene Wilder?" The name fit him I thought.

"I am Pendyse Ra'Vell. *Daughter* of Davood and Allois." The men began a mean, angry muttering, and they began scanning the surroundings. "You will not be allowed to pass." I projected my voice as loud as I could. They fell silent for about a second before saying some vile things about women.

A man stepped up next to the troop leader and raised a bow, nocking an arrow. "Let me skewer the little bitch and clear the road," he said.

"You don't want to do that," I warned.

The man said nothing. Meaning to prove me wrong, he lifted his elbow in preparation for drawing the string. I Rectified him, he fell, his bow and arrow clattering against each other as he dropped next to them. The soldiers gasped and stepped back, looking all around but not seeing another soul or any threat but me.

"You have a choice," I informed them. "You can put down your weapons and go home, for the killing in our world is over, or you can fall like your swordbrother."

"You killed him!" someone shouted, "You talk of no killing, but it's OK for you to kill?"

My free hand was still up in the "halt" sign, and I now used it to point to their fallen man. "Your man merely sleeps; he is not dead. Check him and see."

"The Spirit of the Tree is with me! *The killing must stop!* Murder will no longer be tolerated. It will be up to you to choose a life of freedom for yourselves or a life in a cell because you want to take life or freedom from others."

The men gave the skies a look as if they thought the Creator would drop on them from the clouds. Then a man cried, "Kill the bitch! She is lying. Women lie! It is their nat ... "

I made him fall, cutting his words short in mid-scream. I made the leader fall, too, and then the men were in a state of panic, running in all directions, but they couldn't get away from my well-hidden nonlethal army of eight, who put them all to sleep. It was a pleasant pandemonium, to my way of thinking.

When they were all down, we stripped them of any weapons they carried—even their hunting knives had to go—and any dynamite we could find. We left them their sharp-edged army forks. That was it. They could keep their supplies and pack mules. They would need them for the trip home.

"What will we do with these?" Rifkin asked as he picked up one of their swords.

"We will melt them down and make something useful out of them," said Jorame.

Working together, we raised a tent tarp over their heads to keep the sun off them, or the rain, if it came back, and laid the men out in neat rows to sleep it off. I left them a note stuck to the ground with the arrow the man had meant to use on me. It read:

There will be no more killing!

If you cannot abide by this new law, and you kill someone, you will be hunted down and given a chance to prove your innocence, and if you cannot prove it, you will be detained in prison until you decide killing is no longer beneficial to you or any of our people. GO HOME.

Spread the word. There's a new law in Nueden.

No more killing, beatings or rape.

The one you know as the Voice is dead! Killed by your own Gene Wilder and his men. The Tree at Telling Wood is dead and has been reborn on Ra'Vell Island. The woman, Zee, the Voice, killed thousands at Telling Wood with a wicked science. There will be no more mass murders. If you choose to join us in changing the world, you will be welcomed, but do not think you can fool us ...

The Spirit of Creator will reveal your true hearts and minds. You cannot hide from the Spirit.

I will know if you lie.

We fell back, well out of visual range of the road. With the Oaths' digital monocular, we kept an eye on them. When they woke, they seemed disoriented and confused. They looked for their weapons, and when they didn't find them, they headed back toward Ravenwood, all except three men, who came up the road toward us.

"Fan out," I said. "Check to see if any of the troop besides them are coming our way, circling back on us."

When the three men reached me, I stepped out onto the road. "Have you come to join us?" I walked toward them and stopped about fifteen feet away. "What are your intentions?"

The small, nervous man in the middle ran his tongue over his upper teeth, as if he had a dry mouth, and moved his head in a little involuntary jerk. "We have come to join you."

"And what did your captain think of your decision?"

"He was angry. He tried to kill me with his bare hands, but my friends here stopped him."

I turned from them and began to walk away, and said over my shoulder, "Go home! We have no room for liars. We are tired of being lied to."

Hearing running feet, I just kept going, knowing John, Wydra and Jorame would put the men to sleep without ever showing themselves. This time, we left them lying in the road where they fell.

"No one else is following," Zarek said as he came up on my small, sleek cycle. I got on behind him and we rounded up our small crew and headed to Rose Rock village.

Once we were all settled in, fed and ready for some rest, Rifkin, being the restless type, said, "I would like to go out and head toward Ravenwood to see what the soldiers are saying about what just happened to them."

"I'd like to go with you," John said, surprising me. "Safety in numbers." He quirked an eyebrow at Rifkin, then grinned. Noticing the look Wydra was giving him, he said, "No way! You are not coming! You are not exactly the typical woman from around here. Your hairstyle alone sets you apart, not that *I* mind that ... " John gave her a lopsided smile, "but ... " Wydra rolled her eyes at him, "well ... you know what I mean. You don't exactly blend in."

"That might be useful information," Zarek said, ignoring their little exchange, rolling out a sleeping bag on top of one of the beds in the dormered room we were going to sleep. "Just get in front of them and shield the cycles in a safe place where no one's likely to bump into them, well off the road. If you walk slowly enough, you can let them catch up with up you; then it will look more like they are joining you, not you joining them. Less suspicious that way."

"Yeah, that's good." Rifkin nodded, "That's smart thinking."

"But, kid," John said to Rifkin, "you are going to have to talk like a man. No more of these contractions, otherwise they will know in a second you are not one of them. Blend in... that is the way you get information."

"OK." Rifkin said, still thoughtful. "Of course."

After they left and we set a guard to watch at the window for the first half of the night, Jorame and Wydra said they would take the second watch together, we all settled in for the night. We hadn't used any lights or lit any fires. We were on the third floor of the Rose Rock Inn, facing the road that led south, toward Ravenwood. With our elevated position, we could see well down the road.

"Too bad James couldn't come with us. He would have enjoyed putting those guys to sleep." Wydra murmured, and then yawned as she snuggled down under the warmth of the thin, heated thermal bag.

That turned my thoughts to the sadness of betrayal, the heartbreak of war, the senseless death of so many people. Given the time and freedom, what good things might their potential have given to the world?

Sometimes I just wanted to be a kid again, someone with no other responsibilities than collecting the eggs, or feeding the sheep, or fishing, or ... *But,* I sighed, *that was never my life in the first place.* But how I longed for a simpler world, where people said what they meant and meant what they said. A world with no more hurting people. I knew those feelings were naive, but thought, *If we don't try, what will become of us? Because it seems to me that we are getting worse. From the things written in those books from Library, we started out with the goal of being a unified people, one with our Creator and each other. What happened to them that made them change? Or is murder just part of human nature, like John says? It must be in mine, for I have killed. But was that murder? Is self-defense murder? Is defense of the weak murder?*

I wrestled with the ideas of law and justice, of rules that would help keep everyone safe. But what if the people didn't want to be safe? What if all some wanted was power and control over others, and what if others wanted to give it to them, even if it was not in their best interests? Could we do this with Sleepers only? Could we make enough Rectifiers to keep people safe long enough for them to stop and think about how things had been and how they might be? *Is that taking away people's free will to choose?* I wondered. *But if we don't have laws, that leaves anarchy to rule, and we are back to killing people again to protect ourselves.*

Then I thought about a Sleeper, or more than one, falling into the wrong hands ... and who was I to say whose hands were right? My head hurt with all this thinking. Then I remembered my father saying, "Analysis paralysis. It will kill forward motion every time. You pick the best path you can see, then follow it to the best of your ability."

I fell asleep thinking of my father and wishing I could talk to him now.

In the dream—I knew it was a dream—I saw a great crowd of people cheering and calling my name. We were in the King's Plaza in Telling Wood, and I felt happy.

Father was there, and all of my friends. We had signed a Concord of Peace. It was by common consent, and everyone had had a voice in the process. Everyone raised their hands in agreement.

I felt happy.

Then the dream changed, and I saw Gene with a Rectifier, and he was putting people to sleep, and there weren't enough jails to hold everyone he put to sleep, so once they were asleep, he simply killed them without fuss.

Again the dream changed, and I was in a factory where Rectifiers were being made and programmed for one user. If someone else tried to use them, they would fall asleep, thanks to a default setting.

I woke up with a jerk. The pale light of morning silhouetted the Oaths as they sat at the window and watched the road. They were talking in low tones. I slid out of the bed and tiptoed over to them so as not to wake the others. "Hey," I said softly. "Any action out there?" They turned, smiled and welcomed me into the window alcove.

"No. Quiet all night." Jorame reached for my hand and pulled me onto the bench they had put by the window.

"Did you sleep well?" Wydra asked.

"Well, yes, and no. I just woke from a dream that … well, is there any way to personalize a Rectifier, so that only that one person can use it? Say, if anyone else tried to, it would put them to sleep instead?"

"Hmmm," they both murmured, and cocked their heads in exactly the same way as they thought on this. Soon they were talking excitedly about the kind of technology it would take to do this. I only understood about half of what they were saying about how this could be done and the people they knew who might be able to achieve such a thing. They thought it would be fairly easy to make the Rectifier single person users, but the putting the unauthorized user to sleep might take a bit longer. Before they got much farther along in their speculations, we saw John and Rifkin returning.

We woke the others, gathered our things and headed down stairs. We were putting together some breakfast when they came through the door of the inn.

"Well," said Zarek, "was your foraging fruitful?"

"Pretty much." John rubbed his face with both hands. "We haven't slept a wink all night … but we did eat well."

"Yeah, we went eating and drinking with the troop." Rifkin yawned and blinked, casually, as if this was an everyday occurrence. "They were plenty spooked. Didn't have a clue what had happened to them, and while we were there at the Keg and Grill, their three friends stumbled in just before we left, saying, 'The Great Creator put us to sleep a second time, and he wasn't so nice about it. No tarp and pillow.' The little twitchy one said he was going to have a crick in his neck for the rest of his life because of the way he had to sleep, all twisted up like that."

"They said they even saw his angry face in the clouds as he blew on them and knocked them to the ground," said John. "They think you are some kind of warrior priestess with a steel spine. You weren't even afraid of them: you just turned your back on them and walked away. And as long as the God of the Book and the Tree is on your side, who can fight against you?"

Rifkin started to laugh but it turned into a yawn. When he finished, he said, "They are more scared of what they don't know and can't understand right now than they ever were of the Voice. Your legend is brewing back there in that pub."

"I don't know that's a good thing," I said. "When they stop to think, and when they discover we have a weapon that can put people to sleep—and I am sure they will, sooner or later—I really don't want the people to be afraid of me, of us … " I took a deep breath, my emotions all over the map: I was up, down, happy, then feeling turned inside-out with worry. I wasn't sure what I was feeling. Fear was not what I wanted to engender; that would only breed more of what we already had. And I had walked right into that one. Maybe even promoted it without really thinking what the out come might be.

"*Don't worry! We are here for you. Whatever we can do, we will.*" Zarek's thoughts warmed me and I became calmer. "*Thank you. I needed that. I feel so overwhelmed. I don't know what I'm doing, or where to start.*"

"*We'll get there. You are not alone.*"

"Are you listening to me?" Rifkin was saying when I came back to the conversation. "Great, you didn't hear that." He shook his head and grinned ruefully. "Why is it you always phase out on me? I'm going to bed. Don't wake me unless the sky is falling."

John was nuzzling Wydra's neck in the kitchen doorway. She laughed, and hand in hand they left together.

"Maybe we can all get a little more sleep … after we eat," I suggested, sitting down to a hot plateful of food.

CHAPTER EIGHTEEN

Journal of Pendyse Ra'Vell
At Ra'Vell Island

When we got back from Rose Rock, I moved into Ra'Vell Castle Above Ground to be closer to the hub of things.

Right now I'm sitting at my desk, writing in my journal. I decided it might be important, and I want to keep track of things as they happen and thoughts that come to me. Things are going so fast, though; it is hard to find time to record events. This is my first entry. In the course of the last two months since my return from the Blue Moon, seventy-two short days, we got the solar satellites back on line, the Zap back up and running, and connected the capitals of all nine provinces to com links with people we trust in each capital city. We found Hanni's family alive and well in North Harbor, Carolina Province, all the way over on the other side of the country, on the coast. They are on their way here to reunite with Hanni.

Heronimo, Rifkin's father, has been here for a brief time to see his youngest son and meet with the leaders of the provinces, who have come together to hash out some new rules.

The Code, the Creed and the Women's Law have been abolished, and new freedoms and rules are being established. The Oaths are sharing many new (to us) technologies. (Like the voice recorder.) We record all our meetings, so really, this journal will be just for my personal use, things I want to remember, a way to hash out my thoughts and feelings before voicing them in public.

James's brothers, those who are still alive, the brothers who went to their uncle Heronimo's after the burning, are now working to rebuild their holdings in Telling Wood. And Ferris, who joined the king's guard to spy on the Voice's group for a time, is now visiting on Ra'Vell Island with some of his orphaned nephews who survived the silent death of the orbs and the burning and slaughter before that. They came with Heronimo and decided to stay for a time. Telling Wood, the capital city of Nueden, has been decimated by the orb the Spider left in the center of the city as a test of its reach. Of the four hundred and nine thousand people who lived there, we have only found around ten thousand alive, all the ones who were out of range for one reason or another, and the ones who went with Heronimo and James's brothers. This has rocked our world. When the news began to reach all nine provinces, the shock waves of that event did more to prepare the people for change than any words alone ever could have.

The country was full of mourning. Every household had lost relatives or friends. And as the discs from Library began to be more widely circulated and read, the process of coming together began to be discussed everywhere. It was as if the country had been stunned still for a time. Shock wave upon shock wave rolled out over the land and things began to change.

Opposition may be brewing under the surface of things, but we haven't seen or heard of any in these last two months. But it is early yet. Even the priests of the Voice have been silent. Or maybe they are all dead. Certainly none have been heard from.

There is a push in some of the capitals for weapons of war to be gathered up and melted down to be used for making of or paying for cyna-cycles. Metals of every kind are being shipped to the Oasis Wells, with orders for cyna-cycles from every major city. Everywhere they are heard about, people want them.

Two of the capital cities, North Harbor and Numark, both on the northeast coast of Nueden, have made metal sculptures out of gathered weapons. They have made towers of swords and spears, throat-cutters and other metal devices of torture, and welded them together artfully as monuments to nonviolent ways of getting things done. Both Numark and North Harbor are small cities compared to most other provincial capitals, but they are well educated, with the only other large Library in all the Nine in North Harbor. It is said the Head Librarian was the one who got the monuments started. Bless him. A man I hope to meet someday.

ReMaid is well on its way to being a real town, with solid black stone buildings and a great deal of wealth coming its way because of its mineral rights to Linnaeus stone. They are mining it and the black stone *as they keep building. Some of the men from Ra'Vell have taken their wives and children there to do the building and mining, and are making a life there for their families. Peperling is delighted with the whole arrangement, I hear. They are calling her Mother Peperling, ReMaid's founder and not much gets done there without her approval or agreement. The town is spreading out down to the bottom of the hill, with well-built wooden structures, homes for the mineworkers and stonecutters. They have a temporary school building about halfway down the side of the mountain, where Quill is teaching.*

Quill ...

Quill and Minnari and Panda are coming home for a visit.

It has been three long months, one hundred and eight days since I have seen them. Quill and Minnari are coming home to get married in our chapel. Minnari is pregnant. One hundred and forty-four days left of the two hundred and fifty something of pregnancy. They say that would be nine months on our Old Earth, but here it is only seven, because we have a longer year, more days in a month.

I am going to be an aunt ... again ... for the first time. I wonder ...

A knock sounded at my door. I lay my pen down—I was done anyway, more or less—and went to answer the door. "James. What's up? You look – "

"I know it is early," he said, interrupting me, "but Will wants us up at the east gatehouse. We have some company."

"Bad company or good company?" I asked.

He didn't say another word, just headed down the hall in a hurry, and I followed at a quick pace, heart thumping. *It has been so quiet around here these days that I've been worried about things heating up,* I thought. *Is this it? The heat?*

At the gatehouse, Will, James and I climbed the stairs to the tower, got in the aerial rail car and headed out to the other end of the gate.

When we got there, we looked over the edge of the outer tower and saw forty or fifty cycles coming up the road at a nice, sedate speed. I frowned and took up the binoculars, and homed in on our 'company.'

"It's a large group of Sabostienie on some of the fanciest cyna-cycles I have ever seen," I reported, "and ... an air chair ... Father!" I dropped the binoculars and was back in the car in a flash. Will and James were wearing smiles as big as the sun.

"Well, come on!" I cried. "I've got to get down there."

We went as fast as we could back to the gatehouse and I flew down the stairs, yelling, "Open the gate! Open the gate! That's my father. My father's home!"

The mixed group, of white-skinned Sabostienie, and the pinker hued humans—including my father—met me in the middle of the bridge. I barreled through their ranks and threw myself into Father's arms. We were crying, laughing and hugging all at once. Then Zarek, Wydra, John and Jorame showed up with grins on their faces. That is when I noticed Mergel on the back of a cycle next to Father.

"Mergel," I laughed, tears still running down my cheeks. "It is so good to see you!"

Mergel got off the cycle and hugged me with his one arm. "Thank you for all the kind, encouraging messages you have sent to me since I was hurt. I've been getting to know your father for the last few weeks, and we decided to come see you. "

"Why don't we move our party back to the castle, where we can spread out and really relax with friends?" Jorame suggested. Mergel climbed on the back of Zarek's cycle and I got on with Jorame. A large crowd had gathered around the gatehouse and castle by the time we got back. We gave an open invitation to anyone within hearing distance to come in and celebrate.

Will and the Oaths helped lift Father's air chair up the steps and through the doors into the receiving room, where some people were already gathered. To my surprise, it had been decorated and the tables covered with food. Chet, at the head of one table, grinned like a kid who had just gotten his first star wish. Father and Chet hugged each other and exchanged their "I have missed you" greetings. Chet pulled back to look at Father, then frowned. "Have you been eating properly? You're nothing but skin and bone. It's time you came home to a good meal. Come and eat!"

Laughter rang out around the room, and people began to eat and visit, my people shy around so many folks like Zarek. Some seemed a little nervous to be around so many people not like themselves, but what better occasion to come together for and celebrate than my Father's return… *and a wedding tomorrow.*

That's when I noticed John, Lodar and Wydra standing by the door as if they were waiting for someone. Will was there too… and then Quill stepped through the doorway, hands linked with Minnari's and Panda's. They were all looking toward Father. Chet and I patted his shoulders. I said, "Father, your other daughters are here, too. Minnari and Pandasiea."

He turned his whole chair around to look. A hushed silence stilled the crowd, and then Panda broke away from Quill and raced to Father. "Poppa," she cried, and clung to him like a shuddering leaf to its tree. "I remember you. I remember you, Poppa." She was the only one who had ever called him that.

"How could you, child? You were so young." His twisted, gnarled hands threaded through her long, straight auburn hair, I suddenly remembered he used to do at story times when she was small, before they tucked her in bed. We would all gather in her room for the story at the of the day. I clamped my lips closed and covered my mouth with my hand to keep a sob from escaping. "And I have changed so much," Father said.

"But your eyes are the same," Panda said as she touched the side of his face with a gentle hand. "Your eyes always said I love you. I remember that."

Cheek to cheek, they expressed a bond unbroken, even through all that had happened, through five years of being apart. I realized that Father and I had shared a secret, but not a bond like this. I had shared that with Grandfather. He had always told me I was his favorite, but not to tell anyone, because it would hurt their feelings; then I realized Panda had been Father's favorite. How that must have hurt, to have to let her and Mother go to the Women's Palace. It wasn't that he didn't love me, or my other sisters, but I could see Panda had touched him in a way none of us had, not even his only son, Pelldar.

Quill and Minnari came up to Father. "I remember you well, sir. It has only been a little over two years," Quill said.

"Only?" My father pulled away from Panda's embrace to shake Quill's hand, "And I remember you, son. You were like a son to me then; now you will be." Father turned to Minnari, and she took his hand and brought it to her face, pressing it against her cheek. "Father!" she said softly, then, looking at his large, misshapen hand, she traced a faint scar along the top of it with a delicate finger and kissed it. "I am glad you are here." She brought his hand down to her slightly extended belly and placed his palm there so he could feel the baby within. It must have moved, and he jumped a little in surprise. Then they laughed. Everyone laughed. So did I, until I caught a cold glare from Quill. Three months hadn't mellowed his hostility toward me. I stepped back, letting the crowd swallow them up.

I headed over to John and Wydra and my little brother, Lodar, who looked just like me … and our mother.

I felt so strange. Excluded by a glare in one place, but included by a smile in another.

"A happy family reunion," John said with a bit of a forced grin. He patted my shoulder.

Wydra pulled him by the arm. "Come on, we are not missing out on all this good food." She took Lodar's hand too, and we angled around to the other side of the serving line, filled our plates and drifted to a table in the farthest corner. Soon, Mergel came to join us, then Jorame, and lastly Rifkin and James. Zarek was busy introducing some of the townspeople to the newcomers. I watched the ease with which he mingled among the people, as if he was the one who had lived here all of his life. No matter who they were, everyone seemed to like Zarek, to feel at ease with him, I noticed, not for the first time.

"He has always had that effect on people." Mergel leaned close to my ear and whispered. "You have it too."

That drew my attention from Zarek to Mergel. "What do you mean? I have it? I'm more like a magnet for death."

"Well, I can't say I know you as well as I know Zarek, but I know people gravitate to you. They trust you. You have a knack for seeing the best in people, and folks will always respond to that. And if you haven't noticed, people around you live also, and live well. You care for your people, for all the people. Just like him." Mergel gave a chin nod toward Zarek, who was deep in conversation with a couple, a hand on the shoulder of one of them and a hand on the other one's back. He nodded, reassurance radiating from him. I could feel it all the way over here.

"You are like that." Mergel insisted. "People listen to you."

I could only shake my head and say, "No one is like that but him. He is amazing in so many ways. People may listen to me … but he listens to people. And that makes him great."

We were interrupted then as some people joined our table, and the conversation went off somewhere else. We didn't talk privately again until it was time to find rooms for our guests.

I gave Father my room, as it was on the ground floor with no stairs to negotiate, and we had another, smaller bed brought in for Panda, as she could not bear to be apart from him even for a night. "I want to see him first thing in the morning," she said. "I will bring him breakfast in bed."

Quill and Minnari were staying with Will and Tearveena and their family, so we didn't have to worry about finding them a place. That was a relief. I was going back to my room down under, in the Castle Below Ground. I showed Mergel to his room, next to my old room down below. The fire was already lit in both rooms to pull the chill out of the stone and make things comfortable.

"How are you doing?" I asked. "It must be very hard to adjust to … "

"It's OK, you can say the 'loss of your arm.'" He grimaced. "It isn't going to grow back. Our medical teams did everything they could to save it. But it was just too damaged."

We sat down in overstuffed chairs by the fire.

"Does the loss affect your balance?" I looked at the place where the arm should be. It jarred me, the empty sleeve pinned to the front of his shirt.

"Not really, not when I walk, but sometimes when I lean to reach for something, I forget my arm isn't there, and it has led to a few near tumbles. I can't catch myself from that side any more. It takes some getting used too."

"I am so sorry."

"Why? You didn't do this to me. That one got worse than he gave. He died. You tackled the Voice, or the Spider, or whatever you are calling her these days, and went through the phase port, and we thought she would kill you. You can't imagine the turmoil that put the Oaths in, all three of them. Yes, Zarek was concerned about me, they all were, and they got me to medical care very quickly, but as soon as they knew I would live, they were out of there, down here hunting for any word of you."

"Oh, Mergel, what are we going to do with those horrible, murderous weapons, the orbs that are still on the moon and the three we have here?" I cried. "It plagues me night and day, those people falling dead like that. I felt it, almost at the tip of my nose. I saw people fall like puppets with their strings cut."

"You have seen more horror than any child should."

"But I'm not a child. I'm not sure I've ever been a child. The secret I kept, that my parents and brother kept with me, took away any true childhood I might have had. And if I'd been known as a girl, I would have had even less of a childhood."

Almost before these words were out of my mouth, the image came to me of Quill and me swimming under the falls, running free out in the fields and orchards of the island, and I knew suddenly that Quill had been my childhood. Being with him had been the only time I'd felt free to be a kid, a real kid, someone with few worries or responsibilities. When I looked back, those times seemed all too brief, between the time spent in Library in Telling Wood and my weapons studies here at home. I sighed.

"Some people are called to the burden of responsibility sooner than others," Mergel was saying. "Maybe that is what I see in both you and Zarek. It is not that you couldn't be irresponsible, but that you both chose to assume, even hunt out, responsibility in your lives. That may be what sets you apart. You both have the spirit of an Oath. The spirit of service."

I smiled at him. "Then I am in good company." I rose to leave. "I am right in the next room, one door down if you need anything. If not, I will see you in the morning."

"Good night, then."

"Yes, a very good night." I said and gave him a quick peck on the cheek. "May you be blessed with every good thing!"

"And you."

I walked slowly to my door, thinking Mergel was Zarek's childhood too, a childhood that remained with him. For that, I was glad. I had the strange thought that good friends are like journal pages in our lives, staying with us even after they are gone. *We will always have that memory connection.*

Then my thoughts turned to John Bouyahie. In some ways, he seemed like a father to me too. *Indeed. Life is so strange. I guess we are not confined by birth to only one family. There is family by choice, too. I am learning what that can encompass by the losses in my life.*

I showered and washed my hair, hair that had grown so long it hung down past my collar now, still thick with curls. I snuggled up with a blanket by the fire to read and dry my hair, but I couldn't keep my mind on the words.

Finally, I gave up. I put my coat on over my pajamas and decided to go visit the hounds.

CHAPTER NINETEEN

We had a large area in the kennels for training the growing puppies. They were almost ready to go to the people they'd been promised to as guard dogs. They were not even half-grown, but were big enough to be dangerous, and full of energy all the time, except when they were sleeping. Soon they wouldn't qualify for the name 'pup' any more.

As I came around the corner, I heard a voice. Someone was talking to the dogs. A few of the hounds were growling. I hurried the rest of the way and came into the training area to find Panda standing in front of Ripper's kennel with her hand out.

"Pandasiea, what are you doing here?"

She jerked and stepped back. "I wanted to see my hounds." She seemed afraid of me. That pricked.

"It's OK." The hounds settled down once I was there, and stopped growling. "It is just that you haven't been here in a long time, and they may not remember you."

"How could they forget me? Two of them are mine!" She looked hurt, as if the dogs had betrayed her somehow. "That one, and … " she looked around, "and that one there was Mark's." She glanced at me. "That is, if you are going to keep your word."

I tried to hug her, but she stepped out of my reach. "Of course they are yours." Not wanting to chase her around the training room for a greeting, I squatted down, opened the door of Ripper's kennel and let her out. The huge, purple, long-furred hound with sharp features, long ears, dark purple gums and very long white teeth smiled at Panda. She gave a little whimper and went to Panda, who gave me a look that said, *Liar.*

"See, she has not forgotten me."

"Can we talk?" I sat down on the floor and patted a place in front of me. "Please, come and sit down. It's been so long since I've seen you. I've missed you."

"No you haven't!" she snapped. "If you missed me, you would have come to see me."

"I was off Homeworld for a while. I didn't even get back here for about a month. When I got back and wanted to come visit, Quill ... Well, Quill said you were all too busy and that I should not come. That it wasn't a good time."

She stood there, stone still, her eyes looking inward. I guessed she was examining this bit of information to see if she could believe it. Standing there she crossed her ankles and gracefully lowered herself to the paving stones of the training ground, she said. "You should have come anyway."

I sighed, "Panda, things are ... Well, Quill and I used to be very good friends... "

"Yes. Like brothers," she said flatly. And I knew I was hearing Quill's words.

I remained silent for a time, unable to speak. We just stared at each other. I ran my tongue over my teeth and started again. "Just because Quill doesn't like me anymore doesn't mean you can't like me."

"Yes, I know, but I'm with them now. They are my family."

"But I am your family too. You're my little sister and Minnari's our big sister. We belong to each other. Nothing can change that."

"Yes, something can. As long as I am with them, we can't be sisters. You're supposed to be a brother, anyway. We didn't get all that time with Father that you did. It wasn't fair."

"Ah ... " Now I heard Minnari's words. "You could have more time with Father. You could live here with him."

"He isn't staying."

Shock ripped through me. "What do you mean?"

A look of utter devastation flickered across her face, brief, but real. "He is going back to the Wells after the Wedding."

Devastation doubled between us. "I thought he had come home."

"No. Just for the wedding." Then she was crying, and blinking hard to try to stop the big pumpkin-sized tears that were plopping on her lap. I scooted over, took her in my arms and pulled her into my arms, and we rocked back and forth while Ripper licked our wet faces.

This made us laugh as we tried to push her away, but she wouldn't stop. So we had to. Panda moved off my lap, and then we were face to face, and knee to knee. I could feel the shift that had happened, and we were sisters again … or for the first time; or maybe just for right now.

"You could always go home with him," I said. "Live in the Oasis Wells. I think you would like that. It is beautiful there, with things you can't imagine. And it is safe there."

She looked at me with total amazement. "I never thought of that. Do you think he would want me to?"

"I think he would love it." Standing up, I pulled her to her feet. "Come on. If we don't get some sleep, we will look like a couple of ring-tailed monkeys at the wedding tomorrow."

"What's a ring-tailed monkey?"

"An animal on the Blue Moon, in the jungle."

"What's a jungle?"

"Do you still have that encyclopedia from Old Earth?" I laughed. "When you get a chance, look it up. I understand they came from our Old Earth. Zarek tells me there were jungles there that were as large as all the land on the moon. I am sure that word will be in there. Tonight, though, we need to get some sleep." Seeing the puzzlement on her face, I took her hand. "Ripper, kennel." I latched the kennel door and Panda and I headed back to the castle hand in hand. "A jungle is a very green, wild, and wet place where many of the animals are dangerous, even deadly," I explained.

"Can't be any more deadly than people."

"Hmmm. That is a good observation. We are trying to bring a more sensible way of being human to our world. More like the way the Sabostienie live. They are truly wonderful people."

"Quill says they're not human. That we shouldn't try to copy them."

"Really?" That was a bit of disturbing information I didn't know what to do with.

I changed the subject to Panda's and Mark's puppies, the two she would take with her to ReMaid or the Wells upon leaving here. The rest of the walk back to her bedroom door, my bedroom door, was filled with her animated stories of how big, how good, how beautiful they were.

At the door, she whispered, "Do you think they will let me bring my dogs with me?"

"We have to talk to Father first, about you going with him." I kissed her forehead. "Get some sleep."

She slipped quietly into the room and closed the door.

I stood there for a time, wondering how I could hold two emotions so opposite to each other in one heart without it breaking in half. Father wasn't staying. That broke my heart. Panda wouldn't be staying either, I knew that, but we had connected.

That made me happy.

People had been working in secret for weeks on the wedding plans. Garlands and flower wreaths were hung all over the chapel and out in the streets as well. The mood was festive and light. It was our first wedding since the fall of the Women's Laws, a real wedding, with no take backs or "I changed my mind, you're not the woman for me." Our first. So it was a big deal.

Hanni and her mother took me in hand. "You cannot go to the wedding looking like a soldier. Dress up. Show off that cute willowy figure you're developing," Hanni's mother, Meg, said as we searched through a pile of dresses in all the colors of a rainbow. Meg and Hanni would hold up dress after dress under my chin, turn their heads this way and that way, then put it down and say, "No... not that one."

I was worn out by all this choice. I wanted to shout, "Just pick one! Any one!" but this was fun for them, I could see that, so I settled back and let them search.

"Hey, how's the dress hunt going?" Wydra came in wearing an ice-blue, sheer, long-sleeved, short-skirted confection, a white bodysuit underneath it, and strappy, white, high-heeled sandals that laced all the way up to her knees. She had been growing out her hair on the sides of her head and had had it cut all one length, so it was short and spiky all over. It was very cute.

"What about this one?" Wydra picked up an icy shimmer of purple, an iridescent, sheer, long, coat-like thing.

"You've got to be joking." I said. "It's too snug around the waist and too sheer."

Wydra pulled another garment out of the pile, a neck-to-ankle, light lilac, sparkly bodysuit, which would give me the coverage I craved but would be skintight, if I knew Wydra.

"Try them on," Hanni said, eyes pleading. "Please. The material is so beautiful."

"Oh, all right." I gave in and they had me stripped naked in no time. I covered my plum-sized breasts with my arm and used a hand to cover myself down below.

"Don't be embarrassed, we are all women here," said Meg. "You are a gorgeous young woman. Show it off. You can now, you know." She smiled a motherly smile at me and they all helped me into the bodysuit. The long, tight sleeves formed a point down the backs of my hands. The neck was high, up under my chin. The legs of the thing went all the way down to the ankles. It was like a second skin.

"This came from the Wells, didn't it?" I was turning to look at myself from all angles in the mirror.

"Wow!" Meg said.

"And double wow," said Hanni.

"Not many women could wear that as well as you." Wydra began digging again. "There are short-topped, high-heeled boots to match in here somewhere." Retrieving one, she handed it to me. "Here, put this on." She kept pawing through the pile of things.

I slip on the left boot. It fit perfectly. I became suspicious. "It fits like it was made for me … Wydra?"

She came up with the second boot, bent down and slipped it on my foot.

"I don't need anything to make me taller," I complained. "Don't you think five nine is tall enough? Couldn't you find me some flat slippers instead?"

A chorus of no's shut me up. They slipped the sheer, wispy, long, flowing coat over the bodysuit and stepped back to judge the whole effect. The sheer coat had sleeves that mimicked the bodysuit's, but with more room to them. It was tight at the waist and over the hips, with a thin band that tapered to a point and fastened with a large green jewel just under my navel, suggestively pointing down. The skirt of the coat fell in a graceful shimmering plenty that accentuated my slim hips and made them look fuller. The front part of the skirt opened to the jewel, so it would float around me as I moved. The sheer coat's neckline was a long, low V down to the jewel. My dark eyes were sparkling with … what? I didn't recognize myself. Meg had trimmed up my curly hair around my face, but left its length down around my neck. My black curls framed my face now. Wydra had put some black stuff on my lashes to make them seem even fuller and longer. My eyes … my eyes … were so …

"Beautiful," Meg sang.

I turned to Wydra, "You had this specially made for me, didn't you?" I was dumbstruck at how she could have done it all without me knowing anything about the party yesterday, or the wedding, or the outfit. "How did you...?"

Hanni was jumping up and down in little bounces of joy, and clapped her hands. "I helped."

"Me too." Meg said.

Wydra laughed. "You are the sister I never had. Brothers are OK, but they won't let you dress them up."

That made us all laugh, and Wydra whirled me around the room and danced me back, in the three step, to right in front of the mirror. Then Wydra produced my mother's gold collarbone necklace with the large emerald on it and the emerald ring to match. I slid them on with a sense of reverence.

"OK!" Next to me, Wydra smiled at our reflections in the looking glass. "Let's go to a wedding."

Outside, it was a full moon night, and though the wedding would be in the chapel, the dance and party would be in the town square. We would dance under the moonlight.

The crowd was huge. It seemed everyone on the island was at this wedding. There wouldn't be enough room in the chapel. When Rose Rock had been evacuated and its people had come to Ra'Vell Island, our population had doubled. About thirty new houses had been built, but the villagers who had been in tents had gone home to Rose Rock last month. Even so, we couldn't all fit in the chapel at one time, so much of the crowd was making a corridor of people for the couple to go through on their way into the chapel.

Father, Pandasiea and I and all of Quill's family sat in the front rows, then our closest friends, then as many of the townspeople as could fit inside. Brother Swayne stood up front, dressed in blue robes of three hues. When Quill and Minnari came in the door, we all rose and turned to watch them come up the aisle.

They wore matching dove grey, though his outfit was traditional pants and a fine duster coat, while hers was a long-sleeved velvet dress of exquisite cut and design, with simple, clean lines to show off the thickening of her waist, where their baby grew. They both carried unlit candles on silver candlesticks. Both wore solemn and slightly nervous expressions as they came to a stop in front of Brother Swayne.

"We are gathered here today to celebrate the union of two of our children. Quill and Minnari," he gave a wide smile, looking out on the people.

The people erupted in cheers, and clapped and stamped their feet. Some of us were not expecting that and jumped a bit: Quill and Minnari did as well, but it put grins on their faces. As the people settled down, the couple turned again to Brother Swayne.

"We are starting a new age, when a man and woman can stay together and raise a family together without fear of losing their children or each other," he said.

I glanced at Father, who was holding Panda's hand in one of his and an unlit candle on a sliver candlestick in the other; across the way, Will had one too, and so did Tearveena.

"New times call for new words exchanged, with promises, hope and love, to build a new life together." The Heart of Telling stood in its niche beside the altar. Another candle, on a three-foot-tall silver candlestick, stood close by. The candle was the purest white, at least three inches in diameter and two feet tall.

"This candle has two wicks, and represents the Creator, Father and Mother to us all. As you can see, even though there are two wicks, they burn together with one flame. And where there is a baby," Brother Swayne smiled at Minnari, "there is always a father and a mother."

He motioned for my father in his air chair, Will and Tearveena to come forward with their candles. They went up to the Father-Mother candle and lit their candles, then the three lit Brother Swayne's candle. Once his was lit, the three parents returned to their places.

"Your father's and mother's light and life made each of you. Are you willing to be each other's light?"

"Yes!" they both said. "We are."

Placing their two unlit candles to the one flame, they turned toward each other once their wicks caught and said in unison, "You are the light in my eyes, the flame in my hearth, the warmth in my heart, my helper, my friend, my lover, my life." Then they fitted their two candlesticks together to make one stick, where the two flames blended together as one flame.

"You are now husband and wife. Be blessed. And be a blessing," said Brother Swayne.

Together, holding the unified candlestick, they walked out of the chapel to the cheers and tears of many.

I was dry-eyed.

Beautiful as the wedding was, I would shed no more tears for them. They would either come to see me as a friend and sister or they would not. What they thought of me was no longer any of my business. It was theirs, and they would have to deal with it. I had made my peace. And I loved them as they were, even if that love never came back to me.

I turned and smiled at my father and my sister Panda, then enveloped them in a hug. They hugged me back. That brought a tear to my eye, but I quickly brushed it away. This was a happy occasion that deserved smiles and laughter, dancing and singing.

"Let's take this party outside," Father said, so we did.

CHAPTER TWENTY

Lights and music brought the town square to life like a season festival. People were happier than I had seen them in a long time. There was dancing in the streets and all around the fountain. Every building was lit up in fine fair style. Food booths were giving their wares away for free—or I should say I was, as the funds for the celebration had come from the island's coffers, my gift to the newly married couple, being as I didn't think they would have accepted anything else from me. As it was, they accepted my contribution grudgingly. They were a handsome couple. Their baby would be a beautiful child.

Before I knew what was happening, I had a line of young men vying for a dance with me. I had never stirred so much attention. *It must be the clothes*, I thought. After an hour, I was getting warm from all that dancing, so I begged off and went to sit next to the fountain to cool down. I didn't want to ruin the fabulous outfit Wydra had gone to so much trouble to get me into.

Father glided up next to the stone bench I was on. "I know I won't be the first man this evening to tell you how beautiful you look tonight." He smiled sadly. "So much like your mother. Only taller." His attention fell on the gold necklace and ring. "She loved fine things. How she would have loved to see you now… how grown up you are. How fine a person you've become."

"She knew me," I said, putting the palm of my hand on his cheek. "She dreamed it."

"You know I can't stay," Father said. He kissed my palm and held my hand. We just sat there like that for a long time, until I said, "I know."

"I am taking Panda with me to the Wells," he said. "Quill and Minnari weren't happy about that, but they will have a new baby soon and plenty to occupy their minds." I tracked his gaze to where they were sitting with friends, laughing, happy. "They are a good match." Father said.

"I know. I saw them in the Heart of Telling; I saw they would be happy together."

"You can all come to visit Panda and me in the Wells. We are going to get our own place. I have been living off the Oaths long enough. They have a good education system there, and she is a smart girl. Like you! She will make something of her life." He sighed. "I'm tired. I think I will go find Will to help me up the steps and to my room. You and I will talk in the morning." He kissed my cheek and left.

No sooner was he out of sight than John sat down on the bench next to me. I looked at him, but he just sat there for a while before he turned and looked at me. His eyes were red-rimmed. He swallowed, then sniffed. "Does he know who I am?"

"No. I don't think anyone would dare tell him."

"Good. I've kept Lodar at a distance so he wouldn't … the two of you look so much like her. I don't want him hurt any more than he has been. After what he's been through, it is amazing he is still alive. I just wanted you to know I had nothing to do with that."

"I know."

"I am not saying I am always a good guy, but … "

"John. Stop. You are a good man now; nothing that happened in the past matters. You are my second father, and Mother loved you too. Life before was different than now. Things are changing, have changed. We have changed." He squeezed my hand and stood up. I stood up with him.

"By the way … " He looked across to where Wydra, Jorame, Mergel and Zarek stood. Zarek and Jorame were staring at me. They both looked away when they saw me looking at them.

"Yes? 'By the way … '" I waved my hand in a rolling gesture for him to continue.

"You might let one of those guys off the hook."

I look at him, puzzled as to what he was referring to. He shook his head. "Don't tell me you don't know."

"Don't know what?"

"Oh, my gosh, you *don't* know." He started laughing, which perturbed me no end. "Just tell me, what you are trying to say?" I demanded.

"I know you've grown up with a devastating disadvantage for being a girl, but you are going to have to learn to know when the opposite sex is attracted to you, or head over heels in love with you. And the way you look tonight … " He smiled at me and shook his head. "You are of an age now where men will be showing an interest in you for more than leadership. They are going to want you in other ways. Now do you know what I mean?"

I was stunned. "Are you … saying … that Zarek *and* Jorame are … are … attracted to *me*?"

"Now you've got it." He kissed me on the forehead and walked over to Wydra.

I turned away, flustered. I wanted to run. I wasn't ready for this. Not on top of everything else. Then there was another young man wanting to dance. He led me away and I went with him. It was better than just standing there like a post. I danced and danced till I thought my feet would fall off. I saw Rifkin and James by the fountain, talking to three of the off-duty guards, and near-limped over to them. The guards headed off to find their ladies, and then there was just the three of us. We sat on the rim of the fountain and talked. It felt familiar and almost like old times between us. Safe. People were beginning to drift home. We stood up to go too. Rifkin eyed me up and down and said, "Have I told you how absolutely stunning you look tonight?"

James grinned, one eyebrow lifted, and said, "No one would mistake you for a boy in that."

"I can't imagine how we could have ever been fooled my you." Rifkin grinned.

This was all Wydra's fault. *The sister she never had, but wanted,* I mused. *And if I was with Jorame …* What was she up to? I hightailed it out of there as fast as I could, beat it down to my room, and stripped off that accursed outfit. I folded it up, all nice and neat, and hid it in the bottom of the wardrobe under some work clothes, then hurried off to shower and go to bed.

I climbed into bed, so ready to be off my feet. I pulled the covers up under my chin; the fire was dying down and the shadows leapt with every pop of the cooling flames. The pop and snap comforted me with a fire magic light show and the sound of nature's music. I didn't want to think. I pushed all thought out of my mind and just listened to the fire as it sang me a lullaby. I was about to drift off when …

"Pen."

Wide-awake, I sat up in bed.

"Pen, I must talk to you tonight. I've been looking for you. Calling, but… Can you hear me? I've wanted to talk to you all evening. Can you meet me at the Wonannonda Tree?"

What should I do? I wondered. Should I answer him? I haven't even had an inkling that he was trying to mind touch all evening. My head was so full of … Well, never mind.

OK, I will answer him, I decided. *"Yes, I am here, in my room. Alone. (Why did I think that? I grimaced.) Are you there? By the Tree, I mean? What's this about?"*

"Business."

"Business?"

"Yes. Come."

I sat there a while longer, then slipped out of bed and dressed in the baggiest, most nondescript clothes I had and headed for my personal cycle. I hadn't put on my helmet, so I went slowly, not in a hurry for this meeting. What business could he be talking about? Why did Bouyahie have to go and say those things? Now how am I supposed to be around them and act normal? Maybe it isn't true. Maybe John was just teasing me.

But it didn't feel that way.

Silently, I came up to the Nut Snake grove and parked the cycle close to the Shrine. I walked through the outer ring of Nut Snake Trees and was awestruck at the power and presence of the Wonannonda Tree: the crown full and alive with the many-colored leaves, the branches thick and graceful, reaching up as if dancing toward the Blue Moon.

Every time I went there, it brought me to my knees.

That is where Zarek found me, arms out to my sides, hands palm up, empty, in supplication to the Great Spirit. "Help me know what to do," I whispered as Zarek silently touched my shoulder making me jump.

We sat in the grass ringing the Wonannonda.

"I wanted to talk here because I believe the Tree opens us up to greater understanding and possibilities. And we need that right now," Zarek said.

"All right … but isn't that what we always need? What's up?"

"I have heard from Sam, the councilman from Dakota. He has gathered some others who want to bring the rest of the orbs from the moon down here so they can be destroyed all at once, so no one has the ability to steal or use any of them ever again."

"But the councils have discussed this already. Many times, in fact! What is the Women's Council saying about this?

"They have joined the men."

"Oh." I couldn't understand why the women had changed their minds. "It is so new that women have a voice in these decisions … could it be they have been bullied, or swayed in some way," I said.

Zarek snorted. "Not those women!"

"I wouldn't think so either, but we have discussed this issue so many times, and I thought it was settled that we leave the orbs where they are for now. We have so many other things to deal with at this time. We have barely implemented some of the things we've already voted on."

"I know this could disrupt our forward movement, but the people can only take so much change at a time Pen. And if this is going to work at all, we have to listen to what the people want."

"But is this what the people want? Or is it just what some of the councilors want? Are they always going to be the same thing? How can we know what is the will of the people?" I asked. It all seemed so complicated.

"We vote on things in the council sessions. The women of ReMaid vote on things that have to do with their town. Why not give the people the vote, too, instead of council members only?" Zarek suggested.

"Hmmm."

We sat thinking for a time.

"How would the logistics of that work? And how could we set it up fast enough to head this off?" I asked.

"That's assuming the people's vote would go the way we think it should." Zarek shrugged. "You know it won't always."

"I don't like this! It feels wrong. Not that people would have a right to vote, just like on Old Earth, but that things could be manipulated one way or another somehow. True and real information should be given so people can study it, work it out in their own minds and vote on what makes sense to them."

"You forget, half your population can't even read and have not yet been taught critical thinking," Zarek pointed out. "How are they to use a system of logic they haven't yet learned? You were one of the privileged—you got an education."

Feeling the sting of his words, I said, "Well, there is common sense."

"I wasn't attacking you, Pen, I was just stating a fact."

Sighing, I closed my eyes and scooted up close to him, knee to knee, and took his hands. There was a moment's hesitation before his fingers closed over mine.

"*You asked me here to be close to the Tree. Here we are. Let's be open together.*" My mind expanded like the branches of the Great Tree, following many pathways of thought and possibilities.

"*I am with you. We are one.*" I felt Zarek's inner presence, the unified beat of two hearts. We came together like the set of matching candlesticks that had been used at the wedding. That image almost broke my link to him. And I knew in an instant that he knew the image I had seen of the two of us joined together like that.

We moved into the moment, and it expanded. There was a flash of color, a splash of rainbow, and the calm blue light of the moon on the grass.

"*Can you see this?*" I was breathing slow and steady. "*Did you see the colors?*"

"*Yes … and the moonlight. Like I'm seeing for the first time.*"

We stretched out, and I could feel the shape of his private thoughts, and I knew he felt mine. We could see ourselves sitting in the grove from a distance, as if we were in the branches of the Tree. Two small figures touching … a blue light enveloped us, with a white edge around the blue. It felt as if we were being held in the thought of the Tree.

Then, plain as day, we heard, "*The people will choose wrongly. But you must let them.*"

"*Why?*" I sobbed.

"*Free will.*"

As our consciousness came slowly down from the crown of the embracing Tree and back into our bodies, I found my face wet.

Zarek brushed my cheeks with the palms of his hands, pulled me onto his lap, and cuddled and rocked me like a child. After some time had passed, he asked, "Why does that distress you? Isn't it what we want, for all people to be able to choose for themselves, even if it's wrong? How else do we learn?"

I took a jerky breath. "Yes. But it also means there is more trouble ahead, maybe more death. Why can't this just be easy?"

"Because there are hundreds of thousands of people involved. Sometimes even with two, or three, or ten, things are not easy, and people make bad choices. You know that." He kissed me lightly on the cheek, and then lifted me out of his lap. I turned and gave him a hand up. He hugged me, and I felt him tremble under my return hug. I pulled myself out of his arms, suddenly remembering what John had said.

"Did you bring your cycle?" I asked.

"Yes. But can I catch a ride back with you?"

I let him drive and got on behind him, leaning against his back, my arms around his waist, the way we had ridden together many times. But now, I wondered about him and me as a couple. What would that be like? I felt so young. I wasn't ready for that. But I did have strong feelings for him. The mind touching we had was a powerful thing. But was that love? The kind that Mother and Father had had? Or Mother and John? How can you love two people at the same time? I didn't understand.

The two men that John says are interested in me in that way are both Oaths, I thought. They will stay young, while I will grow old. They may look fifteen, but they have had nearly four times the life experience that I've had. How could they possibly love or want me in that man-woman way?

John had to be wrong. Just had to be.

What if I took the purple tea? Or what if they stopped taking it? What would happen then?

We pulled up to the castle and parked on the side closest to the guardhouse. "We will talk about this in the morning after a good night's sleep," Zarek said.

"Yeah," I said with a small huff, "like I'm going to sleep tonight."

He turned me around, held me by my shoulders and shook me gently, and said, "Stop that! You really would not want to change this even if you could. And you can't."

"But so many people could be hurt."

"Pen, you cannot prevent all the misery in the world. We are going to have to live through it. Somehow. Please, at least try to sleep."

He walked me to the steps and said good night. At the top of the steps, I turned and looked back. I noticed Jorame was leaning against a tree close to the corner of the castle, staring after Zarek as he walked down the street. Zarek hadn't seen him, and Jorame said nothing to Zarek as he passed by without seeing him. My heart sank. I simply could not be the cause of a rift between them. Zarek and Jorame had been friends for a very long time. I couldn't do that to them.

I opened the door quietly and slipped in, and hurried to my room.

CHAPTER TWENTY-ONE

Journal of Pendyse Ra'Vell
At Ra'Vell Island
    The next few days after the wedding were busy ones. Father wanted to see the Wonannonda Tree and the improvements to the hydro plant the Sabostienie had helped us with. He said he would not be back for a long time and wanted to see it all while he could. He is leaving today with Quill, Minnari and Panda for ReMaid, and will go around the west side of the lake, back to Ravenwood, and then home. Panda has to pick up her things from ReMaid, and after only a few sessions with Rifkin on the training of Crown, her Nar Hound, and Mark's hound Sashshari, they will travel kenneled up and go with her to the Wells.
    The Sabostienie love Nar Cats as pets, but they have no Nar Hounds. They say they will welcome the new experience.
    I hope after they see the monsters full grown, they will still welcome them. The hound pups are four months old now, almost five in Old Earth terms. Their crown buttons have grown into an inch of thick, hard bone, and they stand just above a tall man's knees. The hounds are big enough now that they could break a leg with their horns if they rammed someone from the side; when full grown, if they rammed a man in the small of the back, it would paralyze him, put him in a chair like Father's. All the pups are well on their way in basic guard training, so it's only Panda who needs to be trained, in the commands and handling of her hounds. Most everyone who bonds with a hound has that hound at home with them most of the time. A Nar becomes attached to its people very young, and that bond is seldom broken. Even breeders like Hungry, Shadow and Ripper, who were sold to me later in their lives, remember

Rifkin's father and mothers and brothers when they were here, and were excited to see them.

Panda's two will make fine guard dogs, even though in the Wells, she will have little need of guarding.

A day or two after Father and his party leave, we will be loading up to go to Telling Wood for another council session. You can only accomplish so much by com link.

Zarek is the Blue Moon emissary, Jorame and Wydra represent the Wells, and wherever Wydra goes, John goes; they are inseparable. Rifkin and James will go to visit family; Ferris will take his nephews home along with a number of other folks. We will have every cycle's platform piled high with things and people, and our hounds.

The people say I am the leader of the councils. They gave me a gavel and desk at the head of the council chambers. I don't exactly know how that happened—I still cannot quite believe it myself—but they say they don't want to hold a council meeting without me present. Anyway, most of them say that; there are a few who I feel would just as soon see me dead.

Being there suits me just fine, because I like to see for myself the undercurrents and movements of the people's feelings. It is like the effects of a wind blowing on the purple plains grass, I guess you might say: it lets me see which direction the wind is blowing. I don't know why or how I can see this, I just can. I'm not there to voice my opinions. My job is to call the meetings to order, and ask questions for clarification and handle disruptions: me, a mere child—a girl child, at that. The absolute strangeness of this still makes me nervous, and I often stumble because of it. John tells me I will grow into it.

The Oaths, all three of them, Jorame, Wydra and Zarek, keep saying, "It is the time for change. It's what the people want," when I wish I were anywhere but there, and wonder, Why me? I remember my face in the place of visions in the Telling Tree—only then I thought it was my mother—on the day the Tree died, on the day it gave me its twin offspring to bring to Ra'Vell Island.

The Great Spirit of Wonannonda wanted me to shake up the world.

Well, maybe I started it, and maybe the shaking will grow into a groundswell of change, but I am only a small part of this. It is the people who will become the wave. One person alone can't be the wave. One person is only a ripple.

Maybe the Oaths are right, it was just time, and the Great Spirit knew it and used me to help get it all started. I was the pebble dropped in the pond.

As I pulled up to the West Gate Bridge, Father's party was milling about, doing final checks and saying farewells.

I parked my cycle and walked over to Father, bent and gave him a long hug. Mergel came up to us and put his arm around my shoulders. "Don't worry, I will take good care of them," he assured me. "And he will have fun helping the survey crew with the plans for the new road and bridges for that side of the lake. A smoother access to the Linnaeus stone mines. ReMaid will have everything they need there."

"Yes, we will lay that black stone as its surface, four work cycles wide. I'll be back in the stonecutting business," Father said for the hundredth time this visit. I smiled to see him look so confident and content with his life.

Panda came up, and we hugged and said our goodbyes, and when I straightened up, there was Minnari, fidgeting with a soggy hanky.

"I haven't been nice to you … since that night … but I can't go away without … saying … I'm sorry," she said.

I reached out my hand toward her, but she spun around and fled.

Father took my raised hand between his two and patted it, and Mergel patted my shoulder. Panda hugged my middle and patted my butt, which made us all laugh. My wet gaze followed Minnari back to her husband, Quill, who still was not speaking to me. I waved to them and smiled. "Tell them I wish them the very best."

Then I couldn't bear it any longer. I fled into the gatehouse and ran all the way up the stairs, my hound Ibera at my heels, and out across the upper bridge to the outer gate. As they rode out, some looked up as I, along with others up on the gate ramparts, waved to them until they were out the gates and well away.

This was my first seed of hope. And I pulled it close and buried it deep in my heart to nurture and see what would grow.

Journal of Pendyse Ra'Vell
At Telling Wood
Stone doesn't burn, but it does fall when floors burn and joists smolder. Even though some of the interior wooden walls are charred,

the roof remained in place, and the rebuilding began a couple of months ago. Things have been cleaned up, the charring and smoke washed from the stone walls. I thought it would never be livable again, but well-paid workers proved me wrong. We are camping out in the large dining area, as the kitchen and dining hall were on the first floor to be completely rebuilt. We have one working bathroom for ten people, as Rifkin, James and one of his brothers are over at the kennels with Heronimo, Rifkin's father.

After the Voice killed more than three hundred thousand people with the Life Stealer, it took more than a month just to clear away and burn the dead. Telling Wood became a charnel house and a ghost town in the second it took to push a button. I think the smell still clings to the place. Some people wanted to change the name to Ash City, but that was voted down, thank God.

The Ash ceremonies were slow, because of the need to identify the dead and keep an accurate record, as much as possible, so the next of kin could be notified of the vacant property that might belong to them. There were all those burned on the plains who we had no name for. When relatives couldn't be found, many homes were sold at auction to help pay the cost of cleanup. There was an influx of people from all the outlying provinces, to see if they could find family who had lived in the area and to help with the cleanup. Sanitation was a top priority, as dead bodies lying around tend to breed disease.

Red Town, the poorest of the poor areas, was simply burned to the ground with its dead. Hollowhead Inn, the Women's Free House with all those women and children inside ... It makes me shudder every time I see that bare swath of land. All those wooden structures that were some of the oldest buildings in the city are now gone, along with the people in them. The fountain with the man holding the world on his shoulders sticks out like a sore thumb, the only thing remaining in the middle of all that bare land. It is a poignant reminder of the destruction a few people with evil intent can cause.

That vacant land starts right next to the Zap Station, and there has been talk of leaving it bare, as a monument right at the edge of the business district on one side and some of the finest homes on the other, to remind the world that such a thing must never be allowed to happen again.

The old warehouse that belonged to Hannratti's father was one of the buildings that burned ... I mean, Hanni. She doesn't like it when I forget.

Being here in the Capital in my once-beautiful home for another council meeting so soon after the last one doesn't make me happy. I thought we had things sorted out for a while, but the issue of the orbs has come up again. People are nervous.

"Hey, Pen, is it time to go to the meeting yet?" Zarek mumbled from under his arm, covering his eyes to keep the light out as he lay on the cot.

All we had for furniture were cots and a long plank table and benches for meals. *At least we have a roof over our heads and somewhere to sleep*, I thought gratefully. One of the last times we'd been in Telling Wood, we'd slept in Heronimo's kennels.

I put my pen down and stood up to stretch. "I'll need a good long run after this. Want to come?" I asked Zarek. Ibera perked her ears up and looked at me like she wanted to come too. I scratched around her horn and ears, appreciating the velvet feel of her fur juxtaposed with the solid, hard bone of her horn.

Zarek sat up on the edge of the cot and eyed me. "Sure! I could use a little limbering up. All these meetings, as important as they are, make my bones ache."

"Now that we have found the phase port the Voice used to get up to the moon and it has been reprogrammed, that is one more worry to cross off our list." I picked up my journal and pen and stowed them in my shoulder pack for safekeeping.

"Yes, for now it can't be used with tokens." Zarek brushed his hands through his purple hair, making it stand up in a spiky ridge along the top of his head, and ran his hand down his long braid, smoothing it. "The only way to get to the moon now is through the port on Ra'Vell Island and the main one in the Wells, by using limited tokens. We use those ports, and they are guarded at both ends. They are safe, and even faster travel than the cycles between some of our connected locations down here. There is some speculation that every capital city had a phase port nearby. At this point, we don't know of any others for sure, but we hear there are people searching in the areas of every capital city in every province. That some people believe there may have been ports that connected to the Park phase port on the Blue Moon in every major city."

We went into the kitchen to find our friends eating dinner standing up at the counter.

"Why didn't you bring your food out to the table?" I asked, feeling exasperated at the waste of perfectly good benches and a table just a few feet away.

"Well, you were busy writing and he was busy sleeping," said John, nodding his head toward Zarek.

"You can all go sit down now," Zarek said. "I appreciate the courtesy, but I was only half-napping, just drifting, really. You could have come out."

Wydra picked up her bowl of stew and nudged John to move as she spoke to Zarek. "When you were on Blue Moon last time, did you get the jungle port disabled so no one runs the risk of transporting any of the Crimson Death to the island by accident? Or to any other port, for that matter?" A small shudder passed through Wydra. "I don't know why we allow those creatures to live. What possible good are they?"

Jorame laughed and poked her in the side, making her jump. "She's always been this way about them. When we were kids, I used to chase her around the house with a clay snake I'd made and painted to match the Crimson Death. Believe it or not, I could get her to scream and run from me every time. Even when she knew it was only clay." Memory lit his eyes and made him laugh.

"I could have lived another fifty years without you telling that story," Wydra said, mock-glaring at him. "But really, Jorame, a C.D. event right now would be the worst possible thing that could happen."

"You're right," Zarek said as he stretched, "and yes, I not only disabled it, I removed the works, and we've had more Truggils running through that part of the jungle than ever before, and the C.D., as you call them, are down to the lowest levels we've seen in recorded history. So they are not the issue we need to worry about right now."

"It's the orbs!" all of us said at the same time.

"Everyone—anyway, we hope it is everyone—wants to see them destroyed, or at least not be a threat to anyone." I said. "We just don't know how to do it. We found the metal shell of the orb that the Voice used here, and it looked like the sections of an orange that had been peeled back. So we can't smash them for fear of releasing whatever kills from inside them." I filled a bowl with steaming stew, as did Zarek, and we all went out to the table. "We could smash the control device, rendering them useless, but there could be more of the control devices on the ship. Stands to reason there are, and more orbs, possibly. And we don't know if by destroying the triggers, we might be setting off the orbs."

We were all silent, thinking as we ate.

"Why not send them into space in a small shuttle, like the ones we use for taking care of the solar satellites?" Jorame asked.

"Well," Zarek and I said at exactly the same time. We laughed and said "You go ahead," again at the same time. Everyone laughed, except Jorame, who grimaced and glanced away. I paused briefly, wondering why he had been acting so strange lately. After the wedding, he and Zarek had both seemed back to normal, so I just chalked it up, more or less, to John teasing me.

"Well," said Zarek, "we know we are not alone in our galaxy, or the universe, according to the books Pen liberated from Telling Wood Library before it burned. What if someone else got their hands on such a deadly weapon and used it, knowing what it was?"

"Or even not knowing?" I added, horrified at the thought. "They might kill themselves, if not others. It would still be horrible."

"Yes. So we have been going around and around at the council meetings about where the safest place is for those things." Zarek finished. "Where can we put them where everyone feels safe?"

"The Nuedeners don't feel safe that the Sabostienies have them, as they don't quite trust them," I said.

"And the Sabostienies worry that the orbs might be used on them if they are moved down here to Nueden." Zarek shrugged, giving me a look that said *we are at an impasse*. "And who trusts first?"

"That is a dilemma," said John. "Why not dump them in the ocean? There is a lot of water all around Nueden. If the orbs are under tons of water, no one can get to them to use on anyone."

We all looked back and forth, blinking, a little stunned at the simplicity of the solution.

"Could we do that?" I asked, feeling giddy at the possibility and doubtful at the same time.

"Maybe," Wydra said.

"But ... " Zarek held up a finger to make a point.

"I think that would be perfect." Jorame dusted the palms of his hands together. "Problem solved, don't you think?"

"But ... " Zarek started again.

"Tons of water. How would anyone get at them? No way to go that deep with the technology we have right now, is there?" John looked around at the Sabostienie gathered at the table. "Well, is there?"

"But ... "

We all turn to Zarek to let him continue.

"Finally!" he exclaimed. We laughed, a lighter mood lifting our worried minds. "But salt water erodes metal."

There were murmurs of "Oh yeah," "Forgot that" and "Too bad." The previous somber mood descended on our group again.

"If we dumped them in the ocean, we might not see the results for a hundred years or more, but eventually we might kill every living thing in the sea, for who knows how long it would take the metal to erode? Would the seawater kill the active ingredient in the orbs?" Zarek lifted his hands and shrugged. "There is too much we don't know about the orbs. We need more information. Has anyone found any mention of them in the books from Library?"

"But Zarek, there is ocean all around our land. We could take them to the far side, beyond the mountain range to the west," John said. "None but a few would even know where we dumped them. The orbs would be safe from any would-be murderers if they were that far away, location unknown, and what sea life they might kill. It would give us time to settle into peace between all our different groups."

We all fell silent, thinking.

"It bothers me." Zarek shook his head. "We don't know what kind of imbalances that might set off in the future. We simply don't have enough information to make this kind of decision this soon. It seems like whatever we decide could be a risk."

"We haven't come up with any other options. We could put it before the two Councils of Nine and see what they say," I suggested. "And no to your question: we have set people searching for any reference to the Life Stealer, but so far none have been found, other than the same information the Spider found saying they were on the moon on the old ship. Maybe we could find something on the ship itself."

"Who's to say the Councils would trust us to actually dump them in the sea?" Jorame said, heading off in his own direction, shoving his empty bowl away and tossing his spoon into it, making a loud clatter.

"I think we need to choose nine men and nine women of the Sabostienie to match those we have here on Nueden to discuss this," Wydra offered. "And all thirty-six could go on the ship together to see it being done."

"I believe the people are ready for change," John frowned, "but we barely got the men to approve the nine women to a Women's Council. Do you think it's possible to move that quickly for a quadruple council?

"Thirty-six." I murmured, "Thirty-six is the number of days in a month, a complete cycle of moons. I think the people might think it's a good number. They might go for it." I began to get that feeling I had when the Spirit of Wonannonda came to me when something was right.

"I think it is a great idea, and if not now, when?" I went on. "It should be done. We are trying to join our people, all of them—what better way to start than to make it so in the council chambers? If we wait, it may never happen. It will create a balance, just like what we wanted with the Women's Council. And the whole process might take enough time to set aside a decision about what to do with the orbs until we know more about them. We could put proposals to the councils to think about both ideas but not make a final decision yet. I am with Zarek on the questions about what the orbs might do to our ocean. There is just too much we don't know yet." I picked up my shoulder pack and slung it onto my back but didn't move off the bench. Ibera stood ready to follow me. "Let's see what we can find out first. We need to investigate more thoroughly both those ships we found on the moon and learn as much as we can from them. Maybe there is a way to disarm the orbs, and maybe that information is on the *Ark*. We need to go there."

"It would be a dangerous undertaking, but if we outfitted an expedition with as many protections as we can come up with, we might be able to go in and not lose anyone, if we are all working together," Jorame said. "It might be an interesting expedition, making the councils work together."

"That's not a return trip I want to make." John gave Wydra a look I read as saying, *but if you go, I go*. "Just in case you're counting on me to go with."

"A big party … " Wydra smiled, giving him that cocked eyebrow look that said *I have something special for you if you come*.

"You mean like the big party the Voice took in with her," John shot back, standing and turning to scoot up on the table, placing his feet on the bench, so he could look down on Wydra as she spoke.

"… could burn our way through the jungle, making a clear path, now that we all know what we are looking for and how to get there. And the Voice and her men didn't have a clue what they were getting into: we do." Wydra finished.

"What if our going to the ships creates more problems than it resolves?" Jorame asked. "What if there are more problems than we know how to deal with?"

"But isn't it better to know what those problems are than to hide from them?" Zarek stood and took his bowl back to the kitchen, and leaving all of us to stare at each other.

"I guess it is time to go." I picked up my bowl and followed Zarek.

CHAPTER TWENTY-TWO

The Chamber House was one of the finest buildings in Telling Wood. The size of the stone dome was unequaled anywhere in all of Nueden. There were smaller meeting rooms and offices running along the outer walls, with two-foot-thick support walls that created the round hallway that separated the public Council Chamber from the outer offices and held up the dome. This main Council Chamber was directly under the dome; above the main floor was a half-circle gallery that ringed three fourth of the chamber, where the public could come to listen and watch the council proceedings if the main room behind the balustrade was full. The acoustics in this room were perfect. Anyone could be heard from one side to the other without raising his or her voice, despite the size of the room.

There were three black marble stone slabs in the shape of a third of a polygon that indicated the front of the room, over which the public overflow gallery did not extend. These stone slabs had been carved with the Code, the Creed and the Law. The throne of Telling Wood, carved from a branch of Telling Tree two thousand years ago, sat on a raised stone Dias, empty now since King Edward and the Voice were both dead. The throne would remain empty as a reminder that no one person, or small group of people, should have that much power. The words of the Code, Creed and Law had been sanded away, as a sign of our new beginning. Tables and chairs for the council members faced forward in a semicircle. My smaller table faced toward them all, on the same level as the council and the people. Not elevated like the throne.

Behind the council seats was seating for the public. This seating area was shaped like a crescent moon and could hold up to three hundred. A beautiful carved wooden balustrade separated the people from the council. The balustrade wood was from the same branch as the throne, the branch that when cut from Telling Tree, became the place of visions.

The people were welcome to listen to all open council meetings, but like me, were not allowed to speak their opinions at that time. That was for their province meetings, where they had a voice with their own council members, who brought their complaints, comments or petitions to their own council members.

Our group came into the room from the hallway behind the three stone slabs, the last to arrive.

"Something's wrong," John whispered. Instantly twitchy, he scanned the large room. The seating area behind the balustrade was less than half full; *probably because cleanup in the city is still going on*, I thought. I saw John's gaze travel up to the gallery. My gaze followed his. There were men scattered around the balcony, leaning against the pillars, looking down. Some of them I recognized as our own guardsmen from the island, posted with Rectifiers to watch over the council members, but there were a few faces I didn't recognize. We moved to our seats. Ibera, at my side, leaned against my leg as we walked, and I felt the rumble of a silent growl. That was new. It made my skin prickle. I couldn't see anything out of order, other than a few men I didn't recognize in the balcony, but there was something … off.

"*Zarek,*" I silently called to him.

"*Yes. I feel it. There is an unusual amount of tension present. Be careful.*" His glance also went around the gallery above us, and it made me tingle again. My hands itched for my slingshot even though my Sleeper rested in my pocket, bound to my belt. Killing weapons were not allowed in the Chamber House, and such weapons were something we were trying to encourage into being retired altogether. I felt a threat, but if it was real, it was not yet visible. So we began.

I sat at my desk and Ibera lay down under it. She had been to meetings before and had never reacted to the crowds this way; maybe she had picked up on my unease, or she could have been feeling the tension Zarek had mind touched about. Ibera became another warning to be on my guard.

I slammed the gavel on the tabletop. "This council meeting is called to order." I looked out upon the council, then at the people. "If no one has objections, the reading of the record of our last meeting will be dispensed with, as it was so recent. Speak the first item of new business, please."

Councilwoman Jennice from Ravenwood stood up. "I propose two more councils be formed, nine men and nine women, composed of people from the Blue Moon and the Domed Wells. This will give us balance and make a total of thirty-six members. A complete moon cycle."

When had Wydra spoken to her? I was sure she had. Unless it was the Wonannonda Spirit rising up within the council to bring us together on this. Murmurs swirled around the room, some of approval and others of disagreement. Jennice remained standing to lead the discussion, as was customary for those who brought a proposal to the floor. Two of our more regressive men stood to speak. "Councilman Steel from Dakota, you first." I said.

"We are not here to add more complications to our council meetings, we are *here* to get those orbs down from the Blue Moon and destroy them. That is all we are here for, and … "

I banged my gavel. "Out of order. Speak to the issue. If you have a proposal to make, please wait until the discussion of this one is finished."

Rauther Steel glared at me, more venom in his stare than he had ever exhibited before, openly hostile. It shook me up. Ibera stood, bumping her two-inch horn on the bottom of the table. It startled me a bit and broke the lock Steel had on my attention. "Please be seated, councilman, unless you wish to speak to this issue." I banged my gavel a time or two for good measure.

"I do wish to speak to this issue." He rounded on the members of the council and the people. He stepped out from behind his desk to pace the open floor between me, and the council, hands clasped behind his back. His sonorous voice and solid tread resounded in the chamber. He paced for a bit, then spun back to the people.

"When a possible enemy holds the weapons that could utterly destroy us, it is not the time to give them access to the council." He paused and folded his arms over his chest his head slightly turned towards me, an upheld finger bisecting his lips, and struck a thoughtful, pious pose.

"We have just burned our dead from an attack by that very weapon. And we should let those foreigners," he glanced at Zarek, "come in and join our council? It is bad enough we have been *forced* to accept women, and them," indicating with a nod the three Oaths, "as representatives of those foreigners … "

Several of the council members began to knock their fist-size stone balls on their tables in protest. "We all voted on that!" I heard someone yell.

"If they had intended to wipe us out, we would all be dead and gone to Tomorrow Land by now!" a woman shouted.

"It was not them that pushed the button! It was the Voice. One of our own, our *spiritual leader and guide*," the councilman from Carolina said sarcastically, "so sit down and shut up, if you cannot bring a more cogent argument to the floor, Steel."

The stone knocking on tables grew louder. I banged my gavel. "Resume order!" I yelled above the din.

When quiet returned, I spoke. "Your fears are duly noted, Councilman Steel. If you have more to add, please do, but keep to the topic, as we now have five more to speak to this issue."

Steel glared around the room, and then took his seat, as he grumbled in a menacing tone about how sorry we would be if we did not listen to him.

We listened to the councilman from Iowa, the smallest, least-populated province in Nueden, for ten minutes. He spoke along the same lines as Steel, but more moderately, and he made some good points that the people heard with respect.

A tattooed woman from Mugar City, Delaware, stood waiting to be recognized. I had had trouble remembering her name. *As flamboyant as she is, I should know it*, I berated myself.

"Amillil."

I smiled my thanks to Zarek. "Councilwoman May Amillil." She was the first of the women who had taken her mother's name as her last name. She was a bright spot of color in our otherwise drab chamber.

"I would like to know more about the thoughts behind this proposal," she said, and sat back down. "Councilwoman Jennice, would you please speak to the question."

Jennice nodded toward May Amillil and began. "We have talked a great deal in the past few months about the lack of trust between us, the people who live in Nueden and the Sabostienie. How do we break the gridlock of doubt when these orbs are a threat to all of us? One way is to include all the people concerned. Once we have the other two councils in place, we can work together toward a solution that we can all live with. Some of you may think of them as foreigners, or enemies, but they have been here longer than we have, they have known about us and they have never once attacked us in anyway. And I have read in one of the Old Earth books if enemies are talking, they are not fighting. I think talking is better than fighting."

Councilman Steel rubbed his eyes with a thumb and forefinger. "Don't you see what they are doing?" He must really have been stressed to use a contraction; he was one who wanted to keep to the old ways. "If you do this, it will effectively table the talks on the orbs until those new people can be chosen and gathered and brought up to speed with where we are now, and … "

"Then I call for the vote on this proposal," Councilman Belzinger from Califeia Province stood and called out. "They are certainly entitled to a voice and a vote if it has to do with their lives and safety as well as ours, don't you think?"

Stone balls knocked on the tables, calling for the vote. Even though this was what I wanted, I had hoped for more discussion on the matter.

I sounded my gavel with a sharp bang. "The vote has been called for." It became quiet. I saw Councilman Steel glance up at the gallery, looking for someone, it seemed, then the vote was on, and I had to count the votes and note them in the vote ledger. To vote yes was two raps on the table when your name and province was called. A no was one knock; to abstain from knocking was an undecided. Out of the two councils of nine, there were only four no's and one undecided. None of these were councilwomen, except for the undecided fifth member.

"The proposal passes," I said, striking the table with the gavel. "This meeting is adjourned until the time the two new councils can be formed." I stood and struck the gavel one last time in adjournment.

Ibera let out a blood-curdling howl. Everyone froze momentarily. When Ibera bit my pant leg and jerked on me, ripping the cloth, I knew hell would break loose only seconds before it did.

Several things happened at once. Rauther Steel grabbed Wydra by the back of her neck and slung her to the floor; he pulled a knife from inside his boot and fell on Wydra, intending to end her life. John was on him in an instant, both hands locked together, bringing a powerful hammer blow crashing down on the man's skull with terrific force. Cries of battle came from the gallery. One of our guards came flying over the edge with a scream, landing twisted and bloody on a table, a sword through his middle, and then rolled onto the floor. Total panic and pandemonium broke out among the council and the people. They jerked around like fish in a frying pan, trapped, not knowing how to get out or what was happening.

John Bouyahie and Rauther Steel grappled on the marble floor, and Wydra rolled under the table closest to her. I still stood with Ibera, who was adding to the pandemonium with sharp burst of savage barking, but held to my side. Some men I didn't know had joined my dead guardsman on the floor of the council chamber. People screamed and cried in tight clusters. Without weapons, they were helpless, our plans of protection gone awry. Somehow people with weapons had gotten into the gallery.

Finally, someone I recognized strode up from among the people. They parted as if he was poison. I put my hands in my pockets, wrapped one around my Rectifier and waited for him, the leader of the troop that I had routed when they had tried to join Captain Gene Wilder to attack Ra'Vell Island.

He gave me a slow, lopsided grin.

"So, we meet again, Maiden Mother of Steel." He glanced up at his men around the balcony, and then his eyes settled back on me. "I see you have a new name: the Gavel. You will not have it for long. When I am done with you, you will beg me for another name."

He laughed, holding one of my guard's Sleepers in one hand and a bloody sword in the other. "Not only is this meeting adjourned, it is irrelevant. A new council is in town." We both looked around at the men posted along the gallery with bows and arrows aimed at the council members. "If you want to live, you will do as I say. I am the head of the new council." He came within ten feet of me and stopped. "I have unfinished business with you, bitch," he said quietly, but the sound of his words reverberated through the round room, and there were gasps from the people. A restless shuffling began again.

Suddenly some of the people bolted and ran for the doors like foxes for a den. Arrows were flying; some struck home, others hit stone and clattered to the floor. The man never took his eyes off me as people dropped, wounded or dead, and others got out, whether safely or not, I couldn't tell. Steel lay in a crumpled, bloody heap. John and Wydra were gone. Jorame and Zarek, too. Relief, then a momentary panic shot through me; then my training kicked in and galvanized me into calmness, and I stilled my trembling.

"*Don't worry!*" I heard Zarek say in my mind. "*We are giving people naps. Maintain. Keep him talking. John says he is a braggart and a bully, but not too bright. Loves to hear how smart he is. Watch for your best shot. We're going up.*" I gave a quick glance at the balcony, then back at the intruder.

"Shut that thing up or I swear to God I'll cut his tail off behind his ears." He lifted his sword a foot or two in threat. I knew it was not idle.

"Ibera!" I said sharply. Silence fell as she went quiet in the middle of a howl and lay down at my side, pressed against me not in fear, but in alert, still readiness, waiting. "Ibera is a she. Only a puppy, really, but bred for blood," I explained. "The smell of your success has excited her."

He laughed again. "My success has only just begun. You will get in touch with your island on that communication device I have heard so much about and have my friend Gene and his men released. If not, I will kill your friends one by one and make you watch."

I looked around. "You haven't got my friends."

He gave another twisted grin. "Oh, but I *will* have. This building is surrounded by hardened, trained solders who do not mind killing to get what they want. And any who oppose us, we will put to sleep … permanently. Your friends may have run and left you to face me all alone, but I will have them soon enough."

"You talk big," I said and shook my head.

"You blind little bitch, you cannot even see what is coming your way." His gaze trailed down suggestively from my face to my budding breasts to the V between my legs. "The council is mine, and so are you." Holding up the Sleeper and aiming it toward me, he pressed the button. Nothing happened, just as I knew it wouldn't.

His face became suffused with red rage, and he slammed the useless thing to the floor and stomped it to rubble.

"What the hell?" Turning, he raised the sword and paced quickly toward me. I stood my ground till he was within swinging distance from me with his sword held high, then sent a visual to Ibera, just as we had practiced, from my mind to hers, a new thing no one knew we could do. Ibera shot out from under the table and rammed him in the thigh. I heard the bone snap, and he screamed in agony and crumpled to the floor.

In my anguish, I wanted him to suffer. Before he hit the floor, I had two of his men in the gallery down for a nap, then him. I flipped the table on its side, and Ibera and I took refuge behind it.

"Get under the tables!" I yelled to the people who were still standing around in a daze, those who hadn't already made use of whatever cover they could find. There were only a few bowmen left in the gallery by then, and I popped up and put another one down for a long sleep. As I ducked behind my barricade, an arrow thunked into the wood just above my head. For trained soldiers, they were poor shots. The tip of the arrow breaking through my table was a Nar shaft, a bone driller. If that bowman had been as good a shot as I was, I'd have been very dead by now.

When I heard no more arrows flying, I peeked around the table edge at the carnage. One of the five council members who had voted against the proposal, the man who sat next to May Amillil, her province partner, was holding the handle of a knife that was buried chest deep in that bright woman. They both lay together, dead in a conjoined pool of blood, an arrow through his throat. He must have slipped from this world eyes wide with shock, knowing his own allies had killed him even as he did their bidding. Or was this only more proof of their ill training?

An unshed ocean of tears welled up inside of me, but I walled them off.

I had liked that woman, May Amillil. I had wanted to know her better. I would never forget her name again.

Why were some people so dead set on senseless killing?

The sobs and screams grew quieter. In the gallery, I saw John give me a wave and a thumbs-up sign as he moved out of my line of sight.

"We are all right. We are heading outside now," Zarek informed me.

"I'll do what I can for the people here. It's bad. We have dead and wounded. Be safe."

Ibera and I went to check on the people. Three of the women from the people's side of the chamber helped me bind up wounds, using fabric from their dresses. Those who could walk or had suffered only minor injuries in all the confusion helped move the dead to the hallway by the main entrance to the courtyard. Three of the regressives were dead. Twelve of the council altogether. It was a great loss, more than half the council, but I could not allow myself to think about what that might mean for us until I knew the killing was over.

And if we prevailed, our holding cells would be full.

I sighed. There would be no pleasant run for Zarek and me at the end of this day. *Why can't everyone see what is good for all?* I wondered. *Why can't they care about "them" as much as "us"?*

"I'm going outside," I told the three women who had helped me with the wounded. Without a word, they nodded. "Bar the doors behind me. Don't let anyone in but me."

"Be careful," the oldest of the three said, and placed a bloody hand on my arm as I slipped through the narrow opening. Silently, I nodded, and Ibera followed me out, her white fur smudged with the blood of the wounded.

Outside there were dead and dying lying on the long, wide steps, soldiers and citizens together. People who were still upright held clubs, sticks, rocks and other weapons; city folk for the most part, by the look of them. Those I thought might be enemy soldiers I put to sleep. If I were wrong at least they would wake up in the morning with nothing more than a headache. If I was right, they were out of the fight and couldn't kill anyone else.

I took off around the building, looking for my friends, Ibera trotting beside me. We came upon four men with swords at the ready. I put the two closest together to sleep without a peep. The two who were left were two of the three men who had followed me after the troop woke up outside Ravenwood. They were the ones I had put to sleep a second time, and I was about to do so again.

"You must like this." I held up my Sleeper. They ran toward me like berserkers, screaming at the top of their lungs. They were coming at me from two different directions, and I had to choose. I took the biggest one, and Ibera rammed the other one in the groin at full speed, even as the man's sword was swinging down toward her back. She connected; he did not. Then both men were down, swords clanging on stone. A mouth full of savage sounds and long, sharp teeth dripped saliva onto the man's face as Ibera stood on his chest with her front paws. His hands cupped his crushed manhood; his sword lay on the ground, forgotten. Ibera would have been enough to subdue anyone, and she was only half grown, but his face so close to those powerful jaws made the man whimper. I felt pride in my young hound as I called her off. I took mercy on the man and put him out of his misery for at least a good ten hours. It would take that long before any of them would begin to stir.

Jorame, Wydra and John close behind, came running around the building. Zarek brought up the rear, running backwards, Rectifier at the ready.

"It's over," John said, breathing hard. "The people rose up and took them out. They only had a hundred men. What egos they have, to think they could capture the kingdom with a hundred men!"

"Maybe that's all they could get to come with them," I said. "How do you know it was a hundred?"

"They came in on the Zap." Wydra said. "The conductor thought it was strange, so he told some friends to keep an eye on them."

"When they began seeing the soldiers making military moves on the Chamber House, the friends got hold of more friends, and so on. By the time things got ugly inside the Council Chamber, the conductor had close to five hundred citizens ready to storm the soldiers out here," John finished for Wydra.

"It was almost over by the time we came out. We just played Sandman and wrapped things up a bit." Jorame looked down at my four attackers, his eyebrows raised. "What happened to this one?" he asked, using his toe to nudge the man's hands away from his groin.

"Ibera," I said, nodding toward her, my own eyebrows rising in admiration at her impulse to strike where it hurt. "You know what they say about a war hound's horn. Well, it's true. They use it to good effect."

"Wow," Jorame said, with a wince.

Wydra laughed. "No man will bother you who knows that."

"Come on. We have work to do." Zarek began dragging one of the men to the front of the building. By the time we got all four to the courtyard, there were wagons coming to load up all the sleeping men, and the dead: the first bound for the brig or the hospital, the dead for the ice house.

At a loose count, of the hundred who came to Telling Wood, forty some odd were dead, and thirty more had serious, perhaps fatal, injuries, which left only twenty-five or so hale and hardy sleepers who would wake up in a cell.

As the hours stretched into night and people began to wind down and go home, I couldn't help but wonder if this boded well or ill for our efforts toward peace and nonviolence in the long run. But I could see defending home, hearth and loved ones as a powerful motivator.

CHAPTER TWENTY-THREE

It was midnight, and the Blue Moon's light rimed the edges of everything with a soft blue glow. I sat on the steps of the city's guard barracks, where we'd put all the sleepers. Five more of them had died from the wounds they'd suffered before we put them to sleep. I felt lost and hopeless.

So much bloody death! I had even wanted to commit some of it. I rubbed my hands over my face. My bones ached; my eyes were smarting with fatigue; my chest hurt. The depth of regret and sorrow and feelings of guilt pierced me to my core.

If I can't even trust myself not to want to kill, how can I expect others not to want to? Not to do it?

Hearing steps behind me, I turned, brushing tears from my cheeks. *Openly being a girl has turned me into a weeper,* I thought. Zarek sat down next to me on the steps and took my hand in his.

"Don't blame yourself for what others choose to do," he said. "And you may have wanted to kill, but you didn't. You could have, but you didn't. You used the Rectifier. You have those skills, and to protect your life ... I would choose for you to live over any of those soldiers. And for me, that's admitting a lot."

"Was I broadcasting?" I half-laughed, half-sobbed.

He folded me into his arms and brushed the hair from my forehead. I felt his lips lightly touch my skin as he whispered, "Only your feelings; maybe a few words. Mostly a sense of ... guilt, perhaps."

I was cradled there, safe and cared for. *"Thank you."*

We warmed each other in the chill, soft blue light of his home, the Blue Moon.

"Have you wondered why it is so easy for us to mind speak?" he asked.

I pulled back to look in his large, beautiful eyes. *"Well … yes. I still haven't been able to talk to Mergel, Wydra or Jorame, the only other people I think might be able to hear me. But with you it is easy."*

"For the most part, your emotions are clear and deep." Zarek said. *"From the first time we met, I felt them like a current in a river, clean and strong. I knew you would sweep me away if I wasn't careful."*

My heart began to race. My throat went dry; my tongue longed to wet my lips, but I was riveted into stillness. Had I been broadcasting my feeling for him? I thought I had been very careful. I wasn't even sure what my feelings were. I had come to realize I had strong but uncertain feelings for him … and Jorame.

Trying to keep my mind blank and private, like Zarek had taught me to do when I didn't want someone to know what I was thinking, I just stared at him.

"It's OK!" He smiled. *"You don't have to say anything. Just think about it. We have a connection. The strongest I've ever had with anyone, other than the one I had with Father and Mother, and they had a special connection with everyone. They used to call it the empathy line. I think somehow we share that, you and I."*

I was afraid to open that line up to him right then, so I said out loud, "Yes, we do."

I lay my head on his chest, curled there like the child I was, thinking of the years of experience he had and how little I had. Both the men in my life who made my stomach flutter were at least fifty years older than me. The fact that they looked only slightly older often made me forget the age factor. What could I possibly have to offer either one of them?

"Hey, you two! Break it up," John said as he and Wydra came out the door. Rifkin, James, a couple of James's brothers and Jorame all crowded out the door and down the steps as we stood up.

"We have the final count." John pulled a scrap of paper out of his pocket. "Thirty-three living and asleep in locked cells. Sixty-six dead."

"There's one missing, then, if the count from the Zap Station was correct," I said, sighing, scanning the street and the buildings around us. "A man is out there somewhere, and who knows what kind of mischief he could get up too? We need to find him."

"Agreed!" said John. "The missing man left from the hospital, we know that much."

"Where is Ibera?" Rifkin glanced around in the moon shadows. "If she smells this," he held up a bloodstained sheet, "I think she could track him. He must have been pretending to sleep when things turned against them and he saw what was happening. We hauled them off to the cells; we're not sure how this one got out of the hospital ward. We have guards everywhere."

"We are still trying to figure that out," added James. "But we think he's been gone no more than ten or fifteen minutes."

I whistled, a sharp crack of sound that brought Ibera from around the corner of the building. She galloped up to us and greeted Rifkin with a wag.

We all walked around the building to the door we thought the escapee might have left from. Rifkin held the bloody sheet down and Ibera sniffed it with interest. Then she let out a full-throated howl, as if to say, *I'm coming for you* and trotted off down the steps and around the corner to the side of the building, and we followed.

Ibera's nose to the ground, and then she caught the scent in the air and cannonballed into the night as silent as a swooping raven on prey, hot on the fresh trail of our solder from Dunsmier. We ran to keep up, following as quietly as seven people could.

It took less than half an hour to track him down.

He was only a kid with a bloody leg. He made me think of Andraykin, Dray; this boy was maybe a little older, ten, or eleven at most. Just a scared kid. Why would solders' bring a kid with them?

He had taken refuge in the heated water of the fountain of the man-troll who holds the world on his shoulders, giant balls hanging between his legs, in the middle of the old square in the burned-out part of town, now barren. The only thing that hadn't burned in this swath of rubble was this ugly stone monument to manhood. The heat lamps in the water showed that the boy was scantly clad and barefoot.

"Please… please do not kill me." He held up one hand as if to ward us off. "I did not want to come in the first place. Do not kill me," he begged.

Zarek stepped out from the group. The boy was trembling so badly that the water he stood in was quaking in choppy little wavelets of agitated sound.

"What is your name?" Zarek asked in a soothing voice.

The boy drew back against one of the statue's large legs and stopped, trapped. "You are one of them! You are a killer from the moon! You killed hundreds of thousands." His eyes were as round as coins, his mouth agape.

I stepped up next to Zarek. The small crowd behind me was silent.

"We are not going to hurt you," I said. "Zarek killed no one. That was the Voice who did that!"

"You are a girl." If possible, he looked even more frightened than before at seeing me. "You are the Maiden Mother of Steel," he said in a raspy whisper. "You killed the Voice. You want to kill us all. You want to change everything. You are evil."

"That is not true." Zarek took another step closer. "You have been misinformed."

The kid screamed like a girl, trying to dissolve into the servo man's metal legs. He turned his face to the side, weeping. "Father made me come. I did not want to. He said it would make a man of me, be my first battle, my first kill. I just wanted to stay home." The wavering, pleading whimper jerked at my heartstrings so hard I could stand it no longer, and I jumped over the edge of the fountain and into the pool with the boy, Ibera right along with me.

"It's all right," I said, my hands out and turned up to show I had no weapon as I came closer. "We don't want to hurt you." I was only three feet from him when I saw a change come over his face, a murderous, hard look, and, just before he swung up toward my gut, the glint of a knife in his hand. I leapt sideways. He tried to follow, but Ibera was already on him, clamping on the wrist that held the knife. The kid slugged Ibera in the head with his free fist, foolishly. I heard bones crack on the base of her horn. Then he tried to hold her head under water still screaming in pain. This time it was a real scream. I grabbed him by the throat and forced his head under water. My savagery shocked me, but that was my dog he was trying to drown, and I was going to make him let go of her.

Before I knew it, the crowd had joined us in the pool and pulled me off the kid. They had him out on the ground with his hands behind his back, already tied up, before Ibera and I could climb out of the fountain.

Dripping wet and in shock, I stared at the boy as they jerked him to his feet while he choked, coughed and spit up water. His cry of pain was real, his hate-filled eyes burning brightly in the moonlight, blood dripping from his bloody wrist and broken fingers.

"I almost had you!" he gritted out. "You all would have killed me … you all want to kill me!" he gasped, his face twisting in pain, "but it would have been worth it. I almost had her. I did not want to come here. Father made me. This is all your fault." He said looking at me.

"If we all wanted to killed you, why are you still standing here alive?" John said. "That's the most irrational thing I have ever heard."

"Make him walk, Ibera," Rifkin snarled. "We don't kill unless we have too."

Ibera looked over at me for permission. I gave her a nod and she nipped at the boy's bound heels until he shuffled off toward the building he had escaped from, John leading the way.

I sat on the edge of the fountain, shaking, tears joining the water still streaming from my hair. How could I be the leader of anything? I couldn't even tell when someone was acting. He had totally sucked me in. Maybe he had tapped into my emotions; I certainly had not tapped into his. He was afraid, that fear was real. I had wanted to save him. Then I had wanted to … no, I hadn't really wanted to kill him, I'd just wanted him to let go of Ibera.

Wydra sat down next to me on the lip of the stone fountain. "You all right?"

"No!" I shook my head. "This day … "

"Has been too long and devastating." She pulled me to my feet. "Come on, let's get you home."

"Why does he hate me?" I staggered against her. "I only wanted to reassure him we wouldn't hurt him. And he hates me."

"He doesn't hate *you*. What he thinks he hates doesn't exist." She wrapped an arm around my waist to steady me. "You'll see that in the morning. Right now you're just shook up. It's been a long day."

"I don't know." Right now I felt as if he *had* gutted me. I had never felt less self-confident, or more inexperienced. "I am exhausted. Do you think we will be safe at my place? It's so open … if there is any … "

"No, don't worry; we are all sleeping at the barracks tonight. We'll be safe there, and ready when the men wake up tomorrow. You'll be fine after you get some sleep. Trust me. We will all get through this day, and the next, and the next. There are setbacks in life: they teach us valuable things we need to know about ourselves, when we pay attention."

We could see the others ahead of us going around the corner of the first building, leaving the burned-out zone. A funny thing happened to me at that exact moment. I saw a long blade of grass shimmering in the moonlight, dancing in the night wind, growing up through the remaining rubble that hadn't been cleared away yet.

I had a sudden, clear picture of the triumph of spring covering this area in green grass. I could almost hear it singing under my feet, pushing up. It lifted my spirits more than any words could have done. It whispered hope to my heart.

Wydra was right. This was a lesson, something that would make me wiser and more experienced on the other side of it, no matter what I was feeling right now. That boy may have almost had me … but he didn't. And he wouldn't. I would train myself to feel for the emotional heart of a person before I committed to an action with someone I didn't know. I would listen for the truth that is easy to hide. I would practice until I could read the lie plain as a print.

It took us the next few days to get names of the dead, real or fake, who could tell? We only wanted to know who we were releasing in the flames to Tomorrow Land, and send letters home to their families. We finally decided on a single letter informing Dunsmier Dakota, the most military province of the nine, that their men would not be coming home. Not the living or the dead. We sent a list and description of all those we burned and those who would remain in the cells.

We wrote, "When the living become tired of staying in a ten-by-six cell and choose to pledge peace in the presence of the Heart of Telling, which knows your future and cannot be lied too, they will be set free to return home."

Not everyone liked this solution, but along with the remaining six council members, we all agreed there had be an end to the killing somewhere, and a new beginning after that end. With this letter, we informed them that Rauther Steel had been killed in the attack and another council member would have to be voted in to replace him. Annora, their councilwoman, would be arriving with friends to see that accomplished by the end of the week, so we asked them to be thinking of the choices they would put up to vote on: not just men from the gentry class, either. Any man who could read and write and had an upstanding and honest nature could be put on the list.

After burning the dead and doing what we could for the injured on both sides, we began gathering back in the Council Chamber to assess the damage and discuss what to do next.

Twelve out of eighteen of our council members were dead. Both council members from Ravenwood would have to be replaced; also, both councilors from Delaware, Califeia, Carolina and Montana, and the two councilmen from Georgia and Dakota. We were all numb with loss. The Chamber House protocols were being revamped, with greater security measures and rules about checking everyone, even the council members, for smaller hand weapons. A larger number of guards with weapons and Sleepers were to be put on duty in the balcony a full day before a council meeting. We had to face the facts. We, as a nation, were not ready yet to forego weapons completely. But someday, I hoped ... someday, it would happen. Things would get easier between people, all the different kinds of people with all their different ways and ideas.

But for the time being, we had to move forward with caution and care and choose new council members, replacements for the twelve who were gone and two new sets of nine from the Wells and the Blue Moon. Wydra and Jorame were going to the Wells to do that, and Zarek was going to the moon to take care of the choosing there. Annora from Dakota would go home and help with choosing a replacement for Rauther Steel. The other five would be going to the provincial capital cities to help them with the process of voting, and to bring back the new council members.

All seven of Heronimo's sons, Rifkin included, James and five of his brothers and a couple of dozen Nar Hounds were going to accompany Annora home. I was sending four dozen guards from Ra'Vell Island with Sleepers, and the ones who had hounds trained to them were all going to meet the Telling Wood group at the Zap Station in Dunsmier Dakota. My Ravenwood Castle keeper, Brontis, was going along with them. He had a good eye for the lay of things, and was an experienced troop commander himself; he would be in charge. All were going fully armed, with deadly weapons as well as Rectifiers. We would not be caught off guard again.

It was only sixty-three men and Annora that Dunsmier would be expecting were coming from Telling Wood. The forty-eight from Ra'Vell Island and Brontis with his fifty from Ravenwood Castle would be a surprise, to say nothing of the Nar Hounds.

My people from the Island were already on the move, loaded on cyna-cycles, and at Ravenwood Castle by now. We had everyone ready to go that day, not at the end of the week. We didn't want to give Dakota too much time to stew over the failure of their men, or think of possible ways to take revenge, if that was in their minds. I hated not knowing. And I hated not going... but I was staying in Telling Wood. Setting up the security for the Chamber House would fill my time while my friends were gone, that and working on clean up around the city, over seeing the rebuilding of my home here.

At night, at least, I would have time to read more of the journals of Susan Pearl, my Oregon ancestor, from the first Oregon back on Old Earth. Or maybe I'll read more of the *History of Earth*.

All the remaining council members had gone to the provinces that had lost their councilors to help elect new ones. None of us knew for sure how long it would take, but we were aiming for a complete moon cycle, maybe two at most.

Thirty-six days, or seventy-two, I sighed, that's a long time without any of my friends to shave the rough edges off the days that stretched before me.

I stood on the hill at the site of the burned Library and looked out over the city, remembering how all this started a little over a year ago.

Telling Wood is a lonely place, I thought, as Ibera and I walked back toward the barracks alone.

CHAPTER TWENTY-FOUR

For about an hour a day, I went and sat with the prisoners and read to them from one of King Edward's journals. At first, they would try to shout me down, but this only wore them out eventually, so they mostly ignored me. I just kept reading. After a few days, even the snarlers made less noise and fewer nasty comments. A few of them made no comments at all. The ones who were the most quiet I figured were the leaders of this crew. Norman, anyway that was the name he finally gave us, the man I had met on the road, the one who had wanted to kill me the slow and painful way after he taught me how to be a woman, was the worst. When he said anything at all, it was always bad. But they were in there and I was out here, and I was hoping to teach them something. So I read to them.

"11.34.1005. Mother and I killed a man today. We found him in the walled garden looking at the Purple Pearl plant. When we questioned him, he knew far too much about us. We could not let him live, Mother said. She made me kill him. My hands were slick with his blood. I do not like killing, but Mother always says it is better that one stupid man die than we ourselves, and I cannot argue with living. I suppose I would kill a hundred like him, even a thousand, to keep my secrets, and to keep living. I am over a hundred years old and feel like I am twenty. I have seen some of my own children die of old age. Somehow Mother keeps making people believe that God has blessed us with extra years because we serve Him. She puts out the rumors that we are not the same Voice and the same King from a hundred years ago. Somehow she makes people believe. She tells them what they want to hear. She tells them what they see in Telling Tree, and they don't *question it. They are simpletons. Believing whatever she tells them. They think she is a man. She has fooled them all ... "*

"That is a lie. You made that up. Or you are not reading it right," the boy who had tried to gut me snapped out. *Well, at least I finally got a rise out of someone that was more than a catcall*, I thought. It proved that at least one was listening. He was still sullen and hateful, but I treated them all the same, no name calling, no angry outbursts. Even though none of them had done anything to deserve my respect, I still treated them with respect, not because of who they were, but because of who I wanted to be. I wanted to express the dignity and worth of all people, and maybe, just maybe, it might make a difference somewhere down the line, too, even if it was only to open a small window for a question to fly through. Understanding always begins with a question.

The boy looked down the row of cells at the other men. "We all know you killed the Voice. And Gene, and his men."

The men roared with the kid, "Yeah!" "Murderer!" and "You are trying to trick us with your reasonable ways and your made-up stories!" along with other, more unpleasant things about what they would do to me if they ever got out of their cells.

I waited till they settled down, and when some appeared to be asleep on their cots, I returned to reading.

At the end of that session, one of the guards suggested, "Why not read just before the midday meal instead of right after, and read to them while they ate; maybe the worst of them would settle down sooner because they would be eating."

As I was leaving that day, another of the guards said, "Do you have anything more exciting than the king's journal's, maybe a novel? I think the king's journals are too ... real, for them. It reminds them all the time of what you are trying to do to change things. Change is threatening, even for those of us who want it. It makes things so uncertain, and uncertainty is hard to live with."

"You're right. I hadn't thought of it that way. I just wanted them to know and understand ... but that's not working." I sighed. "Maybe we should let them choose whatever they want to read for themselves. Get some readers in here and let them look at what the Voice had been keeping from all of us. Even though they don't seem to be reader types, maybe with nothing to do they might start. I will give them a choice. I know some of them must have gone through Military League, if not Library. So I know they must know how."

The rest of my week was spent in meetings, and making sure things were being made ready for when everyone returned with the new Council of Thirty-Six. I read to the prisoners something about Old Earth and its death, and the diaspora that went out looking for new home planets. The different kinds of people and groups who left Earth actually seemed to catch their interest. Maybe they were longing to find their own world and do the same. Whatever it was, when I received four complete sets of the books I had rescued from Library and gave each prisoner a reader, some of them, at least, started reading. Two of the twenty-eight stomped their readers to pieces. They didn't get another.

The person who surprised me the most was the Kid. He was a voracious reader. He started out with anything that said "History" on it. After that, he moved on to Earth novels called the classics. Not only was he voracious, he was fast. He read as fast as I did. I wondered what he was thinking. Was he retaining what he read? What was going on inside his head? I wanted to listen in on his thoughts and see what direction they were going. But try as I might, all I could pick up was his roiling emotions.

One day, when I went to see the prisoners, as I had been doing every day, they were all listening to Mozart music. Some of them were staring at the back wall and wouldn't turn around when I spoke to them. I remembered when I had first heard Earth music what an effect it had on me. And still did have on me.

When I came to the Kid's cell—we were still calling him the Kid, as he wouldn't give us his real name—he was openly weeping. Tears just rolled down his cheeks. He blinked and brushed them away, then stood and came up to the cell door.

"I know you did not make this up. It is far too beautiful to have come from the mind of a mass murderer." He shook his head and turned his back to me, so I couldn't see his face. "And ... it makes me wonder ... "

Ah, I thought. *His window just opened.* The excitement I felt about that lasted all day.

The next day, they were listening to some of the other Earth music: jazz, blues, rock.

"All you need is love... Da ta da da da ... All you need is love, love. Love is all you need." I remembered that one too, from a group with an odd name, the Bees, or some other bug like that. So many of

the musical groups had strange names; I had to smile, remembering some of them.

That was the day I started to see belief slip in behind their hate, as if they were thinking, *"This is not something from our world. Could it have truly come from another Earth? All these books and music could not have come from one young person making things up."*

Uncertainty crept in, and they were all quieter after that, lost in their own thoughts, and again I wished I could listen in on what they were really thinking. But I resisted the temptation, for the sake of my friendship with Zarek.

It had been two weeks since my friends had gone away to find new council members. It was a long two weeks, as my only close companion was Ibera. Of course, I talked with my friends daily by wrist communicator, to find out how things were going where they were. They all felt that within the coming week, they would have the people's choices and have their first local council sessions. That might take another week or two. Then they would all come to Telling Wood for their first joint council.

Every day, I practiced feeling nature, and people's emotions, and was getting very good at it, I thought. I worked at picking up stray thoughts, cast offs, and sometimes could catch a snippet here or there, but I never could tell where it came from, or whose it was. I knew Zarek might consider even that an invasion of privacy, but I needed to stretch myself. I had spent so much time reading, sampling a little of all kinds of things, that I was now reading about the sciences, of which I understood very little, and mathematics that were far beyond anything I had seen in Library in my school days. It was frustrating and fascinating all at the same time. And there was far too much material to ever get through in a lifetime. I would need to drink the Purple Pearl tea to get through it all. If I read every day for the rest of my natural life, I didn't think I could get through it all. The things those Old Earth people knew … *And they couldn't make society work. What makes me think we can?*

Then the image came to me of Zarek's people and some of our own kind, like Jorame and Wydra, family lines the Sabostienie had taken in over a thousand years of the Voice, Zee, pushing her enemies out into the desert, thinking they would die there. Those people made it work. They lived in communities of respect and believed in each person's worth and dignity. *Why can't we?*

I understood the Sabostienie hadn't done that overnight. Zarek said it was something they'd worked at for a hundred years or more before achieving what they had. And when I thought about that, I realized that their people, at some point, had made the decision to try. All of the people had wanted that vision of a peaceful society. *So that is the place to start. To bring the people to a place where they want to try to work together toward harmony.*

Heronimo had invited me to live at his home, where Ibera and I would be comfortable and among friends, and protected while everyone else was gone.

One night, after dinner, Heronimo and I were sitting around the hearth, talking about what I thought of as the beginning place and how to get people to want to try to get along. I had been working up to talking to Heronimo about what was on my mind, but couldn't find my way to it.

The Oaths and I had not told anyone about the ability to mind touch, except for John. Even though everyone in the Wells and on the Moon knew how to do it, at least on some limited level, no one had felt comfortable telling the Nuedeners that it was even a possibility. I felt uncomfortable keeping things from my friends and my people, but I also felt like it might stir up trouble we didn't need right then. This had not been an issue for the Sabostienie back when they stopped fighting as their mind touching ability had not developed until later, when they were well established in their peace. I simply didn't know what to do with it and needed advice, but I did not know how to broach the subject.

"I sense you have something more you want to talk about tonight," Heronimo said after a few thoughtful minutes of silence. "I'm not a mind reader, but ... "

I snorted a nervous little laugh. Was this a perfect opening, or what? "You are very perceptive. Maybe you would be good at mind reading. You *are* a Hound Master, after all; you have that kind of bond with the hounds you raise."

"Come on, Pendyse, open up. Whatever is on your mind, I can keep it to myself, if that is what worries you."

I gave a long sigh. "Well ... many things worry me, but your ability to hold on to a private conversation isn't one of them. I know I can trust you with a confidence. My problem is not with you. It is with everyone else, I guess."

"Just spit it out, then. Stop chewing on it; spit it out or swallow it."

"OK. This is the thing. You mentioned mind reading. Well, the Sabostienies can. And so can I, on a limited basis."

Heronimo's mouth dropped open, then he sputtered a bit and fell silent.

"I want you to understand that they do not go uninvited into just any mind," I continued. "They have privacy principles. Zarek taught me to sense nature and the weather, and how to feel others' emotions, and I'm surprisingly good at it. I can't really *read, or hear* the thoughts of anyone but Zarek. We mind touch easily."

Heronimo had regained his equanimity. "OK, then, what's the problem?"

"What was your first thought when I told you that?"

"Well." He scratched his stubbly chin, scrunched up his eyes and the bridge of his nose. "I wondered if you had been rummaging around in *my* mind," he admitted.

"That's the problem." I shook my head. "I feel a need to be honest and open with our people. Secrets made known can breed mistrust, but this ... I'm afraid it could really knock the pins out from under us with a lot of people. But if kept, and then found out somewhere down the road. Well, that could even be worse."

Heronimo nodded. "I see your dilemma." He leaned his elbows on the table, folded his big hands and leaned his chin on them, thinking. "Some people might perceive that information as a threat. There is no doubt about that." We were quiet for a time, then he said, "But if you don't and they find out later, they will wonder why you did not disclose that bit of information along with the fact you are female. They might feel like you've been using it on them in some way, and trust could break down. I see what you mean."

"You see my problem exactly! Damned if I do, and damned if I don't."

"I am curious. How does it work? How did you learn?"

"I've always had an affinity with nature." *Not as much as Quill,* I thought, but yes, nature had always touched me to the core of my being. "So Zarek showed me how to feel it more deeply, to see and smell in a new way. He taught me how to join our heartbeats and think thoughts back and forth in complete silence. But he is the only one I can do this with so far." I shrugged. "Well, sometimes it seems like Ibera and I ... " She moved from the warmth of the hearth and came to me at the mention of her name, and put her large head in my lap. "Sometimes it seems like she knows a command before I give it. It's strange, like we are linked in some way I don't understand, like we have this deep connection that thrills me and goes beyond words. It's hard to explain."

The grin that was on Heronimo's face when I looked up from scratching Ibera's head surprised me.

"Now that I totally understand," he said. "That I have felt myself for many a hound over my long years. It is the bond! So, trust is the key to this 'mind touching' of yours."

"It is hardly mine. It's been around for thousands of years with the Sabostienies. The Father and Mother could mind touch with each other no matter how far apart they were. The love they had for each other and for their children, and all the people, was so great they could mind touch with any one of them. And all the people could speak with the Father and Mother in this way, too."

"I see you clearly admire them. They must be wonderful people to have you feel so … "

"They are both dead. I thought you knew? The Voice killed them."

"They were the moon's leaders? Oh!"

"Zarek was their son by birth. He will be the next Father. Actually I guess he is now. If you didn't know Father and Mother were the Sabostienies' leaders, maybe you don't know that Zarek, Jorame and Wydra drink the Purple Pearl tea and they are all nearly seventy years old."

He whistled through the gap in his front teeth with the indrawn breath then clapped his hands to his mouth. "Well, now it makes more sense why Rifkin calls Zarek 'old man' all the time. I thought in was only months he was joking about."

I smiled at him. "You are a good man, Heronimo, a good father and good friend. Thank you for listening to me."

"Since you … I wish I could have kept my two daughters. I had no idea daughters could be like you."

"Maybe we can find them for you. You know Rifkin has an affinity for women: girls, old women, really, females of any age. I think he would love to have sisters. Anyway, if we can come together peacefully on issues of what family once was, and what it might become in the future, maybe the next generation can keep their sons and their daughters. But for a lot of people, we have a wide divide to cross."

He nodded, thoughtful. "I'd like that," he said at last, and nodded again. "Can you teach me this mind touching thing? I'd like to try. I want to see for myself."

"Right now?" I asked wondering how to start.

"Yes."

"Let's sit in the chairs by the fireplace."

We moved them to within knee's width of each other. "Go ahead, sit down." I sat in the chair opposite his, our knees touching. I took his rough, work-worn hands in mine, remembering how Zarek taught me. "First, slow your breathing; relax. Take a deep breath." We breathed quietly for a while. "Close your eyes. Find your heartbeat and hear the song that is yours alone. Feel your heart beat." I found mine quickly and waited. "When you find it, open your eyes and see if you can feel mine by looking into my eyes, feel the connection through our hands." I hoped I was doing it right. Slow enough.

The silence stretched out, attenuated into a fine, thin line I could feel and see, a purple and gold thread that hung loosely between us. We held that way for what seemed like a long time. Then the thread snapped taut, shot out from between us and flew to the kennels, where I saw one of the hounds in labor. She was in trouble, and was howling in pain.

Heronimo shot to his feet, me right behind him. We race for the kennels.

"It is not her time," Heronimo said, out of breath by the time we got to her. "This is too soon. Way too soon."

She squeezed out a deformed pup, two pups, actually, that were connected horn button to horn button. Together, they were too big to birth. I felt Heronimo's fear of losing her. I knew without words that this kind of birth almost never turned out well for mother or pups. I also knew I had not known that fact five minutes before.

Heronimo got right to work soothing Violet, his favorite hound, massaging her tight distended belly. "Come on, Violet, you hang in there." He smoothed her reddish-purple fur and spoke softly the whole time she struggled. She seemed to settle into a calmer, less panicked state just having him with her. I felt them together in his mind. He was shoring up her strength with his. He was willing her to live. Finally, a third pup came out, along with a bloody mess, but none of the three pups were live births; they were not formed right. Violet whined and groaned. Heronimo felt her stomach to see if there were any more to come.

"She's empty now. That was it. I've seen this happen before. If we hadn't seen—or whatever that was—she would have died." He got choked up. "I can hardly believe we … that I could save her. This was some kind of miracle."

We sat with her until her breathing got back to normal.

"I'm going to take her up to the house."

Without being asked, I picked up Violet's water and food bowls, and Heronimo gave me the strangest look. "Did you hear me think that?"

"Oh." I realized I had.

"And the bowls?"

"I just knew you wanted them." I shrugged.

He carried her to the hearth, and I found a large cushion and set it in front of the fireplace. Ibera came over and sniffed Violet as Heronimo lay her down on the cushion. Ibera began to lick Violet's face solicitously, and curled up against Violet's back to keep her company.

We sat in the chairs we had vacated—I looked at my cell watch—less than two hours ago. It had felt like much longer.

Heronimo began to tremble as he looked at me. "What was that? What just happened?"

"I don't know, exactly. Nothing like that has happened to me before." I chewed my bottom lip in deep thought for a bit. "I think a need was revealed …"

" And we met it head on, together. I would not have known that was happening. Violet would be dead now if not for you wanting to talk. If you hadn't shared with me what you did, we would not have felt her distress. I would have gone to bed, and she would have been gone beyond help by morning. Is that how it is supposed to work?"

"Honestly, I don't know. So much of this is new to me too, but I think this shows applications for this linking or mind stretching—or hearing, seeing, whatever it encompasses—that not even the Oaths have experienced before. They tell me they have never seen anything; for them, it is only auditory. They say I'm the only one they've ever known who has seen things."

"Pen, this is not something you can keep to yourself. This could be the very answer to your dilemma of how to bring people together."

CHAPTER TWENTY-FIVE

Days later, I was still chewing on my dilemma. How to reveal this information and bring it to the people in a way that wouldn't scare them? *Should I do it now,* I mused, *or wait for everyone to come back, so they can help me?* I seemed incapable of making a decision about this by myself.

Ibera and I climbed to the top of the rubble that was once Library, now only a ruin, and sat on the rain-washed stones to think. Ibera's head was in my lap, and her beautiful eyes told me of her love and devotion the link between us. I smiled and rubbed her face and around her horn and scratched behind her ears. She sighed in contentment and closed her eyes. As sleep took her deeper, her head became heavier in my lap as she relaxed. I began thinking about the pictures of Earth hounds I'd seen in books about dog breeds. None of them had horns. And the cats the Old Earth people had brought to this planet had no horns either.

Where did the horns come from? And so much purple fur? And the purple cast to some people's hair? Mine among them: hair so black it had a blue-purple shine to it in the right light. I ran my hands through that hair, not certain I liked it longer. I hadn't cut it since this all began. It was now down around my shoulders, long enough to pull back into a ponytail like some girls wore. It was bothersome, and got tangled all the time. I pulled out of my pocket a comb made of seashell, wadded up my hair and wiggled the combs teeth into it, creating a little knob of a bun. Hair out of my way and Ibera asleep with her head on my lap, I settled into meditation.

I was thinking of Zarek. Just drifting, really. Floating on the air. Nowhere. No time. Just a pleasant drift, when suddenly, he spoke to me. *"What are you doing?"*

It almost made me fall out of the sky I was in, but I righted myself, eyes closed, still drifting. *"Are you home?"*

"No. Are you here?"

I felt confused. *"No, I am on top of the ruins of Library in Telling Wood. Where are you?"*

"Still on the moon, in a council meeting. I don't understand how we can mind touch when we are a world apart. No one could do that but Fa-"

"Father and Mother?" I finished for him. *"What does that mean?"*

Confusion swamped me; then all I felt was the hard stone beneath me, and when I opened my eyes, Ibera was standing with her nose just an inch from my face. We stared at each other, eye to eye. Shock trembled through me and Ibera whimpered.

Zarek was on the moon! How was it even possible for us to mind touch? The distance was too great. Had I only imaged it? Had I fallen asleep? Was I dreaming?

No! That was real. It had happened!

I tried to settle back into my meditations, stretched out to search for and touch Zarek's mind again, but try as I might, there was no reconnection.

Finally, I got up, and we climbed down the rubble heap of Library and headed for Heronimo's place. He had to know about this. Who else could I talk to?

That night, after dinner, when Heronimo and I were alone in the great hall, sitting by the hearth with a roaring fire, Violet recovering next to the warmth and Ibera close by, I told him what had happened.

He was quiet for a long time, submerged in thought. When he finally spoke, he asked, "What do you think it means?"

"Beyond having a special bond? I don't know. I like Zarek. I even love him ... but I love all my friends. I like Jorame, too. At one time, when everyone thought I was a boy, I thought I was in love with my friend Quill from Ra'Vell Island, but I always knew that was impossible, not as long as I had to keep my secret. But then I decided to tell, I was hoping for ... Well, that didn't turn out like I thought it might, and Quill married my sister Minnari. They are having a baby."

I fell into a reverie about the last time I'd seen them, at the gate. I felt a half smile creep onto my face. "I just realized, I still love him, but not in the way I once thought I did."

"And so, what does that mean for the way you feel for these other two ... friends?" Heronimo was leaning forward, elbows on knees, head bowed, looking at me from under his shaggy eyebrows, his large head tilted up slightly to see my face.

I rubbed my chin in a manner I used to do, a habit I'd picked up watching men at the Hollowhead. "Well, I ... " I closed my eyes and looked away. "I don't honestly know."

"Do they both love you?"

I sighed. "If I can't even figure out what I feel for them, how could I possibly know what they feel for me?" I stood up and leaned against the stones of the fireplace, then sat on the hearth ledge. "Jorame told me he once loved a girl, but by the time he got around to letting her know what he felt for her, she was with someone else. And the three Oaths, Wydra, Jorame and Zarek, share a loyalty because of the tea they drink and the jobs they do that I feel prevents both Jorame and Zarek from speaking of anything that might hurt the other one."

"But this link you share with the Sabostienie, Zarek, you share with no one else?"

"Only him." I shook my head. "Heronimo, what does it mean?"

"I am not sure. But I have only ever had the two mothers of my children, my seven sons and two daughters. I have only truly loved one woman, Rifkin's mother, Herneta. She captured my heart. I can't imagine life without her. I have feelings for the older boys' mother, Saleea, but not like what I feel for Herneta; but I try never to let them know I have a favorite, to keep peace in my home." He sort of rolled his eyes. "It is not easy keeping two women happy."

"I don't think having two husbands is the answer, if that is what you are thinking," I gasped out with a dry laugh. "Besides, I'm too young for even one husband."

He grinned at me sidewise, his face full of disbelief. "I know you are thirteen now, and I married my Saleea when she was your age, and my beautiful Herneta when she was only fourteen, three years later. I felt my heart leap in my chest the first time I saw her."

"All I know, Heronimo, is that I feel I could be pulling Zarek and Jorame's friendship apart, and it scares me." I got up and went back to my chair, and pulled it up close to my friend's knees. "Could I ever choose one without losing the other as a friend?"

"I don't know. Only time will tell that."

We sat quietly and listened to the snap and crackle of the fire. After sitting a long time in silence as the fire died down, a sense of peace and contentment enveloped me, and I knew life would continue and answers would come. It was my job to trust tomorrow to bring what was needed at the time it was needed.

"Well, these old bones need the comfort of bed and a good night's sleep." Heronimo stood and stretched, and he left me to watch the fire go dark before I found my own way to my own bed.

Now that the prisoners were reading for themselves, I went and checked in on them, but didn't stay as long as I had when I had been reading to them. What was the point? I wasn't reading to them, and they didn't want to talk about anything they were reading—at least not with me, although the guards told me they were doing plenty of talking when they thought they were alone. When the guards were out of sight, some mighty arguments were being waged among them about what all those books were and where they had come from. I thought that was a good sign.

"Don't let optimism blind you," said Gregson, the head guard. "Some people have an endless capacity to lie to themselves, and believe the lie even when the truth is slapping them in the face."

"You are right," I nodded. "I need to remain open, not just to possibilities where they are concerned, but also to what I see as the truth. I must never be so sure of the truth I think I know that I am no longer open to something new myself. We must learn to listen and let the winds of the Spirit move among us. Even when we cannot agree, we must learn to listen until what others meanings behind the words they use comes clear to everyone."

Gregson's brows knit together. "Are you sure you are only thirteen?" He shook his head, "I've been around for a long time. Known a lot of men ... well, maybe that's it. You are a woman," he said, as if I hadn't noticed. "But man or woman, you have a depth of understanding far beyond your years. I suppose you have been told that before." He gave me an intense, searching look. "I wonder sometimes what you will become."

I gave a little laugh, "Sometimes I wonder that myself."

Just then, a guard I didn't know personally but had seen on guard duty came into the office where we were talking. "Norman wants to speak with you," he said to me. "He wondered if you were here yet. And since you are, do you have time for him?"

Gregson stood, and we followed the guard down the hall to the cells.

Norman, the leader of what had been the Hundred from Dakota, was pacing his cell and stopped when he saw us walk up. The Kid was in the cell opposite Norman, watching the older man's every move. Everyone seemed unusually attentive to the moment.

Norman came up to the bars and rested his hands casually on the crossbar, relaxed. His demeanor was different than in the past.

I waited.

"Do you mean what you say about letting us go if we swear to bury our weapons and never kill again?" he asked.

My mind was suddenly buzzing with the sound of many voices, and I realized it was their thoughts, but the one that came through loud and clear was that of the man who stood before me. Norman.

"Will you pledge to bury your weapons?" I asked.

His face held no guile, but the words in his mind were, *Oh, yes, right in your back, you little bitch!* "Yes. I am done with war. I know these books speak the truth. And I am ready to surrender to that truth."

I *knew* he was lying. I could hear it, in his thoughts. I smiled as if I believed him. "Absolutely, I meant it. If we are to have peace, we have to start somewhere. But you will have to stand before the Heart of Telling to see if you speak the truth. You know it is on Ra'Vell Island. We will work something out as soon as the thirty-six councilors come back to Telling Wood."

Behind me I heard the Kid clear his throat. "Save yourself the trouble. He is lying through his teeth." I turned to look at the kid, he said. "I know, because he is my father. He has always been a liar."

Norman exploded against the bars. "You bloody worthless bastard! I will strip the skin from your bones. You just wait." He spit those last words out between clenched teeth. I blanched at the bile he was spewing toward his own son, his glare of complete rejection and the raving of his thoughts.

"Actually, we won't need the Heart of Telling, for that Spirit has given me the ability to hear your thoughts." I looked around the cells, making eye contact with as many men as I could.

"What game are you playing at now, bitch?"

"No game, *Norman.* And by the way, my name is Pendyse, not bitch. I heard what you thought. 'Oh yes. Right in your back.' That is what you thought when I asked if you would pledge to bury your weapons." He went pale. "Do you deny this?"

He stumbled away from the bars and sat down hard on the cot. "How could you know that?" he asked hoarsely.

"Then you don't deny it." He didn't. "I have told you before, the Creator is with me. If you choose to deny that, it is your privilege to believe as you wish. But you can choose to have that same Creator with you too, if you would only listen. Sometimes when people throw their thoughts at me, I hear them."

I turned and stared for a long time at the Kid, and heard, in my mind, his name float from the thoughts of someone in a cell behind me. *Nathan. Damn that brat.*

"Nathan, are you ready to believe? Are you ready to pledge yourself to peace and justice for our world and all the people in it? Are you ready to let go of hate and learn to live the truth?"

Almost! he thought. *Almost.*

"Almost!" I whispered aloud. He stepped back till his knees bumped his cot and he sat down, never taking his eyes from mine.

"I know *you* did not write those books, make that music or kill the Voice, the woman named Zee. I know that is the truth." He looked around at the men within his sight and raised his voice. "I know that is the truth."

His face was as pale as his father's as he stared past me at the man named Norman. "You do not deserve the name Nathan!" the man shouted. "My father was a proper, proud man. From the day you were born, you have been a disappointment to us. I knew *you* never would be a real man. You are too soft. You could not even kill one puny girl when you had the chance. You could not get that *one* simple job done! You are no son of mine. I take back your name. You have no name. Now you have no soul. Tomorrow Land will turn you away at the gate when I kill you with my bare hands the first chance I get."

"I never liked that name anyway!" the Kid screamed back. "All that man ever did was hit me. He was worse than you. And I'm glad he's dead."

Norman shot to his feet and rushed at the bars, thrusting his arms through as if he could reach his son, pointing with both hands. *"You have no name!"*

"Yes! I do! I'm Kid." He said with quiet pride. "She named me." He tipped his chin in my direction. "And she has shone me more kindness and respect in the weeks we've been here than you have in my entire life, even though I tried to kill her. Even though I tried to hate her like you said I should. Even though I have done everything to make you love me, but you never have, and you never will. But … " Kid stood and walked to the bars opposite Norman's cell and shook his head, eyes blazing. "I gladly surrender that name, and you. And accept my fate as a fatherless child."

He spun on his heel, walked back to his cot, flopped down on it and closed his eyes, a slow smile spreading across his face. "I'm free! I'm free at last!" he exclaimed.

The silence that followed was profound. No one moved or spoke, and I could no longer hear the babble of many thoughts. One by one, the men in the cells turned on their readers and became islands to themselves. Gregson, the other guard and I went back to the office.

We all sat down, and Gregson said, "What was that?" The shock of it was beginning to wear off all of us. "What just happened in there?"

"Can you really hear our thoughts?" asked the other guard, whose name, Ron, just popped into my head.

"Yes and no," I said. "This is new to me. The Sabostienie have mind touched for a few thousand years among their own people, and they take privacy very seriously; they would never listen in on the thoughts of anyone who hadn't invited them to do so. But I am only a novice. It has been happening for only a few months with me, and I had never been able to mind touch with anyone except Zarek, and, in some new way, with Heronimo only recently. I am trying to deal with it as best I can. I didn't make what happened in there happen. It just did. And I meant it, when I said, this ability, was given to me by the Creator. It happens when there is a need."

They both stared at me with a mix of awe and fear.

"Please believe me. I would never try to steal your thoughts. They belong to you alone. I would never be so rude. But I'm new at it … and in there … their thoughts seemed to scream at me. I seem to have a capacity, a receptivity that comes natural to me. I think many of our people may have the capacity for it, too."

"Maybe you shouldn't go about telling people," Ron said. "They might not understand."

"Do *you* understand?" I asked, my hand out, open, empty. "I don't! I also don't want to keep it secret but worry, like you, that people will take it wrong."

"No," said Gregson, "what happened in there has to be told. We needed to know. Everyone needs to know, but slowly, like the trickle of a creek, not like the gush of one of the falls on your island. Not a big announcement: a more natural, person-to-person telling. We can be the witnesses of what it was and how it came about. I don't understand it, but I believe you would never use it to hurt us, or anyone."

"But what about the Sabostienie?" Ron gave me a fearful glance.

"Of all the people in our universe," I said, "they are the most trustworthy, and lest likely to hurt anyone." I looked from Ron to Gregson. "Believe me, they have been looking out for our welfare for hundreds of years, but afraid to reveal themselves to us because of our killing ways. Do you think, with their advanced technologies, they couldn't have wiped us out ten times over if that was their desire? They don't even use the power from the solar satellites—they have something far better—but they have kept them working for our benefit, and ours alone."

Ron and Gregson were quiet for a minute, taking this in.

"I've actually heard that before," Ron said. "John Bouyahie was telling that story about his trip to the moon, and the jungle, and the talk you all had one night when something called Fire Flyers had you pinned down. He told that story while you were all staying in the barracks right after the Dakotans attacked us. I'm inclined to believe him, but ..."

"I'm inclined to believe it too," Gregson said. "Why don't we just share this with people who we know have an open mind for now and see where it goes from there?" He looked at me somberly. "You have to trust us too, Pendyse, not to put you—or the hope for our better future—in danger."

CHAPTER TWENTY-SIX

"Well, I hadn't exactly planned it, but my dilemma has taken the bull by the horns," I said to Heronimo. "And like the Earth fiction says, it would be like trying to put the genie back in the bottle to try to take back what has happened."

"It is what it is, and maybe that is the way Creator meant it to be." Heronimo patted my knee as he stood. "Do not worry." He shook his head with an amazed smile on his face. Then puzzlement creased his brow. "What is a genie? And why would you want to put one in a bottle?"

I laughed. "Earth stories. *One Thousand and One Arabian Nights.* A genie is a magical being who lives in a bottle or a lamp, and if you awaken the genie and you let him out of the bottle, he gives you three wishes, but genies are often tricky ... " I fell into a silence for a moment, thinking about what it was I wanted, and Heronimo prompted me to continue. "Well, these wishes are a shortcut to get what you want, but often there were unintended consequences that came along with the wishes when they were granted that could sometimes have an unpleasant backlash."

"Interesting!" He nodded. "I will have to read about this genie business sometime. But right now, I am done for the day. Good night, my young friend. Don't stay up all night worrying about wishes. Stay the course, and you will bring about the justice and peace you desire through hard work and perseverance." He turned and headed for the stairs.

"Good night," I said, and turned on my communicator to check in with my friends before I too retired for the night.

Zarek and I had talked by communicator the day of our strange encounter, and were still unable to make contact by mind touch, though we tried. He thought maybe I was trying too hard, and advised me to let go of it for a few days. The new council members were ready to come to Nueden in another day. They would meet up with the council member from the Wells, then they would come to Telling Wood together by beaming to the phase port close to the city.

I was so ready for them to be home. I missed them all terribly... but I had to admit that I missed Zarek like an ache in my bones, or an emptiness in my eyes, like some part of me was missing, and not being able to mind speak with him only made it worse. It was a longing that could not be slaked. To face these feelings scared me, though, more than facing a man with a sword. I was afraid of what it meant and had no idea how to deal with it. There were so many aspects to it, but I couldn't deny the longing it's self.

Two days later, the council members from all the provinces began to arrive. Because so many houses were vacant, every councilor's family received one as their Telling Wood estate. It was a busy time, with all the little glitches that accompany an endeavor with so many new people all within a short period of time.

Rifkin and his brothers, James and his brothers, and even Brontis from Ravenwood Castle accompanied the Dakota councilors and families. It was great to see the big man of many scars.

Rifkin greeted me in the middle of High Street in front of the Chamber House the way we used to greet when he thought I was a boy. He punched me in the shoulder, and then gave me a bear hug and a hearty slap on the back. I returned the rough greeting with a slap on his back and grinned from ear to ear. *It was so good to see him.*

"So you are no worse for the wear of life without us, I see," he observed.

"Are you kidding? I missed you guys so much I could hardly function without you."

"Yeah, right!" Rifkin laughed.

He seemed taller and broader than I remembered. Creator be blessed, it was a feast for sore eyes to see him, to see them all. James and Ferris walked across the street, and we greeted each other in a gentler exchange then the one Rifkin and I had indulged in.

"Hello, James, Ferris, Brontis." Looking at my four friends, smiling and relaxed, I felt my own tension ease. It had been a crazy day, getting so many people settled in.

"What's this we hear about you reading minds?" Rifkin grinned. "I always suspected you could. You just knew too much about the things people seemed to be thinking. You know what I mean?"

"No," I laughed. "I was only deducing what they might be thinking." I sobered up then, realizing what he had just said, and looked around the ring of friends, hoping to see if I could deduce what *they* were feeling or thinking. "Where did you hear that bit of gossip?"

"Well, is it true?" Brontis beamed at me, his long scar twisting across his face like a delirious serpent. "Can you read minds, like Ron and Gregson say?"

"Doesn't that scare you? The thought of me rummaging about in you head?"

"I welcome you into my mind," Brontis said. "I find it an intriguing idea, and I do not think you would wreck the furniture in there; it is pretty sturdy. We must try it some time."

The emotion I felt coming from Brontis was light, playful, an aspect of him I could not remember ever seeing before, a liveliness that was almost childlike.

My reaction to that was a small snort of relieved laughter. "Well, who would have guessed I'd get that kind of reaction?"

"So what happened? Tell us everything that's been going on here since we left." James scratched behind Ibera's ears and around her horn.

"Well, kids, have fun!" Ferris said. "I am sure this would be a fascinating conversation, but I am off to find the sibs and nephews. I've got gifts I don't want to have spoiled. I'll catch up with you later, James. I'll expect you home when I see you coming." He hurried off in the direction of their family compound.

"Why not come and see what progress has been made at the Ra'Vell Telling Wood estate? Things are coming right along," I said to my friends. "When it's done and I move back in, I will miss your father, Rif. He has been a great support for me while you have all been away."

"Please be seated!" I struck my gavel again on the top of the pitted table I stood behind, and the room quieted and people began to take their seats. "I call to order the first meeting of the Council of Thirty-

Six. The minutes of the last two meetings will be read by Secretary Timothy David." I struck my gavel one more time and sat down.

Once that was done, Timothy read the names of those who had died in this very room almost two months before. I looked down and read along with him the list of names and people I had known and who were no longer with us, and the new ones we would get to know.

"Seven men dead. Five women dead," finished Timothy.

At the end of the reading, someone's thought drifted to me: *"Not enough, and far too many of our own."* I searched around the room, feeling for the thinker, but the level of many people's emotions thwarted me.

"These are the seating partners at the nine new tables that have been added to the council chamber. Keep your handout and learn these people's names." Timothy's voice was deep and resonant, without being loud, never the less it carried, I suspected, even out the open doors. The chambers were packed to capacity, from the loft to the doors and into the hallways beyond.

"I will read the list," called Timothy, and he read the names of the Blue Moon and Domed Wells councilors.

"Four women, five men on the council from the Blue Moon and five women and four men from the Domed Wells. Nine men and nine women," he concluded, and then sat at his own small desk to take notes on the proceedings and record them on the Sabostienie device.

I stood to welcome the council body. "We have come from many places to carry on the business of the people of Nueden, the Domed Wells and the Blue Moon, as what goes on here affects us all. The floor is now open for your discussions." And I sat back down.

My friend Wydra stood and took the floor. She walked slowly to the open center of the room and turned to face the people. "I thank you for giving me this chance to be one of those to speak for the Domed Wells. Those of you who experienced the horrible loss of family and friends because of the Life Stealer understandably have concerns.

So do we in the Wells, and on the moon. This weapon is too horrible to image, let alone to ever be used again. The purpose of adding eighteen new people to the council at this time is so we, too, can have a voice and aid in the solution to this problem. I believe when we talk things out amongst ourselves here and with all our people at home, we can reach an outcome we can all live with safely."

She went back to their table and patted Mergel on the shoulder; he looked nervous as she sat down next to him. John was right behind her in the commons area, with the press of people leaning on the wooden divider between them and the council members, eager to catch every word.

And so it began, our first joint Council of Thirty-Six. We discussed things in a fair, orderly fashion until dinnertime. We were all pretty jubilant that no one had killed anyone, and that for the most part people seemed to be expressing themselves without slurs or name-calling. That seemed like progress to me. But that angry, floating thought I had caught earlier bothered me. Was that man a ticking bomb with mayhem on his mind, or just a mean-spirited, small-minded person? *Maybe after we've had a few days of meetings, the crowds will thin out and I can better follow the trail of a thought that's just thrown out there like that.*

We discussed the Life Stealer for three weeks. And the crowds did thin out. And I did find the person with venom in his heart. I intentionally did not try to listen in on Lucus Tallman, Rauther Steel's replacement councilman from Dakota, but there were times when his thoughts nearly shouted out obscenities and death wishes towards Wydra. I told my friends he was someone to watch out for. He seemed unhinged. The mental and emotional flare-ups were scary, because I couldn't tell in what direction those flare-ups might carry us all: possibly into some dark hell, led by the will and drive of one angry, hurt man who blamed Wydra for Rauther's death. Rauther Steel, an uncle.

I was so disappointed when Zarek did not come back with Mergel, Wydra, Jorame and the new council members. They said he had things to take care of on the moon for the people there. That didn't satisfy my need to see him! I still tried to touch minds with him, but it was as if there was a void there. When I talked to him by communicator, he was distant and distracted. He said he was preparing for the possibility that the council might want to come for the bombs and take them to the ocean. He was still worried about that, but it seemed like the Council of Thirty-Six was leaning more and more toward that as a solution to the obvious mistrust between the different groups of people.

A week later, that is what the decision came down to. The council wanted to go to the moon and retrieve the Life Stealers, all of them together, as the trust issue had not resolved its self. We could not convince them of the potential dangers they would have to face to get to the Old Ship. The men of Nueden didn't trust the Moonies, as they called them, and the Sabostienies were doubtful of the motives of the men of Nueden. Some of the women were suspicious of any of the men and didn't believe they would really relinquish that much power to the sea, and they wanted to make sure the men didn't slip even one of those vicious little bombs into a pocket, knowing what just one had done to our world already.

So we were all preparing to go. My mind reeled at the thought of these people face to face with the Crimson Death, but not even when they were told what was in the jungle did it stop them. *They wanted to go.* Maybe it was the spirit of adventure as well, for I heard some of them talking about the story it would make to tell their grandchildren when they were old. If they were so lucky as to live that long, I thought. I was afraid we would have to choose new members of the council upon our return home. But I did sort of understand that when we abolish the old code, creed and law, we had also abolished the strictures on travel to places we had never been before.

After our trek through the north end of the city, then through the underground route the Voice had brought me down when we had reentered the city six months ago, before the unspeakable had happened, I again found myself in the caverns and wide tunnels where we would be transported up to the moon.

"Rifkin," I said in amazement. I had spotted the Rectifier I had lost the day I'd come down with the Voice. I picked it up and handed it to Rifkin. "Keep this as a spare. Where we're going, you never know when it might come in handy. It may not be an updated version with all the modifications, but it still carries a wallop. This is the one I lost on my way down here last time."

"Lead on. Where you go, I follow," he said, combing his long fingers through his wiry red hair that was longer than I'd ever seen it, a disheveled mess, but somehow endearing.

"Where are James and Ferris?" Brontis looked as large as one of those not-so-mythical elephants, even in these caveways that were not at all small.

"Back a ways with the women. We don't want to lose anyone before we even get to the moon," Rifkin said.

"Have you been keeping an eye on Lucus?" I whispered to Brontis as more and more people crowded into the cave area we were in.

"Oh, yes!" I tracked Brontis's eyes as they found the smaller, younger man and settled on him. "He will behave," Brontis said, "or I'll give him a nap and carry him myself, like a baby."

"Oh, I'm sure he'd like that. Rifkin and I will go up first with our hounds to let them know we are here. They are expecting us; I just don't want them to feel anxious at all," I said, and stepped onto the round metal platform. Rifkin looked serious and a little nervous as he stepped onto the port floor. "Brontis, you will have to break up the group, thirty-five the first trip and forty the second trip. I don't think more would fit on the transport floor with all their paraphernalia, anyway," I said.

He smiled and saluted me with a nod and a soldier's hand sign, then Wydra, at the controls, gave a little wave, and the people and the cave began to disappear. Rifkin was clutching my arm. I could tell he was yelling, but no sound could be heard in that tube of light; then the lights went out and we were enveloped by darkness. Our bodies began to glow with bright swirls of light patterns, and the next thing I knew, we were there, and Rifkin was holding me upright.

Zarek, his sister Skitar, her husband Bex, and Zarek's grandniece Willobee were there to greet us.

CHAPTER TWENTY-SEVEN

Their greeting was very formal, and as the first wave of people came up, Rifkin and I moved off to one side to wait for the second arrivals. I had no time to talk to Zarek or greet him as I'd wanted to. I sent out, *"It is so good to be here. To see you, I've missed you so much."* Nothing came back. Not even a glance. I felt stunned. Shunned. What was wrong? Had I done something to offend him?

The small crowd gathered as the rest of the people and hounds came up to the Blue Moon. A group of Sabostienies guided us to our quarters in the Heart building. The last time I had seen it, it had been a mess and there had been two dead people on the floor. It had been restored to order, and new story panels were up on the walls, and the tables and chairs were polished to a gloss. The many rooms off to both sides of the main gathering hall were designated one half for men, one half for women, with two per room. After settling in, we were invited to a midday meal in the gathering hall.

I still hadn't had a chance to speak with Zarek and felt confused about that.

We were scheduled to see the sights of the moon for the next few days before we had to get to work, and to go through some training about the jungle. We had to inform the Nuedeners of the dangers in more specific detail, and any who decided they didn't want to go could stay here at the Heart. The Sabostienie informed the council that the Life Stealers that had been left here by the Voice were in a safe place and that they would be turned over to the council when they came back from the jungle with any remaining at the Old Ship.

A small group of Librarians had come with us to see what they could find of historical interest that they might be able to take back for the Libraries of Education.

"Many of the councilors seem delighted with Moon City," Rifkin said, craning his neck to extend his view from the balcony off the rooms where I had found the Father dying the last time I was here. They were Zarek's now. Things had been moved around and the place where the Father—*his* father—had died was covered with a fine-quality carpet, two potted plants and a chair positioned to look out onto the balcony and cityscape had replaced the large desk.

"It is one of the most beautiful cities I have ever seen." Rifkin turned and smiled at me. "What's wrong? You haven't been yourself since we got here."

"To many worries, I guess," I said. "You know."

"No, I don't know. I can't read minds like you. So tell me."

I stared at him for a time, and then huffed, "I can't read minds either, Rif. I wish I could." I felt the heat of tears prick the backs of my eyes and turned away from him, looking into the beautifully appointed study where most of our friends were gathered. The Oaths were standing in the center of the room talking with Brontis, James and some of his brothers. They all burst out laughing at some story Jorame was telling. Just then, Zarek happened to look my way. Our gazes met and locked for just a moment. I felt a mix of pain and pleasure. Then he broke contact. *Was that his feeling or mine?* I couldn't tell. Well, I knew I felt that way, but did he, too?

"Come on. Tell me," Rifkin insisted. "I can see you are upset about something."

"I want to see the Heart's Library," I snapped.

Rifkin elongated the sound of each letter as he replied, "Ohhh … Kaaay … then."

I turned back to him. "I *do* want to see the Heart's Library. Zarek promised he would show it to me someday." I knew as I said it that I sounded like a petulant, spoiled child, but I couldn't help myself. I had to say something to shake Rifkin off my dull mood. "This might be my only chance to see it."

"I doubt that." Rifkin stepped away from the rail and walked toward the open door. "Let's go ask."

"No!" I grabbed his arm. "He's busy." He gave me a strange look and frowned, but continued inside.

"Zarek," Rif said, walking right into the circle, "Pen wants to see the Heart's Library. So do I."

Oh, great, I thought. I'd been longing for time alone with Zarek, something I had not had in the four days we'd been there. I glared at Rifkin. He shrugged and said, "Isn't that what you wanted?"

"Can we all go?" asked Ferris. "I would like to see it too. I've been talking to your sister, Skitar, and her husband, Bex. They say it is a treasure trove, much greater than our Library that burned."

Zarek looked around the circle and laughed. "Of course. I did promise Pen that someday I would turn her loose in the Library." He gave me a genuine smile then, and my heart gave a leap. And I knew at that moment that I was in love with him. His smile faltered and he turned away. "Come on. It is on several levels lower, beneath Heart's Home."

What just happened? I wondered. *I thought we were connecting again at last. But then there was that wall between us again.*

I followed along, bringing up the rear. John and Wydra fell back to walk with me. "We wanted you to be the first to know," Wydra said.

"We're getting married." John beamed, his grin spreading wide.

"That's great!" I said, and I really meant it. I hugged Wydra, then John. "I figured that might be coming." And it did lift my spirits. "I am happy for you both. You have told Lodar and Jorame, though, haven't you?"

"No, Lodar told *us.* He said we should do it," said John. "And Jorame—she can't keep anything from him. I know she will always have that bond with her brother. It's a good thing I like him," John laughed, "or we'd have a problem."

"And we saw no reason not to marry." Wydra slid her arm through the crook of John's arm and smiled up at him. "I'm going to quit drinking the tea so we can grow old together."

"She is resigning as an Oath," John said. "It is not really a workable position any more now that she is one of the council members; it's not really needed."

That would be big news on the moon and in the Wells. So much was shifting. Would I ever have a person who loved me and who I loved as much as they loved each other? Two more unlikely people matching up seemed like a miracle of chance. How odd it was to think of their first meeting and how they became a team. Thinking about them distracted me from my inept attempts to make a match of my own, at least.

Well, so be it, I decided. I would live. I already had experience with people I cared about leaving me. I would endure. I would be the best me I could be. I would be my own best friend, and if Zarek didn't long after me as I longed after him, so be it. I would move on. But …

"No 'buts,'" I whispered to myself.

"What was that?" Wydra turned to me and asked.

"Nothing," I said, vowing to put it all away for now. "I get to see this fantastical Heart's Library!"

A huge spiral stone staircase descended from the ground level of the Heart's gathering place in the back corner. On the first floor, there were bookcases that extended out like spokes from the center of a wheel. In between the spokes were small tables and chairs, and more rows of bookcases that radiated out from the center hub. It was like a flower with many petals. I was fascinated, and charmed and delighted to see there were old-fashioned books there, as well as electronic means of communicating information that I was unfamiliar with. They weren't like our disk books, but something different, with an apparatus that fit over the head.

There were flights of smaller metal stairs that went down to the next level, and we took one of these and descended to the second level. We all walked through the aisles as Zarek and Jorame talked about what was on each floor. I listened.

From the fourth level, we descended down the main spiral stairs to the last and fifth floor.

"This whole level is dedicated to history," Zarek said. "Even with all this, our own history is not complete. When Pendyse came to us through the Blue Moon phase port, and we found your Old Ship, we also found another old ship. We believe it was our ship, and that originally we all came from the same world."

There was a rumble of voices that echoed softly in the great chamber before people settled down again.

"And why would you think that?" Ferris asked. "No offense, Zarek, but we don't exactly look alike, your people and ours." He paused, suddenly at a loss for words, then sputtered, "I mean, there are lots of similarities, but … "

"No offense taken, Ferris," Zarek reassured him. "We thought the same thing for the last two thousand years ourselves. But when we found that second ship, which predated yours, we found something on it that confirmed my long-held suspicion that we have some deeper connection. Now I have had time to examine it more closely, though by no means enough to make a final determination about what that means. But … "

"The glass book." I spoke as if in a dream. I saw it in my mind. I knew where it was being kept, in a special display, and walked right to it. I looked down at it and knew with out turning a page that it had star coordinates that were exactly like the ones found in some of the books that had come with our people when they first came here.

"How did you know where to find this book?" Rifkin asked. He brushed up against me and bent low to look closely at the page the book was opened to. "Are you and Zarek mind touching?"

I shot a swift glance toward Zarek. His eyes were on me, hooded, secretive. "No, we can only do that when we both want it," I said, letting him know I had finally figured it out: he didn't want it.

"All of these books are written in our language," Zarek said. "None of you will be able to read them, unless you go back up to the first floor to the language center and learn Latin. There are stations there with neurocaps that can download our language right into your brain. It will take quite a few sessions, and it's true we mostly speak English now ourselves, but these last few levels are all books in Latin. To understand them, you will have to learn Latin."

Zarek paused. "And I think it is your history, too," he added.

We were all quiet, thinking. Then Brontis broke the silence, saying, "Sign me up. I never could stand not knowing a thing that might come in handy."

"Me too," I said, giving Zarek a blank stare. "Starting today, if I can."

Brontis, all the Librarians and I spent a few hours a day with neurocaps on, learning the Sabostienie language or other subjects that caught our interest.

After eight days of preparation for the jungle, we were geared up and ready to go. There were the thirty-six council members, as none of them had opted out of going, which surprised me; nine Librarians; and the other fifty-three of us, all ready to go. The tension and excitement was high.

We gathered in the Heart's social hall, where we had just finished our early breakfast. All of us were dressed in white climate suits, and everyone had had training with the cycles and the many aspects of their usefulness. We had practiced everything we might need to know many times. I thought, *Ready, or not, here we come.*

Jungle explorers had oozed out of the woodwork wanting to join our expedition. Five seasoned men varying in age were chosen to come with us as guides, a father-son team and three of their friends. Only one of them was Sabostienie. All five had been born on the moon and loved the jungle and its denizens. These men had explored everything from the Ice Fangs to the ocean floor in dive gear, working on algae farms. They seemed to thrive on dangerous activities.

Max was the father, Rexon the son. Eos was the one they called the old man; Julius was around John's age, and Nerthus, the Sabostienie, was a little older than Rexon. Eos and Brontis hit it off and became fast friends. They were two of the biggest men I'd ever met. Even though Eos was quite a bit older than Brontis, he was still quick and strong, and had long, flowing, wavy red hair he wore in a ponytail at nape of the neck. It was almost as if they could have been brothers. They both had red hair, but Brontis had a dusting of sandy color around the temples, while Eos's was still a vivid red, red as rust, even though he was older by a decade. *When trouble breaks out, I want to be with the guides and Brontis,* I thought.

Zarek held up his hands to quiet the crowd. "We have done all we can to prepare you for the jungle. Keep calm at all times. Remember your meditations and you will be able to sense your surroundings, even if you should get separated from your cycle or our people. We are not going to split up for any reason. That can only get us in trouble." He pointed to Brontis, who had his hand up. "Yes, Brontis, do you have a question?"

"What happens if we do get separated?"

"Just don't!" Zarek said emphatically. "Stay with the group no matter what. You go off by yourselves, and you most likely will not return home. But if you do, you have the wrist com to call for help. Make contact."

Everyone was quiet for a long time.

"OK, then," Rifkin said finally, blowing out a big breath. "Let's cycle up."

Outside in the courtyard, ninety-eight cycles were loaded up and ready to go. We rode three abreast, and didn't stop till we went underground to the place where Zarek and I had spent some time when I had first beamed up to the moon. There was a large meeting room close to the small room we had eaten in, and that's were we ate our midday meal and got ready to go up the elevator, which would be a first for most of our people from Nueden. *This will be a long and exhausting experience,* I thought, *with so many going up.* It would be thirty-three trips for the elevator.

Our five guides and Brontis went up three at a time to the phase port area. Rifkin, James and I went up next. Upon coming out of the elevator, I saw that much of the jungle had been burned away on both sides all the way to the port, then down Death Alley on both sides as far into the jungle as I could see. Visibility was wide open; the sky was crystal-clear cobalt. This made me feel better. There were no snakes' close by, and the ground was black but bare, except for a few stray shoots coming up here and there, even through the scattered white stuff the Sabostienie use to keep the snakes away. They had spared no expense or trouble in the effort to keep everyone safe while in the jungle.

Jorame, Wydra and John came up next.

Zarek, Mergel and Ferris came up after that, and we began to position ourselves along the wide-open path. Over the helmet com I asked no one in particular, "Who had the idea to burn half the jungle down to broaden our way? That was brilliant thinking with the crowd we– "

"That would be me," Rifkin interrupted. "Zarek and I talked about optimizing our chances on this adventure, and I remembered how you guys burned your path in the last time, and I thought that might be a good idea."

"And I'm sure the crowd behind us will much appreciate it before the day is done," I said.

The jungle was quiet; then I heard the *cack, cack, cack* of a monkey high up in the canopy of some very tall trees. A small troop of Cackler Monkeys sailed from treetop to treetop off to the north. I barely caught a glimpse of them, and wondered what they thought of the disruption of their pathways in the sky and the invasion of their home.

As the members of our party came up three by three, we set out in groups, with three leaders in front of nine people, and three behind. We began to stretch out along the path. At that point, we were all shielded by group, but not linked. All went very well all the way to the ship. *That makes six groups of fifteen and a small group of eight at the end who have come all this way, and no one has died,* I felt greatly relieved at that. If we could get each of our groups to stay together and watch each other's backs, I was beginning to believe we might all make it home alive. Everyone had done well so far.

"Was this what the Mother and Father kept the path clear for?" I asked Zarek once we had set up camp and covered it with a shield before darkness fell. After doing a perimeter walk, we had all met back at the tail end of camp, where Zarek had been talking to John and Wydra.

"I never thought of that." Zarek turned to me with a smile on his face. "With all the preparations and teaching, I hadn't thought much about the purpose of Death Alley. But I believe you're right. They may not have known it, but this path leads right to both ships, almost in a straight line. They knew there was an Old Ship out here in the jungle; that knowledge was passed down from the last Father and Mother before them." That was the most he'd said to me directly in the past eight days.

"In fact, that was why we came this way. The path was already maintained, up to a point." Said Wydra. "All our triangulations led us to Death Alley as the most direct route here, with half the work done already. So we had our guides burn the path five times wider than a work cycle."

"And the decision to go to the other ship while we're out here was a given," Jorame said, walking up to us at the end of Wydra's explanation. "Most of us don't want to be out here more often than we have to be. Normal people don't have the capacity for terror like the adventures in our group."

"This ship looks so much smaller than the one we were at last time, the one you say your people came in." John said, looking at the odd, upright ship. "How could it ever have held nine hundred and ninety-nine people? For some twenty years? Hardly seems big enough." He squinted up through the clear shield at the top of the ship and then down at the four parallel flange footings. "I don't think it is possible." He raised his hand and shaded his eyes. The setting sun was glaring off the metal, even though there were patches of moss on the ship and scorched places where the guides had burned away vegetation. "It looks like it says *The Ark* up there. That is what the book on the first hundred years said the ship was called. There might be another word under the moss at the end of it, but I can't make it out. Maybe starts with an S?"

"It is for sure we will not get the cycles inside that thing," said Jorame, "so it's a good thing we brought portable flame shooters. I don't want to risk lives on the inside of that ship without plenty of firepower. Anything not human or Sabostienie that moves is toast."

"We can get an early start in the morning," Wydra said, yawning and stretching. Then she went inside a small two-person tent, and John followed.

"I'm staying up for the first watch on this end of camp," I said to Jorame. "You want to join me for a few hours?"

Jorame shot an odd look toward Zarek, and then said, "Sure. I'll keep you company."

We had guards posted up and down the camp perimeter inside the shielded area all night. We hadn't brought the hounds out here, not wanting to sacrifice them to the Fire Flyers or the Gorges. Not that they were more precious than people; but we could inform people of what to look out for and how to handle those dangers, while the hounds were another matter altogether. They were fearless and would attack even though these animals could kill them in ways the hounds might never understand. I would never expose Ibera to such circumstances. I had left her in Moon City with the other hounds that had come up with us.

"Look at Homeworld," I said to Jorame once the camp was quiet other than the soft sound of snoring as a backdrop, and the cry of birds or a monkey now and then. "How amazing is that!"

"It is always amazing, no matter how many times you see it." Jorame smiled. "Like the Desert Blaze."

"It is bigger than any moon seen from there. When the moons are bright, they show no light like this one."

There was a thump and a slither. We turned as one, and saw a Fire Flyer slide down the side of the clear shield.

CHAPTER TWENTY-EIGHT

By morning, the jungle side of the shield was dotted with the forms of Fire Flyers. They had been trying all night to burn their way through. *Thank Wonannonda the shield held*, I thought. *But when people begin to wake up, what will we do if we can't get into the Old Ship?* To get inside the ship, we would have to drop the shield. Could we put all the Fire Flyers to sleep before they could cook someone for diner? *Or maybe several some ones* I thought.

"I think I have an idea," Rifkin said, hurrying up to Jorame, Wydra, John and I. "I don't know if you can do it, but what if you could just roll the shield over the Fire Flyers and contain them until we can get all the people into the ship? People are beginning to wake up, and we need to come up with a plan fast, as I think some of them are on the verge of panic." He looked over his shoulder. "I don't think we want that, and we don't have much time. The news is spreading fast."

"That might actually work." Zarek grinned. "Rifkin, you're a genius!"

"Then let's get to it," John snapped. "Tell me *how* it works and I'll be impressed."

"It will take us spreading out along the camp line," Jorame said, "all of us coordinating to the exact second and flipping the shield at the same time."

"Ok, space yourselves out over the camp line and keep your communicators on," Zarek said as he ran for the other end of camp. I ran with him and stopped two-thirds of the way while he kept going. We hadn't mind touched at all, but I knew that was what he wanted me to do. Just like when Heronimo and I saved his hound, Violet. I could see the others taking their places down the line behind me.

"What's happening?" a woman asked, catching at my arm. "Those are Fire Flyers!"

"Will we be safe?" a man asked anxiously. "What are you doing about them?"

"If you back away, I will be able to do my job, and you will be safe," I said, not wanting such interruptions.

That was when Lucus Tallman showed up, screaming, "We are all going to die!" He was acting like a raving lunatic.

The next thing I knew, Eos had him in a headlock. "Shut it," the old man snapped. "You want to start a riot? I don't think you want that, now, do ya?"

Brontis lumbered up at a fast trot. "What can I do to help?" he asked me.

"See that the people are ready to board the ship. The guide crew and you already cleared it of any jungle wildlife last night and we sealed the door, so we should be safe there. As soon as we flip the shield over on the Flyers, you move the people into the ship as quickly as you can, into that main bay area. I think it's the only place we can all fit into comfortably. OK?"

"Will do!" Brontis said, heading off to round people up. Eos followed, dragging Lucus off with him.

"Is everyone ready?" Zarek said over the com units. "Go on three. One … two … three!"

We hit the switches of our remote controls, and the invisashield wobbled like a wet, glistening bubble and then flopped over the Flyers like a net, trapping them inside.

We shared a cheer over the coms and Zarek said, "Genius, Rifkin. Genius."

"It worked!" John said, disbelief in his voice, and I heard Wydra laughing.

The laughter was cut short as a scream rent the air over by the ship.

"Gorges! Gorges!"

Then many people were screaming, and what had been order turned in to chaos. We knotted up around the ship's entryway, and people began to push. I couldn't tell where the Gorges were coming from, but some of our guides were running around the edge of the pushing mass of people with their flamethrowers. I heard the *wubb, wubb* of a slow-moving Gorge calling for his friends. We were down to only a dozen council members on the ramp when I caught a glimpse of the first Gorge, then two more close behind it, *wubb*ing along toward the ramp. A whoosh of flame shot out ten feet, catching the first one in line. It writhed and shrieked, and the ones behind it all looked up to the sky, as if they were looking for Fire Flyers.

I could see four more Gorges coming through the jungle, and that gave me an idea. "As soon as we are all in side, seal the door behind us; but just before we do that, turn the Flyers loose," I shouted.

"Ha," Brontis laughed, eyes glittering. "Smart girl." He nodded. "Let them eat each other."

"Yeah, but then how do we get out of here later with those things flying around?" Lucus Tallman gesticulated at the Flyers. What I heard in his thoughts was, "*Maybe this will afford me the opportunity to avenge Rauther's death, to push Wydra out to those Gorges.*"

I got right in his face and said, "You try that and I'll kill you myself."

Everyone within hearing distance went quiet. I stood glaring at the man, too enraged to not let it show in my face. "Don't you think enough people have died without you plotting another death? Vengeance never brought anyone back. I should know." I stepped away. "It will only get you a replacement on the council. So don't *even* think about it. I'm listening to you."

"But ... " He swallowed and blinked. "But ... how ...?" He must have been one of the few who hadn't heard that some intense thoughts could be broadcast, and that people like me could pick them out of the air. Maybe my warning would be enough, but I would keep my eye on him. *I'm not going to lose another friend,* I thought. Then I took a mental step back from my own thoughts, as I wondered if I might be broadcasting.

"Get moving, Tallman." Brontis grabbed the man's shoulder, pinched it hard, turned him toward the large doorway and gave him a shove up onto the ramp.

Once everyone was inside, the Oaths, John, Rifkin and I remotely turned off the shield that held the Flyers. By that time, there were ten or eleven Gorges moving into the clearing, and the Flyers shot out over their heads. There were a lot of *wubb, wubb*s going on, and the sound of fire whooshing, and shrieks. We stood and watched for a few minutes. It wasn't going to be a fair fight, but the Flyers wouldn't be so hungry when we came out after our explorations. We sealed the cycles and campsite back under the shield to keep them safe, shielded the entry and moved inside the wide bay area.

The Librarians and those more interested in history climbed up the ladder along with the two younger guides to explore the upper reaches of the ship while the rest of us waited to have the jammed hatch opened where we thought the rest of the Life Stealers were. I told everyone what I had overheard Zee tell Gene, "There were more where these came from. I know where they are. I jammed the door. There's a little surprise for anyone trying to break down that door."

"So what do you think Zee did?" James asked. I hadn't seen much of him, as his duties were with a group that was farther up the line from mine.

"Knowing her, most likely something really nasty," I answered. It scared me. Would it be something that would kill us all, or maim or debilitate us in some way? Blow us apart, or kill us without a sound. I shuddered. I wanted to put Lucus Tallman in charge of getting that door open, but I wouldn't, not even if I thought he deserved whatever nasty surprise the Spider could think up. But I wouldn't hesitate to put him to sleep, or even kill him if I had to, to save Wydra from his misguided revengeful actions.

We had no idea if the "surprise" would explode, flare up as a fire or release one of the Life Stealers, in which case we would all die and the cause would be moot. I thought it was crazy not to just leave them where they were, but the council had spoken. They wanted to drop them into the Trillium Sea, even though Zarek and I both still had misgivings about that. I knew that, if nothing else was the same between us. But he would have to deal with the consequence of this decision in a hundred years … I wouldn't. But we, what "we" there was, would bend to the wishes of the people.

Brontis, Eos and a man named Leeson, also a big guy, were the ones elected to work the jammed hatch door open. We moved the rest of the group into the storage bay opposite the door we were breaking into, and those who couldn't fit, we moved up one ladder to the next floor.

"We'll try pry bars first," Brontis said. All three men placed their thick metal bars up against a ridge on the riveted edge of the metal door.

"OK, push!" Eos shouted.

They pushed with all their might. The door didn't budge.

"Again," Brontis and Eos said together.

They tried four or five times, but didn't seem to have moved the door more than a quarter of an inch. But there was a sliver of light shining through that thin crack. Where was the light coming from?

"Can you see where it is stuck?" I asked, coming up behind them to examine the crack. "Maybe we can use a torch on it and cut it open."

The three men's hands and faces were damp with sweat, wiping hands on their climate suits, preparing to try again.

Brontis pointed to the two places that were the most likely sticking points. "That is where I feel the most resistance," he said.

"Yes. I think you're right," Leeson agreed. "We could try a shot of heat on those places, and try again. It couldn't hurt, could it?"

"What do you think that light is?" I asked.

They all shook their heads and shrugged.

After heat was applied to those two places, they tried again, and the door moved an inch more.

"It is a small control room of some kind," Leeson said, his eye pressed to the crack. "There is a window in there above a panel of instruments." Leeson turned his face away for a moment. "What is that awful smell?" Then he pressed his face against the crack again. "I think it is the main hatch or ramp control; it … " He suddenly went rigid, leaning against the door like a brick.

"Leeson!" I ran over and shook him. He fell over like a tree cut down in the forest, stiff. Zidell flashed in my brain, Zidell with his axe, and seeing one of my trees go down just like Leeson had fallen. I shook him. He didn't respond, but his eyes were wide open.

Then I saw something move under his pant leg and screamed, "Snakes!"

I jumped back just as a Crimson Death came slithering over his shoe and out onto the main bay floor.

"Fire!" I shouted. "Use the flame torches on the crack!"

At once, there were more torches flaming on that area than I could count, catching Leeson's clothes on fire, then Leeson. I had a moment of wanting to pull him out, away from the fire, to save him, but I knew it was already too late for him. He was burnt to char in seconds.

The flamethrowers were covering the seams along the floors and up along the ceiling, anywhere they thought a snake could crawl from. After everything in the whole hatch area was scorched black, they stopped, and we all held our breaths and watched the slim line of light against black.

My heart was pounding, my eyes darting here and there, looking for any escapee Crimson Death. I felt a flutter of panic in my chest as my heart tripped into a beat I knew well. Zarek. Where was he?

"Calm down," he said in my mind. *"Follow my heartbeat. Go deep. Listen. Feel for them in your mind first. See if there are any more in the area were you are. Calm your heartbeat."*

I did. I slowed my breathing. My arms relaxed, and I lowered them to my sides. Time felt like it stood still, and I closed my eyes and looked around the large room with my inner sight. I could sense none of the Crimson Death out here, so I entered the control room with my minds eye, and the first thing I saw was what I was sure Leeson had smelled. One of Zee's men was tied to a chair attached to the floor. His body was riddled with holes. He was a mess. Another body in the same condition was lying on the floor at his feet. My repulsion almost snapped me out of there. She had fed two of her men to the Crimson Death. The utter vileness of her shook me again, as it had done many times before. That was why we were here. We could never let anyone like her terrorize the people like this again.

Then my mind caught on the closed crate of Life Stealers sitting on another chair attached to the floor, in front of the small, thick window above the control panel. I could sense no life at all in here. None.

I took a deep breath and came back to myself. *"Good girl!"* and I felt Zarek slip away from me.

Another deep breath "There are no more snakes," I said into the utter silence.

Brontis came up to me. "Are you sure?"

I swallowed and nodded. "Nothing in that room but death … warmed over."

"OK," Eos and Brontis said at the same time.

"But keep your finger on the trigger of those torches, people. We are getting that door open now!" Eos shouted.

After moving the remains of the two snake-riddled men outside and torching them, we moved the camp inside the cargo bay area. We decided to stay there for the night and explore the ship. It would be safer, we hoped, inside the metal womb, since it had been cleared out twice now, so to speak, while the jungle was, without question, wide open.

The clearing outside the ramp area was littered with Gorge carcasses, burned and torn apart. A Fire Flyer body was there too, one wing ripped off and consumed, most likely, as it was nowhere to be seen, and other parts of it were missing also. It looked like a jungle war zone, with blood drenching the ground. Looking at it made my skin crawl and I shuddered, thankful that none of that blood was ours, except for Leeson and he hadn't bleed at all. It had ended mercifully quickly for him.

We managed to open every one of the doors that ringed the bay area on the main floor. The areas behind them were all empty, so we got all our people situated and as comfortable as possible in those empty rooms. We brought one of our cycles in, loaded the Life Stealers onto it and sealed it with a shield, so no one could get to anything that was in that crate, just as the one Zee had brought out of the jungle had been sealed and kept in the Library at the Heart.

That night, many of the party gathered in the main area to talk and eat. There was a relaxed, almost festive air to the group overall. I guessed that with only one of us dead, they all felt like celebrating that it wasn't them. *There are far too many horrible ways to die out here,* I thought. I would be glad to get back to Moon City, where I would feel we were all safe again. *Out here, it's life on the edge.*

The Librarians were gathered with some of the people interested in the history of this ship and the things in it.

"I don't believe this ship could ever hold nine hundred people, let alone those who the disks say were born on board while en route here. It simply is not big enough," said one man, who was sitting on a box of supplies. I walked up, and he jumped to his feet and reached out his hand to shake mine.

"You're Saunders," I said, just as he spoke his name. We laughed, and I nodded. "Please, continue. I'd like to hear your thoughts about that."

James, Rifkin and Jorame were with me, and we all sat on the floor, along with many other people.

"Well, the ship is not big enough," he repeated. "And look what we found." He handed over an ancient-looking reader. "I rigged up a connector out of some of the things we found with this and powered it up—just a small bit of juice at first; I didn't want to blow out whatever circuits it works on—and I found this." He turned on the reader, and the screen showed a moving picture and a huge area where there were lush, green, growing things. Then a young woman who had a remarkable likeness to my sister Minnari, was standing in the middle of the moving picture, and she was speaking. "This is the hydroponics bay. We can feed at least a thousand people from here alone, and we have another hydroponic unit that can be brought online if we have to divert to a different planet in this solar system, there are two, it would take longer to get to the second planet—and we would have more people to feed. We have had fifty-one births so far."

The young woman reached up toward us, saying, "Recorded by Susan Pearl Steel, switching off." The screen went black. Saunders switched it back to start over, and we watched it again. I couldn't believe it: a picture, a moving picture, of my ancestor, Susan Pearl. Saunders lit it up again and started passing it around. Everyone was fascinated with it.

"It's so short. Are there others like it?" I asked.

Saunders grinned and removed the lid of the box he'd been sitting on. "Oh, yes!" he said, he pointed to the five boxes next to it. "I think that many of these are that same kind of moving picture recording."

The awe that went around the circle and the grins on the faces of the Librarians gave me happy chills.

"We found other disks similar to our own kind with only a few modifications," one of the other men said. "There were a couple of these old readers with bigger screens than we use today, but I think they are adaptable."

"And look at this," Saunders said. "This is the one that makes me think this ship is not big enough." He flicked on a new, larger screen. "Watch this."

It was as if we were looking out a window into the darkness of space, seeing the pinpricks of light from stars far away. Then the view panned right and the rim of what looked like a wheel slid into the visual range. The wheel had spokes radiating out from a hub that was lit up on multiple levels. You could see a small part of another wheel, and another below that. Then it blinked out.

"Not only that," Saunders said, "in all the places we looked in this ship, there was no one place big enough for that hydroponics bay thing in the first moving picture."

"We think this ship was only a shuttle, like the Zap, only in space instead." Saunders said.

"Then where is the ship?" James asked, looking stunned.

Saunders slipped in another disk, and a view of part of our world showed on the screen. We all gasped. The row of moons was between us, and Homeworld.

"Is the wheeled ship still out there?" Rifkin asked.

"We don't know," one of the other Librarians said. "We have only looked at a few of these. We brought everything we could find."

"This place is mostly empty," Saunders added. "There are some heavy equipment pieces still here, but nothing else small enough to move, or take with us at this time."

"No," another Librarian said. "We've got everything of interest we could carry."

"And we think we found evidence that Susan Pearl Steel returned to this ship several times over her long life to store some of her findings and hide Earth books and records. One of the records shows her at a very old age."

Saunders beamed. "It will take us a while, maybe years, to catalog everything we've found and boxed up to take back with us. Out of the eight or so recordings we looked at, three of them were of Susan Pearl Steel."

"There was even one of Adam and Eve Steel, and their son Stephen and Susan." The excitement in the group of historians and Librarians was so thick it was palpable. Could it be true? Could a larger ship still be out there? The group broke up into smaller groups for conversation and speculations.

"What do you think?" Jorame asked. "Do we have room for another ship in our pantheon of ships?"

CHAPTER TWENTY-NINE

We arrived back in Moon City nine days later, with crates from both ships and only two more casualties, a woman of the council and one of the Librarians, who died from some kind of poisonous spider's bite, according to Mergel: a flesh-eating poison that kills in a day's time, consuming the skin and organs closest to the location of the bite. We must have picked the spiders up somewhere between ships. All we could do was make the victims as comfortable as possible before they died. It was so quick. We sent them to Tomorrow Land there in the jungle between the ships. It subdued the mood of jubilation that had taken over the whole group when the moving picture disks were found.

Most of the Librarians were staying on in Moon City for a while to take advantage of the Heart's Library and the Language Learning Center. They wanted to spend some time with the teachers in Moon City's schools and learn as much as possible about how they taught and what they taught, as well as share their findings at both ships. They had already discovered that the triple-ringed ship we had seen in that one moving picture was the one that had made the journey from Earth to our world, to New Eden, and that the ship here in the jungle had been used simply as a conveyance from the larger ship to the moon. They were asking, "Is that super ship still out there, behind one of our moons? Could there still be people on it?"

I was ready to go home; Ibera and I were both ready to go home. Rifkin and James and their hounds were off hunting in the forest at the northwest root of the Ice Fangs with John, Wydra and the guide crew. They were staying in a smaller city called Tramon, close to Fang Lake. I was amazed that they hadn't had enough adventure yet.

I was in my room, writing in my journal, when I heard a knock at my door.

"Come," I said, putting my pen down.

Jorame poked his head in, and Ibera yipped a greeting and loped over to him.

"You should get out more. Come on, let's go for a walk," he said.

"Why not?" I stood and stretched. "You're right. Between keeping my records and spending time in Heart's Library, I really haven't been doing anything else. The Library is full of so many interesting things. A walk on the beach would be nice."

He held out his arm. "Then let's go."

I slipped my hand through the crook of his arm and we set off, Ibera beside me. We wandered the old town streets, narrow and curving, hardly wide enough to fit a work cycle through at some places. There were homes with brightly colored doors and potted plants on the stoops, with balconies that hung out over the streets, and some of the tiled roofs twisted at odd angles from the houses next to them to allow for more privacy. Sometimes we could catch a glimpse of a small personal garden in the back of a house, with charming details and garden art.

"Mark would have loved this place," I breathed dreamily. "He loved green, growing things. And ... " I faltered.

"I know." Jorame put his arm around my waist and pulled me close.

"Don't be too sympathetic, or you'll be walking in a lake of tears," I said. I stayed in the comfort of his nearness for a while longer, then pulled away as we came to a single-file spiral staircase that led down the cliffs to the docks and beach area. We walked along the shoreline and were quiet, listening to the waves roll up on the beach, past the last of the homes, we sat on a large rock that jutted out over the ocean as Ibera played on the beach, nipping at the waves. The view of the city as it rose up on the cliffs was spectacular. The cliffs were a blue-grey, squared-off, pillared affair that almost looked man-made, but weren't.

"Thank you," I said, tucking my knees up under my chin, wrapping my arms around my knees and taking it all in. "This is beautiful. I needed this." I shut my eyes and breathed in the scent of sea and warm sand.

"So, what's going on with you and Zarek?" Jorame asked.

I looked at him and shrugged. "Nothing." I shook my head. "What do you mean?"

"Something is not right between the two of you. Wydra and I have both noticed a … a difference."

Turning from him, I looked out over that celestial blue I had first seen on my birthday with Zarek, nearly a year ago. I drifted on the waves of time and pondered the elasticity of it, and how when you look at a period of time one way, it feels long, but when you look at it another way, the same period of time feels short.

"What's going on?" Jorame asked again. He reached for me, placing a hand on my shoulder. "Aren't we friends? You can tell me."

"Nothing. Honestly." I turned back to face him and smiled. "I think he is just preoccupied with all the business of leading his… your people." I shrugged again, remembering that when Zarek had helped calm me, I had thought maybe things were getting back on track, but he hadn't responded to any of my thoughts to him after that, and I'd quickly quit trying. I could only stand so much rejection. "He's just busy." And I refused to let anyone else see how that stung my heart.

Jorame shook his head. "You two were nearly inseparable before we went to Telling Wood the last time. But you have hardly spoken since you came here. Why won't you tell me what has happened?"

"We, you and I, have never tried to mind touch." I took his hand in both of mine and moved so I was facing him. "Could we try?"

He hesitated. "Well, I'm not a great mind communicator, I've only ever been able to speak with family." he said, squeezing my hands in gentle reassurance, "but we can try. I'm not gifted like Zarek, but I'm not absent talent either."

"Maybe I'm not gifted," I said, looking down at our joined hands. "I thought maybe I was, but now … " I shrugged and glanced up into his green eyes and sweet smile.

"Let's see."

We closed our eyes and I found my heartbeat. I waited for a time, and then opened my eyes, and we held each other's gaze. I sought his heartbeat; I followed the path as far as I could, opening myself to his questing mind. I could feel his genuine love and friendship for me, and I sent him mine. We sat there for more than an hour, reaching, but that was all we could do. I sent thought after thought his way, but none of them reached his mind, nor did I receive any of his thoughts directly.

Finally I pulled my hands away and smiled at him. "I could feel your feelings, but could hear none of your thoughts. Maybe it is just something we will have to work on," I said.

"Yeah," Jorame said, standing up and jumping off the rock to the sandy spit below, then holding up his arms to help me down. When I jumped down, I knocked him over, and we both landed in the sand, his arms around me. He drew me close. "You didn't hear any of my thoughts," he whispered into my hair, his warm breath tickling my ear. "You didn't hear me think that I hold you more dear than my own life." He tipped my face up to his, and as our eyes met I knew, with clarity, that I did not feel the same about him as he did about me. It was as clear in my mind as when I realized that I did love Zarek. I pulled away and got to my feet, and gave him a hand up. I didn't know what to say. I felt torn. Would I lose him as a friend too if he knew my love for him was not the same as his for me? Would everything become awkward between us?

I was suddenly tired and depressed, and just wanted to go back to my room. We returned to our rooms, swimming in inconsequential chatter about the places around us. Jorame kissed me on the forehead at my door and left. He seemed as low as I felt. *This would be so much easier if I could feel that kind of love for him,* I thought. *Maybe at one time I could have ... before Zarek. But truly, if not Zarek, there would be no one for me. I know that down to my marrow.*

On the day we beamed down to Telling Wood port, we returned to the council chambers and all the council members slept in the courtyard around the shielded cycle that carried the two crates of Life Stealers, not trusting that someone might try to tamper with them, even though I was the one with the only remote control for the shield. Never mind that they had sat in the great gathering hall for nearly two weeks under shield before we all came back here. Logic and reason don't seem to matter sometimes. People will feel what they will feel and do what they will do despite logic.

But as the first week home wore on, the council members drifted away to more comfortable beds than stone, and the shields kept the sick treasure safe from anyone with a desire to pry.

We had someone keeping a watch on Lucus Tallman. Of course, John was never far away from Wydra when out in the public, so we felt she was relatively safe from Lucus and his ilk. I felt sorry for Jorame sometimes, as John and Wydra were together so much that Jorame spent more time by himself, giving them space to do whatever couples do. Jorame and I were alike in that, both at loose ends. Once we got back to Telling Wood, James and Rifkin went off to spend time with family and to hunt up some of their other friends to see who had survived the Spider, as they had taken to calling her, along with John. The Voice would go down in history as the Black Spider of Death who ate her young.

Over the next few weeks before we left on the Zap for Mugar City, another councilwoman for Telling Wood would have to be chosen, as Susan, who was from here, was one of those who had died of the spider bite and would have to be replaced. Once that was done and a last joint council was behind us, we would be going to Mugar City to take the Life Stealers around the Steel Desert to the west side of the Trillium Sea.

To sea was another place few of us had ever been. It was strange, but I could feel that the trip to the Blue Moon had left us all with a shared experience that somehow drew us together creating a kind of bond in spite of disagreement, and for many of us, the excitement was high to be off on another adventure. I'd already heard that people were outfitting for other adventures, wanting to explore the world openly, for the first time, as we had never done before. And I could feel along with them the desire to know, to do, to go.

But right then, I was tired and just wanted to go home to Ra'Vell Island. It had been over six months since I had been home. I was heart sore and weary of people who always seemed to want something from me. Maybe it would be no different there either, but I had my caves and quiet space to run in. It had been ten months since my thirteenth birthday, so much of my worldview had changed since then.

We, Ibera and I, were back in my home at Telling Wood, as the first floor had been completed. It was still raw and plain, but the structural work was done, though the second story was still being finished. We had guards, and were safe here again.

Although I no longer carried my sword or slingshot on my belt, I always had my Rectifier on the chain around my waist, tucked in my pocket. Sometimes I wore two. *Just for balance,* I always told myself, but wondered if I was catching the general paranoia this city seemed to engender in people.

"Come on, Ibera. Let's take a run." She happily trotted over to the door, tail wagging her whole body, her purple tongue lolling from the side of her mouth. She scared a lot of people, but to me, she just looked like love. At eleven months old, she was nearly full grown. Her long, powerful neck held her elegant head with its pearl-colored horn, now a full four inches of thick, hard bone tapering to a rounded point. She danced around, bobbing that beautiful head. Her long legs made her back reach as high as my waist after her last growth spurt. We could almost stare eye to eye. I figured when her growing was done, she might be head to head with me. She was already bigger than most full-grown hounds. I knelt down to where she sat and hugged her around the neck, burying my face in her silky white fur, breathing in the comfort of her dog scent, clean and reassuring. She put her paw on my shoulder, nearly tipping me over, making me laugh. She wuffle barked, and whined wanting to go out.

Out the door, past the guards and down the street we ran at a slow, steady pace. Before I knew how far we had gone, I was in front of Hannratti's place—and the estate was lit up as if for a festival. Through the windows, I saw people moving about, so I went up to the door and knocked. Hannratti answered the door.

"Pen!" She hugged me so hard I thought I would faint. When she turned me loose, we were both laughing. "I'm so glad to see you. How'd you know we were home? We only just now arrived on the Zap."

"Ibera and I were out for a run and … "

Suddenly the entry hall was packed with people and greetings. "Hannratti, what's going– "

"Hanni," she said, interrupting me, and shook her head. "You forgot. I'm Hanni now."

Suddenly, Hanni's mother and father were hugging me too, and her three little sisters, like stair steps, wearing matching dresses, were dancing around me, making Hanni's hound, Nitro, howl and Ibera joined in, matching her sibling with gusto. The hall was utter pandemonium.

"Let's move this into the front room," Hanni's father said, moving us along. As we were moving into the main entertainment room of the house, I glanced up the curving stairs to see Dray coming down them.

"Dray!" I called. He joined us, giving me a shy hug and Ibera a scratch around the ears as she licked his face. "What are you doing here?" I asked. "I thought you were at the village on the grass sea."

"Well, I missed you guys, and as pleasant as Insuladune is, it's small and sort of dull. I missed all of you." he looked around at Hanni, "so I walked back to the island and hooked up with Hanni's family. They have sort of adopted me. Or I adopted them." He shrugged one shoulder and grinned around at the family circle.

"We adopted each other," Hanni's mother said, smiling. "Now we have a son."

Magic bloomed in my chest, the magic of family, and suddenly I felt my world shift and click into its proper place again. I had been living in my own head far too much. This was what I needed, *family,* the sight, the feel and the joy of it.

They lifted my heart out of the doldrums it had been in, and I felt happier than I'd been in a long time. Even if it wasn't my family, it was beautiful to be in it with them. And I couldn't quit smiling and hugging people as the night expanded with the light of the Blue Moon, bathing the courtyards and balconies that were all being opened up to the family that had returned. It was the most hopeful and worry-free I'd been in weeks, maybe even months. This family had become the symbol of what I wanted to see happen throughout the world.

CHAPTER THIRTY

I banged my gavel. "Silence," I said. "Let the man speak."

"I said," Lucus Tallman spoke with as much enunciation as Rauther Steel, "there is no reason we all have to take this trip. The women do not need to go. We could choose a few representatives to go in their place. Some of us have had enough of this adventuring around in dangerous places. I, for one, would stay home if I could. But the women … "

A feminine grumble began.

"We have already taken the vote on this issue, councilman. We are all going." I banged the gavel. "It has already been decided. Now, is there any other business before this joint council meeting before we adjourn?" Lucus glared at me and sat down.

"Yes!" Talithia. One of the council members from the Domed Wells, had stood to speak, "In view of the fact that this mission will take at least two or maybe three months … " She was at the table next to Jorame and his counterpart Julka from the Steel Desert, so I couldn't help but notice that something extraordinary was happening there. Because so many new tables had had to be added, they were smaller, and the pairs at them had to sit closer together. I was aware the moment their hands accidentally touched that sparks were flying between them, an explosion of sparks, and mind touching I could sense. It was an instant connection I could feel like fire racing along a line of fuel. She was a beautiful, graceful Sabostienie woman I had noticed before, with large silver-blue eyes and purple-black hair, her head bare on both sides above her tiny shell-like ears; her long hair was caught up in five or six gold barrettes gathered down to the nape of her elegant long neck.

Somehow I knew what Jorame had felt for me was just infatuation compared to what he already felt for her. *With one touch.* I breathed a sad sigh of relief suddenly knowing our friendship would survive intact. I was sad, but happy for them, too; then I was brought back to myself as the council erupted in applause. And I didn't know what had just happened. My attention was drawn back to the business at hand.

"I call for a vote. We take our families with us as far as Mugar City, at least." Someone said.

"Vote called for!" I slammed my gavel for quiet, and the knocking began. It was unanimous; families would have a vacation at the expense of the council funds. That was all right by me. I wondered if Dray would like to be my guest.

The lights of Mugar City were bright and sparkling when our contingent of travelers arrived on the Zap. We had reserved an entire inn for our group of one hundred and eight people. The family members would live in those rooms until the council members returned from our Trillium Sea excursion. A few had special permission to take their younger children with them. Our seafaring vessel would be a cruise ship that had never been past the Little Finger of Mugar City. It had only been up and down the eastern coastline and was quite sea worthy though. The Four Fingers of Mugar City are narrow peninsulas' that reach into the Indigo Ocean. The ships never go past that last Little Finger. Some of the largest, most well appointed inns of Nueden are in the fingers. And some of the biggest homes of the wealthiest in all the Provinces are here in the Fingers.

We spent two weeks gathering up supplies and mapping equipment, for we were taking a cartographer along with us to map the coastline around to the Domed Wells, as we'd been told the people of the Wells had built a harbor at the mouth of the river that my father had floated down, nearly dead, close to the first Domed Well. We would stop and stay there for a week. I would get to see Father and Pandasiea. Wydra and Jorame could show John their home there, that is, Wydra, Jorame and Julka. Life is full of odd twists.

A local Mugar theater troupe gave a performance in welcome to the council. It was amazingly eclectic. Someone had gone to a lot of effort to include aspects of song and dance from the Blue Moon and the

Wells as well as some of the most beautiful among the people of Nueden. Even Lucus Tallman seemed impressed.

Dray was having a great time. We went shopping and filled out his wardrobe, which he much needed. Life seemed almost normal. Things in our world seemed to be settling into some new patterns. Not all women liked being free: some felt untethered and afraid they would not be able to take care of themselves, so the Women's Free Houses and the Palaces were shifting into places to shop for a wife, though not for a son anymore. New rules, not so much laws but definitions of conduct regarding women, were being formed all over Nueden, and the people themselves were enforcing these rules. There were groups called the Sleeper Force, and any man or woman who abused another person would be put to sleep and carried off to jail for a few days. Behavior modification, the local Librarians called it. Librarians from all over Nueden were banding together to reform education. They'd been meeting in a conclave in Telling Wood when we left for Mugar. We had spent a day with them discussing ideas and possibilities. Zarek had beamed down to meet with them, the Librarians and council members, and to go with us to release the Life Stealers into the Trillium Sea.

The ship's crew was excited to see a different ocean. I thought that was funny, as the ocean continued on as the same waters; it was only a different shoreline they would see. And I was eager for that as well. Dray, Ibera and I were in a double suite on the main deck and had a wonderful view. The dip and bob of the ship gave Dray a bit of trouble, though.

"I've never been on a ship before," Dray said for about the hundredth time, standing at the ship's rail as if he needed it to hold himself up. "But the ocean is beautiful, with its shifting colors," he added as Mugar City seemed to pull back from view. We left it behind, but we stayed within sight of the land, which quickly changed to the dunes of the Steel Desert.

The main deck was packed with all the people on the ship, not wanting to miss a thing.

John and Wydra moved through the crowd, holding hands. "So, what do you think of sea voyaging?" Wydra asked Dray, smiling.

"Well, it's my first time. So … " Dray began.

"Mine too!" she said. "John tells me I'm a natural."

"I'm still a little wobbly," Dray laughed.

He was one of the three children on board. John and Wydra had left Lodar and Klea back at the inn in Mugar. They were planning a wedding on our return to Mugar City. Things were being prepared while we were away. *How amazing that this could happen*, I thought, *that the man my mother loved as much as she loved my father, the man who is, in many ways, like a father to me, is going to marry the best woman friend I have in this world.* Well, there was Hanni, but that was different, because of our history, when we were both boys. I laughed at the thought.

It would be the event of the century. People from all over Nueden would be there being as it would be the first wedding between the two groups of people.

"It's a beautiful day." John took a deep breath. "I have always loved the ocean. You know my father and my mother spent some time in Califeia? We own a home just outside Crescent Bay."

"No," I said, "I didn't know that. I thought you lived in Telling Wood growing up."

"That was where Father kept Ojilon's mother. My brother Allan was raised in Dunsmier Dakota. My father only brought us together after our First Tellings. We hated each other right off. Father had a dozen or so wives that I know about, scattered in every capital city in every province." He gave Wydra a look that spoke volumes about her singular status. There would not be multiple women in their lives.

"If they had been kept, I would have had—or do have—two or three dozen sisters somewhere in Nueden." He looked at the waters gliding beneath us, and then looked into Wydra's eyes. "I can promise that will never happen to us. No one will ever take a child of ours away. That is a tradition I am more than glad to see gone. Forever."

Shifting from one foot to the other I was feeling like an accidental bystander in someone's private moment when Rifkin and James came crashing in. They had joined the crew as guards, and were riding high in a wave of excitement.

"Hey, look at you, Dray," James said. "You're not even clutching the rail."

At the mention of this, Dray's hand shot out and grabbed the top rail.

"Now see what you've done," I chuckled. "He will be an old hand before you know it."

Rifkin leaned over the side of the ship and watched the water glide by. The slap and slither of the water was a pleasant sound, I had thought so many times on Fell Lake. This was just on a grander scale. Rif gave a big sigh. "I love the water. I didn't know I would love the ocean as much as I do the lakes."

I stepped back to get a wider view of my friends. There was Dray; Ibera sitting next to him, was alert and grinning her happy dog grin; there was James and his hound, Bone Cruncher; and Rifkin and Sky, named because her eyes were sky blue; there were John and Wydra, with eyes more for each other than the scenery; and as I looked down the row of people gathered all the way down the landward side of the ship, I knew we were making history together again. We were living in a time the people, maybe for the first time on this planet, were setting their own course. What we were doing right now was a big deal, a huge beginning.

I just prayed it wouldn't fall apart.

We were on the water for three days and four nights before we came to Well One. We stayed for six days and left on the seventh morning. I had the best time with Father and Panda. She showed me her school and all her favorite places; she was so happy to see me. They had their own place at the second-tier level close to a lot of shops, so Father could get out easily on his own onto the concourse, where he picked up his supplies for the blueprints of the highway they were going to build from Well One up to ReMaid. Things were going so well for them.

Quill and Minnari's baby was due any day, and Father and Panda were planning a trip to see them whenever they got word of the baby's arrival. They would stop at Ravenwood Castle and see Brontis, who had gone home and taken his friends with him, the Blue Moon jungle guide crew, to show them around Ravenwood and Fell Lake. What great news that was. It made me smile; the bonds of new friendships, was a good thing. I guess having to count on each other in order to live through dangerous times is one way of solidifying budding friendship of all kinds.

We got back on board the *Blue Gull* and again set out to sea, for a day and a night. We woke up to shouts of excitement. We had just rounded a curving peninsula of land that curled into a bay and sighted a ruined city perched among the cliffs. It was as white as bleached bones, glistening in the sun. We all wanted to go into the ruined harbor and look the place over.

"I think that is one of the cities our enemies abandoned when we became one people," Zarek said. "I didn't realize it would still be here. There were three major cities along this mountain range on the coast line, according to what Father and Mother knew about our history." He spoke loud enough for everyone on deck to hear. "I believe this one was called Green Atlantis. It's amazing that it hasn't completely crumbled back to earth by now."

"Green?" Rifkin snorted. "There's not a living thing around, only sand and stone and a few scruffy bushes. Why was it called Green?"

"Because at one time it was green. Where people overpopulate, things die." Zarek said, giving me an odd sidelong look. A longing bloomed in me to talk to him, to touch him casually like I used too, when we were friends, but he turned away.

The bay was deep and narrow. The land curled around on the right-hand side. On the left, there was a shorter rock jetty with an inlet opening to the small bay itself. It had been well built, you could see that, but was by now only a crumbling line of large rocks. We crept in slow and easy, using depth testers as we went. We pulled up to within five feet of the rock jetty, dropped anchor and yarded the gangplank over to the rocks.

"Remember," Zarek said, "just like in the jungle, we don't separate. Stay together in your groups. This is unknown territory to *any* of us. We are only going to take a quick look around. We can gear up an exploration team later, once we get the job done we've come to do."

"We don't want any casualties," Jorame added. "We had no idea this was here." He grinned at Wydra. "If we had, we'd have been out here before you."

"I'm glad you didn't," said Julka. "This way it can be *our* adventure." She indicated the council, the larger group, but she gave Jorame that look I was beginning to identify as the "secret couple's look." They were living in their own little world. They didn't realize everyone else already knew or suspected they were a couple, even though she was Wydra's guest.

Rifkin stepped up next to me. "Where's Dray and Ibera?" he said. "We want to keep an eye on those two. We don't want them wandering off alone."

I looked up and up at Rifkin, noticing again how tall he had grown. "When did you get so tall?" I asked. He only grinned. He must have been a good two inches past six feet. "And broad!" He was coming into full manhood before my eyes, even had a ragged scruff of hair on his chin. When had that happened? It seemed that James and I had stopped growing at the same time, with him only slightly taller.

"There's Dray, with James." Rif pointed as they came through the crowd. "Come on, let's go see what the bones of a city look like up close."

CHAPTER THIRTY-ONE

We partnered up like we had done before, nine in a group with guards. We weren't as large a party this time. People went ashore by our lifeboat and climbing up and down the rocks, or hopping from rock to rock, until we all had reached the sand. The ruined city was not as large as Moon City, but climbed the cliffs in much the same fashion. From what looked like the city center, it flared out like a fan, rising up in terraced streets. Most of the buildings' roofs had collapsed, and some walls had fallen, blocking roadways and alleys, but we could see the form the city had once taken, and it must have been beautiful. The center had held a fountain and concentric rings of once-colorful tiles. Now the sand blew over the walls and the floors, filling up the corners and the fountain, robbing everything of its original colors.

The place was empty. As Zarek had said, it looked like these people had abandoned their city to join the Sabostienie. If there had been wooden doors on these buildings once, they had rotted away to blow in the wind, which blew grit in our faces as we came up to the first flight of steps. There was the breath of recognition in the design of things: spirals and swirls, all curving lines, sanded down to only a hint. Up close, reminded me even more of Moon City.

My group was the first to go up to the second-tier street to look around. "Stay out of the buildings; go where the group goes," I told everyone. I noticed as I looked back toward the ship, as we stood here at the ruined city's edge, half of the people just wanted to play in the gentle surf of the harbor, and had taken off their shoes to do so, "Pen," James called. "Come look at this."

Rifkin and I joined James all the way up the crumbling steps. Our group moved to follow. I held my hand up to stop them at the bottom of the steps. Only the three of us went as far up as the second street. My gaze followed James's pointing finger. I saw a track of maybe four sets of wet, webbed feet running along the sandy and rock-paved curving way. The prints disappeared in between some crumbling buildings.

"Whatever animal made those prints was big," James said, "Maybe as big as we are."

"It's time to go back to the ship," I said. "Enough. We know less about what lives here than we did about the jungle. With the jungle, at least we had guides. This place may look empty, but something lives here. I'm not willing to put these people in any further danger for a mere adventure. We're done."

I com linked with the other group leaders below us and said, "We've all got to move back to the ship." I motioned everyone to head back. "We have spotted wildlife signs. Let's leave this place for others to explore. We've got a job to do. This was only a diversion anyway. The fun's over."

"Pen's right." Zarek com linked all of us to uphold my decision. "This has only been a taste of what may lie on this side of our world. There will be time for some of you to come back this way and be more thorough in your investigations of these ruins, but for now… back to the *Blue Gull*."

From that point on, we went northwest at an angle leaving the land behind, on a course only the captain knew, and he was not allowed to mark on any coordinates map the location where we'd be making the dump. We went two full days out to sea and could only see the thinnest dark line of land by the time the second night fell. It was eerie being so far from land, in the dark, with swells that rolled and lifted the ship high and slapped its sides alarmingly when we dropped down in the gully's of the troughs. As soon as there was light, though it was diffused by grey clouds, the people gathered, ready to empty the crates. Being nearly out of sight of land had an unsettling effect on all of us, and we were eager to be done with this whole business and go home, back to land, afraid we might lose the land and be lost at sea forever.

I stepped up to the rail, between the two crates, and disarmed the shields.

"Captain, would you do the honors and open these boxes for us?" I asked.

The captain had a small crowbar, and he jimmied the lids off both of the crates. "I'll go and get us started for home," he said, acting as nervous and I felt.

There was a collective sigh of relief from everyone on deck. I tipped each crate enough to show everyone that none of the orbs had been taken out. We also had the ones Zee had left behind when she fled the moon with only her pockets full. Every single Life Stealer we knew about was here to drop in the ocean, minus the one she had killed some four hundred thousand people with.

"May this bring peace and trust between our people," Zarek said.

And I threw the first white, hateful handful of death into the sea. As we moved toward home, I threw one after another into the waves that slapped the side of the ship, whispering what sounded like *mistake, mistake, mistake,* in the wash of water against the hull. I watched each orb drift down out of sight. *May they never cause us grief again*, I prayed. At one point, I thought I saw faces below the surface, as if they were a vision of those who would be saved from such a wicked instrument of death. One after the other, I pitched them in, until all the white balls and the control pads were lost in the depths of the Trillium Sea.

"It's over," I heard people saying, and "Now we'll be safe," and "We can go home now."

"On to better days," Lucus said sarcastically.

Dray was standing next to me, and Reia, Klea's mother, who was the councilwoman for Ravenwood, had her arm curled around his shoulders. Ibera sat between Dray and me, her bulk a solid and reassuring presence.

We sped over the water as if the ship itself longed for harbor and home. We all retired early that night and woke up to the sight of land rising out of the waves; the next morning, the ruined city gleamed white in the sunlight. We didn't stop. We passed the Domed Wells and went up and around the Steel Desert. We cut our going-out time by a day coming back to Mugar. Everyone was egger for land. It was a glorious afternoon when we arrived back in the Fingers.

When we reach harbor, a spontaneous party erupted; everyone in Mugar City was excited to hear every detail of the sea voyage. We were welcomed back at the docks on Little Finger, the one farthest south in the city like returning heroes. A feast was prepared, and we were taken in welcoming arms. We all stayed up late talking to people: men, woman, Librarians, ship captains, young children. I felt better than I had in a long time. A horrible burden had been lifted from my shoulders; I was carried on waves of jubilation. *Things may work out for our world after all*, I thought.

John and Wydra's wedding was set for the following evening at the rise of the Blue Moon, in the courtyard of the inn. Skitar and her husband, Bex, and Zarek's great grandniece, Willobee, had come to Nueden to be there, as they were all close to Jorame and Wydra. They were more like family than friends, Zarek, Jorame and Wydra, being the Oaths for so long. I couldn't help but wonder where Willobee's parents were. Why was she always with her great grandmother?

At the end of the night, Jorame, Julka and I were sitting on a stone bench in front of the inn, talking, as the crowd began to thin out as folks went home. We knew the party would start up again by midday tomorrow, before the wedding.

"Well, it has been a very long day." I stood to go. "I need some sleep in a bed that doesn't rock."

They laughed, and stood too. "We should all call it a night. There will be another long day tomorrow." Jorame smiled. "Let me walk you ladies to your rooms."

We came to my door first. "Well, good night," they both said and walked down the hall, shoulders touching, hands held loosely, a glow about them, a togetherness that made me ache. And I realized I missed Jorame's attentions toward me. What kind of fickle, immature person was I? I shook my head and shrugged as I heard Quill's voice in my mind saying, "Do you even know who you are?"

No! I had *answered* that question, and those were doubts I was not going to revisit. So much had happened since then. With every discovery, life didn't get easier or simpler, but more complicated and complex. There was so much I didn't understand. Maybe no one did. Maybe that was just the shape of life. And maybe I hadn't arrived at my full, free self yet, my most real self, but I knew the small pieces of me, and they would all come together in the right order eventually. I knew the Wonannonda Spirit was with me and that it would always be my guide. Like in the Earth story, following the North Star straight on till morning. I would make it through the dark. Any dark. As long as I was with the Wonannonda Spirit.

Once in bed, Dray asleep in the other room, Ibera sleeping on the floor at the foot of my bed, I drifted on thoughts of home, Ra'Vell Island, the people there and those in ReMaid, and my father and Panda, happy in their new home in the Wells.

Even though I knew I was not alone, I couldn't help but wonder where *did* I belong? How *did* I fit in this world? Why did I feel so lonely? And why did I feel so responsible for positive out comes. Even though I felt things were moving in the right direction, and that was great, at the same time, there was a subterranean shiver of loss that shot through all my happy moments, like the veins of purple in some of the rose stone from our quarry.

I brought up all the faces of the people I had loved—still loved—and lost: Mark, Grandfather, my great-uncles, Pelldar. Mother. Even Father in some ways was lost to me. Had I just lost too many people? Was one of those small parts of me broken somehow, too empty to ever hold a love like I saw developing between Jorame and Julka, and John and Wydra? Or was I just too young? If emptiness was the sign of future capacity to have and hold onto a love like that... well, that capacity was almost too devastating to think about. Or was it simply the absence of Zarek? Had loving him put an unpatchable hole in my heart, a hole that all my happiness would forever leak out of?

Why had he turned against me? Why could I no longer sense him in my mind? When I stopped to let these thoughts in, it felt like agony, a crimson thread of pain I wanted to ignore but couldn't. I had tried.

The longing for that connection broke me open and a flood of tears poured out. They ran into my ears and soaked my pillow before I found sleep.

The next morning, I felt better, though no less empty, even though I could feel the comforting presence of the Spirit and was more at peace with my condition. I felt loved—maybe not by the one person I wanted it from most; but I knew many people loved me. Maybe that was all I could expect from my life. Mother had said my life would not be easy. *Maybe I'm meant to be alone, to give all of myself to the people,* I thought. *Creator knows their last leader tried to take everything from them. That is, if the people still want a leader; anyway, there are many who seem to think it should be me. Maybe that's what my place is, what I am to become, the Mother to my people, and Zarek, the Father to his people. Not one people but two cooperating nations.*

As I dressed and got ready to go down to the dining hall, I noticed Ibera sniffing something next to the open window. "Hmmm, I don't remember leaving that open," I said.

I went over to see what was on the floor. A large puddle of water spread out on the wooden floorboards. Ibera looked at me and growled, a low-timbered, throaty sound with a question in it. Had it rained last night? I looked out the window. We were on the ocean side of the inn, and I could see the waves two stories below crashing on the cliff edge directly beneath me. *No, it can't be seawater we're too far up.* I shook my head, "Come on, girl, let us go eat."

I sat down at the table with James, Rifkin, Dray and Ferris. "Did it rain last night?" I asked as I buttered a piece of bread.

"No," Ferris said, smiling dreamily. "It was a beautiful night. A lady and I took a walk in the gardens. It was lovely."

James and Rifkin exchanged glances. Rifkin ginned and James rolled his eyes.

"Were you guys also out in the gardens?" I asked. They both took on sappy, satisfied looks, like a hound that had caught a rabbit. "No. Don't tell me. I don't want to hear. I get the picture."

I set to eating, and wondered where the water at my window had come from. After we ate, we all went out to the gardens and walked our hounds. Too much in door time for Ibera, maybe? I had never seen Ibera not be able to hold her water before, but could she have had an accident? But I was sure the window had been closed when I got in bed. So who had opened it?

"Dray, I know you like fresh air. Did you by any chance open our windows last night before going to sleep?" I asked.

He shook his head. "Can I take Ibera around to the bay? She really likes running in the waves."

"Go ahead," I laughed, "but be careful."

I watched them go, and saw John coming down the path. James and Rifkin had some mysterious thing afoot and took off, and Ferris slapped John on the back in passing and went in search of the lady from his garden walk the night before.

"Well, they all seem happy with life," John said as he watched Ferris leave.

John and I walked down one of the paths to an ocean lookout. There was a stone bench there, and we sat down.

"Where is Lodar?" I asked.

"With Wydra. They are having a morning together." John smiled. "She is really good with him."

"That is a wonderful thing to see," I said. "I really love that kid. You can see she does too."

He laughed. "She says it was like she already knew him, because of you."

"Well, we do look alike." I said. "Can I ask you something?"

"What do you want to know?"

"How did you get into my house in Telling Wood that day? I've tried and tried to figure it out, but … "

John grinned. "So, you're still trying to puzzle that one out." He rubbed his chin and began, "Well, it is a trade secret, but being as we are family now, I guess I can tell you."

He rubbed his hands together as if he was getting ready to work on some tough project, then leaned his elbows on his knees, folded his hands and made a steeple of his index fingers. "You see, most folks don't lock their back doors, the ones out to the gardens. They almost never get locked, especially if they have walls like your place had before the bombing and burning. People feel safe behind high walls. Now, your heavens glass was a bit of a problem. I worked on that one for a good while to figure out a way to cross it without tearing myself up. But really, once I put my mind to it, it was simple. I had a metalworker make me a two-foot-wide metal cap to set on top the glass, with a chain-link ladder going down to your side of the garden. It was so easy I didn't even mess up my clothes."

He dusted his hands off and leaned back against the bench. "Then I just walked right in." He grinned.

"I thought you had had to come over the wall. I just couldn't figure out how else you could get in. We usually lock the garden door too, but… Mark had been out there."

"I wanted to scare you enough to make you go home." He was quiet for a while before he spoke again. "Your mother used to talk about you and Pelldar, and the girls. Leaving your father and you was a hard thing for her. She loved you all. Life for a woman in our world is hard. So many losses, no matter what her few choices are. I met her in Telling Wood. I fell just as hard as a man can for a woman. She was beautiful, all the way from the inside out. She fascinated me, and made me laugh. When we discovered she was pregnant with Lodar, I convinced her to marry me and come live in my home. Ojilon wanted her too, and I knew he had been devising a plan to force her to marry him. When I told her that, she agreed to marry me; she did come to love me, though. My father died shortly after we married. I also had a home in Ravenwood as well as Telling Wood, but my brothers thought any place that was mine was also theirs. My mother was still alive, and Allois was a great companion to her in her last years. We had gone down to Ravenwood to be with them when Father fell ill."

I waited as he thought about them. I could see the memories form behind his eyes as he thought. "Your mother … " He paused, then said, "She was my heart and soul." He sniffed and turned to look out over the sea. "She was the best part of me. And I knew she would have wanted me to protect her other children too, if I could, but I failed Pelldar … and Mark."

A tear slipped down my cheek as I listened.

"Allois had a way of making me want to be a better person, a good man. My mother was like that too. But Father expected me to go into the family business, which was GBI, and Free Houses and Palaces.

"When I met your mother, I was already trying to work my way into a different kind a work for the GBI, finding lost or stolen things. That was working well, but then Ojilon spied on Allois and saw her writing a letter to your family. He became incensed and dragged her out in the street … "

"Stop." I held my hand up. "I've seen too many of my family dead or dying; I don't need to see what he did to her too."

"You're right." He wiped at his eyes. "I apologize. I know. They are images no one should ever have to see."

"Teia and Reia said Panda and Klea saw it all. That they were there."

"Yes, Allois and I found your sisters and Klea. Panda was with us from time to time, but had to take training at whatever Palace we were near. I could move the girls around to Free Houses or Palaces in whatever city we were in to keep them with us, close, at any particular time. This was not smart, as Ojilon was watching us closely. I did not know. I didn't realize how deep his hate and jealousy went. If I had known … "

"Don't do that!" I shook my head. "Too much time is wasted in this life on what we should have, could have, would have done, if we had only known. We can only know what we know."

"You're right." He looked me in the eyes. "I feel like I've been given a second chance at happiness, here, with Wydra. I never thought I would ever feel this way again, but here I am, on my wedding day, and I can promise I will take better care this time." He shrugged and smiled. "Your mother was right."

"About what?"

"That you would grow into a person people would follow; that you would be wise and deep, and gracious, with a spacious mind."

"She said that?"

"All the time!" He sighed. "She had dreams. She called them True Dreams, and she saw you often as you grew up. I felt like I knew you before I met you. But she didn't tell me you were a girl. That was a secret she kept to herself. But when I went into your library and saw all the little touches that were Allois, I could have … well, even your face was enough to drop me. You had no idea how you affected me. I just wanted you to be safe, and I knew the king had you on his list. They wanted Ra'Vell Island one way or another. Ojilon was after my son, and I couldn't allow my focus to be split, so I tried to scare you away. I thought if you were back on you island you would be out of their reach."

"You were the most intimidating, scary man I'd ever met, until I saw you brother, Ojilon," I said, laughing. "Now I feel like, somehow, you're my father too." I looked at him. "Do you mind that?"

"Not at all." He stood and pulled me up into a hug. "You honor me, and I will not let you down."

CHAPTER THIRTY-TWO

No matter where we went, Wydra was able to find the most amazing clothes. Her wedding dress was floor-length and midnight blue, a gem-spangled thing that swayed with grace as she moved. She looked like a star-studded piece of heaven. Her spiky white hair had grown out on the sides and was all one short length. That night, she wore a smile that would have made the sun jealous, if it had been out. She sparkled with happiness.

John could not take his eyes off of her.

Since our talk, I understood his need to stick so close to her. The fear of Wydra vanishing out of his life as my mother had done when she had been killed was a real and possible danger in his mind. The happy couple was the first on the dance floor, twirling under the stars, her gown billowing about them, a reflection of the night sky.

Jorame and Julka joined them, and before long, the floor was full of people celebrating what had been a beautiful wedding.

James and Rifkin had surprised the wedding party by throwing rice in copious amounts at everyone there, saying they had read that was what the Old Earthers did at weddings back on the true Earth. It would take me forever to remove all those little pieces from my dress and hair, but it made me smile even as I felt another piece poke me somewhere down my bodice. As I danced with a number of men, more of the rice worked its way down to the floor, which was now as white as snow.

We ate, and some drank; the mood was light, and the warm air was scented with flowers from the garden surrounding the courtyard of the inn. My feet hurt when I wore those ridiculous shoes with the three-inch heels that I always let Wydra talk me into, so I went to sit on the sidelines and watch. I kicked off the accursed shoes, crossed my legs and tucked my feet up under my dress. I was still not used to dresses. I would rather wear pants any day in the Nine. But I did always feel strangely feminine when I was dressed like this; even if it felt abnormal, there was still some allure to it that caught me.

Someone sat down next to me on the garden bench and I turned, smiling a greeting. To my surprise, it was Lucus Tallman.

"And you think all this will lead to some kind of peace and equality?" he said, his hand making a flourish around at the wedding party going on. "I hope you're right, because I feel like... " He seemed agitated, fretful, "something is terribly wrong and something bad is about to happen."

"Are you trying to tell me you *know* something is about to happen that will disrupt our progress toward peace?"

"No. Just that something is off. I think someone was in my ... oh, never mind, why would you believe me anyway? I have not exactly endeared you to me. You most likely wonder if this is some kind of trick, but I am ... I feel ... I just know ... "

"If we don't believe in peace, we will never look for it, or prepare to live with it," I said. "We are going home to Telling Wood tomorrow. We will work out an agreement that we can all live with, a concord of peace. I promise you. We don't have to be enemies. We will all have a chance to speak. We will listen to everyone and bring an acceptable rule of law, justice and mercy to all the people."

"But I don't understand why we have to change so much so fast." His usual petulant sarcasm was back. "Things were working just fine for us the way they were."

"Except for the ones it wasn't working for at all," I said. "We need to make that right. I'm sorry that it makes you feel– "

He stood as if he had spotted someone in the crowd and abruptly walked off into the throng. I followed him with my questing mind, wanting to see if I could catch any cast-off thoughts. I settled down comfortably, resting my open, empty hands on my unladylike crossed legs, and breathed deeply, exhaling, inhaling. Settling into my search. What I felt was a genuine feeling of dread flowing off Lucus like the heat waves from a banked fire, but no thoughts.

I expanded my field of search and ran into ... *What was that*? I felt the hairs on the back of my neck rise, knowing someone was watching me. I stood up slowly and stretched, then turned to face the garden behind me. I saw a shadowy figure melt back into invisibility, and thought maybe Lucus was right. Just because we were rid of the Life Stealers didn't mean we were out of danger. Who had been standing there watching? The mind I had felt was different; its shape and form … different. I wasn't sure exactly how, but …

I was too tired right then to make sense of any of this. I looked for my shoes, but couldn't find them in the bushes where I thought they had tossed them to my left, so I got down on my hands and knees to look under the bench. But they were gone. I no longer saw Lucus. Could he have taken them somehow? But he couldn't have, and why would he do such a strange thing anyway?

"OK. I'm going to bed. I've had enough. Whoever has my shoes, you're welcome to keep them. They hurt my feet anyway," I shouted, and went to find Dray and Ibera. Lodar was spending the night with us to leave his Father and Wydra to be free for the night.

Up in our room, Lodar asked, "Do I get to sleep on the lounger in the main room?"

"If you want to." I took his small hand in mine. "There is a perfectly good bed in Dray's room, you know. There are two."

He shook his head.

"Of course, we can make up a bed for you in the main room if that is where you would like to sleep."

"Yes, there are no windows in here." He looked around, pleased. "And can Ibera sleep with me?" he asked. "That way I won't be scared."

"Why are you scared?" Dray asked. "Nothing could get past Ibera. You will be perfectly safe with us."

"There is something out there watching us," Lodar said, and my skin crawled over my bones. I was afraid to ask any questions for fear that would only alarm the child further.

"You just feel that way because we're in a strange town. Things are different here, that is all," said Dray.

"We will be back home tomorrow. You'll see. We'll get on the Zap and be there in no time at all," I said.

I made sure the door and windows were closed and locked. My skin was still twitchy, creeping around my back like a wind shivering the surface of Lake Fell.

I brushed my hair until it was snapping with electricity. Finally I felt calm enough to sleep. In bed, I lay on my back, my favorite sleeping position, and did my breathing exercises to calm myself even further. I drifted into sleep on the memory of a sound, a gentle slap of water on the side of a boat, the lulling reassurance of small waves pushing me ever forward, and I felt peace float on the blossom scent of the great Wonannonda tree.

A cool breeze woke me. Early morning light was coming in the window. Suddenly I realized my face was wet, as if I had been crying or had been out in the rain. I was confused. Then the previous night snapped back into place, and I was out of bed and in a fighting stance, looking around. Realization dawned that I'd perceived a form standing by the open window only a split second before. I ran to the window and, leaning out, I caught the splash of someone going into the water. Then I felt the puddle under my bare feet and, looking down, I saw the wet print of a webbed foot, just like the ones we had seen in the ruined city. It hadn't been a some*one*, it had been a some*thing* that had been in my room. I slammed the window shut and locked it. There was a puddle next to my bed. I followed the webbed prints from the window into the other rooms to find the boys still sound asleep, small puddles pooling on the floor next to their beds. Ibera was sound asleep too.

Now that was weird!

Going back into my room, I examined the small wet spot next to my bed as well. The "rain" on my face … that must have been what woke me. I looked into every corner and behind all the chairs, but there was no other sign that anything had been disturbed or was out of order. I knew I hadn't dreamt it. The wet spots were still on the floors. But what kind of animal could open locked windows, two stories up? And subdue Ibera, was more to the point.

I dressed and got the boys up. "Come on, get dressed. Let's go down for breakfast. I want to talk to John, Rifkin, James and the Oaths. Oh, she's not an Oath any more," I corrected myself. Or is she?

Lodar grinned. "Nope. Now Wydra is like me. She is a Bouyahie! She is like my mother now." He got quiet, then he said, "I know I had another mother before, and that you and I look like her, but I don't quite remember her." He was silent again, looking at me. "Sometimes, I think I almost remember her. Sometimes I hear her voice in my head."

I knelt down by him and gave him a hug. "Our mother loved you very much." I knew Dray had entered the room and was just behind us.

"I know, Father told me. He tells me that a lot," Lodar said.

"And now Wydra loves you too, and you are a very lucky boy, because you will get to grow up with two people who love you," I said.

Dray put one hand on my shoulder and one on Lodar's. "Actually, you will have lots of people who love you, Lodar: Pen and all her friends. Me. It's a good thing to belong to a family, even if you have to pick them yourself."

I smiled in spite of my worry over Webfoot and a few puddles. I hugged them both in a big bear hug. "Come on, we need food. Let's go eat."

As we trooped down the stairs, they laughed and played a word game Dray had made up to entertain Lodar. I couldn't wait to leave the Fingers of Mugar. I would even welcome being back in Telling Wood. Once back there, the real work would begin. There were laws to hammer out. What form that law and peace would take to keep the most people from being discontent until we could move farther along, I could not guess. Yes, that would be hard work.

But the others would need to know we were being followed by … by whatever Webfoot was. Maybe they had always been around these parts, creatures from the sea, and the people who lived here knew about them. But that didn't seem right to me either; I had never heard of such a thing, and I was sure there would have been talk about something like Webfoot.

As it happened, when we were finished with our meal, Wydra came and took Lodar away to pack up their things. The move back to Telling Wood was already in full swing, and Dray and I had to be packing and loading our belongings on the Zap same as all of our friends.

There was no chance to talk privately with anyone without causing alarm among some of the people around us. *Like Lucus Tallman*, I thought. There were a number of reasons I didn't want to do that. Some of the council members were sensitive to fear and might use any whiff of alarm to set people at odds with each other. So I would just wait till we got home and I could have my friends alone. *Besides*, I decided, *it may mean nothing. Wait*, I counseled myself. *Give it time.*

The Zap was full to capacity, and it was as if the entire wedding party was on the move. A light, jovial mood that was contagious caught me up and moved me along with it. *I will tell them later*, I thought. Right then, I just wanted to be happy for them, with them, and revel in the joy I saw around me. There would be plenty of time later. And besides, we would be about as far from any ocean as we could get in Telling Wood, at the center of the country. But the thought following that one was, *what about the people of Mugar City, will they be in any danger from Webfoot or its kind?*

CHAPTER THIRTY-THREE

By the time we arrived back at Telling Wood, the city was being flooded with people from all over the nation looking for work, mostly poor men, but some women, too, who had left the Houses and Palaces looking for a different life.

"There are people sleeping in the streets." Rifkin shook his head. "We have to do something, Pen. These are people who have found jobs, they are hard workers, but have nowhere to live."

"Well," I indicated my mostly rebuilt home, "I could turn this over to the people. We could bring cots in and maybe house sixty or maybe even seventy people."

John, Wydra and Lodar came in just then from the back gardens, where they were helping get things cleaned up. "I heard that," John said. "Maybe we could move in here with you and we could turn my home into boarding for those who need housing. It's far larger than your home, and has close to a hundred rooms they could use. It has never felt like a home to me, far to large for a real family." John bent and kissed Wydra on the top of the head, and reaching out his hand, ruffled Lodar's dark curls, with affectionate.

"They could pay a small amount for a room," Wydra said, "maybe share a room and general access to the living spaces, library and so on. We could have a fully staffed kitchen where they could have their meals. It would be like a permanent inn, only cheaper."

"I like that idea." John said.

"Me too." said Lodar. "That way my Nar Hound, Shell, will have a brother around to keep her company. We're going to live here for ever, aren't we Father? I like it here."

"New opportunities, new beginnings" Rifkin repeated the city slogan. "It will be one of the best places to live Lodar. We will make it that way."

John owned one of the largest unburned homes on the city square. It was not far from the complex of James's family, which was a few city blocks away but also on the square. At least half of James's family complex had not been completely destroyed, and what damage there was to the remaining building had been repaired before we returned from the Fingers of Mugar. It was enough room for them, as their family was one of those that had suffered many losses and was greatly reduced in size.

On the one hand, things in Telling Wood were in a state of active chaos, but on the other hand, there was a sense of order and progress, even in the midst of that chaos. There had been much improvement with the cleanup and rebuilding. There was a sense of purpose and excitement along with the grumbling and complaining.

We had been home for five days before I told anyone about my visitor, simply because we had so much to do: new laws to form, council meetings to attend, citywide problems to deal with. By the time I had the time or the energy to speak of it, I had begun to downplay it in my own mind, yet I couldn't deny it altogether. It still nagged at me.

James, Rifkin, John, Wydra, Lodar, Dray, Jorame and Julka were all living at my house, and the adults were all gathered around the long table in the dining area next to the kitchen to discuss some issues we thought should be brought up at the council meeting that evening.

At the end of our talk, I asked, "Did any of you have any strange things happen to you while we were in Mugar that last couple of days?"

"What kind of strange things?" John asked, going still. Then he glanced at Wydra and said, "Elaborate. I was sort of preoccupied." That ultra protective look shadowed his eyes, and he touched Wydra's hand lightly.

"Well, I woke up with a wet floor that last morning, what sleep I got." Rifkin said, "and I couldn't find any leak from anywhere. Is that the kind of strange you mean?"

I nodded my head in confirmation. "Yes. Not only was my floor wet, so was my face. And so was the floor over by my bedroom window, which was also open when I know I closed and locked it before going to bed."

"Well," said James, "there you have it. Maybe it rained a bit and got your floor wet. What is so strange about that?"

"And did the rain also unlock and open my window?" I asked James.

"It didn't rain," Jorame said. "It was a beautiful clear night. I was up early; Rifkin was in late. I met him coming in as I was going out. He said it had been a glorious night all night, and he said it with a grin."

Rifkin wiggled his eyebrows. "Oh yes!" Then he frowned. "Come to think of it, my window was open too, and I don't remember leaving it that way when I went down for the wedding."

"Anyone else with wet floors?" I asked.

"If they were, I didn't notice," Jorame shrugged, "but my window was open." He shook his head and shrugged again. "And I don't remember if I left it that way when I went to bed either," he said, glancing at Rifkin.

"So, what's the big deal about open windows and wet floors?" John gave me a dark look. "I know you're not afraid of a little water, so spill it."

"You know the webbed footprints we saw in the ruined city on the other side of the mountain range?"

"Yeah," they all chorused.

"Well, I found the same webbed prints on my floor in front of the open window."

"Webbed footprints?" John sat up a little straighter. "And you are just telling us this now? Are you sure you locked your windows? All of them?"

"Yes," I said. "Quite sure. I did it because I had wet floors the night before, too."

They all sat a little taller, an etching of tightness about their faces, as if they were thinking, *What now?*

"Well, we are away from the ocean." John stood up and stretched. "Whatever they are will hardly bother us here, but we should get in touch with the Mugar City fathers and let them know to keep an eye out for anything odd now that we know what to look for."

"I already called the City Father and talked to him. He'd never heard of anything like that, but he is aware to keep an eye out for anything unusual now." I said.

"Well! There's nothing more we can do about it now." Rifkin also stood. "It's time to go to the council meeting anyway."

"One thing at a time," James agreed. "Maybe it's nothing."

"No, this is something." Julka, who had been quiet through most of our planning, now spoke with an authority that sent chills down my spine.

"We need to talk to Zarek," Julka and Jorame said together.

"All of us." Jorame said. "I'm in touch with him now." He fell into silence for a space of time, and then said, "He will meet with us at the council library. We should leave now, so we have some time before meeting."

I felt a pang of sadness at that quick response afforded Jorame, when I couldn't even feel Zarek's presence anymore. Just more proof I couldn't get it right, somehow. Trying to communicate with him was taking a stab in the dark. I sucked in a breath and rose from the table, as did the rest of them, and headed for the door.

Zarek. Where did you go? Why?

CHAPTER THIRTY-FOUR

We gathered in council, all chairs full, ready for business, and Timothy read off the roll call, then I banged my gavel and called us to order. All morning, we had listened to the stories of women and the poor, hearing about what their lives had been like. We had even heard from children who had been orphaned and had lived in the cracks of our society that I had never known about. We had had a very productive first half of our day. The life stories moved many in the council chambers, and the quiet we took with us at the end of that session was testament to the power of the people's own words.

We all have a story. We all are *a story,* I thought as I looked out over the full chamber. The council chambers had been full to bursting at every meeting we had had since we'd gotten home.

"Lucus Tallman," Timothy intoned in his deep, loud voice. "Councilman from Dakota.

"You have the floor," I said, with one sharp rap of my gavel to quiet the crowd.

"Most of you know my concerns of going too far and too fast," he began. "I am concerned about the rumblings I hear of a more conservative group of men who are agitating for an army to rise up and put things back to the way they were. They are calling themselves The Natural Order. I am sure some of you, at least, have heard of them too." There was a soft, sibilant shimmer of disturbance throughout the chamber, then it settled back into quiet. Lucus continued.

"I have come to see, to understand what most of you want. I can even see it is time for change, but it disturbs me that these malcontents from every province in the nation might overwhelm us."

He stopped, taking a deep breath. "I have a bad feeling I cannot shake, and I am not calling for any kind of vote on this, I just want to be a voice of caution."

And with this, he turned toward me and half smiled. "I know. I am sounding like the Gavel. When we let her speak, she is always saying, 'Talk about everything; think about the consequences of each decision we make today and how they might affect us tomorrow. Look for the unintended consequences of our actions today, and we may see ways to avoid backtracking tomorrow.'" He turned back to the people. "To my utter surprise, I think I am hearing her. But still I am full of fear, and not totally without anger. Fear that our tender start might be squashed. Anger that people I love may die if there is war. So please, do be careful with the decisions we make this night." And he sat down.

I pounded my gavel, and when Lucus looked up at me, I nodded, a quick little sign of respect and thanks. He had surprised me. And I seriously hoped he wasn't being duplicitous.

We had opened this series of meetings to the public, and as long as they maintained order, we were allowing them to speak.

Behind the balustrade that separated the council members from the public, our security was high on all levels of the chamber and at every point of entry to the building. There were not just two or three, but five or six guards at every door and throughout the chamber, all equipped with Sleepers that were set to their own thumbprints and biologics. And every one of them had communicators on their wrists. Outside, we had a small army that patrolled the entire perimeter of the building day and night so no one could enter without notice or record. People also watched out for things that didn't seem right to them.

Maybe we were overdoing it, but we had heard of the group that didn't want any change. And we were trying to be ready for anything, determined not to have a repeat of when Norman had brought his men into town and killed so many of our council members and some city people.

Timothy called out, "Daniel Block. Councilman from Iowa Province."

"I have recently read in the journals of Susan Pearl that there is a plant that can give us very long life, and good health." Daniel said. "I have talked with people from my province, and they want this plant. What I want to know is when can we have it?" Then he sat down, calling for discussion.

I had known this idea was being pushed around the circles of some of the province's social parties and had wondered when it would come to the surface. My friends and I had had our own talks about this very question coming up.

Wydra stood to speak to the question.

"I am one who has been chosen to carry the responsibility and burden of the tea from the Purple Pearl." She walked out into the open area at the front of the room, where she could look out at all the people. "In the culture of the Sabostienie, they willingly gave up the use of it on a wide scale, as the population could foreseeably live so long and have so many births that the moon and Homeworld would be overused, which could lead to starvation and wars. At present, there are only three people who are drinking the purple tea that we know of: myself; my brother, Jorame; and Zarek. Zarek's father and mother also drank the tea. They both died at the hands of the Voice when she and her men invaded Moon City. Camison and Trisaine were the Father and Mother of our people. They were our leaders, you would say, but to us they were more than that. They were Father and Mother." Wydra paused and looked out over the crowded chamber. Daniel Block rose to ask a question.

"Councilman Block." She nodded at him. "Do you have a question?"

"Why do you consider it a burden? I can understand, to some extent, the burden of leadership, but it seems to me having hundreds of years would be a blessing." Then he sat down, looking almost angry.

"There are two points to be considered here," Wydra said, and her voice carried in a clear, precise tone, filling the dome and greater chamber.

"Burden. Responsibility." She walked across the open space, stopping close to where John stood behind the Telling Tree banister, leaning against the wall. "An Oath usually starts drinking the tea when they are fifteen or sixteen. We have been taking it for approximately fifty years. We were the only children of our parents ... Jorame and I. The Sabostienie don't always have children right away. We are twins. We limit ourselves to only one or two children per family."

There was a collective gasp of surprise, for many Nuedeners hadn't heard this before.

"But what if someone only had a girl," A man shouted out. "Who would carry on you family name?"

"We just don't see it that way." Then she continued with what she had been saying, "It doesn't take long to see your grandparents and older friends and other family members wither before your eyes. People you love and treasure, die, and you still look like you're sixteen. You have the experience and knowledge you've gained from those fifty years, but you are still physically sixteen or seventeen. And every one of the threads of connection around you age and die. In a hundred years, they are all gone. Without the people we know and love, who are we? There is a loneliness to being an Oath. And it doesn't just happen once, the new connections you make, will also grow old and die. Then you may do this again ... Oh, eight, nine, maybe ten times in your life. There is a burden to losing loved ones." There was a thoughtful silence blanketing the hall. People were hanging on her every word.

"Which brings us to the responsibility part," Wydra said. "The plant is rare and hard to cultivate. It has the most awful, bitter taste, but it has healing, restorative properties, so we use it for grievous wounds among our people, in small doses or topically with people who are injured in accidents—not much, because the effects are addictive. All Sabostienie know this, and the medical people are careful with its use.

"And for us who take it daily, it is a responsibility, because we are the leading edge of our people. We have to see which way to go to keep our people safe and living in harmony. We strive for balance and continuity as a people, by having a few we know who can see the long view of life."

"We had the Voice who took it," someone yelled out of the crowd, "and we were damaged by that long view."

"Exactly!" Wydra shot back. "None of you knew what she and the king were doing. They did it for themselves, not for the good of the people. They did it to gain advantage over you. And without a great love for the people, there is no desire to be a responsible leader. Is that a person you want living beyond their natural life?"

A rush of no's swept through the hall, rising to a crescendo of shouts and the rustling of people getting to their feet.

Wydra held up her hands for quiet. When the people settled down, she continued. "The other part of that responsibility is that to lead or care for the people means a loss of personal freedom for the Oaths, because you live for the people. Your first thought in the morning and your last thought at night is for the people, like a mother for her daughters and a father for his sons. Like parents for their children.

"The issue we need to discuss now," Wydra turned and walked back to the center of the floor, "is that with a rare substance like the Purple Pearl, some will think it should be for everyone, but will soon learn there is not enough to go around. Then the thinking follows that the chosen elect should be the only ones to have it. And with the past history of abuse of this gift, or curse, to our world, who should get it? The rich? Those who can exert the most force to take it? Or maybe only the educated should have it, the Librarians of the world. And then, how many children would be brought into the world with all those extra years of birth productivity? How long would it take before resources stretch to the breaking point? Who then gets the limited food supplies? Again, the weak and the poor will lose out on what should and could be an abundant life for all."

Councilman Block stood up. "Those are all pretty words from someone who has the privilege of extended life like you have. I bet you wouldn't give it up … " He turned and gave the crowd a long look, "for the people," he finished, and sat down.

"Actually, my brother and I have both cut back on it to every other day. Our intention is to stop taking the tea. We are drinking less every time," Wydra said, looking directly at Block "It may have been easier to decide to start drinking it than to stop. No one in the history of our people has ever made this choice that we know of. And I can tell you, it is not easy." She faced John, who was standing away from the wall now, a tremble passing through her, and said, "But I want to grow old with my husband like normal people do. These are new times for all of us. Our lives will not continue exactly as they have been. We will have to make adjustments even as you are. We may never have a Father and Mother again … "

At this, she gave another quiet shudder, swayed on her feet then went to sit down with Mergel, her council partner, at their table. He patted her hand, a look of sympathy on his face.

"Councilwoman Emmalynn, from Georgia Province," Timothy called out.

"So what should we do with this Purple Pearl?" the councilwoman asked. "Should we use it for everyone and anyone? Should we destroy it? Should we use it for healing only? How can we know it is being used correctly? How can we know a person like the Voice, that evil woman Zee, is not going to get their hands on it and deceive us all again?"

Murmurs swept through the chamber, and I felt the fear lying beneath those murmurs. As I watched the audience, I spotted Zarek standing among the outer rim of people, leaning against the wall, ankles crossed, arms crossed tight over his chest. A sense of sadness that nearly floored me was rolling off him in waves. A deluge of the feeling of isolation and loss so great that I wanted to weep, but kept myself upright and dry-eyed. At that moment, he caught sight of me looking at him, and all that emotion just turned off. Blinked out. Blank. He closed up, and I felt nothing of him, only my own reaction to what I had felt he had been feeling.

The discussion moved on. Many people spoke on the issue of the Purple Pearl. I tried to pay attention, but my thoughts returned again and again to Zarek and what I knew were feelings that mirrored my own, that sad loneliness that hollows out the soul.

CHAPTER THIRTY-FIVE

We spent the next few days in council discussing all the possibilities of the Purple Pearl. At the end of it, we all agreed to table the matter in order to think about it and sit with it for awhile, let people get used to the idea of its very existence, the good and the bad of it.

It was a beautiful fall morning, the light in the sky a golden stillness, the scent of pink pine in the air. I longed for my island home, but I talked to Will every day to discuss the needs of the island, and things were going well there. I also talked with Brontis on a weekly basis. He was still entertaining his new friends from the Blue Moon at Castle Ra'Vell near Ravenswood.

Sighing, I walked up the steps to the Chamber House for another meeting. Hundreds of people were already milling about the entrance, talking, when we heard shouts and saw a commotion happening far down the main street in direct site of the Chamber House.

Rifkin, Dray, Jorame and Julka and I were standing on the top steps near the plaza of the Chamber House, shading our eyes, trying to see what the commotion was about, when we saw some small objects in the sky, coming closer. As the flying things approached Telling Wood, people began to run for cover behind buildings. Even some of our security forces lost their nerve and broke their line. Most of the guards got behind building corners in battle stance, ready to face whatever these bright white flying things were. The memory of the Oaths' first appearance flashed through my mind. Where these friend or foe? Could we be that lucky twice?

John, Wydra and Zarek ran out of the council building and came up behind us. James and his brother Ferris came up from the other side of the steps. We all stood there watching the objects become larger, like moving, shiny stars of white light glinting in the sun.

The flying things reminded me of the cyna-cycles, but larger with long thin wings along the bodies of sleek, fat, cylinder-shaped bodies.

"They look sort of like the ships we use to maintain the solar satellites," Zarek said, "but those are not ours."

"I think we should take cover," John said, pulling Wydra down behind the stone edge of the fountain in front of the Chamber House. We all followed suit. Ibera, Bone Crusher and Sky Blue, James and Rifkin's hounds, were circling around us, not understanding the threat but sensing our uncertainty. They went from whining to a howl that nearly deafened us with the high pitch of that baying. People who had not already taken cover were running behind the largest buildings they were close to as the white machines came near and stopped, hovering in mid-air above the square.

There were sixteen ships. We could see they carried people inside, but they were too high up to see how many. They dropped down to the ground, and their clear covers dissolved almost like the invisashields on the cycles. The technology seemed similar, but much more advanced. People began to step out of the podlike flying machines, three per the first nine machines, and gathered in the empty square in front of the Council House.

Most of them looked like Sabostienie, except for their skin tone, which was an opalescent light green. There were three who were brighter green shot through with colorful stripes down the length of their bodies, and one had jewel-tone spots. Those three were completely naked, one man and two women, and they had flanges of thick skin on their legs and arms and backs that looked like the fins of a fish. Their longish hair shimmered with many colors, like fish scales caught in the light. Those three had odd flaps of skin on both sides of their necks. Then I noticed their feet, which were large and webbed, as were their hands.

"Look at their feet!" Wydra said with a gasp, as if she had heard me think it.

One of the women who looked more like a Sabostienie, but with a full head of hair instead of bare skin on the sides, stepped forward, and the air around her shimmered, and I thought they were being shielded by something similar to the cycles' shields. She was dressed elaborately. A knot of stunningly bright blue hair was twisted in a towering design on top of her head, a fringed collar that looked like a fish fin but was some kind of fine material stood up around her neck and head, and she was wearing a long-sleeved, black, shimmering robe that swept the ground in flowing waves as she moved. An undergarment of jewel blue covered her body beneath the flowing robe.

I felt cowardly crouching behind a barrier. That was no way to lead a people. *And if these people were here to kill us*, I thought, *they would have done it by now*. So I stood, and Ibera and I walked to the edge of the steps.

"I am Pendyse Ra'Vell," I announced, in a loud voice. "Who are you, and why have you come here?"

The woman backed up a step as if alarmed, and I noticed my family of best friends had come to gather behind me.

"What do you want?" I asked again.

Zarek came and stood beside me.

The woman spoke in another language. I thought it sounded like Sabostienie and Zarek struggled to understand her. I could only understand one word in ten, and only because of the time I'd spent in the Sabostienie Library in Moon City. I thought I heard her say "War," then I lost all sense of the conversation as fear darkened my mind.

Two large, strong-looking men from the flying machines came up to us with a large box and tipped its contents out on the paving stones at our feet. The clatter of ninty-nine white Life Stealers rattled up against the steps, around my feet, behind me, every last one of the Life Stealers I had pitched into the sea hoping to never to see them again.

"She says we have declared war on her people, and she wants to know why," Zarek said. "She says we can never win in a fight against them. They have all the advantages of superior technology beyond anything we know."

"Have you told her we didn't know they even existed?" I asked Zarek.

"She said her witnesses saw you cast these orbs down on the, I think she said the … Obaskillian … 'fish children,' who gathered them up and brought them to the … city … underwater?" He shook his head. "That doesn't make sense, and I'm not sure I got that right. It is the same language, but has differences I'd have to get used to before I could fully understand all its nuances. But I think that is what she said. And her name is Verity; her title is Second Woman."

"If that is the second woman, I'd like to see the first," Rifkin quipped under his breath next to my ear. "She is gorgeous."

"Don't be so pleased, they may be here to kill us." I said quietly.

After Zarek and Verity talked some more, she said they would consider a peace exchange so we could learn each other's ways in order to avoid a war. "If this is rejected, she said they will not hesitate to protect themselves," Zarek informed us, "and that the weapons we have to put people to sleep will not work on them."

I finished that sentence with Zarek. "Yeah, yeah, I already figured their physiology was more like yours than ours."

"She also told me that they have similar weapons, but they don't make you sleep, they make you dead."

"So, what is this exchange she wants to do?" I asked.

"Nine of our people of her choosing to go with her, back to Hadria, her city, for a full cycle of the sun, four hundred and thirty two days. I think she means a year."

"Where is the exchange in that?" I said. "Tell her she can take me and no other."

"The exchange is that they leave nine of their most valued children to learn our ways, and our language as well. And if a hair on their heads is disturbed, or something like that, they will kill us all, down to the last person. They will sweep the land clear."

"Oh, sweet," Ferris said. "Like I'd want to live with them for a year. What about the hair on our heads?" he snapped, sounding confrontational.

Just then, nine of them stepped forward, making a line. One dark green-haired female stepped out from the line and shouted the word "Zagora!"

"That is her name," Zarek said in my ear.

Then, one after the other, they shouted out their names.

Another female. "Mirabella!"

A young man. "Keto!"

A girl. "Fabianna!"

A young boy was next, maybe five or six, or nine, who could tell, how were we to know? "Cyrus," he shouted in a child's voice.

An older woman. "Lupa."

"Jason." Another man.

"Rexxon." An old man shouted out his name.

"Iola," the last woman in line said.

The Second Woman, Verity, was speaking again. We all listened, even though only those among us who spoke the language of the Sabostienie could understand any of it. I saw a steep learning curve ahead of me if I was to live through this and be granted a return trip home. *It just goes to show there is always someone bigger and stronger than you are that wants to impose their will on you,* I thought. *I hate this!* And suddenly I had the insight to know what the ones calling themselves The Natural Order felt. They were losing power and control, their way of life, and I could see why they might want to fight to get it back. Why they might see us as the aggressors. I felt chagrined that the Spirit of Wonannonda always seemed to point these moments out to me when I least wanted them.

"Verity says that she will leave three of the Stinger ships to patrol this city where their children are to live, for their protection," Zarek said to me.

"Why does she call them children? I asked, "They are of many ages."

"I think it is like the Father and Mother called us their children." Zarek shrugged his shoulders, "She will choose the ones to be taken to Hadria. She wants to talk to you in private."

John stepped up and said, "Hell no. That is not going to happen! She will talk to all of us, or not talk at all." He was shaking, barely containing his anger. "That woman is not getting close to Pen alone, you tell her that!" he barked out at Zarek. Zarek looked at me, and I could tell for the first time in ages what he was thinking. And like John, it was protective.

"They want to know what kind of beast guards you, Pen," Wydra said, distracting the men.

"Don't tell them war hound, whatever you do," I said. "I want to take her with me if I must go. If I can convince them to leave everyone else, at least I'll have my Ibera." Ibera whimpered, staring at the Second Woman, then looked up at me with her large, liquid eyes, waiting for a command. "Sit. Greet." I said. "Be nice."

Verity's people and my people all agreed to meet in the council chambers, leaving their flying machines shielded as they stepped away from them. The staff Verity carried seemed to be the controller for not only the ships' shields, but also individual shields for her thirty or so people. As they came up the steps, two men rushed out from the far corner of the building with swords raised to attack the strangers.

Before they got ten feet, Verity tipped her staff and blue fire consumed the two men to nothing. Pandemonium and screams ensued. People were dropping to the ground: some were dead, some only frightened. The people from the flying machines had small handheld devices that were dropping people who got too close to them. They could fire through their shields without dropping their shields. They were still protected, while my people had nothing to protect them.

"Stop!" I screamed. "Sistite!" I yelled, over and over. "Stop!" I held out my arms, holding up my hands to my people and their people, running down into the open ground between them, hoping I was saying the word I seemed to remember meant stop.

Finally, motion ceased, and it became quiet again. As some of the people rose from the ground, I saw four bodies that remained motionless and recognized them as four of our own peacekeepers from Ra'Vell Island.

"You didn't have to do that!" I yelled at the Second Woman. "You have a shield around you. This was unnecessary."

"A show of power," Zarek, next to me, whispered. "I think she is as afraid of us as we are of her. I have her mind mapped. And she may not show it, but she feels sick at what they have just done. Remember your training. Feel for her mind, and you will see what I say is true."

"Please don't try to retaliate for this!" I yelled loud enough for any Nuedeners around the square to hear. "We want no more deaths. Let me talk to her; we will work this out. Please. Don't do anything. Don't attack them. They have shielding. It will only get us all killed if you attack again." Zarek was repeating what I was saying to Verity and her people. Our frozen tableau looked like colorful carved statues in a mausoleum garden.

Before anyone could stop us, Ibera and I rushed back up the steps, almost tripping on the small white Life Stealers, and halted right in front of the Second Woman's shield. My hands were held high. Ibera was silent beside me, her size and bulk a reassurance to me even though I knew these people could obliterate both of us in a blink of time.

"Let's talk," I said, staring at Verity, eye to eye. Zarek repeated what I said to her. Verity's eyes were round like mine, not the cat eyes of the Sabostienie, and they were as blue as her hair and her dress. No one spoke for a time, then I motioned for her to follow me, she nodded. I turned around and led them up the steps and into the Chamber House. My friends followed.

CHAPTER THIRTY-SIX

When we were inside and the doors were closed, Verity spoke in an attempt at English, with an accent that sounded vaguely Sabostienie. "We take. Pendyse Ra'Vell. Rifkin Steel. Andraykin Wilks. Jorame Oath. Willobee. Lucus Tallman. Reia. Kid. LaBo."

Nine names.

"Is there no way I can convince you to leave one of your people and take only me?" I asked, and after Zarek gave me a long, hard stare, he repeated what I said.

She recited the list a second time as she walked around the room touching the tables, and went and sat on the Telling Wood throne, carved from Telling Tree two thousand years ago. Then she came back to us.

Verity gazed up at the dome and nodded. Zarek repeating her words, "This is very impressive. Big!" she had said. "We watch and listen … from time and again. We have learned about you." She spoke in a fast flow of words that seemed to tumble over each other. How was I ever going to understand? She spoke too fast. When I'd used the neurocap at the Language Center, it was all slow and measured, and I only had a few hours of time spent at the Center. And how did she know about Kid, Willobee or Lebo? And why would she choose these people?

Zarek interpreted what she'd said. "'Your warriors had slicing weapons and I reacted with haste and little thought. I regret the loss to you.'" Zarek added, "Those kinds of weapons seem to hold great terror for these people. Some tribal memory of destruction from our shared history, I think. From before the joining. Maybe they were some of the people who split off from the other side before we became one people."

"We are … " she turned to me, trying to speak English "Stella Mara. Sea… " She stopped again, looking frustrated.

"Star of the Sea?" Zarek asked. "Or … Sea Star?"

The Second woman nodded, "Sea Star," Verity repeated carefully. Then she spoke again in her own tongue, and Zarek translated it for us.

"They would never have revealed themselves but for the threat we made against their children." He paused for her to talk. "Those white things have bad waves that scramble the minds and speech of the Obaskillian, 'Fish Children'. Sonic." Zarek shook his head, frowning. "Not sure. Sonic language … maybe."

"No," Wydra said. "Not sonic; I think it's infrasonic. They speak by some kind of sound waves carried in the water. It is the way those bombs killed people, only those waves carried through the air. I think their Fish Children can feel what's inside those bombs."

"The bombs!" I ran from the chamber and out to the steps to see our security men in a circle facing out, guarding them. I sighed in relief and began to pick them up and put them back in the box, counting every one. I put the lid on the finely carved box and asked two of my guards to take it back inside the Chamber House with me.

Between the Second Woman's people and my friends, there was a small crowd standing in the center of the room, under the dome that seemed to impress these people so greatly as they were all staring up at it when I returned.

"Thank you," I said to the security guards. "I am so sorry about our men." I said to the guards, "I will do everything I can to keep this from happening again. Even if it means I have to go with them, leave for a year. And if that should be the case, I'm asking you to make sure the Stella Mara people left here are kept safe, too, while I am gone. Treat them as you would treat me."

I indicated my scarred-up gavel table, and they placed the box on it while everyone watched in silence, a feeling of resignation settling over us. I walked the guards to the Chamber House doors.

"I promise," I said to them, "I'll do my best, whatever it takes, to keep this world safe. You tell all our people. I promise!"

It took about six hours to get ready to leave Telling Wood. We took the Sea Star people to my home, where their nine would live during the coming year. We made sure they each had a personal set of guards they could get to know and feel comfortable with.

We packed what we would need to live in Hadria, even though we knew nothing of that place. I would take my journal, along with a set of the liberated books from Library, and food for Ibera, at least enough to last until we could see what was available there. Verity said they would make shuttle runs for us if we discovered we needed anything more. She seemed quite civilized about all the arrangements, even though she was a hammer over our heads.

Lucus Tallman wailed that he didn't want to go. But there was no moving the Second Woman, Verity, about any of her choices, and he finally, grudgingly agreed. Reia was eager to go. This new place seemed to hold a great attraction for her. She was excited to see what Hadria was like, as they seemed to be saying it was under the sea, which seemed totally impossible to me. Maybe it wasn't and they just wanted us to think that, so that none of our people would look for Hadria. But that name did make we wonder if Hadria meant something to do with water, like hydro.

Rifkin, Dray and Jorame, all three, would not have let me leave without them. Dray said, "If they hadn't picked me, I'd have to swim all the way there by myself." Jorame and Julka spent their last hours alone together. Rifkin went home to Heronimo. He didn't want to take Sky, so Heronimo would keep her. Ibera would be the only Nar Hound under the sea, if that was really where we were going.

Kid. Why had they chosen him? How had they even known about him? When I went to tell him what was happening and that the Sea Star people had him on their list, and I had no idea what that might mean to him or for him. But he simply said, "Yes! I want to go! Any place on this planet would be better than next to the man who fathered me." He glanced over at Norman. "He is my past. You are my future. I have decided." I perceived no deception in him, so I took him home with me to make ready.

LaBo and Willobee had to come from the Blue Moon. LaBo was one of their top historians/Librarians and practically lived in the Library, according to Zarek. I remembered meeting her while I was spending some time as a beginner trying to learn their language. She was a tall, thin, older woman with purple-gray hair she wore long and loose. Willobee, of course, was Zarek's great grandniece, and very hard for the family to let go, but we were all making sacrifices to keep the Stella Mara from doing something unthinkable or irreversible to our people. We had had that happen with the Voice, and we couldn't let it happen again.

Verity and her people seemed reasonable, and obviously wanted to reach some kind of peace accord or they wouldn't have been leaving nine of their own here, in this wild, dangerous world they didn't trust. The more people with differing views of things, the more chances for misunderstandings, and things to go wrong—but also for new discoveries, if we could stand the pace of change without cracking wide open.

All I could do was put it to rest in the Heart of the Great Spirit of Wonannonda, and do my best. I was not smart enough, quick enough or experienced enough to do anything else.

The sun was setting by the time we were loaded into the Stingers, and the streets were full of people to see us off. It was a solemn crowd. It was so quiet you could hear their collective breathing. I stepped up on the edge of the fountain in front of the Chamber House and said, "We will return." I looked out over the silent crowd. "Trust the council members to lead you in this year. Listen to them, and to John, Wydra and Zarek. We have our communicators and will keep in touch. Verity, the Second Woman tells me everyone going with me will be able to talk to family when they want to. So can the Stella Mara talk to their own people? We will all make it through this unusual exchange and be the stronger for it."

I stepped down off the fountain edge and turned to John and Wydra, gave them both tight hugs, and whispered to John, "Keep things on track. Watch out for the Natural Order. I love you guys. Good luck, and many blessings."

They reluctantly let me go. Hurrying down the steps, I climbed into the Stinger and waved. The others were already in the ships in which they would be traveling. The shields went up, and Telling Wood was out of sight in no time at all, and we were over the Wells before we could even register the distance we had gone.

"I thought the cyna-cycles were fast," I said not expecting an answer, for I was traveling with Verity. But she nodded and repeated the word, "Fast! Yes."

At that point, attempting conversation was pointless, so I just watched as the Trillium Sea rose up beneath us and the Blue Moon laced the choppy waters with reflected shards of light. It would be a full moon tomorrow night. I wondered if I'd be able to see it from Hadria. I would be fourteen, or fifteen and a half, if you counted by Old Earth years. I'd accept anything to comfort myself in a time when I felt far too young for such responsibility, and making myself older seemed to help.

Then, to my astonishment, we slipped beneath the waves and glided underwater for what seemed like forever in a dark world, with occasional flashes of neon colors on my left and right, until we slowed, and I saw a city of incomparable beauty grow closer. The dome over it glowed like a million star-pricked night-lights radiating down on some of the most fantastically shaped buildings imaginable.

"Hadria," I breathed.

Verity turned and smiled at me. "Home!" she said. "Mea cara Hadria."

This I knew.

Looking at that sparkling beauty, I breathed her words in English, "My dear Hadria."

ABOUT THE AUTHOR

Linda lives in Bend Oregon with her husband, Duncan, and their magical cat, Panga. Duncan is also a writer. They met in a writer's group thirty-four years ago and married in the fall of that year. A year later they bought Pegasus Books of Bend. Fourteen years ago the couple started a used bookstore, The Bookmark.

From an early age books of all kinds, fiction and non-fiction, fairytales and fantasy, poetry and dictionaries all intrigued her. But it is the character's living at the edge of her dreams that whisper their stories over her shoulders catching her in a web of words. Stories of far away places, different ways of living, strange worlds or our world seen from a different angle, no matter, the character's from those places always whisper, like waves on a beach, **"Write, write, write."**

TRILLIUM TRILOGY

TELLING TREE
ONCE ON A BLUE MOON
UNDER THE TRILLIUM SEA

llmcgeary@gmail.com

Made in the USA
Columbia, SC
29 October 2017